Unsinkable

"An intriguing and tho[...] time journeys of Viole[...] three separate shipwre[...] son, a brilliant young [...] during the dark days [...] expert hands, separat[...] create a remarkable d[...] the bravery of women and the stunning lengths they will go to protect others. It is a heart-stirring story of women who risk everything in order to claim their proper place in this world. Walsh takes readers on an exhilarating voyage of danger, sacrifice, and ultimate triumph."

—Lynda Cohen Loigman, *USA TODAY* bestselling author of *Two-Family House, The Wartime Sisters*, and *The Matchmaker's Gift*

"With elegant prose and superb attention to detail, Walsh pulls you instantly onboard this beautiful tale of two determined, whip-smart, and truly unsinkable women. I was intrigued from page one, both Violet's and Daphne's stories sweeping me along through every harrowing moment until that perfect twist and captivating ending. A must-read for fans of unstoppable, courageous women."

—Noelle Salazar, *USA TODAY* bestselling author of *The Flight Girls*

"Jenni L. Walsh spins an incredible tale of survival and heartbreak in this riveting novel. Inspired by true events, the rich historical detail and tense plotting make for an unforgettable read. Historical fiction lovers, add this one to your list!"

—Sara Ackerman, *USA TODAY* bestselling author of *The Codebreaker's Secret* and *The Uncharted Flight of Olivia West*

"A stunning dual narrative spanning some of the marquee events of the early twentieth century. Violet and Daphne are compelling heroines of the first order, and one cannot help but root for their triumph from the first page through to the seamless, satisfying conclusion. Walsh is a master storyteller, and *Unsinkable* shows her skill at its best. Not to be missed by anyone who loves historical fiction and resilient heroines."

—Aimie K. Runyan, bestselling author of
The School for German Brides and *A Bakery in Paris*

"An extraordinary story of two extraordinary women. Jenni L. Walsh expertly weaves together Violet's and Daphne's histories—Violet is real, Daphne an amalgamation of several real-life women—to craft a historical novel that is vivid and enthralling. There is intrigue and bravery, duty and love in these pages, and readers will keep turning them to the very end, eager to learn the fates of these two inspiring women. A joy to read."

—Kate Albus, award-winning author of
A Place to Hang the Moon and *Nothing Else but Miracles*

"I fell headfirst into this historical fiction tale featuring two powerful and resilient women, Violet and Daphne. Walsh seamlessly weaves together fact and fiction in a dual-timeline narrative that keeps the reader guessing, culminating in a satisfying conclusion. The courage of both main characters lingered with me long after I turned the final page. I am so looking forward to whatever Walsh writes next!"

—Amita Parikh, bestselling author of *The Circus Train*

The Call of the Wrens

"In *The Call of the Wrens*, Jenni L. Walsh chronicles two volunteers in the Women's Royal Naval Service during the First and Second World Wars. Spanning decades in a story that is both epic and intimate, *The Call of the Wrens* is an original and compelling tale of sisterhood and strength."

—Pam Jenoff, *New York Times* bestselling author of
The Woman with the Blue Star

"What a lovely surprise. The heroines in Walsh's latest can be found racing around war-torn Europe on motorbikes, relaying secret messages and undertaking daring missions as part of the real-life women's branch of the Royal Navy. There's also giddy romance, family secrets, and shocking twists, making it an absolute treat for historical fiction lovers."

—Fiona Davis, *New York Times* bestselling author of
The Magnolia Palace

"The lives of two women in two different world wars collide in unexpected ways in this powerful exploration of the British Women's Royal Naval Service, commonly known as the Wrens, a daring group of real-life women who were instrumental in both World War I and World War II. Laced with triumph and tragedy, bravery and redemption, this tale of finding oneself in modern history's darkest hours will break your heart and put it back together again, all in one delightful read."

—Kristin Harmel, *New York Times* bestselling author of
The Forest of Vanishing Stars

"*The Call of the Wrens* by Jenni L. Walsh is a beautifully written gem of a historical novel, shedding light on a little-known group of women, the Wrens, during both world wars. Walsh skillfully entwines the stories of Evelyn and Marion as they journey to find their voices and, ultimately, their calling. I was completely captivated by this richly drawn portrait of strength, survival, and love."

—Jillian Cantor, *USA TODAY* bestselling author of
Beautiful Little Fools

"In *The Call of the Wrens*, Jenni L. Walsh has woven a wonderful tale inspired by the real-life women's branch of the United Kingdom's Royal Navy. This dual-timeline novel features two courageous heroines, Marion and Evelyn, roaring around Europe on motorbikes during both world wars. Thrilling missions, family secrets, romance—it's all here. We need more books like this that show the remarkable contributions made by adventurous women during the darkest of times."

—Elise Hooper, author of *Angels of the Pacific*

"In *The Call of the Wrens*, Jenni L. Walsh lends her remarkable voice to the little-known, intrepid women of the Women's Royal Naval Service, women who revved up their motorcycles and risked their necks to heed Britain's call to win the world wars. Packed full of action and with a heart-wrenching twist, Marion and Evelyn's story reads like a battle cry for anyone who's had to fight against other people's expectations and find her own place, and her chosen family, in this world."

—Caroline Woods, author of *The Lunar Housewife*

"With a winning blend of adventure and romance, Walsh highlights the bravery and intrepid spirits of women destined to forge a path beyond the restrictive expectations of their era and circumstance. A winning treatise on courage and sisterhood, *The Call of the Wrens* will have fans of Kate Quinn and Erika Robuck rejoicing with each compulsively readable page."

—Rachel McMillan, author of *The Mozart Code*

UNSINKABLE

ALSO BY JENNI L. WALSH

Adult Fiction
The Call of the Wrens
A Betting Woman
Side by Side
Becoming Bonnie

Middle Grade
Operation: Happy
Over and Out
By the Light of Fireflies
I Am Defiance
Hettie and the London Blitz
She Dared: Malala Yousafzai
She Dared: Bethany Hamilton

UNSINKABLE

Jenni L. Walsh

HARPER MUSE

Published by Harper Muse, an imprint of HarperCollins Focus LLC.

This book is a work of fiction. All incidents, dialogue, and letters, and all characters with the exception of some well-known historical figures, are products of the author's imagination. Where real-life historical persons appear, the situations, incidents, and dialogues concerning those personas are entirely fictional and are not intended to depict actual events or to change the entirely fictional nature of the work. In all other respects, any resemblance to persons living or dead is entirely coincidental.

Any internet addresses (websites, blogs, etc.) in this book are offered as a resource. They are not intended in any way to be or imply an endorsement by HarperCollins Focus LLC, nor does HarperCollins Focus LLC vouch for the content of these sites for the life of this book.

Library of Congress Cataloging-in-Publication Data

Names: Walsh, Jenni L., author.
Title: Unsinkable / Jenni L. Walsh.
Description: Nashville, Tennessee : Harper Muse, 2024. | Summary: "Unsinkable is a stand-alone historical novel about two women who survive against all odds and become legends. Violet Jessop is Miss Unsinkable. Daphne has survived calamity of her own"--Provided by publisher.
Identifiers: LCCN 2023031681 (print) | LCCN 2023031682 (ebook) | ISBN 9781400233946 (paperback) | ISBN 9781400233953 (epub) | ISBN 9781400233960
Subjects: LCGFT: Novels.
Classification: LCC PS3623.A446218 U57 2024 (print) | LCC PS3623.A446218 (ebook) | DDC 813/.6--dc23/eng/20230714
LC record available at https://lccn.loc.gov/2023031681
LC ebook record available at https://lccn.loc.gov/2023031682
Printed in the United States of America

23 24 25 26 27 LBC 5 4 3 2 1

CHAPTER 1

Violet

—

Southampton Port aboard *Titanic*
April 10, 1912

"VIOLET," SHE CALLS AT MY BACK.

I ignore her. Not to be rude. Not to be cruel. I like Ann just fine. What's more, she's a cabinmate who doesn't snore.

"Vi," she tries again.

I ignore her because I know exactly what she's after. And I can't give it to her. I, too, am in search of more vases. A task that has left me slightly breathless.

There's humor in Ann's voice as she imitates a high-maintenance passenger. "Miss Jessop! Oh, Miss Jessop!"

I respond in a singsong manner, the Irish lilt to my voice emphasized, "I'll be right with you."

Ann laughs, the sounds of her footsteps thudding against the hallway runner, gaining on me in the first-class corridor, the paneled walls so white I almost need to squint. "Liar," she says.

I chuckle. I know without looking that her arms are full of flowers. Mine are as well. The new Mrs. John Jacob Astor has been gifted eight bouquets alone by those sending her off on *Titanic*'s maiden voyage. My allotment for my *entire* section is ten vases.

A final horn sounds, muffled from being below the A and B decks.

It is noon, departure time.

I look up at the equally white ceiling, as if I could see straight through those upper decks to this perfect springtime day, imagining those high-maintenance passengers in their fancy dresses, suits, and hats, waving their embroidered handkerchiefs, shouting their goodbyes, our majestic ship being led by tugs, tooting their own farewells. I should like to see it, the excitement of leaving port, but there's too much to do before the passengers proceed to their staterooms and locate the electric call button above their beds that'll signal they need me for any number of things. Bicarbonate of soda to alleviate indigestion and heartburn. Help putting their clothing away. Directions to the swimming pool, the gymnasium, the squash courts. A request for me to schedule a bathing time with the bath stewards. An *additional* vase. At the thought, my muscles tense around my armful of tulips, peonies, and dahlias.

"Actually," I say, spinning toward Ann, "I could use another tall vase if you have an extra."

I know full well she does not. But my comment is worth the playful glower she shoots my way. She says, "This must be a record. This ship has created a new level of excitement."

I nod just as the ship tilts and—practiced after twenty-four voyages—I widen my stance, unable to use my occupied hands to steady myself.

"So many notable passengers too," Ann says. "Mr. Guggenheim, Mr. Thayer, Lady Duff Gordon, Edith Rosenbaum, Mr. Astor . . ."

I raise my arms at the mention of him, denoting that this grandiose assortment of bouquets, ones currently working an itch up my nose, are for his stateroom. *Titanic* tilts back, leveling us, and Ann goes on, "Dorothy Gibson, Old Miss Townsend"— we both groan at her name—"Mr. and Mrs. Straus . . ."

A soft smile spreads on my lips at the mention of Isidor and Ida, though I'd never dare let anyone hear me call them anything other than Mr. and Mrs. Straus. I'd been seeing to them for years, by far my favorite of all our passengers.

I like to play a game with myself, making presumptions about what a prominent person will actually be like. Once upon a time I had guessed the older couple would be warm, gracious, and respectful, despite Isidor being a co-owner of Macy's and Ida being a prominent member of New York's high society.

I won.

I'll soon see if Dorothy Gibson's captivating smile is real or reserved only for motion pictures. Or if Madeleine Astor is indeed as radiant as I have pictured in my imagination. She is, after all, a young woman who is said to be brilliant at drawing room conversation, who's an accomplished horsewoman, who's been educated at Miss Ely's School. Not only that, but a woman who's rejected the fervent opposition of her marriage to John Jacob Astor IV and wed him all the same. Him forty-seven, her eighteen.

I like a woman who goes after what she wants.

I wish I could be more like that. Alas, circumstances don't always allow for what a person wants. Only what is necessary.

Which is why I'm on this very ship.

"I'm off, then," Ann says. "Little good you've done me."

"*Adios,*" I say and smile at my friend, then I continue on, turning down another long corridor, my destination the C Deck cabins, one of which will be the Astor suite. Along the way, I pop my head into staterooms until I find a coveted vase just sitting there for the taking.

I take it.

At C-62–64 I knock, announcing myself, though I'm certain Mr. and Mrs. Astor are still waving their goodbyes and not yet in their cabin.

Flowers successfully in place and after a final sweep of their room to ensure all is in order, I nod curtly to myself.

Their suite is impressive, known as the "French cabin" because it is Louis XV–inspired. Varnished oak paneling. Cabriolet furniture. Every dressing table, armchair, sofa, wardrobe, and washstand, along with the light fixtures and upholstery, has been recreated with an obsessive care for accuracy.

"Miss Violet!" I hear.

Stanley. Good old Stanley. With a steward uniform that is perfectly pressed, without a crease in sight, but who himself is as wrinkled as a prune. *"Aged to perfection,"* he once quipped.

I adore him, despite my initial resistance at getting to know him. Getting to know anybody. I'm aboard for a job, a purpose, an income.

But over the past two years, Stanley and I have worked together on the *Olympic* and *Majestic* and he's worked his way into my heart.

It's hard to believe I've been a cabin stewardess for four years. It's even harder to believe both Stanley and I are on this ship right now after what we experienced on the *Olympic* last year.

As if plucking that unsettling day from my brain, Stanley says, "We almost had another *Olympic* imbroglio."

I twist my body, a prick to my nerves, to look through the window and beyond the Astors' small private deck, only forty feet above the water. The sky is blue. The sea is a lazy calm. No other ship is in sight. "What happened?" I ask him.

"Didn't you feel it?" He must mean the ship's heel, when *Titanic* rocked. I nod, and he says, "We had a near collision with the SS *New York*, just past the peninsular. Eerily similar, I say, to what happened with the *Hawke* last year."

Nothing more needs to be said. We were both there. We both remember when the *Olympic* collided with the warship. Both thrown off our feet. It was only her fifth voyage and almost her last. *Hawke* was designed to sink ships by ramming them, and when she accidentally did just that, two large holes were torn into *Olympic*'s hull, one above the waterline and the other beneath. Two of her watertight compartments were flooded. Her propeller shaft had been twisted.

I'd clutched the life belt I'd put on, instructing others to do the same. My voice was panicked as I tried to calm my passengers. But in the end, *Olympic* was able to return the ten or so miles back to Southampton without sinking. No one was seriously hurt. The ship's damage was remedied. In fact, she was back on the water, bound again for New York in only two months' time.

I was bound again, too, despite feeling at odds with myself about the idea of returning to the sea. In one breath, I hadn't been certain my legs would be sure enough to carry me aboard another so-called grand ship. In another breath, I'd felt like I'd been cheating death and testing fate ever since I was a young girl. Sometimes I feel as if I'm living on borrowed time. Or maybe it's an ongoing, never-ending mentality of simply surviving. Whatever the case, all there's left to do is continue on, one foot in front of the other, only ever looking toward that next footfall.

My mother made countless pleas for me to secure another job after almost sinking. A hundred years ago, maritime disasters were common. One out of every seven ships made their way to the sea floor. But that was then, and this is now, when ships have state-of-the-art radios. When—eliminating an instance last month where a steamer struck a rock—there hasn't been a notable sinking in eight years.

Besides, finding work in another vocation isn't a piece of cake. Lord knows why, but when stewards apply for jobs ashore, we're treated like pariahs, somehow unsuitable for work except in our own line. Are we hardworking? Some of the most. Enduring, patient? We have to be. Can we adapt to people of varying temperaments and to varying circumstances? *Sí.*

But there are times it matters little. In the rare cases where onshore work was actually found, I often heard stories of my fellow stewards returning with their pockets empty and talk of missing one thing: the tips.

Our wealthy passengers generally tip very well. It's not our salaries as stewards; it's the gratuities that add up.

To pay rent and coalman's bills. Tuition for my brothers. Clothing and shoes for us all. Doctor fees for my mother. Even more doctor fees for my sister's hearing, still unresolved, the effects of the rheumatic fever she experienced in Argentina having followed her across the sea to England. A mastoid operation has seemed to help, but the poor child is still mostly deaf and not a stranger to hospitals.

If Mother and Father were also contributing to the household, I think we'd be just fine. But Mother is unable to work. Father's in heaven.

So here I am, twenty-five years old, the oldest of six living siblings, and the only breadwinner for our family. Here I am, still at sea, nearly colliding with other ships that could quite literally sink me and bring my family down too.

Stanley offers me a gentle smile, one of the few on board who knows my predicament. "Smooth sailing from here, Miss Violet."

"Smooth sailing," I repeat, just as voices begin to trail down the corridors and float through the salty air.

Quickly, Stanley and I report to the pantry where the stewards and stewardesses congregate, waiting for orders. I stare at the billboard, knowing it'll soon begin twinkling with calls from passengers no longer waving goodbye but now in their rooms . . . and quick to be in the need of assistance.

We set bets on whose section will ring first.

We don't have to wait long.

* * *

I'M EXHAUSTED—ACHING FEET, STIFF BACK, THE WHOLE shebang. Sailing days are always mayhem.

I've answered summons, most commonly the need for refreshments.

I've arranged flowers, put away clothing, and tidied cabins as guests have sashayed in and out of their rooms.

I've swept and dusted the alleyways and corridors.

I've cosseted the seasick and brought food trays for those unable to leave their rooms.

I've turned down beds I'll strip and remake in the morning.

I've run errands. "Could you please check on my Hercules in the kennels? Every hour would be preferable," one of my passengers, Miss Walton, asked, motioning to her father to retrieve his billfold from his vest. "My pleasure," I quickly obliged, accepting his money.

When we docked shortly after departure in Cherbourg, France, allowing for tender ships to ferry more passengers aboard, I comforted my existing passengers that this stop was indeed planned and that there will be another one tomorrow in Queenstown, Ireland. "Remember," I told them, "you are traveling on an unsinkable ship."

That verbiage was used in the White Star's advertising, for both the *Titanic* and the *Olympic*.

AS FAR AS IT IS POSSIBLE TO DO SO,
THESE TWO WONDERFUL VESSELS ARE DESIGNED
TO BE UNSINKABLE.

"I've experienced as much on the *Olympic*," I added, continuing to reassure my passengers and myself alike. "She lived up to the name of 'Unsinkable.'"

Even still, tomorrow my passengers will inevitably forget that the second planned stop in Queenstown is nothing to be concerned with and I'll have to offer a new round of consoling.

Tonight, even as knackered as I am, I can't help pausing on the first-class promenade to watch as a young man lines up a young

woman from behind the lens of a movie camera, memorializing
their first night aboard *Titanic* under a crescent moon.

The setting is idyllic. He's completely rearranged the deck furniture. In the middle of the walkway, the young woman lounges
on a chair, one arm perfectly poised behind her head. Trying to
find just the right angle, he's moving about her in a semicircle,
muttering to himself how the moon's glow is perfectly capturing
her beauty.

I snort and continue to tiptoe by, not wanting to interrupt.

Besides them, the alleyways are mostly deserted except for a
few stewards on late watch. A man passes by. Judging by the smell
of him, he's returning from the smoke room. I return my attention
to the young couple. I imagine him to be a young film director.
Maybe she aspires to be a starlet. Maybe not. What's obvious to
me is that they are newlyweds. I've seen many. The young man
straightens from his camera, supported on a tripod.

"Perfection, my dear. The perfect balance of light and dark,"
he says, and his accent is clearly American. Ah, another piece of
the puzzle: they are returning to New York rather than visiting.
My guess is they've honeymooned overseas. The way she touches
her stomach tenderly tells me she's also likely already with child.

How wonderful for them.

I continue on toward my cabin with a familiar pit in my stomach. When I signed on to work aboard a ship, I experienced a
multitude of emotions. A deep ache at cutting short my schooling
and my dreams of medicine. Determination to fulfill a duty to my
family. Gratitude that I was able to step into my mother's stewardess role after she could no longer work. Apprehension regarding
the lurid stories of sea life. Yet a fascination with ships from my
childhood in Argentina, when jolly men in blue suits and brass
buttons would arrive at port, always with a gift, tins of marma-
lade or a box of chocolate creams. And finally exhilaration at the
compensation for my hard work, at the changing of scenes, at
the rotation of faces, and perhaps . . . at the prospect of romance.

Though that last seems to be the most unobtainable. What's the point of galivanting with another crew member or passenger when they'll only disembark? And how could I accept a proposal—I've received two thus far—when I have Mother, William, Philip, Patrick, Jack, and Eileen to look after? A large number that is counting on me. It's not lost on me that the total could be even higher, if we hadn't buried Father, Ray, Denis, and Molly.

But we have, and my shoulders rise and fall at the loss, my body stilling mid-breath as I painfully remember my personal fault over Ray's death. Then I swallow roughly, telling myself I cannot fail a second time.

Father's words dance through my head.

"What butter and whiskey won't cure, there is no cure for."

And, it seemed, there was no option other than me stepping into Mother's job. After Father died, Mother's heart and head, already chiseled away from the deaths of my siblings, died with him. She tried to work at sea, but Mother was a ghost of herself. The ship's doctor advised she abandon her post and take a complete rest. In England, Dr. Cree concurred, confining her to bed.

I was twenty years old and at the convent, studying for my examinations, when Sister Majorie sat me down to tell me of my mother's prognosis. My sister Eileen was there, too, though she shouldn't have been. She was only five years old, too young to be at the convent, but also too young for her to be on her own while our mother worked. At least my sister and I were together. She could've been at an orphanage, like my brothers. With Mother being unable to afford a boarding school, that's where my brothers resided.

"I do not like this for you," Sister Majorie had said.

She meant a shipboard life.

I gave her my reasons—the changing of scenes, the rotation of faces—to which she said, "You'll only be wasting your studies."

I sighed. "The root of the word *scholarship* comes from the Greek word for 'luxury,' does it not? It doesn't appear I have such a thing any longer."

Sister Majorie had frowned. "So what of your desire to heal others? Is that gone?"

Not to be a nurse. Not to work in medicine. But, specifically, to heal. That is what she'd said. And hadn't I lain awake many nights wondering how life could've been different if I had that seemingly fantastical ability? Her words had cut me like a knife. I had no rebuttal except, "What other choice do I have?"

I had been speaking of my familial obligation. The root word of *obligation* is "to bind," and I was—and am—bonded to my family in every way possible.

"*Family first,*" my mother had been known to say.

"There are other vocations," Sister Majorie had tried. "A housekeeper, teacher, stenographer, bookkeeper, laundress. Shall I go on?"

"No," I said. She'd made her point. But those vocations were missing something Mother had relied on: again, the tips.

"*Americans,*" my mother once told me. "*They are the most generous. They recognize you are there to make their trip more comfortable and pleasant, and they pay you for it. They don't expect you to hang about like beggars outside a church, waiting for alms. They tip freely, often, handsomely.*"

And I knew Mother's wages, along with the checks from Father's old company and the occasional trip to a pawnshop to part with another heirloom—but most importantly the gratuities she earned—were enough to keep my family afloat. I wasn't about to disrupt the cog, especially not after the promise I'd made to Father before he died.

I'm on the E Deck without even realizing I've passed the most ornate of rooms, the first-class lounge, with its glimmering chandelier and oversized fireplace, where passengers go to blissfully pass their time, reading, playing games, gossiping, and sipping their afternoon tea, and I've descended the aft grand staircase four floors, with only two decks remaining below me on our grand ship. One for the second- and third-class cabins and the final for the control, turbine, engine, boiler, and kennel rooms.

"There you are," Ann says as I walk into our quaint cabin, so unlike the grandeur of the rest of the ship. "I was about to send out a search party."

I huff a laugh. "I got caught up watching a newlywed couple on the promenade. He was filming her."

Ann fakes a gag. "Mr. and Mrs. Marvin. They're one of mine. Sickeningly in love. Though"—Ann tilts her head—"quick to anger too. At one point today I thought Mrs. Marvin was about to remove her shoe and use it as a projectile intended for her husband's head."

I widen my eyes. "Ah, young love."

"Stanley brought us a hammer," she says, holding it up. The length of her narrow bed is filled with family photographs. With a quick *tap, tap* she adds a calendar to the bulkhead. Twelve months of restful country scenes was gifted to every member of the crew at the start of the New Year.

Ann flips to April, and my heart nearly skips a beat when I recognize the landscape of the Andes Mountains, at the base of which stretches a well-tilled vineyard where white muscatel grapes grow like weeds and old, gnarled vines form a perfect arbor.

A similar setting was once my home, a place of mixed emotions. It was the fifth place I'd lived. Where we'd journeyed to save my life, the subtropical heat a last shot for curing my lung ailment from tuberculosis. It worked. But it was also where my father died due to his own complications from surgery. From there, we resorted to England. Colleagues of Father thought it best. The schools were better. But also my brothers would be plucked up for the Argentine Republic in the war against the natives if they came of age in Argentina. Mother paled at the thought.

But . . . the Andes . . .

Before Father had fallen ill, the Andes had been the location of my last happy family memory. An evening where we did nothing more than sit around the dinner table. Father, Mother, William, Philip, the twins, Eileen, and myself. All laughing. All telling jokes, Mother too. My pet armadillo curled atop my feet. More than once I'd held my breath, waiting for Mother to declare it was time for bed. But she'd let the night roll on and on. It'd felt like a gift. I often long to return to that time in the Andes.

"Picturesque," Ann comments as she strikes an X through today's date. She counts forward seven days, marking a star on when we're due at Pier 59 in New York. Another seven days after that is when we'll tie up again in Southampton's Ocean Dock. From there, turnaround time varies before a new voyage begins. Sometimes the wait is four days, other times a week. In either case, it'll be enough time to sign off and hasten up to London to check on Mother. By the calendar's end, we're likely to have completed twelve voyages.

There's something comforting about having the same position day in, day out. It's not something my father had. He'd first emigrated from Ireland to Buenos Aires to be a sheep farmer, spending everything he had to start again, Mother taking the risk with him. But after tiring of the sheep, he'd worked at the port, then for the railway. During my childhood, my father held five different jobs—always pivoting, always struggling to make ends meet. As a family, we were constantly reinventing ourselves and learning a new place.

On *Titanic*, there'll be a routine. The occurrences of my days will be mostly expected, save for the whims of fussy passengers. Like Old Miss Townsend, an ornery, self-righteous woman who once demanded on a previous voyage aboard *Olympic* that mirrors be added to nearly every wall and surface of her cabin and for the furniture in her already luxurious stateroom to be changed at once.

Ann offers me the small hammer. The sounds of busy hammers float through the thin walls of other crew cabins. There's a whole slew of us. Many have worked the White Star Line for years. Others have voyaged on the Cunard Line, the Red Star Line, or aboard the Royal Mail Ships traveling to the West Indies, where I first cut my teeth.

I'll bypass the family photos within my luggage that I bring from ship to ship but never hang. I need no visual reminders of my family on the wall. And, odd as it may seem until explained, I prefer to love them from afar—where I can't see something so silly as the inch of skin between my brothers' trousers and their shoes or, more heart-wrenching, watch as Mother's health diminishes further or as my sister loses her hearing in totality.

Instead, I hang a photograph of Mary Pickford, signed to me as *Miss Violet Jessop.*

Beside it, I add a headshot of Charles Labine. He's yet to sign it, yet to sail during one of my voyages. But if he ever does, I plan to work up the courage to ask for his autograph. He's young, handsome, both an actor and a director. I saw his most recent film, *Caesar,* on two separate occasions.

"Tell me," Ann says as I switch to unpacking my trunk, beginning with a small jewelry box. "Did you win with Mrs. Astor? Is she as radiant as you predicted her to be?"

I twist my lips and turn toward my friend. "Much to my dismay, I believe I've lost. She hung listlessly on Mr. Astor's arm. Quiet. Pale. Sad-faced. It pains me to say it, but she came across as rather dull. At least in the interactions I had with her."

"How unfortunate," Ann remarks. "Who could be miserable on the arm of the richest man aboard this ship?"

So unfortunate, indeed. What I could do with those riches. Not having to worry about finances would mean I could explore what happiness truly looks like. It's not something I've allowed myself to imagine. But maybe one day . . . someday . . . things will be better and I can pursue a vocation that lights a fire in my insides. Maybe one day . . . someday . . . something good will come my way that is all my own.

CHAPTER 2

Daphne

London
April 10, 1942

I'M QUITE INTRIGUED WITH WHAT TODAY CAN BRING. WHAT that is . . . I'm not sure. Why I'm here . . . I'm also uncertain. I passed another woman with a perplexed yet unsettled expression as she was leaving and as I was entering this small room, with little more to it than a desk and a visitor chair.

I lick my lips and square my shoulders as I hear footsteps approaching, then a male's deep voice. "Sorry to keep you waiting, Miss Chaundanson."

The man who enters the room rivals a young Allan Jeayes. Severe side part, dark hair, round spectacles. Handsome. Allan starred in one of the last films before the war broke out. Father said it was quite good, high praise coming from him.

As he passes by me toward his desk, he pauses to shake my hand. While he takes his seat, I fold my hands in my lap, ever poised. "No need to apologize for the delay. But please, call me Daphne."

"Very well," the man says, zero intonation in his voice. He could be reciting something from a grocer list. Seems fitting. All I know about him is that he's part of a clandestine operation.

There's something utterly provocative about anything clandestine. While I attended Oxford, my eyes and ears were perpetually alert for any notion of a secret society for women, something resembling the Bullingdon Club, an elusive and exclusively male dining—though really drinking—club.

Alas, it's for the best that no such club existed for my sex. My father wouldn't be pleased if I engaged in any mayhem that would put my name in the tabloids. That's reserved for him.

The man settles behind the desk. He does not respond to my name with his own. But he does continue to stare at me overtop his oversized spectacles. I don't squirm. I'm as cool as a cucumber, or at least I attempt for that casualness. I remind myself: this man, and whoever else is involved in his clandestine operation, are the ones who invited *me* here.

When my father first began in the film business, he had to dazzle in order to win parts and notoriety. Now that he's renowned, he's the one who needs to be dazzled.

Dazzle me, Young Allan Jeayes.

At the very least, tell me why you've lured me from Paris to London.

This whole adventure began only weeks ago . . . over a year ago, if the onset of war is included. For context, it's best to start when the war turned France upside down.

Last summer Germany marched into Paris. I woke to a voice over a loudspeaker. Something my father has said, when he thinks he's being amusing, is that a man should speak German to his horse, French to a woman, Italian to another man, and Spanish to God.

The man over the loudspeaker was very clearly speaking French, but in a German accent—and he was imposing a curfew of eight o'clock.

This turn of event wasn't wholly a surprise. Parisians were rightfully terrified after Germany's air force had inflicted a deadly bombing. Then city officials and citizens alike had been fleeing after the Germans circumvented the Maginot Line—a defense strategy the historian in me could ruminate over at great length.

But still, it was awful that not a thing was done to try to stop the Germans from occupying the capital. In fact, it struck me as altogether cowardly and rightfully embarrassing. My birth country simply rolled over. Though I can recognize the hypocrisy of criticizing someone for not being more defiant, as many decisions throughout my three decades on this earth haven't been made by me but for me . . . by my otherwise absentee father, whose wishes I routinely abide by as a means to stay present in his life.

As such, self-preservation appears to have been the case with Paris too. The Arc de Triomphe has gone untouched. The avenues and streets aren't marked with gunfire. The Eiffel Tower still stands, even if the German forces have raised the swastika flag at its top.

Only eight days after the Germans took Paris, an armistice was signed and the Germans made themselves comfortable in Vichy, the new capital for the new puppetlike France.

But I can see not everyone wishes to be a puppet. I recognize those angered by our limited freedom, with shop owners being told when and for how long they can open their stores. Other cafés, restaurants, and shops have been taken over entirely. Many are frustrated with the food queues and the rationing of bread, flour, milk, butter, cheese, and meat—only fifty grams of meat a week, including bones and gristle. My stomach turns at the alternative meats some are resigned to ingest. Many watch stone-faced as German soldiers march daily down the Champs-Élysées but grumble in private about how only the Nazis are allowed to ride in autos, the rest of us limited to the bus or metro. I often ride a bike.

I, too, am angered.

My father, who'd already left France for England, wrote to me, demanding that I, also a British citizen, should leave immediately for our London town house.

But I couldn't leave Paris. I'd heard the four-minute speech Charles de Gaulle gave from London over a BBC broadcast. Just three hundred sixty words, fifteen of which were how *"the flame of the French Resistance must not be extinguished and will not be extinguished."*

It struck a chord with me, the type of woman who does not give up easily. I suppose I have my father to credit for that. Absentee, as I've said, though also someone with incredibly high standards. My friend Josette from boarding school once jested, rather spot-on if I'm being honest with myself, that I'm forever chasing after the next accomplishment to dangle in front of my father's face to maintain his fleeting attention, perhaps because he's all I have.

And in Paris, I found myself pursuing ways to fan the fire. I began rationing my own rations to help those in need and covertly opening the doors of the art gallery in which I worked for those who wanted to meet in secrecy, where they recounted the shooting of hostages, the rounding up of the innocent for deportation, and the mounting cruelty of the Gestapo.

It was on one such night at the gallery that a woman walked in. She was tall, confident, a red tint to her hair. I noticed a slight limp. That evening the numbers in attendance were larger than normal, sending a nervous ache into my stomach. In English, thinking the foreign language would go unnoticed, I let out an expletive.

It turned the woman's head. "You speak English?" she responded in French, in a voice so low I barely heard her.

It's not often I don't seize the opportunity to grandstand, so I replied, "Yes, along with fluent Italian, Spanish, French, and German."

The woman's eyes had lit up. "But you're English?"

In part I am. I nod. And I placed her as American.

"Remarkable. Your accent is perfectly French. I'll find you again," she said simply. And she did, despite the Germans taking control of the gallery. I don't know if they were suspicious of activity there or merely greedy to have it for themselves. In the end, my position had been eliminated and the woman, seemingly coming out of nowhere, approached me on the street, discreetly hand-delivering a letter to report to London and a low whisper in my ear that I could do more in this war.

It felt serendipitous, to have this flashier way to help in the war's efforts, and thus I fled to England, found the address within the letter, and handed over my invitation to a doorkeeper who studied it astutely before bringing me to this room, across from Young Allan Jeayes.

"I'm late, you see," he says, "because I've just learned that havoc is being wreaked at Bataan. Only yesterday, thousands of American troops surrendered there. And now the USS *Finch* has been sunk. These are a very bad turn of events. By any chance, is Japanese one of the languages you speak?"

My pulse quickens, at both the mention of a sinking ship and at his question. Already I feel as if I'm failing whatever this interview is. "No," I say. "But I can learn it."

He waves off my response. "I'm told you fluently speak six languages already."

"Yes," I'm quick to say, and then to also add, "I also have a diploma in Arabic language from the University of Cairo."

"Quite impressive, Miss Chaundanson."

I take a calming breath. "Daphne."

He dips his head. "I'm curious, as I am related to someone in the film industry, do you hold a relation to Charles Labine?"

I startle. I hate that I react in this manner. It gives me away. But I've never fielded this question before. And now, after my response, there's no use denying the relation. "How do you know I do?"

"Naturally we've looked into you. Charles Labine is the benefactor attached to all your schooling."

I nod. "Very well, yes. We're related, though he prefers no one knows it."

"Hmm. Interesting."

I expect another question, but he's silent. Merely watching me, annoyingly so. Waiting for me to divulge more of my past? I could tell him that I was around five when I realized my father had an actual first name. In fact, he was so often called Charles Labine, rather than simply Charles, that I thought his full name was Charleslabine Chaundanson, incorrectly thinking the two of us shared a surname.

It was at a Parent's Day at my earliest day school that I realized my oversight, if that's even the proper word choice. I had no parent in attendance that day. I'd known my mother was deceased. I rarely saw my father. Yet I expected him to be there because everyone else's parents were oohing and aahing over artwork hung on the walls and the neatness of their desks. I told everyone how "my father, Charleslabine, should be arriving shortly."

Only I was quickly ushered to the headmaster's office and handed a telephone. It was my father.

"Where are you?" I asked him.

I don't remember an answer to my question. I only recall his tin-sounding voice over the telephone telling me that I can't tell anyone that I'm his daughter.

I had scrunched my nose. "But why?"

For a heartbeat I'd thought he'd hung up. But he finally said, "Because of Papa's job. Be a good girl and do as you're told."

"Yes, Father," I had agreed.

His voice softened. "I'm told your watercolor is being showcased. Well done, Katherine. I should like to see it next time I am in town."

Even at my young age, I could feel the end of our conversation, and so I quickly spat out, "Who should I say my father is, then?"

But no answer came. The line had gone dead.

And I had gone on, never speaking of my father by any name again.

Young Allan Jeayes steeples his fingers. I can tell he's finally going to speak. What leaves his mouth is scarily astute as he says, "I get the sense you're an actress in your own right."

I swallow roughly. "If I must be."

"I'll be candid that we were quite surprised to learn of your connection. Now that you're right in front of me, I can see the resemblance, but I assume you more so take after your mother."

"Yes." Her brown hair and eyes. Her height and slender figure. It's only a cleft chin and an ambitious disposition my father and I seem to share. "So you know a lot about me, then?" I'm both alarmed and charmed by the notion.

"Some. I'll admit there are gaps." He pauses, and I think he may begin the next great inquisition, but then he says, "We wouldn't have invited you here unless we thought you could be a fit for our efforts. I'm pleased to find you quite articulate. I'd also wager quick-witted."

"If appropriately rewarded."

He smirks. "Humor as a defense mechanism, I'm coming to see."

It feels too expected to reply with a quip, and there's no need. Young Allan Jeayes continues, "What if that reward was the Paris you once knew?"

A solid hint as to why I could be here. Now I'm even more intrigued.

"I wonder," he says, "if we could continue only in French."

I smile politely and oblige him, speaking a language as familiar as English. "It makes no difference to me."

"A result of your schooling."

He doesn't say it like a question, more of a suggestion for me to talk about myself.

"Yes," I continue in French. "I studied at various day schools before being educated at the International Boarding School in Geneva, Oxford University, Slade School of Art, and I took a course at the Sorbonne."

He adds, "Along with time spent at the University of Cairo."

"That's right," I say. "Collecting degrees and languages is a hobby of sorts."

The man leans back in his chair, folding his hands atop his chest. "Miss Chaundanson, I would very much like to see you again."

"I'm flattered," I say, maintaining a straight face, though inside I'm doing a jig at passing this first test. "Only I don't date."

★ ★ ★

I GET THE SENSE MY INTERVIEWER IS AS EQUALLY INTRIGUED with me as I am with why I could be here.

Enough, at least, for both of us to be sitting across from each other a second time only a day later. In between, Young Allan Jeayes suggested that I "go home to my London townhome and await further contact."

I could've told him it's not my home. Not really. It's just one of the residences my father owns. But then he'd likely ask where home is. And I don't know how to answer that. The most recent place I lived was Paris, while I worked at the gallery. I suspect he'll eventually ask me about my interest in art too.

My father's not at the London townhome, nor do I have a way to track him down unless I want to call on Higgins, his skeleton-like manager. I do not. Nor do I currently have a reason to contact my father.

I'm eager to return to this little nondescript room, where Young Allan Jeayes has learned I'm multilingual and, when after asked a simple question—"Did you see the woman who interviewed before you yesterday?" "Yes, momentarily." "And her appearance?" "Medium-length curly blonde hair, brown eyes, a mole on her neck, pale green blouse, checkered skirt, purse over her right shoulder, pink polish on her nails"—he has gathered that I have a near photographic memory.

On my end, I've gathered he's part of the French Resistance, but from within a British organization.

It seems we both want to know more about each other.

"So tell me," he says—he still hasn't given me his name, which feels very one-sided, though not an unfamiliar dynamic—"is there anyone besides you and your father? I heard you loud and clear you don't date, so I assume no beau or husband. Where is your mother? Any other children Charles Labine is hiding?"

I avert my eyes before I can stop myself. The simple answer: "It's just me and my father."

He taps a pen rhythmically against his desk. "Describe your father to me."

"Accomplished, hardworking, charismatic, intelligent."

He pushes his chair away from his desk to cross his leg over his knee, gripping his ankle, his finger tapping. "And does your father know you're here?"

I should scoff. I'm thirty, clearly not a child. I don't need my father's permission. I shake my head before I say, "No. He's busy on a project. A propaganda film, last I heard."

"Ah, doing his part to aid in the war. That is, from a safe distance. Some aid can be more dangerous."

"Like what you're proposing?"

He smiles. "I haven't proposed anything yet."

I return his smile. "But if you were to propose?"

I've teed up a teasing response, but I get the sense this second conversation is more serious than our first. His response confirms it. "It'd be dangerous. Does that scare you?"

"Honestly?"

"That'd be preferred."

In my lap, I massage one hand into another. "Yes."

He lays down his pen, rotating it until it's perfectly pointed north. "I would stop this conversation here and now if you said you weren't scared. Now, how about this . . . are you capable of keeping everything said here and that may be asked of you confidential?"

I don't hesitate. "Absolutely."

I never tell my father anything until afterward, until I'm certain I've done something that'll make him say, "Well, that's something, Katherine."

Yes, Katherine. He never calls me Daphne, my given name. Given to me, that is, by my *maman*. My father supplied my middle name, named after his own mother. For as long as I can remember, I've been Katherine to him. Kitty, if he's feeling especially paternal in that very moment in time. "Just remarkable, Kitty," he'd tack on.

The first time he praised me was when I began speaking French at the age of three, after nothing more than spending endless amounts of time with my *au pair*. The astonishment on his face is seared into my photographic memory.

"You sound quite certain of your abilities, Miss Chaundanson. What if you were in the hands of the Germans? What if you were being tortured?"

I sit straighter at that.

I've read of torture in various history books. Like how the Tower of London contained a "Rats Dungeon." The Dutch Revolt used rats as well. The Spanish Inquisition had the "Heretic's Fork" and "Neck Traps" to keep a person in an uncomfortable position, not allowing the head to droop or else risk sharp prongs jutting into their neck. Henry VIII boiled people alive. The Middle Ages had the "Breaking Wheel."

I could go on and on, though I'd rather not. I quickly skimmed over descriptions of torture while reading.

But I know something for certain. Reading about it and seeing it firsthand are two very different things, and I've seen what the Gestapo is capable of. I've seen them silence a man by putting a thick bottle in his mouth and shoving it deeper and deeper until the man's lips slipped and his teeth cracked from the pressure.

I touch my own mouth, gently running a finger back and forth over my unmarred bottom lip. But then, answering his question—could I keep a secret even if I'm being tortured?—I attempt a nod.

It's not very convincing, even to me, but still, Young Allan Jeayes continues. "I'd like you to really think about my next question." He pauses, then asks, "Could you kill someone?"

"Kill someone?" I say, tripping over the question.

"That's right, Miss Chaundanson."

My chest rises, falls. I have an aversion even to stepping on bugs. But these aren't bugs I'll be facing. These are scum who think Jews are nothing more than fleas, who do many worse things than splitting lips and crushing teeth. I swallow. "Yes. I could take a life to save a life."

Just saying the words allows me to regain my composure.

Young Allan Jeayes sees this. He nods. But then he says something surprising and not a little off-putting. "I think joining us is something that'd impress your father."

"Excuse me?" Even I can hear the defensiveness in my voice. "I've never said a thing about impressing my father."

But, good grief, Young Allan Jeayes is seeing straight through me.

My father asked me recently, before the war began, *"What are you doing with your life, Katherine? If art is to be your life now, then by thirty you should own a gallery, not simply work at one."*

He went on, reminding me how by thirty he was not only starring in films but also directing and producing them.

At thirty, I still only worked at a gallery, and now I don't even have that anymore. I have this war. This opportunity.

"You're right," Young Allan Jeayes says. "You haven't mentioned impressing your father. Call it instincts. Call it fascinating that you respect your father instead of resenting him. Up until a few days ago, I had no notion Charles Labine even had a daughter. And like I said, my brother is in the industry. I've rubbed elbows with quite a few industry folk. And your father in particular is quite accomplished, like you said yourself. That's quite the shadow to live in."

I allow my lips to twist, not bothering to hide the emotion on my face this time. If he's trying to get under my skin, it's working. And it appears Young Allan Jeayes likes to see my vulnerability. So I give it to him, saying, "If you must know, I only ever pass through his shadow."

"Well, helping to encourage the French to discreetly oppose the Germans, helping to liberate France, ultimately helping to end this war could cast your own. You'd be a secret agent, Miss Chaundanson, and not just on film." He raises a brow. "That's something your father can't say, yes? Your feet would be on French soil, seeing to the success of your assigned mission. And while you can speak nothing of your actions during the war, once this war is won, I imagine those actions would make any father proud."

"Yes, one would imagine so."

And I can all but hear my father's approval and see the same expression from when I was three. Each accomplishment in my life—each degree, language, promotion, rare acquisition for the gallery—my father would send flowers, always with a note inviting me to whichever villa or flat or château he was currently in residence at. Usually he mostly exists on-screen as Hamlet, Caesar, the Earl of Essex, Napoleon II. But for a few short days, he'd exist as simply Charleslabine. Then off he'd go. And off I'd go, to work toward the next great achievement.

And now, Young Allan Jeayes has placed one on a silver platter—albeit a very dangerous silver platter. What's more: he wants *me*.

I'm feeling dazzled.

Young Allan Jeayes begins tapping his pen again. "I've one last question. Why an art gallery?"

"You mean as a place of work?"

He nods. "Sure, why art?"

And there it is, the question I'd been waiting for. It also happens to be a loaded question, but I answer simply, "Art is history."

"And history is a particular interest of yours?"

"I study it, yes. Disasters. War. All those moments that precede us yet can still affect us now. That we can learn from. And when we don't, we risk history repeating itself."

"Anything in particular?" The pen's end goes between his teeth.

I consider, and a topic I've studied extensively in photographs, accounts, and conspiracies, even, comes to mind. "Are you familiar with Morgan Robertson's novel *Futility*?"

My handsome interviewer shakes his head.

I find a more comfortable position in my chair. "The novel tells the story of the *Titan*, billed as the largest ship ever built—and also unsinkable. But of course, calling it such is the kiss of death. In the story, the grand ship strikes an iceberg."

"And sinks," he finishes.

"Yes, in the month of April."

He removes the pen from his mouth, and I can tell he's about to point it at me and conclude where my story is going.

I continue quickly, "Because there aren't enough lifeboats, more than half of the passengers perish."

"I take it this novel was written shortly after the *Titanic* disaster? A recounting of history?"

"No." I shake my head. "Morgan Robertson's book was published in 1898, fourteen years before *Titanic* sank."

I watch as goose bumps erupt on my interviewer's skin, his shirtsleeves rolled up his forearms.

"There's a second work of fiction too. This one by a W. T. Stead, who wrote a short story about an unnamed ocean liner where the protagonist noted the lack of lifeboats. The ship ends up colliding with a barge in a fog bank and sinks. Fortunately for the protagonist, he's pulled from the water. The last line, how-ever, is chilling. The author gives a warning that while the story is merely an anecdote, it's a cautionary tale of what could happen if a ship is put to sea without enough lifeboats."

"And when was this published?"

"In 1886."

"Fascinating."

I bob my head. "And rather ironic, considering Willian Thomas Stead himself later died on *Titanic*."

My interviewer bristles. "It appears art can be predictive too. Why would he ever step foot on a ship without ample lifeboats after his own warnings?"

"*Titanic* was supposed to be unsinkable. The White Star Line wanted their own trio of ships to compete with Cunard's ocean liners. So they built ships nearly a hundred feet longer, ten thousand tons larger, and with only the most extravagant of features. Originally *Titanic* was supposed to carry sixty-four lifeboats, but God forbid the decks be cluttered, so she set sail with only twenty. And perhaps her maiden voyage would've been successful, but *Titanic* didn't leave port when she was sup-posed to."

"And why's that?"

"*Olympic*, which was the first of White Star's trio, had her own collision. Fixing her up delayed *Titanic's* completion, also delay-ing her planned departure in March and instead putting her in April's iceberg-infested waters."

Young Allan Jeayes shakes his head. "I can't quite recall, how many people survived?"

"Not enough," I say, keeping emotion from my voice. "The history books say nine-week-old Millvina Dean was the young-est to survive with her mother and brother." I almost add more about this historical record, but I stop myself. I think I've shared enough from what I know about that horrific night.

It's horrifying to think how 2,241 passengers and crew set

sail that April with no clue that in four short days, their lives and history would be forever altered.

Ironically enough, it's now another April and Young Allan Jeayes forever alters my life when he says, "I've heard enough. Will you join the SOE, Miss Chaundanson?"

"The—"

"Special Operations Executive," he provides.

"Yes." There is no way I can leave this room with a different answer. History has seen its share of sinking ships, but also wars. And I plan to have a hand in ending this one. My course is set.

CHAPTER 3

Violet

—

At sea aboard *Titanic*
April 14, 1912

LAUGHTER NEARLY SPLITS MY SIDE. WE'RE OFF DUTY AFTER our fourth day aboard the *Titanic*, somewhere, I believe, near Newfoundland. Or at the very least, it feels like we're closer to Canada due to the cooler temperatures. Last time I was on the boat deck, wisps of icy mist wafted on board from the sea and left a chill all over me. I looked forward to my bed, warm and cozy.

But first my friends and I are shaking off the day. Shaking off how Miss Walton didn't believe me when I said her Great Dane was just fine, and still she sent me to check on him for the umpteenth time. Shaking off how Mr. Astor misplaced a necklace he intended for Mrs. Astor and insisted I find it, despite how I needed to clean up after the latest cocktail party. However, I will give him credit for not assuming I stole the jewelry. Besides, if I had the gall to do such a thing, it's Mrs. Widener's $250,000 pearl necklace that I'd have my eye—and hands—on.

Every steward and stewardess—of the deck, smoking room, linen, bath, bedroom, plate, and saloon variations—has their own shaking-off story, for which we now reel with laugher and admonish the ridiculousness with the wobble of our heads. Sometimes we even nod appreciatively when a passenger surprises us.

Like the film star Dorothy Gibson, who is as captivating in real life as she is on the screen.

Stanley takes a long pull from his drink. "You may've trekked to the kennels an absurd amount of times, Miss Violet," he says, "but I can do one better." He clears his throat, then begins again in a feminine tone. "My dear, I don't wish to bother coming in off the deck. You can understand how it is much cooler than inside. I know you won't mind giving dear Fifi her lamb cutlet and green peas."

I snort. Ann does, too, along with the other crew members who have gathered with us in the Pig & Whistle, the staff's own private sanctuary. Raising pints, shooting doubles, and inciting gossip has become our routine, even for those who don't wish to imbibe.

Stanley's not done, continuing in the same voice, waving away a cloud of smoke. "But please be sure they are fresh peas, won't you? Well-mashed-up and spoon-fed—"

"She did not!" Ann interjects.

"Fine, not that last portion," Stanley jibes with a wink, the wrinkles in his face multiplying. "But see, Miss Violet, it could be worse."

"But why," I say, "can't it be better?"

We each shrug. Such is the life of a steward or stewardess. Hearing each other's stories is a balm. Knowing my job would not be needed if this ilk did not travel, a bandage. I ask Ann, "How about you? Tell us of your day."

"Well, one of mine told me she couldn't possibly take her lunch in the saloon today. Insisted it was too noisy. And that she didn't like the persons seated near her."

"You mean the replicas of her?" Stanley asks playfully.

"Indeed. So she asked that I bring it to her cabin." Ann holds up her pointer finger. "But not before two o'clock because she shalt not have an appetite before then."

We all laugh. I ask, "She didn't say *shalt*, did she?"

"Creative license." Ann smiles. "But, oh! Speaking of creative." She prematurely laughs, and unable to help myself I join in without knowing what she's about to say. "The honeymooners," she finally composes herself enough to say. "Mrs. Marvin did it. She finally did it and actually threw her shoe. Mr. Marvin was filming her on the promenade. I guess she'd had enough of his documentation. The surprise on his face nearly doubled me over."

I suggest, "Mrs. Astor could use some of Mrs. Marvin's fire."

"And I could use some sleep," Stanley announces, to which we all agree.

We're off, then, Ann taking my arm. A friendship with Ann, like with Stanley, is something I fell into, despite my hesitance. Now she's someone else for my heart to fret over.

In our cabin and furthermore in my narrow top bunk, I pull a magazine from beneath my pillow and flick on the light beside my bed. To my good fortune, the *Tatler* has a spread all about Charles Labine. Dark eyes. Dark hair. He's English but spends a lot of time in France—apparently wooing the lassies. The gossip is that he's been seen with a plethora over the past few months and years. The most notable of late is an heiress named Charlene Anderson.

I chuckle to myself. He's too handsome for his own good. My laugh is cut short. *Titanic* gives a good rock, nearly tipping me from my bunk. A low rending, crunching, ripping sound follows.

It's as if the ship shivers, shudders, then the sound of her engines is cut off.

There's silence. Dead silence. I don't even call out to Ann. There's no way she didn't feel that. There's no way she doesn't know the engines have been off for nearly an entire minute now. I'm still, barely breathing as I listen for any new sounds.

In the hall, doors open. There's the hum of questioning voices.

I don't dare move. Nor do I put words to what I know has happened. If I'd been on my feet, I would've been knocked off them. Just like last time.

Finally, I lean over the side of my bunk. "Ann?"

Only her fingertips are visible over her blanket, the quilt pulled to her chin. She licks her lips. I expect alarm in her voice, but she's calm. "Sounds as if something has happened."

There's not a thing funny about what she's said. And I know what she's said to be correct. But, Lord help me, a laugh bubbles out of me.

I roar with laughter.

How is a sea-related calamity happening a second time to me? First the *Olympic*. Now the *Titanic*? I've long felt I've been surviving on borrowed time, but how unlucky must I be?

Dios mios. My mother will have a cow.

I try to visualize the closest port for us to limp to if we've struck something and need repairs. Six hundred nautical miles? Seven hundred? And that'd be to Halifax. It's even greater to New York, if our path doesn't alter. It'll be a job for *Titanic* to get to either. Likewise, it'll be a job for me to comfort my passengers every mile of the way.

That puts an end to my laughter. It's fifteen till midnight. The last thing I want to do is put my shoes, apron, and hat back on and trudge up four decks. I groan. "We should do our rounds."

Ann nods, looking more nervous than when I'd first hung myself over her bunk, perhaps on account of my slightly unhinged crowing.

"We'll be fine," I assure her. "*Salvo.* Now let's go make sure our passengers are too."

★ ★ ★

NOT FIFTEEN MINUTES LATER, THERE'S AN EXPLOSION. MY hands pause on the life belt I'm tightening around Miss Walton.

"What was that?" she gasps, teeth chattering as much from the cold air seeping in as from the excitement.

"I'm not sure." *Sincero.*

Last year *Hawke* thrust eight feet into *Olympic*'s hull and tore a forty-foot gash below the waterline, but I don't recall hearing any blasts. A number of flooded compartments, *sí*. But explosions, no. And to me, a flooding ship is arguably worse than a tiny boom.

While the inner workings of a ship are not my forte, I'd wager we are fine on this second unsinkable ship, just as we were on the first. At the time, I'd been more interested in the buzz that followed *Olympic*'s collision. The incident was a huge financial disaster for my employer. There was the obvious—the cost of repairs. But also mounting legal fees since it was claimed the larger *Olympic* sucked the smaller *Hawke* into its side. Then there was the cannibalization from this very ship—a propeller shaft and other materials from the *Titanic*—to get the *Olympic* back in service as quickly as possible that resulted in a delay getting *Titanic* in the water. I could've begun sooner with *Olympic*, but the allure of *Titanic* enticed me to await her maiden voyage. That, and the larger salary.

This late at night—rather, this early in the morning— exhaustion is written on Miss Walton's face, competing with a pinched expression. "All is well," I dutifully assure her. "Your life belt is on." I give it a final tug. "Why don't you go above deck for some fresh air? It looks as if many are headed that way. In these unique circumstances, I bet you can even request to have Hercules brought up to you too."

All around us, other stewards and stewardesses are doing the same and directing everyone to the boat deck. Some passengers have yet to change from their silk evening gowns. Others are practically sleepwalking from their rooms, fumbling with buttons and still in their slippers. Mr. and Mrs. Marvin emerge, hair mussed, Daniel's motion camera tucked under one arm.

I touch Miss Walton's elbow, gently pushing her toward her father, who is conversing with Stanley. I give her my most reassuring smile. "If I see someone from the kennels, I will put in a good word for Hercules."

Miss Walton visibly calms. "I'd appreciate that very much." Then she presses coins into my hand.

I'd have made this offer nevertheless, but very much appreciate the gratuity I slip into my apron.

Once Miss Walton is firmly clinging to her father's arm, I look for Mrs. Astor, but she must already be above deck. I bend to untie and readjust a child's life belt, the child barely registering me in her sleepy bewilderment. I stop to instruct a woman to put her life belt beneath her coat instead of over it.

"Why should it matter?"

"It's how it's properly worn," I answer.

"But what does it matter if I won't be in the water?"

I smile sweetly. In an actual moment of emergency, the weight of the coat, if worn over clothing, could easily be discarded. But I don't see the need to say that. Instead, I reply, "It's your decision, but I'd advise wearing it correctly."

I'm met with twisted lips and suddenly, Stanley is by our sides.

"Ma'am," he begins, "we've just been instructed that everyone should board the lifeboats."

The woman blanches. "That seems entirely unnecessary."

My thoughts exactly.

"It's a precaution. Once we know the ship is in tip-top condition, everyone will return to their warm cabins."

He smiles earnestly.

She huffs off.

Additional questions are not only asked of me but of all the stewards and stewardesses mulling about. "Are we safe?" "What is to happen?" "Should we bring anything?"

It seems we all have the same answer, a shared line: "Wear your warmest clothing and board the lifeboats, but just as a precautionary measure, of course."

We all use the same calm, unemotional voices. All my remaining passengers are vacant from their rooms, some leaving their doors thrown open and their belongings in disarray. Jewels sparkle atop various dressing tables, and a pair of silver slippers are lying just where they'd been kicked off. In complete contrast, others start upstairs unhurried and unconcerned, taking their time.

I'm in the second camp, choosing to go down to my room first. Absentmindedly, I begin tidying up, folding my nightgown and putting things in place. I nearly pull a neck muscle at the abrupt hurling of my name.

"What?" I say, twirling around to see Stanley's hulking figure in my open doorway.

"Miss Violet? What do you think you're doing?" He rushes into my cabin, clutching both my arms. "You understand it's all hogwash we're feeding them, don't you?" I smell the liquor on his breath. Stanley is excitable, even more so when he's enjoyed himself like he has earlier tonight. "We've hit an iceberg. We're not coming back on this ship. Not ever again."

"Oh?"

"She's sinking, Miss Violet."

Sinking?

He goes on, "Our only hope is that the lifeboats will sustain us until another vessel can reach us in time to pick us up."

Hundiendose? I repeat silently, as if it'd make better sense in my second language. It does not.

"That's not possible," I say, lightly touching my collarbone.

"Get your coat, Violet. Go up to the boat deck. Get on a life-boat. Where's Ann?"

I look around as if just now realizing that she's not here and that I'm uncertain of her whereabouts. I've never seen Stanley more serious, the lines of his face so deep. All I can do is nod, even if I think he's more concerned than he needs to be.

Still, he stands there. He means for me to get on some type of outerwear this very second. I fumble in my wardrobe but then remember I have no such thing. It's spring. The weather's

been beautiful. I left such a garment in Ealing after the change
of seasons. Ann has a beautiful mackintosh coat she had the
wherewithal to keep on hand, though. It's already gone.

"Ann is upstairs," I surmise.

"Your coat?" he asks.

I shake my head. "I don't have one."

"Come on," he says, all but pulling me from my cabin.

We proceed up the stairs and onto a first-class deck. At the
first open room he sees, Stanley runs inside, returning with a
silk eiderdown blanket that he wraps around my shoulders. He
pauses before he unlatches his wristwatch.

"Here," he says, pressing it into my hand. "For you. An audible reassurance that another moment is forthcoming." He tries
for a smile. "As long as you keep her wound, that is."

"No." I swallow. "This is yours."

"It's yours now. Now, up we go."

I allow him to lead me. The uppermost first-class boat deck is
quiet with the hum of curious voices. By a doorway, I spy Captain
Smith chatting with the manager of our line, our chief purser, and
Dr. O'Loughlin. They have their hands in their pockets like men
do who are casually waiting for something. I test them, throwing a smile in their direction. Nonchalantly, they wave back.
Dr. O'Loughlin, whom I've grown close with, also offers me a
warm smile.

I let out a breath.

Stanley is overly worked up, is all.

Besides the officers and men who are briskly getting lifeboats
ready to lower, there are very few serious faces. More than anything, the passengers look put out and dispirited.

It doesn't surprise me that my friend Jock is gathering his
bandmates. I overhear him say, "Let's give them a tune to cheer
things up a bit."

A grand idea.

String music begins.

I turn to see Mr. Marvin with his camera rolling. For once, Mrs. Marvin isn't in the shot. He's capturing the happenings, which, again, feel rather dull at the moment. He proceeds to the railing, trying to angle his camera down.

I don't know what he intends to see in the darkness, but curiosity does strike me. Stanley says we're sinking, that we've hit an iceberg. But is there a hole? I only heard that single explosion, which hasn't been mentioned since. Surely there'd be more concern from the captain and more urgency with loading the boats if this is truly a serious matter.

I pivot, assessing further. Miss Walton is stroking Hercules's ginormous head. The Great Dane is nearly as tall as she is, even as she stands. She catches my eye and waves, mouthing, "Thank you."

I wish I actually had a hand in bringing her beast to the boat deck. But it matters little. She has what she needs, including her father, who is nearby conversing with Mr. Astor. Mrs. Astor sits stoically on a deck chair. Par for the course.

In a steady, loud voice, an announcement is made that the first boat is ready. No one makes a move to board. It's no wonder, as there's still no sense of urgency. And, *Dios, ayúdame*, the lifeboat dangles off the side of the ship, suspended from what feels like miles overtop the yawning blackness of the sea.

So far that's the most alarming thing I've seen.

It's certainly not *Titanic* herself. She's steady, her engines still off. It'd be easy to confuse us being at port and not in the middle of the Atlantic.

"Look!" I hear.

The whole of the deck's inhabitants seem to turn at once. On the horizon, there's a light. A ship's light, as it can't be anything else.

The discovery is chorused by many saying how another ship has come for us. That leaves many—myself included—content to bide our time to see what actually needs to happen next instead of boarding that dangling lifeboat. Perhaps *Titanic* will move again. Perhaps we'll board that other ship. But to lower precariously in a lifeboat, what's the need?

Still, one lowers, with very few people on it. Maybe ten, twelve? I recognize Lady Lucy Duff Gordon and her husband, Sir Cosmo. There was room for plenty more, at least fifty. I note—and I'm sure others note as well—how it descended well enough.

One of the officers, Mason, quite disgruntled by the tone of his voice, comical as he's usually so good-natured, calls out, "If each boat is lowered at that capacity, nearly all of you will be stranded."

Ears perk at his word choice. No one wishes to be stranded. Nor does the ship's light we spotted on the horizon appear to be any closer. Anxious energy sparks in the chilly air. The effect is a surge of people forward to embark. Mason certainly wasn't expecting the flurry of chaos. The second boat lowers very full, almost too full.

Directions are called out for people to calm themselves. Funny, moments ago everyone was arguably too calm in Mason's mind, and now they rush at him and the other officers like banshees.

Miss Walton's voice screeches above the rest, her hand tightly wound around her dog's leash. "I will not leave without my father and Hercules."

"Only women and children at this time," she's told, despite the fact we all just watched Sir Cosmo be lowered.

Miss Walton points to a woman in the lifeboat holding a Pekingese. The woman lifts her nose. "Fifi fits in my lap. *That* dog would take up the space of three women. And there, see, my husband has agreed to get a later lifeboat."

Her husband—one of Stanley's passengers—agrees valiantly.

"Well," Miss Walton asserts, "I will not board without my father or my dog."

The officer loading the boat wears a pained expression but still insists, "Then you must stand aside, miss."

She does.

Mrs. Astor takes her place, boarding. I expect for an exception to be made for John Jacob Astor IV as it had for Sir Cosmo, but he doesn't try to climb into the lifeboat. He chastely kisses his wife on the cheek, says a few private words into her ear, then steps back into the ever-increasing crowd of men. She offers him the most genuine smile I've seen from her yet.

As if my heart is being tested, I notice Mrs. Marvin being pushed forward next. Mr. Marvin's kiss is not chaste. Over the past few days, I've heard stories of their coupling. They first married in secret, knowing their parents wouldn't approve because of their young ages. After Mary fell pregnant, they couldn't keep their secret any longer. And thus, they were married a second time. Afterward, they traveled, as I had correctly guessed, to England for their honeymoon. And now the couple is on their way back to New York to begin their life together.

Only they are no longer together in this moment. Daniel is left on the deck. He calls out, "It's all right, Mary. I promise. I've my life belt. I'll jump off and swim after you. Keep an eye out, my love. I'll be in need of you to warm me up." He gives Mary a wink as the boat lowers. She rubs a finger beneath her nose, a choked laugh leaving her mouth, but then waves, the enthusiasm clearly forced.

He raises his camera, begins filming.

"And, darling," he calls, "I endeavor to save the film. Imagine the memories I've captured, ones to show our grandchildren when we're old and gray."

Mary's hand lowers to her stomach.

Tears spring to my eyes.

Watching family taken from family or otherwise determined to stay with family brings up emotions I know all too well. To protect my own heart, it's why I now put an ocean between myself and those I love. But now is not the time for tears. I'm to set an example. I encourage a young woman to board a lifeboat. Then I urge another.

I notice another steward standing by, his back to the white bulkhead, a cigarette in his mouth, surrounded by our distinguished guests. It's jarring to see. Never would such a disciplinary erosion be tolerated under normal circumstances.

But tonight is far from normal.

"There you are," Ann says, slipping her arm in mine.

"Where have you been?" I ask, my words spilling out.

"I was around the other side. Most of the lifeboats over there are gone. Are many left here?"

"I'm un—"

Shots ring out.

I twist toward the noise, a hand on Ann's arm. A streak of white light is high in the sky. A baby cries in reaction.

"A distress rocket," I mumble.

"To call that ship closer?"

The light we saw from the other ship is still there. But I can't determine, yet again, if it has moved closer. I think it may be moving. Or it may just be my tired eyes playing tricks on me.

Another rocket is shot off just as there's a second commotion. Stanley leads a group of people wearing heavy woolen clothing to the first-class deck. I place them as third-class passengers, ones I'm surprised to see. The uptick of whispers tells me I'm not the only one. Though, now that the upper-class women and children have been given the opportunity to board, why shouldn't they have their turn?

How sad, them being forced to wait in the first place. How scary for them too. A few of the women cry freely, even more so when hands are pressed on their husbands' chests to keep them behind.

"Nie," one of the women protests, her words nearly drowned out by the sounds of Jock and his musicians.

My heart goes out to these foreigners. They likely do not

speak English. How horrible to be among a crowd in such a situation and not be able to understand what is being said.

The few remaining lifeboats are now being lowered more rapidly. Too hastily. One end of the lifeboat is higher than the other, then reversed, the cries of the women aligning with the jerky movements.

I look away. My brows scrunch. Thomas Andrew, the ship's architect, and Charles, the chief baker, are throwing anything wooden—deck chairs, rafters—over the side of the ship.

But why on earth would they be doing such a thing? My mind churns through the possible reasons. To lessen the weight aboard the ship? For floatable items in the water?

The latter is frightening. I cannot swim. I never learned, not with having a part of my lung removed as a child.

Suddenly the crowd of people around me parts, allowing room for a man who pushes through. He darts to the ship's side, and before he can be stopped, hurls himself into a descending boat.

"*Increíble*," I say, turning to Ann. "We'll all get a turn." But just as I say it, my heart stands still. I notice now how the forward part of *Titanic* is lower. Much lower. And in that moment, my unshaken faith in this ship is shaken.

A strained breath later, one of the mailmen from our sorting office has joined Ann and me. "The mail is floating up to the F Deck with water," he tells us choppily. "I've raced up."

I grip the mailman. "Tell me, is there a hole? One too damaging for our ship?"

His mouth hangs open, but all he says is "I'll pray for you, Miss Jessop." Then he rushes off.

Too much has happened in the past few moments.

Items being thrown overboard.

A man making a daring escape.

The mail floating beneath us.

The mailman praying for what . . . my survival?

I've taken each blow as it has come, determined to stay level-headed. I've been in a similar situation before and walked off the ship without a scratch. But . . . is Stanley correct? Is this unsinkable ship to sink?

Where is Stanley anyway? With Ann's grip tight on my arm, my gaze passes over the crowd remaining on deck. Mostly men. A few bullheaded women. No Stanley, though.

I'm still holding his wristwatch. I put it on, the size of it too large for my slender wrist.

At the nearest lifeboat, Mason catches my eye. It looks like he's been trying to capture my attention for some time. He motions urgently toward the boat he's filling. His face looks weary and tired.

I recognize the sounds of Jock's men. "Nearer My God to Thee."

"It's time," Ann says. "There's nothing else for us to do. Our passengers, those who can and will leave, have done so. I've seen other crew go down. It's our turn."

My survival instinct kicks in, knowing full well if I go into the water, I have no known skills to keep myself above water. I nod, my heart in my throat.

Mason helps me onto the small boat, already nearly full with twenty, maybe thirty foreigners wearing bewildered expressions. He turns toward another passenger on deck when it is Ann's turn to climb in. In helping her board, I nearly fall over the tackle and oars, but finally she is beside me, the very last spot.

I return my attention to Mason to thank him, earnestly for me and mockingly in regard to Ann, when he holds up a bundle. It seems as if he's about to throw whatever it is at me. Instead, he leans down, extending the wrapped parcel to me. "Look after this, will you?" he says.

I reach out, curious. As soon as my hands touch it, I recognize the shape, the softness yet firmness of it.

A baby.

CHAPTER 4

Daphne

London
April 15, 1942

EVEN THOUGH I ALREADY TOLD YOUNG ALLAN JEAYES I'D join his clandestine operation, he makes me say it a second time during our third meeting. Then he slides the Official Secrets Act across his desk to me.

It's dated, and today's date isn't lost on me: thirty years since *Titanic* sank. On that day, many lives were saved, while even more were lost or had their trajectories greatly changed. I read that the passengers had boarded for various reasons: a better life, a business opportunity, a honeymoon, a holiday, a way to begin again.

Signing this document feels like my own precipice, an opportunity to do something extraordinary. I can only hope it has a better outcome.

"Everything all right, Miss Chaundanson?"

I scoff lightly at myself. Dramatics run in my blood.

I answer with my signature.

"Very good," he says. "Now, there's no guarantee of this, but after you've been given an officer rank, you'd ideally be treated as a prisoner of war under the Geneva Convention if captured."

"Which is different how?"

"You wouldn't be tortured."

"But you already said I could be tortured at the hands of the Germans."

"Yes, which is why I say you'd *ideally* be treated as a POW. There is a strong likelihood that you'd be tortured. We've already had agents shot, killed, taken to Nazi camps. But they've all been men. We do have a woman in France, but she's yet to be caught. You're to be within our first group of women to officially be trained and dropped in. There's no telling if you'd be treated more humanely than the men have been."

I shiver involuntarily.

Of course Young Allan Jeayes doesn't miss my reaction. "Would you like me to tear up your signature and you can go on your way? It'd be like these conversations never happened."

"No," I say firmly.

He smiles. "Last thing we'll need you to do before training begins is to enlist with FANY."

"Which is?"

"The First Aid Nursing Yeomanry."

"First aid?"

"It's merely a cover. Every bit of you will have a cover, Madame Irene du Tertre."

"Oh, I'm married now?"

The thought is somewhat comical. I wouldn't say I've had positive experiences with men. Sure, I've had dalliances, but the two past relationships I've had haven't gone well. Since then, some would say I've kept men *on the back burner*. Better them than me.

"Yes," he says, "you are now married to a milner, who you'll say has joined the German Wehrmacht, if you're ever asked."

I scrunch my nose. "It appears I do not respect my own husband."

"Well, he's off doing Germany's bidding so you won't have to feign an in-person relationship with him. And if you'd like, we can make you a widow in time."

"Better."

A soft snorting sound escapes Young Allan Jeayes, but then he clears his throat. "In all seriousness, this *is* very serious, and you'll need to know every aspect of your new life inside and out."

"Understood."

"And your code name, which you'll use with us and any contacts in France, will be Katherine."

"How ironic."

"Yes, we're aware it's your middle name."

I rattle my head. "Yes, but it's also what my father has always called me."

In fact, I went by Katherine much of my life. It was not until attending the Sorbonne, where I studied journalism, that I envisioned my byline as Daphne Chaundanson instead of Katherine Chaundanson. If I'd be writing my truths, it'd be important to be fully myself.

The idea of writing under the name Daphne felt like I'd be putting on a new skin, a reinvention, but only partly so as I'd still retain my surname. And now, the dogged part of me that has always been Katherine is about to join the war. How fitting.

* * *

WHAT'S ILL-FITTING ARE MY BOOTS. AND ALSO MY OVERALL physical makeup for the current task at hand during my SOE agent training. I'm a tall girl. I have long arms, long legs. I'm an academic. I am not meant for athletics.

Although, no, there are many tall women who are athletic. Barbara Burke comes to mind. In the last Olympics she medaled in one of the running races. A relay, perhaps. And I recall her being quite statuesque in photographs. Same with Alice Bridges, or maybe it was Lenore Wingard. I'm having trouble separating them. Both were American swimmers, but one was noticeably taller.

So there goes that theory. It's simply me who is lanky and uncoordinated, quite obvious in how I'm currently struggling to army-crawl beneath crisscrossing barbed wire.

I blow hair from my face and renew my concentration. During the preceding timed run, I'd distracted myself from my seldom-used, now-throbbing muscles by searching for a particular tree. I've studied Queen Victoria and I recall how she liked to plant plane trees. She did so at Buckingham Palace, an obvious location. But I also recall the mention of Wanborough Manor—this very manor—as one of the places she'd planted. I'm still not sure which tree is hers, but wondering blessedly occupied my mind while running and has successfully resulted in me here, beneath this barbed wire—where another recruit would rightfully pass me, if there was anyone left behind me.

I finally emerge, push to my feet, and jog the final bit to join the three other women and ten men who've already completed the run and obstacles.

Their cheers only make me feel foolish for being the last to finish. Hands on my hips, I turn away and struggle for breath.

Four weeks, I remind myself. The first part of our training consists of "only" four weeks of physical conditioning, basic weapons training, and hand-to-hand combat here in Surrey before we're off to our next training locale. What awaits us there, I'm not sure. But it's still a light at the end of the tunnel, an end I must reach.

Not everyone will be asked to continue. Getting asked to leave is unfathomable. What do I have to go home to? *Where* do I have to go home to? An empty London town house? Returning to Paris, my life there, my job there, my few close companions there, isn't an option. People are fleeing the city, not flocking to it. Nor do I think I'd even be allowed back in to my birth country with the state of things, severing one of the few connections to my *maman* I have. Young Allan Jeayes mentioned how we'll be snuck into France when the time comes. *If* the time comes, unless I take this opportunity by the horns.

I face the group.

I feared I'd be—how do you say it?—a bit aged compared to the other women here. But I'm shocked that Suzanne and Adele are older by at least a decade, maybe two. Denise is the youngest, twenty-two I heard her say.

Of course, none of those are their real names. We aren't supposed to share private information, but after our arrival and before we started today, Adele insisted on knowing why each of us is here.

"I'll go first," Adele said in French. All communication should be in French. "My husband is also part of SOE. I'm here for him. It's important that he comes back. It's important you ladies know that."

Her eyes were kind when she said it, but her voice couldn't have been more serious. Suzanne squeezed her hand. She has a motherly look to her with short wavy hair. "I'm divorced," Suzanne began, "so I don't share the same fondness for my husband, but it's clear you care about yours. I'm here because the Germans bombed my home last year. Got my blood boiling. Guess it got really boiling because apparently I was overheard quite a few times when I was working as a receptionist in a hotel about how angry I was about it. Wasn't long before I was approached to come here. They say looks can be deceiving. I may appear to be a sweet old lady, but I can be a lion."

Denise talked next. "I'm here for me and for France." She said it so matter-of-factly that I envied her confidence. "I was already working with the Resistance," she went on. "I still have a lot of work to do. I came across a German once. He was sleeping. For some reason, the adage 'let sleeping giants lie' stuck in my head. Though I think it was the fear of the noise I'd make killing him that really stopped me. So I let him live. And then the next day I saw that exact German torture an innocent man. I won't make the same mistake again."

After, Denise didn't blink; she stared at each of us like she was waiting for us to challenge her. I very quickly gathered she's tough, no-nonsense, another lion through and through. Her eyes locked on mine.

"I'm here for France too," I said, trying to infuse the same passion into my own speech. "It's embarrassing how nothing was done. So I want to help do something." What I said is true. What I didn't say is how I'm also here to make Daddy proud. *That* sounds more like a mouse.

A pathetic thirty-year-old mouse who shouldn't place impressing her father as a top priority. But I can't shake the feeling that maybe if I do enough, I'll be enough. Then, when questioned by the press and people in his industry, my father won't laugh me off as an overzealous fan when I'm captured in photographs with him. More than Higgins and various house staff will know my true identity, instead of being misidentified as one of his many young lovers when we're seen together.

I'd simply be his daughter. That day on the telephone during Parent's Day, he never answered me, not fully, on why I must be kept a secret.

"Because of Papa's job," he had said.

I asked him again, sometime later. His response then wasn't much better. *"To protect you from my life, Katherine."*

It wasn't his protection I wanted. It was his love.

Adele had clapped her hands. "All right then, ladies. We've all got our reasons for being here. Now let's get to work."

That work continues at the firing range.

"What we've got here," Major McKennan says, "is a metal tube. About a foot long." He taps it against his hand. "Easy to conceal. Then we've got these two other pieces. You push the barrel into the tube. You tighten the barrel nut. Slide the stock into place. And voilà, a Sten gun. I want you to practice putting it together. I want you to be able to do it in your sleep. When you're in France, you'll likely receive the gun just like this, in three parts."

Major McKennan drops a box in front of each of us. "Go on, put it together. Quickly."

I scramble to open my box. Push. Tighten. Slide.

My father's given me many material gifts over the years.

Jewelry, books, even the most delicious macarons—by the by, thank you to Queen Catherine de Medici for introducing them to France. My father may be short on in-person time, but never on gifts sent from afar. But the best thing my actor father has ever given me is a brain for remembering.

In no time, I have the gun together.

In fact, I have it together before anyone else, the men included.

I place it atop the lid of my box and pull my hands back like it doesn't count if I'm still touching it.

"Well done, Katherine," Major McKennan says.

I hide a smile, mostly because Denise doesn't hide a growl. Though I don't get the sense the reaction is directed at me, but more so at herself for failing to be first.

One of the men, with a strong aura of Cary Grant to him, is next to complete the task. "Nice work, Gabriel."

Denise shoots him a look.

He shoots me a look, like he's a bit intimidated by Denise. I don't blame him. But then he smirks and asks me quietly, "Hey, how much does a polar bear weigh?"

A polar bear? I can't say that's ever come up in my many years of schooling. I pull a face.

"Enough," he says, clearly amused with himself, "to break the ice."

I can't help it, I laugh, because there's surely plenty of tension and awkwardness at the moment.

Denise slams down her completed gun. Soon we all have assembled guns in front of us.

"Next," Major McKennan says, motioning toward various target boards, "we shoot. Two short bursts, in your own time. Go on."

I swallow. I've never shot a gun before. But the spurt of noise from the other guns jolts my own finger into action. My body rocks with the power of it, and suddenly this feels very real.

It only becomes even more so when we're no longer lined up

in front of wooden targets but lifelike dummies. This time we're told to use nothing but our hands, knees, and feet.

I chop at its neck. I chop across the bridge of the nose. I scrape my nails down the burlap. *Face tearing*, this is called. *Testicle crushing* with our knees seems self-explanatory.

It does me good to continue to picture it as a dummy and not a human being. Though I remember what I told Young Allan Jeayes: "*I could take a life to save a life.*"

And it's as if Major McKennan is inside my head and can sense my hesitation. He questions the group, "Now, who here feels comfortable striking another person?"

Denise's hand shoots up so quickly she rouses a string of birds from a nearby tree. We shouldn't laugh. But we do, even the major.

His next question: "Who would like to be partnered with Denise?"

"Don't everyone volunteer at once," one of the men, Hector, jokes, which Major McKennan says earns him the honor. Hector curses as he steps forward.

"Denise, attack Hector from behind."

I'm not sure what I'm expecting, but it's not for all five feet of her to run at Hector, leap onto his back, and dangle from his neck while twisting her body side to side.

Denise brings him down, landing deftly on her feet. Casually she dusts off her hands, then looks to Major McKennan for his next orders. Hector is still on the ground.

Beside me, the Cary Grant recruit lets out a long, slow breath. "She's horrifying."

"Uh-huh," I say just as quietly.

"Partners?" he asks me. Gabriel is his code name, I remember. "You look tough, don't get me wrong, but you also don't give off the vibe you'd like to dismantle my C1 and C2 vertebrae."

"That's oddly specific."

He shrugs. "I'm a physician."

"Of polar bears?"

He chuckles. "Humans."

"A shame. Well, I work with priceless art. Ripping and shredding aren't exactly in my nature."

"A match made in heaven," Gabriel says playfully, but then his expression startles. "That came out wrong. I have a girl back home."

Such a man, thinking I assumed we were exchanging flirtations. Even if it's likely that women often *do* flirt with him. But that's not me. Why put myself in a position for another man to come in and out of my life?

Gabriel confuses my reaction. "Listen, I didn't mean—"

"It's fine," I say just as Major McKennan announces for everyone to find a second.

"Partners," I affirm.

"Great," Gabriel says, smiling.

And of course he has a dimple, just on the one side, somehow having a more charming effect than if he had two.

We practice attacking each other from behind. When Gabriel grabs me, I stomp on his foot or plunge an elbow into his stomach. His breath rushes out.

"Okay, on to something new," the major begins. "Place your palm beneath your partner's chin." I do as he says. "The head will go back, yes. Put some pressure there. Then your hand closes over his face, your fingers lining perfectly with his eyes. During an actual incident, you can dig your fingers there. At the same time, strike your knee into the groin. Aiming for the balls is almost never a poor decision."

I really sell the *testicle crush*, winding up my knee and stopping a mere inch away.

"Very good," Major McKennan calls out just as Gabriel releases a relieved exhale. "Again."

And again and again, along with other hand-to-hand combat techniques.

"Now we'll use sticks."

"Dear God," Gabriel whispers.

The major adds, "On our dummies."

"Oh, thank God," Gabriel revises.

"I need maximum aggression!" Major McKennan shouts. "This is about killing, the difference between your life and his."

I jab beneath the neck. In the stomach. The ever-popular groin.

"Life or death, Katherine!"

I picture a German with venom in his eyes coming for me. I whack the dummy upside the head.

Coming for another woman, a child, anyone vulnerable.

Torturing. Raping.

I strike the spleen—Gabriel had pointed out that one for me earlier. The kneecaps. Again, the head.

I'm breathless.

"And stop!" the major yells. "That's it for today."

Gabriel is catching his own breath at the dummy beside mine. "A hell of a first day."

That it was. Does it make me more of a lion that I cannot wait for more? I find it comical, the girl who grew up with her nose in a book is now eager to break someone else's.

CHAPTER 5

Violet

—

Atlantic Ocean
April 15, 1912

MY CHILDHOOD WAS SPENT HOLDING BABIES, MUCH LIKE the one I hold now, as I'm about to be lowered from the *Titanic*.

It's such a familiar weight in my arms. I was around five when my first sibling, Ray, was born. Two years later, William was on the scene, then Philip. Patrick and Jack came together, only minutes apart. Then Denis, Molly, Eileen. All spread out over fifteen years.

There was one more, but Mother was too heartbroken at that point to name her. Father had just died, and this final baby was a stillborn.

But ever since Ray, Mother counted on me to see to our one-roomed home and to each new sibling who came along. I remember raising my chin, accepting of the challenge even at my young age, watching as my mother and father left our *puesto* to see to the sheep that first brought them seven thousand miles to Bahía Blanca from Ireland. They worked so hard to make ends meet.

I worked so hard to do what they could not do at home. At the end of each day, I collapsed with exhaustion into the gin box I used as a cot and reluctantly, anxiously listened to the shrill, high-pitched calls of the viscachas outside.

More often than not, the rabbitlike creatures would awaken Ray, his cries just as shrill and high-pitched, and I'd drag myself across the dirt floor to his own gin box, pulling him into my arms, rocking him, wondering what predator caused the viscachas such alarm.

Another distress rocket whistles into the air, sounding eerily like those damned rodents. It yanks me back to the here and now.

Aboard a lifeboat.

Holding someone's child.

About to be lowered from the *Titanic* to the dark waters below.

Por favor, I think, *don't let me touch those waters.* Not only are they bone-chilling cold, but there's this child in my care I'd have to also keep afloat and somehow warm.

A dog barks.

My regard jumps to the deck. Miss Walton stands there, her face blank, Hercules by her side. He's agitated, twisting on his lead. Another bark, the thundering sound vibrating through my body.

I jerk as Mason lowers one side of our lifeboat.

Ann grips my knee.

"Stanley," I breathe, finally spotting him on the deck, feeling the weight of his watch on my wrist. He's farther down the ship, the vessel pitched, raising him higher than where Miss Walton stands. I scan what little I can still see of the promenade.

We're lower now.

The only lifeboat currently going down.

Stanley is leaning over the railing. He blows me a kiss, and a realization so sharp and so painful crashes into me that I truly cannot breathe.

It's a goodbye.

Are there no other lifeboats?

How had I not seen that when Mason ushered me forward?

I would have insisted Stanley board. That Miss Walton, even Hercules, be given a spot.

This lifeboat is full. Six crew members. Ann, me, and another stewardess. Upwards of thirty foreigners. But we'd cram in.

Mr. Astor.

Mr. Walton.

Mr. Marvin—filming.

They're all still there.

The lifeboat groans and jerks so abruptly I almost drop what's in my lap. So second nature, I've forgotten I'd been holding the child.

Someone's child.

A forgotten child?

How is this innocent child so unlucky to be in this situation? Or perhaps lucky to be in my arms within this lifeboat instead of still on the ship?

I wrap the eiderdown blanket around us both.

None of this feels real. *Surely it's a dream*, I think as we lower down the ship's side. Each deck we pass is alive with blinding porthole lights, so close I could reach out and touch them.

But there is nothing dreamlike about the impact when the lifeboat thuds against the dark water. Women let out shrieks, cries, and exclamations, some in languages I cannot understand.

Ann's crying now.

I hold tight to what's in my arms, focusing my attention there. And not on how we're in a crowded, tiny boat in the middle of the Atlantic.

I'm momentarily confused when I hear the cry of a baby, the noise not coming from my own arms but from across the lifeboat. A second baby. The child I hold starts to whimper as well. A lad or a lass, I do not know. I haven't gotten a good look yet. And right now I frantically scan the moonless night for Stanley.

If only I can keep my eyes on him, then he'll stay safe. *Titanic* will remain afloat long enough for whatever vessel I'd seen earlier to get here. I look in that direction again, the light of the ship still in the distance. But closer? No, it doesn't seem so.

When I turn back, *Titanic* looks lower.

Imposible.

There's simply no way she could have dipped so severely in

only the blink of an eye. There are ten decks on the *Titanic*. Seven above water. Eight if the boat deck is included.

I crane my head back and count the rows of lights that designate each floor.

One, two, three, four, five, six.

No, that cannot be correct. I'm mistaken, *eso es todo.*

I begin again—*one, two, three, four, five . . .*

A crew member in the forepart of the lifeboat calls out for the oars.

It interrupts my counting.

I lick my lips, my heart pounding.

Uno, dos, tres, quatro . . .

I stop. I shake my head. My eyes and the ship's lights are playing tricks on me, that's all. The baby whimpers again. I hush it.

I begin again, but there's no need. I'm not mistaken. This is no trick. The ship is lower in the water.

Sinking.

With so many people still aboard. Given the number of lifeboats in the water, over a thousand people could be saved. Yet, as I already witnessed, not all the boats were filled to capacity. Nor would there be enough, regardless. How can that be? Over two thousand boarded our unsinkable ship, yet over half will suffer her same fate?

It's as if the others on this boat are connecting the same dots, counting the lifeboats, counting the remaining decks above water, coming to the same realization that so many will be plunged into the frigid Atlantic with nothing more than coats, life belts, and prayers. The women collectively weep. Some silently. Some unrestrained. And for as much as I needed to train my eyes on Stanley only heartbeats ago, now I cannot look.

* * *

IN THE END, I DO WATCH.

A tiny breeze, the first bit of wind I'd felt the entire night so far, slices icily across my face and my eyes shoot open. My life-boat has been rowed a greater distance from *Titanic*. Her bow is significantly lower in the sea than her stern. People are jumping.

Men.

Women.

Children.

Bodies of all shapes and sizes, jackets and dresses billowing in the air, plunging into the water, only to emerge bulging on the water's surface. Screams and cries ring out, from both the far-off people and from those on the lifeboats.

Then *Titanic*'s lights flicker off, a blessing and a curse, leaving me only with ghastly shadows and an ongoing, agonizing sound of the ship tearing itself apart.

First comes a large crack. *Titanic* lurches forward, breaking in two. With a thunderous crash, one of her four funnels topples off and into the sea, like it'd been made of nothing more than cardboard.

The oddest, most trivial thought passes through my brain in that very moment. Only three of the four funnels were functional in releasing smoke, heat, and steam from the boiler rooms. The fourth had been added merely for aesthetics, because *Titanic* is supposed to be beautiful. Grand. Majestic.

It was all a ruse.

That funnel.

The claim she could not sink, when now she's in two pieces.

Her bow begins to drop away. It's gone in heartbeats, leaving the stern to elevate, barely seen in the darkness, to rise, and then to right itself into the sky. There it stands, for another heartbeat, before it grates with a groan and plunges back down, her submersion echoed by a rumbling roar of underwater explosions.

Until she is gone.

I hold a hand to my mouth, unable to stop my brain from conjuring the image of people being pulled beneath the surface by the ship's suction as she goes down and down, and it's as if the whole of the ocean wails as one, an unforgettable, agonizing cry. Then, soon, there is silence.

I sit paralyzed with cold, with misery, with disbelief.

Sometime later, I still sit numb, both in mind and in body. The night grows even colder as the wind howls, as the sea mists and the waves have their way with our tiny boat. Our bodies heap together. It's easier to huddle than to try to retain our own personal space. Besides, I'm glad to be packed in, far from the lifeboat's edge and the seemingly depthless waters. No one speaks, though many pray. All I do is rock the small, fragile life in my arms, her—I've come to see it's likely a lass—red cheek pressed against the hard cork of my life belt. Every once in a while she fusses or reflexively tries to suckle. I put my finger in her mouth, so frozen I cannot feel her futile attempts to nurse.

The second baby howls until exhaustion or until he's succumbed to the elements. I'm too afraid to know which.

I raise Stanley's watch to my ear, listening to the steady *tick, tick, tick*.

"*An audible reassurance that another moment is forthcoming.*"

My eyes water with more tears.

Oh, Stanley, I think.

Even with the consistent, promised click of the second hand, I'm scared the dawn will never come. That we'll forever remain aboard this lifeboat or perish before we ever see the sun again. No others are in sight. Our six crewmen, one I recognize as a fireman from the stokehold, rowed us away from the *Titanic* and in the direction of the light we'd seen originally. That, too, is now gone. And the men have become too tired and too cold to do anything more than let the sea take us wherever it wishes.

I try not to allow myself to think and merely to exist. But it only reminds me of Stanley and the many other passengers who were left to go down with the ship.

Had Stanley jumped? Had he pulled himself onto one of

the deck chairs that'd been thrown overboard? Better yet, had he made his way to a lifeboat, just as Daniel promised Mary he would do? They'd be frozen stiff, but they'd be alive.

Alive. A life. Life. Lie.

My head is heavy, my body drooping forward as much as the rigid life belt and baby will allow.

I've a thought. In heaven, there'll be ample family members to greet me. My father. I'm picturing him—fair hair, even fairer skin—just as a woman's hoarse voice startles me. A clearing of her throat. Then another gravelly call. It's a language I do not understand. But with a trembling finger the woman points. A dark speck on the horizon.

A ship.

I stare at it. I stare so long it wobbles in my vision. But then the ship decidedly moves closer. With every minute, that closeness becomes more distinct.

We're to be saved. And I've been spared, once again.

CHAPTER 6

Daphne

CODE NAME KATHERINE
Alias Madame Irene du Tertre

Inverness-shire, Scotland
June 12, 1942

SOMETIMES I WONDER WHY MY FATHER EVEN AGREED TO take me.

He met my French mother in France. She was an artist, a great one.

"She didn't know who I was. She didn't even care who I was," my father told me years ago. "I loved that about her."

I'll give my father credit for that . . . for never having an ego. He easily could. But instead, he continues to work endlessly hard for the next film, the next award, the next what have you.

Why that same enthusiasm doesn't extend to our relationship, I don't know. Josette from boarding school, the only person I've told of my true paternity after that first oops on Parent's Day, would say it's because I never make a fuss when he sends me away. But making a fuss, in my mind, would only serve to make me even more unwanted.

When my father first learned about me, when I was nothing

more than a missed monthly, my *maman* gave him an out, saying he didn't need to be part of our lives.

"Your mother didn't need me," my father said. "She had no interest in my money. My connections. She disliked the limelight. She only wanted you. And . . . and I only wished for no one to know about you."

To protect me? I go back to his answer from years prior. My father claims to always be honest with me, painfully so. He insists he's incapable of lying to me. He does too much pretending onstage and behind the camera, he says. In real life, he's a bona fide straight shooter, right from the hip and into my heart.

Only I'm not sure I believe his honesty. How can I when he's lying about something as big as my existence? Regardless, in the end, both my *maman* and my father gave each other what they wanted. My *maman* left with me to start anew far from my father. And he was free of me.

Then *Maman* died. And after a change of heart, my father took me in. Well, in part he did.

I kept my *maman*'s last name.

An *au pair*, instead of my father, met my every need. As soon as I was old enough for boarding school, that began. Then on to another school, then another. Always well taken care of and looked after, just not by my father.

I'd been with the gallery for only a year—finally feeling like I was gaining my footing as an adult, living as Daphne instead of Katherine—when the war broke out.

Now, after I help end this war, I wonder if I'll be in his presence long enough to recount all I'll have done and if maybe this time it'll be enough to hold his attention.

Today begins my second round of training.

"I was in the wilds of Scotland," I can imagine telling my father as I approach a sheer rock face, one I'm meant to climb.

"Yes, the wilds, where the weather could be as hostile as the environment beautiful. You'd love it as a film set."

I wonder how much I'll love it as the location where we'll be practicing guerrilla combat. I've read about it, a type of warfare of ambushes, sabotage, and raids, dating back to the sixth century BC, that is usually successful and usually with few casualties. But I'm reminded again how reading and seeing and, especially, experiencing can be very different.

Over the coming days, I excel with arms again, in all German, British, and American variations. While I'm good with the mechanisms of a gun, there's something about setting a bomb that I find unsettling.

Perhaps it's because a gun is immediate. Instant gratification. Or, adversely, instant failure if the target is missed. But with bombs—and in our case, timed explosives that detonate on a delay—I can't be certain it'll go off as I planned.

I have an 83 percent success rate.

I hope my success rate at climbing is no less than one hundred, as I begin to ascend a ladder that's drilled into the sheer rock face that connects to a second, then third ladder.

"Yes, Father," I'd tell him. "It culminated to one hell of a climb. What a view at the top, though."

I'll be able to go on and tell my father how I traversed the rough country, the goal not to be seen but to creep undiscovered through the undergrowth.

We do it at night.

We do it during the day.

Today it brings us to a rock-strewn stream, where I wager we'll be able to hop from stone to stone the majority of the way.

"Shall we hop to it, then?" Hector says in French. Always in French. Those who struggled with the language are no longer here. Thankfully, the three other women have all advanced. Same with Gabriel and a few of the men.

"And I thought my jokes were bad," Gabriel remarks.

I raise a brow at that. He's made some rather poor ones. For a woman with an amazing memory, it's saying something that I cannot recall his punch lines.

It's not surprising that Denise is first to cross the stream. She one-steps the smaller rocks, stopping toward the river's center.

"I think we'll have to swim," she calls back. Without hesitating, she slips into the water, letting out a whooping sound.

"Cold?" Adele calls out.

Gabriel enters next. "It's certainly not Cyprus."

The group laughs. I feign amusement as I inch closer to the first stepping stone. In general, I have a wariness and dislike of bodies of water. I understand the necessity of crossing them. I spent practically my whole life going back and forth between France and England via the *Forde*. It's a two-hour trip where I've clutched the railing and focused on my breathing for all those one hundred twenty minutes.

Leaving Paris through Calais a few months ago was even more nerve-racking, having to travel a greater distance and through potentially dangerous waters.

Give me a train any day of the week, like how we got here to Inverness-shire from London.

Trains follow tracks, it's as simple as that.

I've even ridden "loop-the-loop" roller coasters. They lock to the tracks. There's a science to it, and I trust they'll stay locked because very smart individuals designed them to do exactly that.

That's not to say that disasters can't happen, but Mother Nature . . . she does as she pleases, whenever she pleases. I trust an engineer more than I trust her, with her rogue waves, icebergs, and deadly storms.

I'm being dramatic, of course. In front of me stretches what I observe to be a relatively mild stream. Denise is already to the other side. Gabriel is wading up to his waist. Adele is just fine.

And here I am, wondering if the current will suddenly change.

A freak rainstorm, despite today's sunny skies? An undertow? I don't even know if rivers can have such a thing. We're in the wilds, after all.

I puff out my cheeks, hating how my pulse is quickening over such a trivial body of water. I've experienced worse. Gabriel and Adele are across now. Suzanne is waist-deep.

"Gonna go for it, Katherine?" Hector says. "Ladies first."

I can feel Adele's eyes on me, wondering what on earth has me stuck in the mud. I suck in breath to respond, to say, "I'm going," but instead of doing so, I hold the air in my lungs. My chest tightens; my pulse jumps even higher.

"Katherine?" Hector questions.

Adele asks, "You okay, sweetie?"

I let out my breath in a rush and press my thumb and forefinger into my eyes. "I'm going," I finally say.

Crossing the rocks are fine. I even feel in control when I have to leap from one to another. I trust myself to land on the other side. But when I ease myself into the water, that's when all trust is lost.

My boots sink into the streambed. I yank free, pushing through the water's resistance to take another step. The river's stronger than I thought. Colder too. I fight against the current, seemingly even swifter than only moments ago.

My breath comes quick.

Arms raised, I step and step and step, certain each time my foot will forever be stuck, a flash flood will occur, and I'll be doomed. I stare upriver so hard, so long that I stumble into the rocks at the other side without even realizing I'd made it there.

I thrust both palms onto the large boulder, feeling grounded, just as a scream erupts.

Adele.

I turn to find her swept up in the river. An arm flails. A leg kicks. Within another breath, she's another stone's throw downstream.

Her name is shouted.

There's a splash. Gabriel.

Only a few strides into the water, Hector dives, surfacing into a swim.

They reach her at the same time, each pulling her from the current's grasp. Within moments, she's musing, "I'm okay. I'm okay. Just got caught up in it, that's all. Thank you, boys."

I realize my palms are still pressed into the rock. I haven't moved. I did nothing, only watched.

On the shore, Adele is waving off the concern from the other women. *They didn't jump in either*, I tell myself. And as I climb wobbly onto dry land and hurry toward them, I act as if nothing is amiss, joining in by saying, "You really gave us all a scare," and pretending my bout of aquaphobia and my inability to help my friend never happened.

This is part of my training I won't tell my father. I'm great at pretending.

* * *

I'M FORCED TO PRETEND MORE OFTEN THAN NOT IN THE coming weeks.

One such occurrence is when we view a propaganda film, produced by none other than my father. It's brilliant work. He and a New Zealand artist by the name of Len Lye bring the efforts of a British sniper to life very well.

Too soberingly well, if you ask me.

In three parts, we watch as a Sergeant Smith crawls through a forest, much like the one I've navigated. His goal: to kill a Nazi. Within minutes of the film opening, the Nazi is found and the shot is made. The documentary then begins again, the second act backtracking to show the suspenseful manhunt from Sergeant Smith's perspective, as if we're seeing it through his own eyes. Chilling. The third act continues with the Nazi's dead body being used as a decoy to lure other Nazi soldiers into a clearing. Smith picks off each of them.

Kill or Be Killed, that's the title. And while the film ends with an undeniable tone of triumph, and while I'm not disgusted with Sergeant Smith's actions, I'm scared to think that my mission may result in me having to use the skills I've learned here to track someone in a similar manner or, even worse, for me to be hunted by a Nazi.

I haven't been told my mission yet, only that I'll be a courier of sorts. A go-between among my network leader, our wireless operator, and any resistance groups we'll be coordinating with. I'm antsy to begin, especially after watching my father's work, him already having done something so profound and instrumental to improve morale during this war.

Another instance where I have to pretend that I'm not unnerved happens when Major McKennan gives us an update on what we may encounter once we land on French soil.

"It appears," he says, "France's prime minister is allowing German forces to enter Vichy to ferret out hidden radio transmitters."

Mutters go through our small group. Vichy is part of the unoccupied Free Zone, south of the demarcation line. There isn't supposed to be a German military presence in these parts.

"You should be prepared," Major McKennan goes on, "to be hunted as well, and they'll use your transceivers to do so. Gestapo headquarters in Paris will search—day and night—for signals from our wireless operators. Picture it." His gaze passes slowly over each of us. "Thirty German clerks hawkeyed on their cathode-ray tubes on every available frequency, searching for any new blip to appear. When it happens—and it will—they'll pass the information to their direction finders, who'll take up the hunt on the streets. Their equipment is sensitive. Quite sensitive. We know Germans are good with their technology. They'll establish a triangle around where you're transmitting. Within it a smaller triangle will be identified, and another—until they are within a mile of you. They'll go on foot at this point. Long raincoats, high turned-up collars to hide their earphones, and a large wristwatch, which is actually a meter . . . That's what you should look for. And if you see this description, run. Hide. They've pinpointed the very location you've been signaling from."

I swallow. The direction finders sound like bad-guy characters in a comic book or a spy role pulled straight from the pages of a script. But no, they are real—long raincoats and all—and they'll begin trying to find us as soon as we send our first transmission.

If they do . . . part of me worries what I'll do. If I'll freeze. If I'll be unable to help my fellow agents . . .

"This is why," the major informs us, "you only ever transmit for no more than twenty minutes and remain in the same location for no more than a few days. Everyone here will receive an understanding of how to code, decode, and transmit messages. Our future wireless technician will undergo another sixteen weeks of training."

I glance at Hector. He mentioned at dinner the other night that he's been earmarked for such a role. He's nodding along, his chest puffed, accepting of and proud of the extensive training for such an important role.

"The rest of you will progress to Beaulieu, where you'll undergo classroom and specialty training. Forgery. Microphotography. Picking locks. Safe breaking. Industrial sabotage. Those of you arriving in France by air will practice parachuting. Buckle up, ladies and gentlemen. You're only weeks away from having your feet on French soil."

* * *

"ONCE I DO MY FIRST SKYDIVE, I'LL BE FINE," I SAY TO THE other women in French.

I'll know I can successfully land in France without the fear of breaking a leg. I'll have practiced. Until then . . . I wring my hands, especially when I think about stepping out of a plane into nothing but an inky sky.

We turn down the cloister at Beaulieu Abbey and toward a workshop outbuilding on our way to today's lesson.

Yesterday we learned how to recognize the ranks of the ordinary French police and the uniformed French militia.

The latter are much more dangerous. Native Frenchmen who understand local dialects, who have intimate knowledge of the towns and countryside, who know the local people and informants.

They remain in France to fight against the French Resistance.

I'd be in France to fight *with* the local Resistance, with the Maquis.

In what way, I'm still not certain. Much of our work is on a need-to-know basis.

Next month, when I'm set to leave, I'll need to know.

But first, tomorrow I'm leaving the abbey for a few days to go to Tatton Park for parachute training. Manchester is a journey away, but Ringway Airfield is where all the troops train in parachuting.

The goal: five drops, with at least one at night and one with a leg bag for carrying equipment. We'll work on landing. We'll work on being quick off the mark to get away. *"We can't be sure what you'll be jumping into,"* Major Barrett warned.

"I hear the training film is boring," Denise says, her boots clomping against the cobblestone of the cloister.

"You'll have to let me know," Suzanne says. "I won't be going to Tatton."

"You're not?" I ask. I've spent nearly every waking moment with these women the past few months. It'll be strange being apart.

"Too old," she says, seemingly unbothered by her prohibitive age.

"I'm even older," Adele says with a shrug. "I won't parachute in either."

"So how are you getting there?" Denise wants to know.

"Seadog," Adele says.

Suzanne: "Same."

"Seadog?" I ask. Just the name makes me shiver and it's a seasonably warm summer day, though I eye dark clouds that look to be rolling in.

Suzanne says, "It's a tiny sailing boat."

"A *felucca*, the major called it," Adele adds. "We'll fly to Gibraltar, then take the boat from there to the South of France." She punctuates with another shrug.

Me, I wouldn't be shrugging. Going in a tiny sailing boat is the last thing I want to do. Suddenly falling into black nothingness isn't scary at all.

"Rain's coming," Denise utters in a deadpan voice.

I look to the darkening skies as we enter the workshop to a bunch of unusual chatter.

"What's going on?" I ask Gabriel, already seated at the long worktable.

Ever the gentleman, he pushes out the chair beside him. "Apparently the Germans debuted a gruesome tank during a battle yesterday."

"Of course they did," I say, shaking my head while accepting the seat. More and more, the Germans are sending the wind up me.

Denise plops down next to us and begins spinning a pencil on the table. "I'm already so sick of the Germans and I'm not even back in France yet. I'll tell you what . . . if I ever come upon a sleeping German again, I won't be so nice this time around."

"Oh, Denise," Adele says, also joining us across the table. Suzanne too. "I'm almost too afraid to ask what you'll do."

Denise grips her pencil and jams it into the tabletop. "I'd stab him through the ear into the brain."

And how on earth am I supposed to respond to that besides letting my mouth hang open?

Gabriel gives it a try. In between shocked laughter he says,

"I sure hope you and I are in the same network. I'll sleep better knowing you're around."

The major enters—perfect timing, saving the rest of us from a response. "All right, ladies and gentlemen. Being it's Sunday and a few of you are off tomorrow to Tatton, we'll take it easy today. We'll be writing letters."

He explains: We're to have no contact with any friends or family while we are on French soil. However, letters will be sent at regular intervals. We're to write those letters now, a dozen in all.

Instantly, my bottom lip goes between my teeth. When looseleaf paper is placed in front of me, I'm no closer to knowing who to write or even what to say.

I never write my father unless I have something to share that'll evoke his response: "Well, that's something, Katherine. Just remarkable, Kitty."

Then there's Josette. She's in America, where she stayed after traveling abroad and meeting her now husband. We exchange letters, but not often, especially now that she has two children underfoot. I twist my lips. I could write her, if I must have letters sent.

I shouldn't . . . but I'm tempted to see who Denise is writing. She's obviously peculiar. Rough around the edges, yet passionate to a fault.

I peek.

Her *maman*.

I wasn't expecting that. A friend, a sister, even. But her *maman*. It feels intimate, and it stirs a longing inside me for a mother I haven't had for nearly all my life.

The scratching of pencils fills the room, some already on their second letter.

We were told to write sentiments like *I am well . . . All is right*. The letters will be sent even if all contact with us is lost and our fates are unknown.

I let out a long, slow breath at the thought that I could be killed and no one would know it.

Gabriel finishes a letter, turning it face down, and begins his next.

I shouldn't look at what he's writing, but at this point, snooping won't make me feel any worse.

Dearest Evelyn, it starts.

All is well, he begins.

The way his arm is positioned keeps me from seeing what he pens next. But after another few lines, he scratches his nose, and I see his salutation.

With love, Percy

Ah, his real name, I think. But I also must have let out a sound. Percy/Gabriel's head ticks toward me.

"Sorry," I say instinctively. "Nosy."

He smiles.

I take it as an invitation. "The girl back home you mentioned?"

"Yeah. I wish I could tell her more about what I'm doing. She's not going to like the vagueness, especially since she knows I'm with the SOE."

"Oh?" I prompt, the Official Secrets Act we signed coming to mind.

"She found out a while back, before I came here for training. She was a motorcycle dispatch rider for the Wrens and caught me red-handed one time when I was coming out of Baker Street."

"That'll do it," I say.

He shakes his head, a dimple-inducing smile on his face. Clearly he's completely beguiled by this woman. "Evie's something."

"Is she still in London?"

He shakes his head. "She's doing her own secret stuff in Portsmouth."

"Quite the dynamic duo."

He laughs. "She'd actually loved to be called that. How about you? Any lucky fella back home?"

I'm almost tempted to lie, slipping into the role of being in a loving, committed relationship. The problem is, Gabriel has eyes and the sheets before me are completely blank. "In Paris? No." I could leave it at that, but those eyes of his also seem caring, the kind I don't get the sense will judge me. "It's just me. I haven't dated much. There were always classes and lectures. Then long hours at the gallery. Took me ages to sign Thérèse Lemoine-Lagron to showcase her watercolors with us. I made a go once or twice at a relationship, I guess. The first time, the guy said he felt like he never could get to know me. I was closed off, wouldn't let him in." I shrug, and part of me can't believe I'm opening up like this. But in a world of secrets, it somehow feels safe. So I keep going. "The second relationship I made an attempt to really let down my walls. I couldn't tell if he was interested or not, but I kept at it, and, well, that came back to bite me in the . . . you know. Turns out he was married . . . with two kids."

Gabriel cringes. "Ouch."

"So, yes, it's just me."

Denise lets out a sharp exhale. "That may be the saddest thing I've ever heard."

I roll my eyes. "We're at war. Surely you've heard sadder."

"I meant pitiful, Katherine."

My God. "Tell me how you really feel, Denise."

Her body language screams indifference. And at that, she returns to writing her dear old mum.

Gabriel returns to his letter writing, too, but I see his shoulders rocking as he stifles a laugh. I elbow him. "Still want her in your network?"

He drops his head, letting out another silent laugh.

"Katherine," I hear in a booming voice.

My head bolts up.

Major Barrett has his eyes locked on me. "A word?"

I'm quick to stand, the blood rushing straight to my head. My feet boom in the quiet room as I cross toward him. As I near, he begins to lead me outside to the covered walkway.

It's begun to rain since we've been inside. The air's thick with humidity. When he stops, I salute, then clasp my hands tightly behind my back.

"Katherine," the major begins. I'm ready for him to chastise me for talking instead of completing the assigned task. "You won't be continuing on to parachute training tomorrow."

I go hot all over.

"You were set to leave for France the end of October, but there's to be a change."

I brace myself, feeling emotion build, knowing the dams will break if I'm to be sent back to London.

"We're moving up your mission, Katherine. There's a need for you straightaway. As such, you'll be leaving tomorrow."

Tomorrow? I question silently, relief but also alarm now bouncing around my insides. I haven't prepped at Tatton yet: My five jumps. How to use the fan, a machine that'd help hone my landing. My quick getaway once I'm on the ground.

I open my mouth, not wanting to question him but terrified to step out of a plane without any practice.

"You also will no longer be parachuting in, Katherine."

"What?" I can't help asking.

But without him even answering me, I know how I'm meant to get to France.

A seadog.

CHAPTER 7

Violet

—

At sea aboard *Carpathia*
April 15, 1912

I WISH TO BE ANYWHERE BUT THE SEA. SO MANY LIVES HAVE been lost, but—somehow—here I stand on *Carpathia*.

I should sit. I will sit. I shift my feet lethargically—my mind feeling as if it's a second behind my body—in search of a chair. As I shuffle forward, my numbed fingertips don't register the child in my arms, yet I can still detect the weight of her.

She's sleeping now, her blue lips pursed. Every so often she twitches.

Then the weight of her is gone.

I startle. Instinctively, my empty arms reach out for the child a woman has taken from me. I part my lips, but no words are spoken—by either of us. The child is merely whisked away.

My arm is taken then. I slowly turn to find a kind face, a *Carpathia* crew member, and I'm led inside the dining saloon to a chair.

"Thank you," I mutter and there, with my hands folded in my lap, my bedspread replaced by a much warmer coat, I finally allow myself to think through how I got here.

I'd taken one of the final seats on one of the final lifeboats. Lifeboat sixteen.

That spot could've been filled by Stanley or Miss Walton or

one of the hundreds of second- and third-class passengers who'd been left on that ship.

But no, it was me, when there were over two thousand passengers and crew who boarded the *Titanic*.

Moments ago, as I stood stoically, I was approached about a list of survivors, us lucky souls who made it onto a lifeboat or who were plucked from the water clinging to life.

My name was asked. My name was added.

The child's? I didn't know. No name was added.

I asked to see the list.

At first, the names only danced across my vision. Then I saw ones I knew. John and Joe from the deck crew were on it. Kate, Emma, Eddie, and Bertie from the victualing crew. I recognized others from the engineering crew. Those of us on the list are the only ones who had been saved.

But Stanley, Dr. O'Loughlin, Mason, George, Frederick, Charlie, Willie . . .

So many others . . .

I did not see their names.

I shake my head now, staring blankly at the commotion in the *Carpathia*'s dining saloon.

She's so different from *Titanic*. A workhorse, I've heard her called. Not glamorous. Not designed to resemble Versailles. She'll never compete for the Blue Riband, awarded to the fastest trans-atlantic crossing. She'll never arrive at the New York port met by swarms of photographers and fanfare like the *Olympic* has, like *Titanic* was supposed to in three short days. *Carpathia* carries solely immigrant and emigrant passengers, not the wealthy and upper class.

Yet she has come to our rescue. I should be on my feet, helping to soothe sobbing widows and offering to help hand out blankets, tea, coffee, and soup to the survivors. I am a stewardess. But I cannot; my throat feels too thick and my mind is stuck on my own grief. It's stuck on Stanley.

I had let him in. A poetic man who reminded me of my father, who cared for me as a parent would. Now, like my father, he's gone.

And I can't help feeling angry that I allowed myself a closeness with him. Hadn't I learned my lesson from all the loss I've endured before? Hadn't I long wondered why them and not me? It's not as if I haven't had the chance to die. I've cheated death a number of times. An accidental poisoning, typhoid fever, tuberculosis, jaundice attacks, gallstones, malaria, scarlatina.

I've had them all. I've survived them all. And that last one—the scarlet fever—may not have had the long-term physical effects like my tuberculosis has had, but Ray getting scarlatina has haunted me for years.

It was my fault.

Not Ray's, who was only two years old. Maybe three. He was very young, that I remember.

When we lived in Bahía Blanca, we had very few neighbors. One of the closest was widow Doña Rosa who ran the *bolichi*, a tiny tavern, store, and meeting place.

Ray wanted no part of the *bolichi* or Doña Rosa with her squinted eyes and the exaggerated curve to her back. While I found her interesting and I'd follow Father inside, Ray would go no farther than the door.

One day while at Doña Rosa's, we learned that a woman traveler had stopped in with her child. Both looked ill. With the nearest doctor at a great distance, Mother surprised us by offering to check in on the woman.

It was very un-Mother-like. It wasn't that she wasn't caring. She was and still is. But Mother has always been more concerned with our own happenings.

"Family first," as she always says.

And exposing herself to a potential illness seemed unfathomable. Because of that, I followed her. And Ray followed me. He always did.

We weren't there long. Mother spotted us by the woman's door. "Out with you," she demanded.

The next day the woman died. Mother was unfazed, both her and Father so busy with our sheep, waking at dawn each day to divide our livestock from our neighbor's since we could not afford a fence. By that time I was taking care of both the house and Ray. As usual, we went off to play, creating our own fun amidst the seemingly endless fields.

We came upon a heap of clothing. Some of them had been burned. Others were just fine. New clothing wasn't something we were often able to afford. We thought it'd be fun to dress up, pretend to be royalty.

Sir Ray.

Lady Violet.

Giggling, we sashayed home in time to wash up for supper. Without fail, Mother always dressed in the best she had for dinner. That night we'd do the same.

Father's brow scrunched. Mother's tired eyes took a moment to register what we were wearing. Then panic bloomed. "Off! Off!" she screamed. "Get it off!"

The clothing? It'd taken me my own moment to understand. But *sí*, she'd meant the clothing we'd found. Unbeknownst to us, they'd been the sick woman's and her child's.

Three days later, I woke from a stupor. My whole body felt wizened, as if all the liquid parts of me had been wrung dry. My eyes were more gray than blue. My dark auburn hair had been shaved to relieve the heat of my body. But worst of all, the infection had taken Ray from me. From us. From Mother.

And it'd been all my fault.

After that, everything changed.

Mother no longer sang and hummed. She'd sit with a far-off look in her eyes, muttering and thumbing her rosary.

At first I thought little of it. Mother was grieving. We all were. But then Father approached me. "Violet, your mother will

need you. God's given us each gifts. Yours is your resilience. Your
strength. Will you promise to always be there for your mother?
For our family?"

I had nodded, desperate to mend the wounds I created. "Family first. I promise, Father."

"Good girl," he told me. "My brave, loyal girl."

Father's foresight was without error. Ray's death was the beginning of Mother's illness, only to worsen with the death of my
baby brother, Denis—for reasons unknown beyond him never
waking one morning—my sister Molly from meningitis, my
father, and the stillborn.

"Are you okay?" I hear, looking up to see Ann. She shakes her
head woefully and takes the seat beside me in the dining saloon.
"A moronic question," she corrects. "None of us are okay."

Ann cups her hand over mine in my lap. I pull my hand away,
making as if I need to tuck hair behind my ear. But I know my
action is driven by fear of someday losing her too.

"Hey," she says, a question in her voice and a rise to a brow.
"The baby?"

Tomada, I think, but I say, "A woman came out of nowhere
and snatched her away. Didn't say a single word. Just took her."

Ann sighs. "Some way to say thank you. It's better this way,
though. It's a lot to look after someone else's child."

Her words impact me more than she knows. I've cared for my
siblings for what feels like my entire life. I've already failed once
with Ray. I can't fail again, not with a family to support. Not with
the promise I made to my father. But right now the weight of that
obligation is too much. Last night has been too much.

Why was I spared all those years ago?

Why have I been spared now?

It's as if the universe took that precise moment to remind me
of those who have not been spared.

Words are whispered, but also spoken in a way where the
gossip is loud enough to be heard. "John Astor? He's not aboard?"

The answer comes in an incredulous tone, "He's not on any lists."

"Neither are the Strauses."

"No," a woman breathes.

No, I parrot, squeezing my eyes shut. Not Isidor and Ida too.

But yes, John, Isidor, Ida, those three names in particular are repeated again and again and again, the focus of conversations, just as they were a focus of New York society.

"Mr. Straus refused to get on a boat," another woman says. "Not until all women and children had a seat. So Mrs. Straus gave up hers. She handed her fur coat to her maid and she climbed right back onto the deck to be with her husband."

"Did you hear what her final words were?"

"'As we have lived, so we will die, together.'"

A muffled sob.

Is it remorse over Isidor and Ida? Is it guilt that no man sits by this woman's side, her husband presumably one of the victims while she still lives?

I cannot help myself; I morbidly search for Madeleine Astor. But she's not in the dining saloon. I don't see her on any decks, when I finally have enough gumption to go in search of fresh air. I picture her in a private room, mourning. To be widowed at eighteen. Would it have been better for her not to have loved at all?

It's a question I think again when I see Mrs. Marvin, her hands tightly wound around her middle, her eyes nearly swollen shut.

Both women—and so many other women on this ship—took the biggest risk of all by giving themselves to another and now are being forced to live without that person.

I do not think I could ever allow that to be me. Nor do my life's circumstances allow for it, not with living for my family's future instead of my own.

CHAPTER 8

Daphne

CODE NAME KATHERINE
Alias Madame Irene du Tertre

Beaulieu Abbey, Hampshire, England
August 31, 1942

I FEEL TOO SHOOK UP TO SLEEP. I SHOULD BE RESTING, LET-
ting my energy accumulate for whatever awaits me tomorrow . . .
on that dang seadog and beyond.

Still, I haven't been informed of my mission yet.

But I'm less concerned with what will happen after I arrive
and more about how I'll get there.

It's why my left eyelid keeps twitching. I wish it'd just give up,
close, and let me sleep.

But no, it's nearly three in the morning and my brain won't
shut off. Especially after I hear voices outside my one-room cottage. We each have our own little place to call home in these final
weeks of training.

Who could be out this late?

I sit up just as my door is flung open, knocking into a small
table. The lamp crashes to the floor.

I hate that I do it, but I yelp a scream as my brain struggles to
make sense of what is happening.

And *who* is entering my cottage. "Major Barrett?" I question. There are two men. Is he one of them? Am I to leave earlier than expected? My mission has been moved up an entire month. Advancing the timeline by a few more hours isn't unreasonable.

But no, the uniform is wrong.

Major Barrett always wears a khaki-colored, open-collared, single-breasted four-pocket jacket. There should be four brass buttons, one to each breast pocket and each of the two epaulettes.

On his uniform he'd have a metal crown to indicate he's a major, two bronzed collar badges, a shield-shaped badge, three medal ribbons, and a badge of a qualified army parachutist.

And that's not what I see.

His hat is all wrong, an emblem with wings, a skull, and crossbones.

Even in the darkness, I see gray-green uniforms. Red bands around their arms. It's impossible to miss the black and white swastika on it.

It's the uniform of the Gestapo.

Here . . . in my cottage in Hampshire.

From my bed, I try to stand, but my legs get trapped in my sheets. I yank and pull, freeing myself. I lurch forward. My bare feet only just touch the wooden planks of the floor when the men are on me.

"Get her," one of them says in German.

There's coffee on their breath. A tight grip to their hands.

I'm outnumbered, unable to use the one-on-one training I've learned, nothing I can do beyond wrenching an arm, kicking a foot, twisting my torso, demanding they take their hands off me, snapping my teeth whenever any part of them passes anywhere near my mouth.

It does me no good.

My arms are forced behind my back.

The dark room goes darker.

A blindfold.

I'm pushed, pulled, and prodded outside.

"Quiet," one demands, this time in French. But I haven't called for help. I wouldn't dare. I've been taught not to. Involving other agents, who can potentially be added to whatever situation I'm being forced into, isn't an option.

It doesn't stop me from wishing Denise were here. She wouldn't have let them get her. Or at the very least, they would've been mauled in the process.

I stumble forward, around, then down. I quickly lose my bearings, unfamiliar with the grounds of the abbey.

But the air soon smells dank. The floor beneath me is stone or cement. Until I'm hoisted onto something wooden. A table? Somewhere underground?

Suddenly hands no longer grip my arms. The sensation of being free causes me to lose my balance and I tumble to the side. Nothing is there to catch me, but I stay on my feet, picturing myself only inches from the table's edge.

My breathing comes fast. Instinctively I move my eyes around behind the blindfold. The room isn't well lit, that much I can tell from the sliver of light that seeps in through the space around my nose.

Then the blindfold is torn off, not delicately, strands of my hair going with it.

I blink, it taking valuable seconds for my vision to return to me.

There's a single hanging light above my head. Rather, alongside my ear, so close it's difficult to see clearly unless I turn my head away.

Against the back wall is a man in a Gestapo uniform.

A cough comes from behind me. I don't turn. I keep my eyes trained in front of me. On the greater danger?

"Don't let her fool you," I hear in German from one of those men behind me.

The man in front of me pushes away from the wall, shooting

daggers at me. No, at the comrade who spoke. He walks closer to me slowly, deliberately, his hands clasped behind his back.

"Hello," he says in a low voice. "Welcome to France. We own it now."

France? That's not possible. He may have spoken French, but it means nothing. I haven't used anything but French in months despite never leaving the United Kingdom.

I've never left.

The Gestapo man continues to stare at me.

Have I?

No. I run a hand across my forehead. "What do you want?" I demand, and quickly realize I shouldn't have spoken at all. The question and my nonverbal movement broadcast my unease.

A slow smile spreads on his face. "I want to know why you're here. In France. How did they get you here?"

My eyes dart around the poorly lit room. The walls are stone. The ground is dirt. A cellar.

At the abbey.

I haven't left . . . This evening I went to bed at the abbey. I blink hard. He's wrong. He's trying to confuse me so I'll make a mistake. Reveal something.

"This is England," I insist. "I'm still in England."

He doesn't respond. He doesn't so much as twitch. And if I am correct, if I haven't left, that means the Gestapo are somehow here. Are they German spies? Have they invaded Beaulieu Abbey? What of the others? Are they being questioned at this very moment, too, as the enemy tries to get information from us about where we'll land when we actually do go to France?

I startle at the man's voice and the abruptness of a single word: "Fine." He lets out an exaggerated sigh. "It's true. We are in England. Now, how about we get to know each other better?"

I swallow discreetly and work to erase all tension from my expression.

"Name," he orders.

I've spoken my alias to myself so many times. "Irene du Tertre" flows off my tongue.

He sniffs loudly. "And your date of birth?"

Don't flinch, I demand of myself. "The ninth of January, 1912."

The bulb is so bright on my right side that I begin to sway, disoriented, and a pain starts behind my eyes.

"Hmm," he says. "Where did you live?"

"Paris."

An honest answer, but also the correct answer for my cover story.

"Then what are you doing here?"

I press my palms into my outer thighs or else I know I'll fidget. My cover story never accounted for me being in Hampshire. "Um, holiday. I'm on holiday."

"Is that so?" His next question piggybacks. "For how long?"

"Two weeks."

"But you'll return?"

"Yes."

"When?"

"Two weeks."

"What's your father's name?"

His initial questions had been spat so quickly, then this one comes out of left field. But alliteration helps pull it to the forefront of my brain. "Samuel Seigneur Simonet."

"Your mother's?"

My *maman* . . . my mind blanks on her fictional name. I lick my lips. The man cocks his head, a malicious grin beginning on his face. I clear my throat. "Please, forgive me. It's hard to talk about my mother. She, um, died last May. It's still a raw emotion for me. But her name . . . her name was Micheline Irene Simonet."

"Are you sure?"

I nod.

His eyes narrow.

"Yes," I say, putting as much faux confidence in my voice as

I can muster. Despite the coolness of the room, my body grows increasingly clammy.

"When did you say your mother died?"

When *did* I say? I blow out a shallow breath, hoping it goes unnoticed. I search my brain, cursing myself for adding a detail. *Last year*, I think. I should've said that. But no . . . what did I say? It comes to me. At least I hope it does. "May."

"May? But you said June."

Heat surges into me. All I can think to do is deny and stick to my answer. I shake my head. "May."

The man twists his lips, staring. He holds his gaze for one . . . two . . . three seconds. It might as well be a lifetime. Finally, he blinks and asks, "You're married?"

"Yes."

I glance down at the floor, needing a break from the intensity of his blue eyes. The table isn't more than a few feet off the ground, but it feels like miles.

"Who is your husband?"

I answer, "Mateo du Tertre."

"He's not on holiday with you?"

"No, he's joined the German Wehrmacht."

"When?"

"As soon as he could."

"Hmm," he says a second time. "What did he do before?"

"Milner."

He snorts. "In Paris?"

"The outskirts. He worked a windmill in Montmartre to grind flour and press local grapes."

The hard lines around his eyes ease just as a burst of laugher comes from behind me.

"You're not breaking her, Monroe," I hear.

What's that supposed to mean? And Monroe, that's certainly more Scottish than German.

I'm jostled forward when my back is patted.

"Nice work, Katherine," I hear next in another man's voice, one I recognize.

I turn. Major Barrett stands there—in his normal uniform—beaming. "Looks to me like you're ready for France."

★ ★ ★

EVERYONE HAS A GOOD LAUGH AT MY EXPENSE.

"Yeah, yeah," I say to them as I'm led aboveground again. Inside, my nerves are as tight as a drum. On the outside, I try not to let it show. A cup of cocoa is pressed into my hand.

My shaking hand.

I squeeze the cup tightly, willing away the lingering fear. The interrogation felt real. Too real. Too scary.

But I've passed.

That's what matters.

And my reward is a few hours back where it all began in my cottage to "get some shut-eye" before I'm briefed—minute by minute—about my practice interrogation and what I can do better if next time it's for real.

"Don't ask questions."

"Remain stoic."

"Retain eye contact."

"Avoid the use of *um*."

"No unnecessary details."

"It could be a matter of life and death, Katherine."

I hear him loud and clear.

Next, I'm shuttled off to Orchard Court in Portman Square.

The building, with its brick, stone detailing, and giant classical columns and pilasters, looks like any other in central London. But not every other building is used as an undercover location for the SOE Section F. That *F* standing for France.

Inside, I finally meet the man in charge of the SOE.

"Welcome," Colonel Maurice Buckmaster says, "and congratulations."

"Thank you, sir," I say, taking the seat across from him at his desk.

"We have high hopes for you, Katherine, and are appreciative of your flexibility in moving up your mission."

"Of course."

"We've not a minute to lose. You'll be off this evening. Now, for your particulars."

Finally.

I'm told how I'll be part of a network called FAME.

When I arrive, I'm to make contact with my network leader, a man aliased Lucas. Then we'll rendezvous with our wireless technician, this one by the name of Louis.

Once the three of us are together, FAME is officially ready to begin.

Our mission: sabotage.

My particular mission: to find drop sites to receive materials from London, to locate safe houses for Louis to transmit from, and to establish relationships with the local French Resistance.

"This is for you," the colonel says. He slides a small gold powder compact across the desk. "A parting gift." He smiles. "In case you need to sell it or pawn it, if you need money in an emergency."

I nod, accepting it. "Thank you, sir."

"And also this." He slides a small pill across the table. "It's an L-pill. Some hide it in their buttons."

"Sir, if it's okay to ask, what does the *L* stand for?"

"Lethal."

The word hangs in the air.

I don't reach for it. I can't imagine taking such a thing. If I'm to die in this war, I'm going to make it as difficult as possible for the Germans. Instead, I fold my hands in my lap.

With a curt nod, and I suspect pride in my decision, Colonel Buckmaster stands. I'm dismissed.

★　★　★

I CANNOT BELIEVE IT. I AM FINALLY OFF TO FRANCE. BACK to France, actually, where I've always felt I belonged more than anywhere else.

And now I have a renewed purpose, a chance to do something great.

If I can survive getting there.

The plane ride to Gibraltar was uneventful, despite the fact it should've been eventful. Before tonight—rather, last night, as a new day is dawning—I'd never been in an aircraft before.

If it'd been day instead of night, I would've pressed as close to the window as possible, watching the buildings and trees turn to specks.

Instead, there's only darkness.

And instead of jumping from the plane, as originally planned, we landed and I was escorted with bated breath onto this rickety fishing boat.

I'm convinced at any moment something will sink us. A torpedo. A mine. Hell, a rough breeze. It wouldn't take much. The seadog resembles a lifeboat more than a ship, with sails instead of an engine and a crew of Polish men I can only barely understand who prefer grunts over words.

I squeeze my knees inward, more securely holding my suitcase between my feet, and hold my breath, only to release it and promptly hold it again. I fear it's only making my motion sickness worse. But I keep at it, my breathing the only thing I can control. Certainly not our speed, which is faster than I expected of such a vessel. Nor the waves, which are miserably larger than anticipated for waters sheltered by so much land.

The crew laughs at each yip I release as we rise and fall over one of those waves. Unfortunately, laughter is universal, no need for interpretation. So are their expressions when I lean over the side to retch.

Their response—and frankly, my reaction to being on water—leaves me feeling ashamed. But it's not something I can help. My aquaphobia feels as much a part of me as does my brown hair and eyes, my impatient nature, and my aptitude for ill-timed jokes. I only wish this water-related part of me was something I had outgrown. But no, it's been with me for as long as I can remember.

My father has always chastised me, balking when I take a longer route to avoid water for my visits. *"Face your fears,"* he'd say.

I roll my head to one side, then the other, feeling the pull down my back.

Finally, I hear something in Polish that sounds close enough to understand. So much of the language borrows words from German, French, and English, and has similarities to Russian.

I lean forward, staring into the dark night.

And yes, there's land ahead.

Cliché or not, when my feet hit the beach of a small cove, I could kiss it. I barely have time to appreciate how my voyage is complete when I hear the splashing boots of the Polish men.

They're gone.

I'm left with half a moon, an empty beach, and the hope that this unoccupied portion of France is truly without many Germans.

I have no plans to linger to find out. The directions I memorized before departing told me to spend the rest of the night in a villa.

I let myself in.

I don't light a lamp, don't dillydally. At the first soft location I can find, I sink into sleep.

In the morning I pull another address from my memory. This one in Cannes. The train ride up the coast takes less than an hour. When I step from the train, a rush of memories comes upon me.

The last time I visited Cannes, I was with my father. Sort of. He'd invited me to a film festival held in the holiday town after I told him about securing a position at the gallery.

"To celebrate the start of your great success," he'd told me.

It was the most public affair he'd invited me to yet. MGM even chartered an ocean liner to bring a number of Hollywood's biggest stars to opening night: Gary Cooper, Cary Grant, Douglas Fairbanks Jr., Mae West, James Cagney, Spencer Tracy.

And right in front of them all, my father swooped me into a hug, whispering his congratulations into my ear. After our embrace, I looked around, wondering what would be made of me. No eyelashes seemed to be batting. When I turned back to my father, I saw why. His arms were around another woman, this one considerably younger than me, in her early twenties.

Undeterred, wanting to continue our celebratory time together, I took the seat beside my father at the screening of Dieterle's *The Hunchback of Notre Dame*, only for it to be cut short as news of the day's events began to circulate.

Germany had invaded Poland. The French government ordered a general mobilization of its army. An ultimatum was issued to the German government: withdraw troops or war will be declared.

War was declared.

The film festival was canceled. Father was immediately caught up in the buzzing excitement, already putting his head together with another director about how their talents could best be put to use.

He left for England and I went north to Paris, reassuring my father I'd join him in England if necessary. "I have more important artists to sign," I'd said during our goodbye. I saw a glimmer of something then. Concern for me? But I further assured my father I'd leave if Paris became a part of the war.

I had wondered, not without a hiccup of my own concern, if that'd be sooner rather than later. During the first war, Paris was under the bombs from the get-go.

Now here I am, doing my own part to aid in this war, on my way to assemble with an agent named Lucas, who'll be the leader of our network FAME. My instructions are to go to a beauty shop, a place I assume won't raise questions when I walk in. But would it raise suspicion for a man, not likely to come in for a set of victory rolls?

I push open the door, a bell announcing my arrival. I smile politely when a woman greets me. "Just a trim," I quickly recite, as I've been instructed—maybe a touch too hastily.

"Ah, yes," the woman says, as if she does this every day. Perhaps she does. "This way, please."

She leads me past several women in various stages of haircuts, dyes, and rollers. None of the women give me any mind, their noses in magazines or mid-conversation with their stylists. An older woman looks to be asleep, her head under a dryer. At a back door, the stylist gestures for me to proceed, but doesn't enter herself.

Despite having explicit directions to come here, nerves encroach. This is it. All will change after I pass through this doorway.

Though all is not as I expected.

Instead of a man, Lucas to be exact, a woman is slumped comfortably in a chair. The hem of her trousers is raised, revealing a prosthetic foot. She's a woman I immediately place. The last time I saw her was in Paris, when she came to my gallery.

"You're the one who recommended me to London," I say, a bit astonished to be seeing her again. "Thank you."

"Don't thank me yet," she responds, both of us speaking in French, hers with a clear American accent. She stands from a chair and sets aside a book. Hemingway, I notice. "Also, I'd prefer if you don't bugger my recommendation. I've been told I possess a temper."

I can tell she wants to smile. She doesn't, though. Instead, her already stoic expression hardens. "Unfortunately, Lucas won't be meeting you here as planned. He's been captured."

"What?" It's late summer. In the South of France. The salon itself is warm. Yet a shiver passes through me. "Arrested?"

The American nods. "Yes, he's been compromised and is now

imprisoned. We communicated it to London last night. A new network leader will be sent, but it'll take up to a week. In the meantime, you're to proceed to Lyon. Go here," she says, handing me paper with an address. "Memorize it."

I lick my lips, my mind still trying to catch up to this development. Already things are going astray. I've been in France for less than a day, awake for even less. I run a hand over my brow as I read the address to myself.

"Have it?" she asks me.

"Memorized?" I question back.

"Yes."

I clear my throat, concentrating on the words and numbers. "Yes, I know it."

In a snap, the woman has the paper back in her hands. Like a magician, she has a match not only within her fingers but also lit, and the paper above it. I watch it catch fire, then the American drops it in a rubbish bin. She sets her brown eyes on me. "Good. Now, once you arrive at the safe house, get to know the area, the people. You'll need to find a few additional safe houses for your wireless op to use. Note any flat land that'll be ideal for London to use for drops. Hey," she says, softening her voice.

And it's in that moment I realize my facial muscles and my shoulders are so tense that I haven't done so much as blink.

I'm tall myself, but she dips to my level. "You'll be just fine. Your new network leader will find you at the safe house, which is at . . ."

I rattle off the address.

"That a girl."

I'd laugh if her stare weren't so serious. The way she handles herself tells me she's seen a lot. The fact she once lost a foot and now uses a prosthetic tells me she's experienced a lot.

I immediately respect her. And oddly, I trust her.

"I'll be fine," I parrot.

CHAPTER 9

Violet

—

The Hudson River aboard *Carpathia*
April 18, 1912

I'M WRONG. I THOUGHT THE *Carpathia* WOULD NEVER ARRIVE in New York with light bulbs flashing. But here we are.

Now, as nighttime fully forms, we make our way up the Hudson, flagged by tugboats that are little more than shadows.

Ann is beside me on the bench where we've slept the past two nights, distancing ourselves from the dialogue and discourse I cannot bear to hear. While I ached to push Ann away, we've rarely left each other, save for the use of the loo.

Voices intensified by megaphones filter through the cool air. The reporters want to confirm how many lives have been saved. How many have been lost. If it's true that John Jacob Astor IV, Benjamin Guggenheim, Isidor Straus—the notables—have been lost.

Not enough.

Too many.

Sí.

And I'll have you know, those who aren't "notable" have perished too. What a stupid question to fling at a ship full of widows and fatherless children.

Ann lets out a long breath. "Won't they stop?"

I mumble, "I think they've only just begun."

And as Pier 54 comes into view, illuminated by lamps and nearby buildings, I know this to be true. It appears as if thousands upon thousands of people have gathered. Thousands of people who are hoping against hope that the messages received in the three days since *Titanic* sank are false and that their loved ones will be among the 703 survivors.

The camera bulbs flash.

I close my eyes, preparing myself to step off the ship.

My turn comes too soon and not fast enough.

The pier is a cacophony of sobs, footsteps, horns, barks, whistles, and voices.

"Is it true," a reporter calls out, "only a single woman was pulled from the water?"

Is it? I don't know.

Another voice volleys back, "A Mrs. Rhoda Abbott. Is this the woman from the water?"

Then the woman's named is called, again and again, in an attempt to locate and interview her, no doubt.

News has traveled faster than the *Carpathia*, and she'd traveled faster than she'd ever gone, a feat considering the extra weight aboard with her own passengers and those rescued from *Titanic*. I wonder if my own family has heard word of me. Are they left wondering about my fate? It nearly doubles me over, imagining my mother in her chair by the window, staring blankly, yet her mind a kaleidoscope of memories, many of them not good.

I lower my head, my arm tucked into Ann's, and forge on. A body bumps mine. I twist through the crowd. A man, I assume a reporter, touches my arm. The flash of a camera steals my vision for a heartbeat. When my eyesight returns, he's all but salivating to talk with me. "You worked on the *Titanic*?"

How does he know? But I realize I'm wearing my uniform beneath my borrowed, unbuttoned coat. It strikes me I don't know its owner, if that person is dead or alive.

Then something else strikes me. This uniform and coat are all

I currently own. Everything else sank with the *Titanic*. My meager personal possessions, I'm not upset about that. My clothing, it'll be expensive to replace, but even that isn't dire. It's my tips. Five days' worth of American-sized tips that I didn't have the foresight to safeguard in my apron.

How could I have been so careless, so obtuse?

"Miss?" the man prods.

I ignore him, my mind whirling.

But then something brings my head up. "So sad," I hear a woman say. "They say she was found with him. A woman with her dog. A Great Dane. Both dead."

If Ann wasn't beside me, I'd topple to the dock.

Miss Walton. Hercules.

"How horrible," her companion, another woman, responds.

"Yes. It breaks my heart. I heard her arms were frozen around the dog. At least they didn't drown."

The second woman counters, "You'd rather freeze to death?"

I cannot hear anymore. I bully on, pulling Ann with me.

I need to be away from here. Away from this pier. These survivors. These vultures.

* * *

IT'S TAKEN TEN DAYS, BUT I RELUCTANTLY STAND OUTSIDE the gate to 22 Vallis Way in Ealing. This has been my address ever since we moved to London years ago. It's where my mother lives, where my sister comes when she's not at the convent, where my brothers reside now that I've been able to move them from the orphanage to a daily school, where I've come during my ship leaves. Yet it's never felt like home.

I think I made certain it never would.

It's a place where I check in on my family, then hightail it back onto a ship.

It's where I come to pay the bills.

Only this time I've come nearly empty-handed.

I feel as if I've survived the sinking only to fail my family. As such, I'm hesitant to release the gate latch and approach our small two-story duplex. I inhale deeply and proceed. I've no bags to carry.

White Star paid us our full wages, of which I spent the bare minimum at a rummage sale in New York City after our arrival there.

A "new" dress, a "new" coat. I was more than happy to exchange the coat I'd been given aboard the *Carpathia*. I didn't like the idea of wearing someone's coat. I realize I'm still wearing someone else's coat, but at least this individual had nothing to do with *Titanic*'s sinking. I can imagine its owner simply outgrowing it or wishing to wear something from this season's fashion.

The stone walkway to my home is cracked. The grass is overgrown in the front garden. The paint on the door is chipped. No sound comes from inside, but it is late.

I arrived in Plymouth only this morning after spending eight days aboard *Lapland*, at White Star's expense. My desire to be away from the hordes in New York was greater than my fear of boarding another ship. And, thank the Lord, the captain chose a more southerly route for our return, far from the location where so many of my friends are lost at sea.

The relief I felt at stepping off the *Lapland* was so intense that I wondered if it could be physically seen. I wondered if a person could simply set their gaze upon me during the many hours I sat aboard the Great Western Railway—at my own expense—and see the ordeal I had experienced.

I retrieve a spare key from beneath a pot and enter the house, the door creakily announcing my arrival. Because of the late hour, I assume my presence will go unnoticed until the morning. I'll be given time to run a hand over our family photos, look in on my brothers safely in their beds, kiss Mother's forehead as she soundly sleeps.

But as soon as I press the door closed and turn the lock, I hear a cough. By the window, where she is known to stare unseeing, Mother sits in the glow of the streetlights that filter through the thin curtains.

"Mother," I whisper. "You startled me."

Her head slowly turns toward me. She's aged since I saw her only weeks ago. Her eyes pool with tears.

I cross to her as fast as my legs will carry me and drop to my knees, taking her hands.

"I'm okay," I lie. "I'm here. I survived."

In her lap is the *London Daily Mail*. I make out in the dim light a headline: "*Titanic* Sunk, No Lives Lost."

It's dated the sixteenth of April, only two days after the *Titanic* sunk.

"Oh, Mama," I say. I know she must've received word that I had survived, the White Star contacting the families of those who lived. She saw this headline that no lives were lost. But then true reports came in.

I imagine the corrected headlines. "*Titanic* Sunk, Thousands Lost."

She would have doubted that I'd be coming home.

"I'm here," I repeat. "I'm fine."

Mother's lips quake. Then she says two simple words. "No more."

Those words haunt me as I lead her to her bed, kiss her forehead, and retreat to a second bed in her room. *No more.*

She never wanted me to work the *Titanic* after the incident with the *Olympic*. It makes sense she won't want me to return to the sea.

But no more? How is that possible when I can't fathom how we'll have enough to pay this month's bills? When we'll have next month's, and the months thereafter.

That night pure exhaustion, both physically and mentally, is the only reason I sleep.

I wake first, intent on going through the pile of unpaid bills. I start a fire to chase away the chill in the air, put on the kettle, then settle into a kitchen chair.

I open each envelope.

I make little stacks of golden sovereigns.

Rather ruefully, I wish that sovereigns were more elastic.

But they are not.

Nor will there be enough.

I feel my brother before I see him. His arms wrap around me from behind, his head leaning against mine. "Violet. You're home."

I know immediately it's Patrick. Despite him being a twin with Jack, he has a deep voice all his own. Hearing the tenor of it brings tears to my eyes. I swallow before I say, "I'm back, yes."

"Tell me you're not going to sea again."

It helps I can't see his face, still tucked next to mine. "I have to."

"Violet, no."

I pull on Patrick's arm, unwinding him from around me, and guide him into a chair. "You sound like Mother."

His eyebrow quirks. "I'm surprised. She's worse."

"Ever since . . ."

"*Sí*."

I lick my lips.

My brother asks, "Could you not get a different job?"

"And take the time to look? The time to train?"

The questions are mainly for myself. But my brother quickly counters, "Steward a private family instead, then?"

Instinctively I shake my head. Putting aside the fact I'd be paid a wage and nothing more, I imagine the colorless and slavish life of a servant, even while traveling with their employers to summer estates and holidays around the world. I think more on it, consider what it'd really mean . . . for my family. And with no set calendar of voyages, it'd mean less structure to check in on Mother.

I recall the gray along her hairline, the deep lines etched across her face, but most importantly, the distant look in her eyes.

I can't lose the comfort of my schedule. Nor do I have the convenience of time to find a job that would align with our needs.

Patrick offers, "I could get a job."

I give him a smile, but still I counter, "You're fourteen."

He shrugs.

To which I shake my head. "You will not forfeit your school." I leave off, *Like I have.*

"Fine." A cheeky smile appears on Patrick's face. That's more like him. William is serious. Philip is cautious. Jack is mischievous. Patrick is goofy. And the goof says, "Please just don't undertake another disaster without first making sure of your toothbrush. Have you been without it for days?"

I let out a laugh, my first in days. "Sound advice, Paddy. Maybe I'll carry a backup, just to be safe."

"You'll really return? You're not scared?"

Oh, I'm horrified. But I cannot let Patrick see that.

"You're too young to remember Father's sayings, but there's one ever so fitting to this scenario."

My brother cocks his head.

I say, "The devil you know is better than the devil you don't."

And I've seen the worst the sea can do, or so I must tell myself I have.

CHAPTER 10

Daphne

CODE NAME KATHERINE
Alias Madame Irene du Tertre

Lyon, France
September 2, 1942

THE DEVILS. THEY'RE EVERYWHERE. WHILE LYON IS TECH-
nically in the unoccupied zone, this detail has done nothing to
reduce the number of German soldiers walking about.

With the city being a rumored hotbed of resistance, it's clear
to see why. It's not as if men and women wear signs around their
necks that declare them to be with the Germans or with the
French. Who is on what's side . . . it's a gamble, one that could
cost me my life if I put my trust in the wrong person.

I will need to be Katherine—the helpful and dependable secret agent, familiarizing myself with the area and people, finding
additional safe houses, locating flat land to use for drops—and
also Madame Irene du Tertre, the dutiful wife of a man who's
joined up with the Germans.

It's this latter role I need to slip on as soon as I step from the
train at the depot. I'm immediately questioned by an officer in
the gray-green Gestapo uniform.

"I'm visiting a sick aunt on Juiverie," I say, offering him my travel papers and the preestablished lie. "My husband is with the German Wehrmacht," I add, thinking he'll like that, "which has given me more flexibility to travel, though I'll admit to being a novice at doing that. I feared I'd get off at the wrong stop. This is Lyon, is it not?"

I hope I haven't said too much, but my acting lands. The officer sees me as a feeble, confused woman. "You're in exactly the right spot," he answers.

I smile, feeling a surge of confidence. Yes, I am.

I ask him to direct me toward one address, of my imaginary sick aunt, while I go toward another, to the address I committed to memory before the American woman set it ablaze. Even while I think he believes me, as his attention is quickly turned to another passenger, my confidence wavers. That was one man to convince, but now I must pass man after man, any of whom could question who I truly am. I look over my shoulder after every turn, using the Basilica of Notre-Dame de Fourvière as a beacon toward the safe house.

I remember from my readings how the basilica is atop a hill, seen from almost anywhere in Lyon. It was built to give thanks to the Virgin Mary for having spared the city from invasion during the Franco-Prussian war.

Sadly, I fear Lyon won't be spared this time.

The safe house is an apartment on the second floor of a bar. I find the key beneath a loose floorboard and let myself in. It's dark, but I keep the blinds closed. It's better no one knows I'm here. For a moment, I sit on the sofa with my hands in my lap, letting my mind and body catch up. Then I want nothing more than to get to work.

Within moments, I'm back on the street and climbing Fourvière Hill. From there, I'm awarded a panoramic view of the city: Lyon's two rivers, converging at the city's center; the Grand Theatre, where the gladiators once fought; courtyards, gardens, and narrow stone corridors that I know can only be accessed by traboules, so easily missed they're practically secret passageways; the noticeably taller buildings, which double as both homes and silk factories; and somewhere, though I can't pinpoint where exactly, is the Museum of Fine Arts, home to one of the largest art collections in France, including works by Rembrandt and Monet.

As much as I want to nail down the museum's location and leisurely walk its rooms, it's the secret passageways and their tucked-away homes that draw back my attention.

They appear to be perfect spots for additional safe houses or Resistance meetings. Though it's not as if I can simply knock on their doors. First, I have to let the Resistance people get to know me as Katherine, while blending in as Irene.

I'll purchase a bicycle and ride about, making myself visible, visiting markets and shops—all under the guise of procuring medicines and necessities for a sickly aunt.

But more importantly, I'll also do simply nothing.

Before coming here, I was taught in the favorite pastimes of the Lyonnais. That is, to simply sit for hours at an outdoor café or pontificate along the riverbanks.

So I'll sit, I'll watch, I'll listen, and I'll determine who is with me and who is against me.

* * *

IN A FEW DAYS' TIME I NOTICE A GROUP OF MEN WHO CON-gregate at the same *bouchon* both yesterday and today.

I notice a woman who flinches when a Gestapo man strikes a man on the streets. Though who wouldn't blanch?

I have to train my own expression from alarm to compliance.

I wish there was a way to react in such a manner while also broadcasting to anyone in support of the Resistance that I'm only playing along. When a man passing by nods in approval, I wonder if he's also acting the same as me. It's not as if I can simply ask him.

But I do wonder, especially as there seems to be more German presence, even compared to when I arrived only days ago.

I bike the narrow streets, accustoming myself to the city, the people, the buildings. I let myself be seen. Women on bikes are commonplace. When I purchase medicine for my "sick aunt," I also inquire if the pharmacist knows of any rooms for rent.

"It may be best if I sleep elsewhere, you see," I tell him. "I'm a night owl and I worry my moving around will disturb her sleep. Plus, she's quite infectious, I fear."

The pharmacist, who takes a discreet step backward, is quick to make a suggestion for an apartment and have me on my way.

At the market, I inquire about the nearby farms. "With my husband away, I'm interested in a job milking," I say casually. This of course is a separate story from my poor sick aunt. I should probably find a way to consolidate the two. A rare illness where she drinks large quantities of milk? I'll think on it.

But I'm quite interested in these farmers, not only because they'd be the ones to have flat land—where our planes can make supply drops—but also because railwaymen, dockers, and farmers are the most likely to oppose the Germans.

I'll be sure to poke my nose around the depots and docks too.

At night, I risk listening to the radio, needing to know the state of the war while also fully aware that the Germans are actively trying to ferret out hidden radio transmitters all over the so-called free zone.

Still, I keep the volume low, having to press the device to my ear to hear over the sounds of the barroom beneath me.

The Germans captured a port in Russia.

The Germans sank a submarine. The Germans sank a ship. Both so frighteningly commonplace.

The Germans took an airfield in Stalingrad.

The Germans, the Germans, the Germans.

I close my eyes. They are everywhere, controlling all of western Europe, with the exception of Britain.

The radio broadcast continues. The Gestapo have captured two prominent members of the Red Orchestra resistance group. Details are given, but I twist the knob, silencing the transmission.

Hearing this will do me zero good. In fact, all it'll do is paint a more vivid picture of the Gestapo in my head.

It's horrific enough my network leader has already been arrested, the replacement not set to come until some unannounced day. The American woman didn't give an exact date.

In search of a glass for water, I shuffle toward the kitchen area, noticing an ache in my legs from biking all over God's kingdom. I yawn, the excitement of the last few days taking its toll on me. Finally, the bar-goers are making their way home, the noise considerably less. The apartment is stuffy, and I pinch my blouse to shake the thin fabric.

That's when I hear footsteps on the stairs, then on the landing.

I drop to my hands and knees.

Feet stop just beyond my door.

CHAPTER 11

Violet

—

Aboard *Olympic*
June 5, 1912

WHAT'S A PERSON TO DO WHEN FACED WITH GREAT UNCERtainty and fear? Remember the reason for being.

That promise.

Those bills.

And so I've stepped upon a ship again. In this case, the patched-up, refurbished *Olympic*, sister to the *Titanic*. And here I am, readying rooms for my new passengers.

In the weeks prior, there'd been constant reminders of what has happened.

The *New York Times* devoted seventy-five pages to *Titanic* in the first week alone, I'm told.

Official investigations began into the sinking.

I was called on for press interviews. They went ignored.

An invitation was sent to me and the other surviving crew members to meet with the mayor, during which he awarded us each a gift of ten pounds.

The mayor then asked for the compensation *back*, after I'd already mentally spent it on tuitions and a new stewardess uniform. All under the ridiculous logic that the *Daily Telegraph* was kind enough to offer each of the 703 survivors a gift of twenty-four pounds. I suppose that's enough reparation in the mayor's eyes.

Ann wrote to tell me that she wouldn't be returning to work. While my stomach tightened at this loss, and I chastised myself for growing so fond of her, I'm glad to think of her alive and well on land.

Then, a month after the sinking, a film released. The star was none other than Dorothy Gibson. I couldn't watch it.

But if Miss Gibson could make a film about her very own harrowing experience after only thirty-one days, then surely I could swallow my fears and complete a job I could do in my sleep.

And that meant seeing to my new passengers.

There's a charge in the air, both below deck and above. I can't quite put my finger on what it is. A nervousness, perhaps, to be on a nearly identical ship to the *Titanic* in many ways. But also a morbid excitement to be on a surviving sister ship.

I overheard a man say into a woman's ear, "The embellishments, the carpet, the structure of the grand staircase is the same, I've heard."

It's true. But I noticed the differences, too, and it's those dissimilarities I latched onto.

In the palm court, *Olympic*'s tables are round, whereas *Titanic*'s were square.

In the smoking room, the tile flooring on *Olympic* is buff and gray. *Titanic*'s were red and blue.

But the greatest of differences: the lifeboats.

Here, there's a lifeboat for all.

I checked. I think this is why I'm able to settle my heartbeat, to put a smile on my face and welcome Miss Anderson to her rooms.

She'd like some tea. Strike that, some wine. I cringe internally, thinking of my own harried past with the drink as a young girl. While recovering from my lung ailment in the Andes, my doctor often prescribed a common red wine to help reduce inflammation in my lungs. Whether the remedy was successful or not, I soon began to refuse it after witnessing how it was made: with bare, unwashed feet.

I shudder now, just as Miss Anderson holds up a finger. "On second thought, the drink can wait. I need your help with the closet first. I have no idea how all of this will fit."

I pat her hand. "Please, allow me to see to your clothing."

The finest of garments too. But I realize as I hang one after another, I feel less charmed by her brand-name clothing and her expensive perfumes than I have in the past.

Miss Anderson herself is well-to-do. A young heiress who'd been linked to the filmmaker Charles Labine in the pages of the *Tatler*.

Yet I'm less enamored with her. I didn't even speculate on her like I had with Madeleine Astor and so many before her. I've no desire to get attached to her like I did Ida Straus after her many voyages with me.

This is merely a job. *Como un media para un fin.*

The sentiment is punctuated when Miss Anderson compensates me for the "above and beyond" assistance.

And so it begins again.

And so it continues. I complete my voyage on *Olympic*—without incident, I should add. I spend four days at home with Mother, again stacking my sovereigns, then I'm back at sea.

This is my rhythm, my schedule for thirteen, fourteen—I've lost count—more voyages. It all adds up to two years.

And while my life is much the same throughout that time—mundane, at best—the world is regrettably more exciting.

Archduke Franz Ferdinand is assassinated. The very same day, Austria-Hungary declares war on Serbia.

Just this week, our ship's radio picked up reports that Germany has invaded Luxembourg and Belgium. France has invaded somewhere, too, but there's too much varying chatter about where. There's more solid talk, however, about how our British forces are arriving in France to help.

I find it all very frightening.

Other ships have been recommissioned for war efforts. We

suspect the same will be *Olympic*'s fate and, as such, this is to be our last return trip to England.

Thus, I'm faced with the age-old question that haunts me. How will I support my family? I can only pray the war will be short-lived or that I can quickly find work elsewhere. Already, men are volunteering to enlist in droves. Logically, women will be needed to fill in for jobs.

Do I want to work in a factory? Absolutely not. Will I? If I must.

War talk and speculations are all the crew can speak of. And if I'm being honest, I also can't help being swept up in the rush of patriotic fervor.

It's only days to November, just a few months after the war's outbreak. I wake to a beautiful autumn morning. I open the porthole in my stateroom and instantly I know we're near land, beyond the fact I know our route to be moving along the coast of northern Ireland. I can smell the difference between land and sea, and a satisfying odor of peat fires mixes with the salt air. It's difficult to describe the exact aroma, but peat smells different from wood. More sour.

Though now's not the time to debate peat versus wood. I have to dress and hurry upstairs to the pantry before the billboard begins lighting up with calls. My Americans do not like to be kept waiting, always running around, always working, always wanting more and more.

I do too. Though I haven't allowed myself to think it for some time. But that notion, that dream I once had . . .

Maybe one day . . . someday . . . things will be better and I can pursue a vocation that lights a fire in my insides. Maybe one day . . . someday . . . something good will come my way that is all my own.

A call comes in and off I go.

On my way up, I notice a few gray shapes in the distance. "Cruisers out for target practice," I'm told by a sweet lad named Henry. "That's what Willie said anyhow."

I smile in agreement. I've no information otherwise. I haven't grown close with the other stewards, Willie included, the way I did with Stanley. I know little about my cabinmate beyond her first name. Henry's the only one I've created any type of kinship with and only because he reminds me of my brothers—and I'd never deny them or him a thing.

I see to my first passenger, before I'm rushing back down the passageway to my next, when I see there's more of a hubbub on deck.

I spot Henry again. "What's all the fuss about?"

He's shaking his head. "Now Willie's saying something is amiss. Captain got a distress call from *Audacious.*"

"Oh?" I say, fighting to keep any panic or concern from my voice. Henry can't be more than sixteen, the same age as my Patrick and Jack. All too young to enlist, in my opinion, yet Henry told me there's no law against him doing just that. It turns my stomach inside out.

"Yep," he says in regard to us receiving a distress call, "and we're putting on speed to help 'em."

I scrunch my brows, but I keep a question between my lips: *Are they sinking?*

With a tightness in my chest, I pat his arm. "So much excitement, but I'm sure all is fine. I'm off to ensure Miss Anderson has all she needs."

But as I go about my morning, I keep a watchful eye on Henry and a keen ear to all that's being said.

"*Audacious* hit a mine."

"She's flooding."

"Has taken a list to port of up to fifteen degrees."

"Swells are heavy."

That much I can feel. I reach for the handrail as I search the waters. I see her, indeed tilting to one side.

I turn, frantically gripping the forearm of the first person who passes by who's a member of our crew. I don't even know his name. "Are there many people on board?"

The man looks startled by my voice and firm grip. "I don't know, miss. It's a battleship. No passengers, just crew."

I nod, and he quickly goes on his way. I still have no wish to alarm Henry, but he's my well-informed *amigo*. I find him. "What more do you know?"

"Only that we're preparing our lifeboats."

I want to shout the question at him, but I somehow manage to calmly say, "To bring them here?"

He nods.

I look again at the great battleship. The swells seem to have grown in size. The deck of our ship looks to be twice the distance above the water, if not greater. The huge warship rises and dips in the swells, where men in blue await our help.

I cannot look away.

Voices ring out, with loud and clear instructions on lowering the lifeboats. In no time, the boats hit water and are being deployed across the churning sea that separates us from them.

To my relief, the list of the other vessel lessens. And while I'm still not advanced in the inner workings of a ship, I've gained enough knowledge in recent years to know it's likely on account of counter-flooding compartments. They'll balance the ship, but they won't stop her from sinking. The men need off.

I give a silent thanks that it is not me rowing from here to there. At any moment I fear a lifeboat will take on too much water or capsize.

More often than not, I hold my breath.

In one instance I'm already breathless when the largest swell I've ever seen washes across the deck of *Audacious*, sweeping the men straight off their feet and into the sea.

"Holy cow," a passenger remarks. Fleetingly I whip my attention to him. He's filming it all. In that moment I'm reminded so starkly of Mr. Marvin filming his new wife as she was lowered from *Titanic* that my head spins and I nearly empty my stomach.

The communal gasp of those on our ship rights me. Miraculously, a second ginormous wave returns the navy men to their ship. I pray it brought them all—and without a slew of broken bones.

As the first lifeboat returns, I rush to meet the men, joining other crewmen and stewards. The navy men outweigh me three-fold, even if I were the one dripping wet, but still I do my best to grab their sleeves, hands, whatever I can grasp, and heave them aboard.

Their faces are cheery, grateful—even those with arms and elbows at painful-looking angles.

Even knowing the lot of them have broken bones, I release a giddy chuckle, the moment seeming to call for it. They're safe now.

They've cheated death. A commonality between us.

"Here, this way," I say, leading them to deck chairs. "I'll fetch towels. Water—"

"I've had my fair share of water, miss, but thank you," one of the men quips.

I chuckle again. "That you have."

Soon I'm wrapping men in blankets and making myself useful while seeing to the sporadic needs of my normal passengers. Some, like Miss Anderson, have graciously put aside their own demands, even pitching in to help the naval men. It certainly doesn't hurt how attractive they are in uniform.

And soon, all so-called nonessential crew are aboard *Olympic*. But that still leaves over two hundred men on the sinking battle-ship.

By this time, the day has grown to midafternoon and the ship has lowered considerably closer to the water's surface.

Suddenly Henry's at my side. "Captain's going to try to tow her. Hope is to breach her on land."

Hope. It's a word I dislike. From my studies, I know *hope* to originally mean a confidence in the future. But in medicine, in life, in reality, how can that exist? It's not a burden I'll put on the young lad. Instead, I ask, "And how far is land?"

"Twenty-five miles."

We don't make it a single mile. The towline snaps, a loud whistling noise as *Audacious* tries, again and again, to turn into the wind.

Others try, too, a light cruiser and a cargo ship having also arrived to help. Their lines break just the same.

All the while, *Audacious* lowers and lowers.

As afternoon creeps toward evening, she's only four feet above the water, her stern at only a foot. All but fifty men are called from the ship. And soon even those men are told to risk the lifeboats to board our ship.

I welcome them, even hugging the last man who comes aboard. Then, for the first time in hours, I slump into a chair.

All the men are accounted for. No man will go into the water. I feel such relief that emotion overcomes me. I release a hiccupped sob just as our ship's passengers let out a collective gasp that brings me back to my feet. *Audacious* is heeling sharply. The incline and the pause that follows remind me so keenly of *Titanic* that I press a hand over my heart. Then the wounded and tired giant gives in, falling backward.

I stare blankly at the capsized battleship.

It's done.

The mine the battleship has hit is the victor.

I begin to lower myself to the chair again when there's an explosion.

I feel the blast even from such a distance. Wreckage is thrown in the air. "Take cover!" is yelled.

Before I can seek shelter, there's a second explosion, then a third.

CHAPTER 12

Daphne

___

CODE NAME KATHERINE
Alias Madame Irene du Tertre

Lyon, France
September 6, 1942

I COULD COMBUST WITH THE LEVEL OF NERVES AND ANXIETY that courses through me. On my hands and knees, I stare at the feet on the other side of my door. They do not move.

There is no noise.

No knock.

My gaze bounces around, my mind whirling wildly. Have I already been compromised? It seems unfathomable. But I've been overconfident before. At the Sorbonne, I studied journalism, convinced I'd graduate and promptly be presented a job in the industry. Soon after, I'd win an award. It didn't go as planned. No publication would have me. Too verbose. Too bland. Too opinionated. Too female.

I panicked, my father expecting news that I was with the *Daily Telegraph*, the *Times*, the *Guardian*, or any publication of note.

Instead, jobless, I telephoned him with a plot twist: I had enrolled at the University of Cairo.

"To study what?" my father asked.

"To earn a diploma in Arabic language."

Which was the hardest language I could think of learning. Written right to left, verbs are based on gender, letters change shape based on whether they're in the beginning, the middle, or the end of a word. It sounded difficult through and through.

My father had guffawed. "You astound me, Katherine."

Exactly as I had hoped.

Harder than I had expected, too, to earn that diploma.

Was I being overconfident now that no one had questioned my presence in Lyon or followed me here? Heard my radio?

Though, of course, the most logical of explanations, I try to convince myself, is that an overserved bar patron has lost his sense of direction and wandered this way.

And his feet have grown roots outside my door. The door to my safe house.

If he realizes there's someone inside, or better yet thinks that I am not alone, perhaps it'll spark him to go on his merry way.

"I'll be there in a moment, darling," I call theatrically, louder than necessary. "Just tidying up."

I'm still on my hands and knees.

The feet remain, though they shuffle, repositioning.

"Yes," I call, even louder. "I'll be there in a jiffy."

To my astonishment, laughter filters in from the hall. "Not a jiffy," I hear.

And I know that voice.

I fumble through the locks and throw open the door.

"Gabriel?" He seems out of place here in France and not in one of our training rooms, even if he's an agent same as me. Still. "What on earth are you doing here?"

He tips an invisible hat, leaning closer to whisper, "I've been told FAME has a vacancy."

A hand goes on my hip. "Well, that's an interesting way to put it."

His smile is replaced with a cringe. "I know. It was bad form. Is it unmanly of me to admit I'm nervous to replace someone who's now in prison? I knew the Gestapo were here, but damn."

"I know," I say, motioning him inside. Then, like the paranoid person I've become, I stick my head into the hallway, look both ways to ensure no one has seen our exchange, and close the door.

"Thanks for tidying up," Gabriel says, gesturing toward the small room consisting of a table, couch, and kitchenette.

"Thanks for arriving *days* earlier than I thought you'd come."

Truly, I wasn't expecting Gabriel at all, but him being my network leader is a pleasant surprise. I'm sure Lucas would've been fine. Actually, I don't know that. I knew nothing about him. He could've been compulsive, sloppy, a bad liar. Whatever he was, it was enough to catch the attention of the Gestapo.

If only I knew what'd gone wrong.

At least I know a thing or two about Gabriel. Intelligent, mostly funny, capable, willing to jump into a river to help a girl out, and smitten with another woman.

All qualities I am happy to have in a man I'll be working with closely.

A recent memory comes to mind. "So I have to ask, how disappointed are you that it's me here and not Denise? Remember back in training when you said—"

"Oh, I remember. I also remember how she said she'd stab a German through his ear. She terrifies me."

I laugh. "We'll make a less terrifying but still effective team."

"Cheers to that." Gabriel begins to examine our small safe house. It takes exactly ten steps and just as many seconds. "So, Louis should be arriving tomorrow."

And Louis does.

Our network is officially operational.

FAME, I muse.

Ironic, even.

The best way I can describe Louis, our wireless operator, is overgrown. Bushy eyebrows. Shaggy hair. Soft in the middle. Baggy clothing.

And maybe overage. He looks too old to be throwing his hat into the war. But perhaps that's all part of his deception.

He arrives with "precious cargo," as he puts it.

"What I've got here"—he shows us, laying down a suitcase—"is my B2 set, short for B Mark II Transmitters. The *B* means I've got a reach up to fifteen hundred miles."

"Take that, A," I say.

Louis nods, either missing or not caring my comment was in jest. In fact, I didn't know there was an A model until he says, "The A's only got four hundred miles in her. Good only for northern France."

Gabriel shoots me an amused look, as if saying, "He told you."

He did, and with a click, Louis has the suitcase open. There are four compartments, Louis explaining each one.

The left: accessories, such as the aerial, Morse key, headphones, et cetera.

The middle top part: the transmitter.

The middle bottom part: the receiver.

The right: the power fittings.

"She comes with a lot, and she's heavy," Louis says, "but the beauty of how she functions is that I can quickly switch from the main electricity current to battery if those direction finders are trying to trace me."

"Amen to that," Gabriel says.

"My thoughts exactly."

"My thought," Louis says, shutting the suitcase again, "is I need you two to get me stuff to transmit. London and I set a pre-arranged schedule. I'll be shooting off code about three times a week. First one in two days. I need to know when we can do our first drop and where."

Well, okay. A rush of nerves and excitement courses through

me and I turn to Gabriel. "Looks like we've got some work to do. And I know just the farm to start with."

* * *

THE NEXT MORNING GABRIEL AND I BOARD A BUS.

I biked to various farms before his arrival. My objective was mostly to scope out potential reception sites for London to make drops; however, during one of my rides, my eye caught on a discoloration in the grass. It turned out to be a paper with a coded message.

Quite careless, if you ask me, but also a stroke of good fortune. The Resistance communicated in codes. And made me think supporters were nearby, like at the farm farther down the road.

The farm we'll be approaching today.

As I climb the final step onto the bus, I realize the transport is more crowded than expected.

"Always smile," my father has told me my whole life.

The first time—oh, the naive young girl I was—I responded that I knew why: because it could lift someone's day.

My father chuckled. "Sure, Kitty Kat," he said, ruffling my hair, "but also because people who smile are more well-liked."

Right now I want to be well-liked. I give the bus driver my best Katharine Hepburn smile. He's an older gentleman. The way I picture a grandfather to look, if I had one. My *maman* left home at sixteen and never looked back. And my father's parents both died during a typhoid fever outbreak a few years before I was born.

As I pass, the driver grabs my arm. Not in a predatory type of way. But I wasn't expecting the contact, and I startle. Behind me, I sense Gabriel tensing.

"Madame," he says. "Not many seats left. The ones in the back are next to a broken window. Why don't you," he says, clearing a jacket and bag off a seat close by, "take this one. Right by the engine. It'll keep the rear end toasty."

I laugh. "That's very kind of you, thank you."

I accept the seat, watching out of my peripheral vision as Gabriel has no choice but to take the seat next to the broken window. I also have no choice but to hide another laugh, especially after I feel his eyes on me as if he wants me to acknowledge the fact that he got the shorter end of the stick.

At our stop in Oullins, I give the driver another award-winning grin, lightly touching and squeezing his arm. "See you tomorrow. And thank you again."

Gabriel and I had decided I'll do the trip every day, even if we have no business out this way. Routine. Routine is rarely suspected of anything nefarious.

I begin walking in the direction of the farm as soon as I get off. I count in my head: ten, nine, eight . . .

Three, two, and right on schedule . . .

"Talk about preferential treatment," Gabriel quips, coming up beside me.

I give a fake shiver. "Is it unseasonably cold today? Or is it just me?"

He chuckles.

I smirk, then refocus. "So the farm isn't far from here. There's a barn and another outbuilding that'd be great for two safe house options. How are you going to play things with the farmer?"

"London told me a man code-named Gaspar is moving in our circles in Oullins. If it's him, we're golden. He's connected to some railwaymen, dockmen. We'll be up and running in no time."

"And you'll do what? Go up and greet him as Gaspar?"

Gabriel looks over at me, one of his dimples showing. "Yup."

I guess the approach makes sense, but when we have boots on his porch and Gabriel's about to knock on his farmhouse door, I'm nervous as hell.

I just about swallow my tongue when a curtain moves aside in a nearby window—with the help of a rifle's barrel.

"Gabriel," I whisper.

But instead of responding to me, Gabriel calls out, "Gaspar? We're looking for a Gaspar."

The curtain falls back into place.

Once I was almost in an automobile accident, and when the car was careening past me, I clenched my bum, as if it would've done a dang thing to help shrink our car and allow the other auto to squeeze past us unscathed.

I clench again now.

The door opens. A grizzly man barks, "Who's asking?"

Gabriel touches his chest and cites his own code name. "And this is Katherine." He then nods with his head over his shoulder toward the stretch of land. "We could really use your fields."

There's a clunk, which I realize is Gaspar putting his gun down on his side of the door. He smiles—I like him more already—and says, "About damn time."

* * *

AND IN NO TIME, LOUIS HAS COMMUNICATED WITH LONDON and a night and time are established.

Our first drop goes off without a hitch.

Our first month of drops, in fact.

My alarm would wake me at 2:00 a.m. on these planned nights. I'd discreetly leave my apartment and even more discreetly bike to the reception site—be it the farm or another parcel of land I've identified, such as a sewage farm, not my favorite of spots. There, I'd mark the drop zone with lights, a beacon for the approaching pilots. Then, as they approached, I'd flash Morse code to let them know it's safe to drop their loads.

Every time, the sight of the large canisters swinging down, parachutes above them, was both nerve-racking and exhilarating. Each weighed about four hundred pounds. It'd be very easy for the Germans to catch us red-handed.

So, of course, we worked like maniacs to pry open the canisters.

We quickly assembled any guns and broke up the other supplies in more manageable pieces for us to cart away.

The key was quickly. Efficiently. And a sheen of sweat covered me when I was done. I'd bike home under the noses of the Germans and fall back into bed, catching what little sleep was left until morning.

In total, we receive around four hundred fifty containers, resulting in loads of dynamite and enough arms for about two thousand resistants.

That amount is staggering to me. *Two thousand resistants.* Gabriel and Gaspar have been busy, and we're nearly ready for our first act of sabotage.

But unfortunately, the Germans have been busy too.

One afternoon in November I'm walking down a quiet, cobblestoned street on my way toward the safe house when I turn onto a larger street—and stop in my tracks.

It's a parade of Germans. Trucks. Men on foot. A Lyonnais man is struck. I don't know why. Nor do I want to find out in this very moment. Other people are scattering, hiding, and I need to do the same.

I take a step backward as I hear a hissing. Actually more of a *psst* sound. A woman is motioning for me from her second-story window and pointing toward a wall beside her building. "Traboule," she mouths.

I wouldn't have seen the secret passageway if she didn't point it out.

I hastily run a hand down the dense ivy, my hand hitting a knob, turn it, and slip inside the courtyard.

The woman already has a door ajar. "In here," she says.

For a moment I question if I should trust her. But I quickly follow her inside. Two walls between me and the Germans is better than one.

The woman is already rounding a staircase to the second floor. I follow, noting how there's a stockpile of clothing and food neatly placed beneath a table. I find her at the upstairs window, discreetly turned so the drapery all but conceals her. Her movements and her stance look practiced. She raises a hand to her mouth, her head shaking. "So much for the free zone. Nowhere in France is free anymore."

Together, we watch as the Germans march past. There's a man who stands out. Not in the Gestapo uniform, but a member of the SS. He looks sure of himself. The rise of his chin screams confidence and self-righteousness.

Already I despise him.

Without breaking eye contact from the streets, the woman finds my hand, her fingers wrapping around mine.

"Worse," she whispers. "It'll get so much worse in Lyon."

I want to offer her some type of comfort. "For them it will," I say back.

At first I regret my words. It was brazen to so candidly show my disgust for the Germans. But later as I lie in bed at the safe house, Louis and Gabriel on the couch and floor nearby, I'm glad I offered her those few words.

After I spoke them, she tightened her grasp on my hand. And then she nodded, her lips pressed firmly together, as if she believed without a doubt I'd stay true to my word.

I sigh.

I hear the ruffling of a pillow. "Are you awake?" Gabriel asks, his low voice traveling across the room.

"Unfortunately," I say.

He's silent for a few beats, and I think that'll be it, just the need to know he's not alone after the events of today. But then Gabriel goes on, "Do you think they've begun sending out our letters yet?"

I twist my lips. "I don't know. They never said when they'd start."

Louis's deep voice is added to the room, "I'd think so."

Gabriel asks, "Who did you write?"

The question could be for either of us. I'm relieved when Louis answers, "My daughter." He pauses, clears his throat. "My old woman passed away ages ago. Here, then gone. I'll tell you what, though. I'd give anything, I'd relive all the pain of her leaving me on this earth without her, for one more moment with her. At least I still have our little girl." He sniffs. "Not so little anymore. Even with the letters, she'll worry about me. Make a fuss and all that. She always does, that one. Always does."

I hear a thump, Gabriel's hand against Louis's arm or back is my guess. Gabriel doesn't need words to respond; that touch speaks volumes.

And me? I don't have a clue what to say. I've never experienced that type of companionship. That type of love.

Enough time passes where it'd be strange if I did respond, so I lie there, quietness wrapping around us again, and stare at a crack in the ceiling, wondering if my father would have thought anything of my insignificant letters, if I'd written a single one. Or if he would have tossed them aside, nothing within its contents mind-blowing.

CHAPTER 13

Violet

Aboard *Olympic*
October 27, 1914

Audacious EXPLODES A THIRD TIME. THE FORCE OF IT PUSHES me back into my chair. Debris flies, striking the deck of *Olympic* even with us at a distance of half a mile.

Men call out, asking if anybody's been hurt.

I pat myself. I check myself over. With the exception of my heart being in my throat, everything else is where it should be, unharmed. But what of the others?

My head's on a swivel, visually examining the many men for injuries as Henry takes my elbow. Together we watch as *Audacious* disappears, leaving nothing behind but rippling water.

It's a harrowing feeling, watching another ship go under. But this time, I remind myself that everyone is miraculously accounted for. Alive and well, most with nothing more than one hell of a story to tell.

I find myself gravitating to the few in need of medical attention. I've often found myself gravitating toward these types of situations. A curiosity about how a person can be well one moment, ill or injured the next, and with the right care, they have the chance to be whole again.

I helped Mother recover after childbirths, William of

diphtheria, took a keen interest in my own many illnesses. I've bandaged, administered, kept watch, offered soothing words.

When my sister Eileen was born, I was fifteen or so. Mother, already disappearing into herself after the losses of Ray, Denis, and Molly, couldn't care for our newest arrival. Eileen became my responsibility. I buggered it tremendously my first day. I bathed her, ever so carefully, but I made the mistake of using pure acetic lotion to clean her naval. She screamed. I cried. Mother barely noticed.

Finally, I was rescued when the doctor came by to check on Mother and Eileen. He didn't go easy on me. What was his name? I can't recall, but I can now appreciate the severe talking-to he gave me. There was a moment, though, when his voice softened and he explained to me the proper care. It was in that moment that I realized healing was truly something within my reach if I continued to learn.

My desire was reinforced the following week. My poor mother needed an operation on her breast, which the doctor saw to. Only, immediately after the surgery he was called away to the mountains where an English explorer was in need of an amputation because of a frostbitten foot.

"Violet," the doctor had started before he left. I wish I could remember his name. Such an informative time in my life, yet he's only "the doctor" to me all these years later. "I'll need your help," he went on. "Can you see to your mother's dressings while I'm gone?"

I nodded.

"Just like this," he said, showing me.

I watched and absorbed and committed the process to memory. Each and every day I saw to Mother exactly as I'd been taught.

"Just marvelous," the doctor had said upon his return. "Well done."

"Miss Violet," I hear now. It's a different doctor, Dr. Wilson. He asks me, "Could you be of aid?"

I rush to his side. I help bandage and heal, pulling from what I learned all those years ago, as *Olympic* carries on and up the coast toward Lough Swilly, through the night and into the morning. The aroma of the peat fires grows stronger until I can make out tiny spirals of smoke. The tinkling of church bells travels through the cool air, announcing the start of Mass.

I attend the ship's services, much to be thankful for. When I emerge from Mass, my deliverer of news is eager to fill me in. "Miss Violet," Henry says, "we're not to talk of what happened yesterday to anyone. It's all to be kept a secret."

I think of the American, the one filming it all. "I think that'll be difficult."

The lad shakes his head. "Direction is coming from the top. Can't have Germany finding out a single mine took down one of our battleships."

I press my lips together. *Sí*, I can see how that'd be poor information to share with the enemy. I also don't like the idea of other mines lurking beneath the surface, our servicemen never the wiser.

* * *

BY MID-NOVEMBER WE'VE DOCKED AND DISEMBARKED— many thankful to be alive—and I've begun my journey to Ealing to check on things there, but thoughts of war are still at the forefront of my mind, as well as on the front page of my newspaper.

"Allies' Left Gains 37 Miles."

I find the headline confusing. The article helps.

"The Allies in the last four days of fighting have pushed the Germans back 37 miles along the left of their great battle line . . . The British and French, according to the French official report, have crossed the Marne and are 'pursuing the enemy, who is in retreat.'"

I like the sound of that.

I read on, tapping my foot, my bus only two turns from my

final stop. It also appears the Germans have made some progress in France.

I do *not* like that, though . . . There's a rumor that our army forced the Germans to evacuate a French town last Sunday.

Of course the article adds, "There is no confirmation of the rumor."

Seems a silly thing to put in an article unless it's been proven true. Did they learn nothing from the false reporting after *Titanic*?

Earlier today I saw a woman saying goodbye to her husband at the train depot. She'd want the rumor that the Germans are fleeing to be true. She'd want the speculations that the war will be short-lived—over by Christmas, in fact—to be an indisputable fact.

"*Don't you worry, Maude,*" a man had said to her so casually. "*Robert will be home by Christmas. If I know him, he won't miss your roast goose.*"

The man rubbed his belly, and while I smiled at his mannerisms, I worried that the sentiment felt too much like propaganda. "Over by Christmas" is plastered on posters, signs, newspapers—right next to posters that say, "Your King and Country Need You. Enlist Now." Beside yet another poster that reads "Are We Afraid? No!"

That one shows our Union Flag, with a bulldog at the center. Along the edges are five other smaller dogs, one for each colony of Australia, Canada, India, South Africa, and New Zealand.

It's my favorite of the posters.

It makes no promises. It's a state of mind, one I can get behind. I can't deny getting caught up in the hoopla of the war. I'd love nothing more than to get back at the Germans after the ordeal they put the naval men and us through.

I also can't help but still hate the idea of our men going off to fight, Henry especially. He's too young.

The bus stops and I offer the driver a warm smile. My smile grows when I see the many flags on our street. The same fervor I felt on the ship exists here, only tenfold.

I hasten inside, rain beginning to fall, only to stop in my tracks. I blink. My brothers stand in a row inside the door.

"Hello?" I say, amusement in my voice. "What are you four up to?"

It's in that moment I notice they aren't in their daily school uniforms. They're in different uniforms, clad in khaki.

I shake my head. "No."

William is nineteen, and I've endeavored to keep him in courses for as long as I can. But Philip, he's only seventeen. The twins are newly sixteen. I don't want any of them going to war. One of the reasons for leaving Argentina was to avoid conscription. I shake my head again. "No, you all have school."

They exchange cheeky looks. "No, Vi. You do."

I glance at Mother in her usual corner. She pays us no mind. She looks content, and I hear her nurse in the kitchen. I tear my attention back to my brothers. "What does that mean?"

"Vi," Philip says, stepping forward as the most practical of my brothers. "You gave up school to see to us." He motions to my brothers. "Well, the war needs us. The war will *pay* us. And you"—he smiles so wide I see each and every one of his teeth I've hounded him to brush each and every night I've been at the house—"are free to do something you've always wanted."

I raise a brow.

My brothers smile again.

"Medicine," Patrick chimes in. "Specifically, nursing for the Voluntary Aid Detachment."

"The VAD," Jack says. "We've already put your name in as a volunteer."

"So it's all settled," William punctuates, the oldest of them, the one who usually has the final say. "We've all got our papers."

Despite all I have done to keep them in school, to keep food on the table and boots on their feet, I can feel the control slipping through my fingers. My four brothers, suddenly so big and broad, have gone rogue.

And it appears that I, too, am going to war.

CHAPTER 14

Daphne

CODE NAME KATHERINE
Alias Madame Irene du Tertre

Lyon, France
November 16, 1942

IT WAS INEVITABLE. LYON IS OFFICIALLY OCCUPIED, AND
now that the Germans have enacted a curfew here, too, sneaking
out of my safe house apartment in the middle of the night has
become exponentially harder.

It begins with a panicked slam of my alarm, quieting the high-
pitched noise. From there, every creak of the floorboards, every
groan on the hallway stairs, every squeak of the door feels like
my undoing. On the dark streets, every shadow masks a German
officer waiting to seize me as I ride my bike to the reception site,
then home afterward by dawn.

Exhausted, I sleep for another few hours. Then I'm up, set
again for Oullins, this time via my usual bus ride, which is essen-
tially the same route I covertly rode during the witching hours.

I leave the apartment, turning to lock my door, when a man
from a neighboring apartment stops me.

"Strange hours you keep, madame."

"Me?" But who else could he be talking to? It's only the two of us in the hall. "Oh, yes, well"—my brain quickly formulates a story within my original story—"I'm in town to care for my aunt. She's horribly sick." I realize I must tweak my cover on account of the curfew. I wouldn't be able to go from my apartment to hers. "She needs her medication around the clock, you see, and considering I sleep like the dead, the alarm is necessary for me to wake and see to her. I do hope it's not waking you up too. I'd hate to disrupt your sleep with the long hours you keep."

Yes, I've been watchful as well. He works at one of the factories in the city. It's good for him to know I have eyes and ears too. The question is: Is he on my side or the Germans'? I cannot tell.

Also, if he accepts my narrative, I likewise cannot tell.

He only nods, wishes me a good day, and is on his way. I think about following him again. To the factory or not to the factory? Perhaps he'll head straight to Hôtel Terminus and report me. It's where the Germans have set up their headquarters in Lyon. A beautiful building, now marred by the ugliness of who occupies it.

I decide to stay with my usual routine, heading toward the bus depot. At every shop window I pass, I catch my reflection but, more importantly, the reflection of anyone who could be following me.

The Gestapo don't always wear uniforms. They think they're sly in their plain clothes. I think they are wretched.

My bus driver, on the other hand, is a breath of fresh air. When I board, he greets me with nothing but genuine warmth. As usual, he removes his belongings on the seat he's taken to saving for me.

"A good morning, madame."

"It is, isn't it," I say, wanting it to be exactly that.

He coughs, banging on his chest with a clenched fist.

I lean forward, asking, "Are you unwell?"

He gives one last bang. "Gets me every year around this time. Nothing to fret over."

I offer him a smile and settle into my seat, watching the city thin to a smaller town with homes, farms, and fields. Conversations happen all around me. A woman is reminding another about how the Federation of Jewish Societies of France is giving out free medical treatment and food this afternoon. Another woman is pleased to have found all she needed at the market that morning. A man shows a photograph of a new grandchild to a fellow rider.

How wonderful to hear of wonderful goings-on.

I reposition more comfortably.

The bus driver turns his head, not enough to fully face me, as he needs eyes on the road, but it's clear his words are directed at me. "Been wondering what brings you out here each day."

"The cows," I say in an upbeat tone. "Needy, stubborn creatures. But I've taken to my job working with them. There's something utterly rewarding about starting with something cold and empty and filling it up with something of substance. I suppose it's a bit like your bus, isn't it?"

He guffaws. "The more the bus fills, the nosier and smellier it gets."

I laugh. "We can't win them all, can we?"

"No, we cannot." Surprising me, his tone has taken on a more somber tone, which is accented by another fit of coughing. I'm tempted to reach out and squeeze his shoulder. But my stop's approaching and I slip my wrists through the loops of my purse. Inside, I have new crystals for Louis's radio set. He's working from the barn the next few days and he needs them to determine the wavelength of the transmission and the best way of controlling the stability of it.

"Madame," the driver says, his voice hoarse. He doesn't turn at all this time. His body is stiff, his gaze fixed ahead. In fact, I nearly miss him addressing me. "Why don't you sit a bit longer? Get off at the stop after, yeah? Such a beautiful day for a walk."

I cock my head but say nothing. And at the next stop, I don't rise, but I finally see what he must've seen from his vantage point. A sea of gray-green uniforms is waiting at the stop.

Ever since marching in, they're seemingly everywhere. I remain sitting, my pulse quickening, but a few bus patrons hesitantly pass by to disembark. As soon as they step off the bus, there's a demand to see their identity papers.

I expect the Germans to board the bus to do a sweep of those of us who didn't get off. Leave no stone unturned—or something like that. I clench my bag, where yes, I have papers that say my name is Irene du Tertre. But would they be accepted? Or would they suspect me? Worse, would they search my bag?

Instinctively I let out a soft curse in English. Then I realize what I've done. It's the first time I've spoken anything but French in months. One of the most obvious ways to out myself as a British agent. Every conversation, every comment, every exchange has been in French. Recruits were sent home for botching this rule.

When I lived in Paris, English expressions often slipped out. Moments ago, when I said, "utterly rewarding," I likely would've made a joke of saying "udderly rewarding" for my own enjoyment. In response, I know I would've received blank stares.

Then it was okay. Now it is not.

Heart pounding, I keep my head still and move only my eyes to see if anyone has heard my blunder.

It's a relief but also horrifying as to why no one has given me any mind. All the remaining bus patrons are focused outside, some on the closest soldier, likely wondering the same as I am: Will he come on the bus?

Outside, the woman who had commented on the free medical supplies and food is yanked by the arm, pulled and jerked and wrenched until she's thrust in the direction of another officer. He makes her kneel. A number of others are forced to do the same.

What's going to happen next? I don't think I want to know, though it feels important that I do. The situation feels too much like a ticking bomb.

I eye the officer closest to the bus again.

Then I'm knocked back into my seat, a direct result of how intensely the bus driver pushes the accelerator.

The officer shouts something at the bus. Otherwise, the bus is eerily quiet, a handful of us still remaining.

At the next stop I stand, my knees feeling wobbly. I don't say thank you as I pass by the driver. But I meet his gaze, and he nods, knowing I'm grateful for his help. The real question is . . . how did he know I, specifically, would need it?

★ ★ ★

AFTER SEEING TO LOUIS AND ALSO TO THE COWS—I'VE TAKEN to actually milking them now and again to ensure I know how to, and today it doubles as something soothing to do after this morning's unsettling events—I return to Lyon for an afternoon of people-watching at a café.

As I'm positioned on a cobblestoned circle, there's much to see. Unfortunately that includes the Germans.

They aren't doing anything of note, but their simple presence is an aggravation in and of itself. Their guns. Their smug expressions . . .

Disgusting human beings. There's an overconfidence to them that makes my knee bounce in anticipation for this evening.

It's to be our first act of sabotage.

We've debated what to do first.

While we assembled at the farm, one resistant sported about arranging a consignment of itching powder to be left with the local laundry and sprinkled into German uniforms.

No one said no. But other more destructive suggestions were also made.

The dockmen we've become friendly with advocated for breaking the lock gates. One man insisted, "It'll cause the canal water to drop about, say, twenty inches. And I'll tell ya, twenty inches can do a lot to delay a heavy canal barge that's carrying important military supplies to the Germans."

This got some head nods.

"But you know what'd be even better," Gaspar said, running a hand through his already disheveled hair. "Targeting the trains."

The railwaymen agreed, saying how we could damage track, signal boxes, shunting sheds. It'd all create delays for repair. Better yet, we could use abrasive grease on the train parts, to wear away instead of lubricate. In enough time, the locomotives would be put out of commission entirely.

But Gaspar shook his head. He wanted more of a bang. More instant gratification. Blowing up bridges, blowing up train cars, blowing up engines—that was more his thing. And the railways were crucial the same way the canals were to move vital supplies.

While suggestions were being made, I ran my finger along a map, following the water, following the tracks.

My finger trailed over a large patch of land, one I identified as a depot.

"Right here," I said to the group—a rather intimidating group, I should add, of big burly men. I stood to my full height as their eyes fell on me. Then I circled a portion of the map. "This is where we should target."

They all crowded around.

"Father," I picture myself saying after this war's been won, "I suggested that we target a former French Army depot that the Germans had commandeered for themselves. Fifty acres of suspected ammunition, shells, bombs, and train equipment."

"A very dangerous task," he'll note.

"Yes," I'll say, letting out a quick breath. "But it achieved what we wanted: slowing down the Germans. Naturally, the depot was heavily guarded. But we had connections. The Germans used forced labor, and some of those men were brave enough to help us get past the guards, electrified fences, and dogs."

In the end, it was my suggestion that was chosen.

Sitting at the café, I smile to myself, while an uptick of nerves also overcomes me. We've each been given our own task for the evening, myself included. Once inside the depot, I'm to set explosives on three spare railway engines. I've practiced and I can do it within minutes. But adding in getting to the shed and getting back . . . "I think I can do it in twelve to fifteen minutes," I had told Gaspar.

"Ten would be better," he'd insisted.

I rub my lips together, people-watching and musing about my task. Ten minutes will be difficult. Mentally I begin running through the route to get to the shed, along with the steps of setting up the primers, the time pencils, and the plastic explosives. All things I practiced in training. But not all things I have pulled off successfully, noting that blasted 83 percent success rate.

A disgruntled baby distracts me. The child, no more than a few months old, has a set of lungs and the poor mother looks beside herself. They've entered the circle from a smaller street.

Every few steps the mother peers over her shoulder. Anxious-looking. In fact, she's walking so quickly I'm afraid her foot will catch on the cobblestone. She doesn't console her child. She doesn't slow. She just hastily walks—no, it seems like she's escaping—until I can see her no longer.

A chill runs down my spine. I tell myself it's because the day's getting long and the air is quickly requiring a scarf, one I do not have with me. I should be getting back to the safe house atop the bar anyway. The plan is for Gabriel and me to leave together from there, shortly after the sun sets around five.

I stand to go when a man appears, similarly distraught as the mother, and from the same street she came from. His skin is pale. He stumbles, catching himself by putting a hand on a man's shoulder. In his other hand he holds his identity papers. I don't know if he knows the man or the man simply has ears to listen to whatever it is that's just happened to him. I watch as he leans in, his lips moving so rapidly it's likely his words blend together.

I squint, as if this'll help my hearing too. It does not.

The distraught man is swiftly helped along, the good Samaritan supporting his weight.

Others are gawking just as I am.

More follow in the same direction, peering with mistrust down the narrow street from which he came.

I should walk away too. I should go to my safe house. But I'm not in France to walk away.

My heels clicking against the stones, I proceed cautiously down Saint-Polycarpe, where the man and the mother came from. Nothing appears amiss. It's a street too narrow for cars, lined with stone buildings that house a bookstore, another café, a restaurant.

But my ears perk at a rising noise. Voices. Crying. Shouting.

I quicken my pace, finally rounding a corner onto Sainte-Catherine. It's another narrow street, yet two lorries are parked front to back on the far end.

A handful of people—eight, I count—are being led from a building toward the lorry. No, they are being forced toward the vehicles, guns pointed at their backs. The men brutishly shoving them are not in uniform. I know they must be Germans, though. They're enjoying this too much not to be.

Nine more people are brought out.

I'm standing in no-man's-land, around the corner but not yet fully in the street. Then I see him, as pompous-looking as when I saw him on the day he marched into Lyon, and I inch backward, putting my body behind the stone corner. I've since learned his name, Klaus Barbie, sent to lead the Gestapo in Lyon.

And that is exactly what he's doing now. In German, Barbie barks directions and orders. He hollers about not letting any of "these Jews" out of their sights.

My breath catches and my eyes dart from one horrified innocent face to another. Another round of people is brought out of the building. I notice now the name on the signage.

"The Federation of Jewish Societies of France."

The name instantly registers in my mind.

And how the woman on the bus said the federation would be handing out free medicine and food this afternoon.

A woman in a neat skirt and blouse stands shivering by the entrance, her eyes red rimmed. A man in business clothing is by her side, his fists clenching and unclenching, his lip trembling with emotion.

It's as if they're being forced to watch. Forced to participate.

Have the Germans used the federation's charity as a trap? And now . . . they're rounding up the Jews who have come?

I swallow roughly and press my fingertips into the mortar gap between the stone blocks of the building where I hide.

Unbelievably, more people are still being brought out. People of all ages: thirties, forties, fifties. Seventies. Then I see a girl so young she cannot be more than thirteen or fourteen. She clings to a woman I assume to be her mother. The mother leans protectively over her, an umbrella to her daughter's body. They do not resist. When the daughter stumbles, her mother quickly takes hold of her arm, avoiding eye contact with the German officer who glares at them with such undeniable hatred.

Tears fall when I watch even more men and women brought out of the green-painted federation building, resigned to their fates, perhaps too afraid to act out. Resisters would be shot. Resisters would be made into cautionary tales. This isn't the first roundup of Jews that has happened in France, nor will it be the last. But earlier this year, something even more horrific took hold. Word spread of camps that are not meant for labor or detention. They were created to kill. They are *called* killing camps.

The presence of such a place—*places*—makes me sick. Yet I cannot move. I cannot do anything to help. Nor can I leave. What if I am the last person to set eyes on them before they are unloaded at one of these camps? Where they'll be forced to labor until they are nothing but disposable skin and bones. Or will they be killed upon arrival? It feels important that I look at each of their faces, hear each of their cries, be someone who will remember what has happened here, who will not forget them.

The total reaches fifty, sixty, seventy, eighty people.

How many more can there be?

My gaze jumps from those being shoved into the back of the dark lorries to those still leaving the building, and that's when I see him.

"No," I say on an exhale. "Not him."

Not any of them, but not him. I close my eyes. But when I open them, he's still there, walking obediently, his eyes downcast, his shoulders slumped in submission.

My bus driver.

I do not know his name. He does not know mine. It doesn't matter; this suddenly feels personal. I dig my fingernails into the building's mortar, helpless to do anything but witness his arrest.

The engines of the lorries roar to life, exhaust sputtering. The doors are slammed closed, the noise vibrating through my bones.

I've seen worse. I've heard stories of worse. I've feared worse happening to myself, even. And while nothing violent happened here today—no gunfire, no bloodshed, no one dying in front of my very eyes—it does not make the roundup of *eighty-six* innocent human beings any less painful to bear witness to.

* * *

AT EXACTLY FIFTEEN PAST THE HOUR, THE SUN IS GONE. I'M not sure I can wait a minute more.

"Breathe," Gabriel tells me.

I shake my head, my lips pressed firmly together. We're sitting side by side on the ridiculously small sofa in our safe house. Louis has rotated to a new safe house I've found us, ironically next door to the Hôtel Terminus, the Gestapo headquarters, where Klaus Barbie is likely congratulating himself on a job well done.

I, on the other hand, would like him to get pummeled by a moving bus.

Gabriel says, "You're angry."

I snort out a breath.

"Really angry," he corrects. "I am, too, and I didn't see what you saw."

"Can we go now?"

If blood could boil, mine would be bubbling over. And right now, the only way I can see to help balm the fury I currently feel is to blow up German shit.

Gabriel nods.

"Don't think I don't see how you're looking at me," I snap at him.

He holds up his palms and doesn't say a word.

"You think I'm coming unhinged."

He shakes his head. "No, I think you care. But in our line of work, that can be a very dangerous thing to do. Are you going to be okay out there tonight?"

I run a hand over the top of my head and down the length of hair I've clipped back. Then I press off my knees to stand. "I'll feel a lot better after I blow up the engines of future trains that could be transporting people like the ones I saw today to Nazi camps."

"Okay," Gabriel says. "Okay." He checks his watch. "It's time."

This is the moment my father's character in a film would crack his knuckles and say something overly confident about bringing down the enemy. But honestly, I don't want to think about my father right now. When the other women agents and I exchanged reasons for going to France, Denise had answered that she came for herself and for France.

Me, on the other hand, I had stumbled over a reply, eventually saying that I was here for France too. And it was true—still is. I still think it's embarrassing how nothing was done when the Germans took Paris. But what I left unsaid then was how I wanted to come to France for the purpose of making my father proud, so that I'd have a big shiny achievement to wave in his face.

After what I witnessed today—all those innocent human

beings whose deaths are probably only being delayed so the Germans can eke out every ounce of work and energy from them at a camp—I don't care anymore, not even a little, about impressing my father.

Being in France is bigger than him. It's bigger than me.

And tonight I'm going to set the fuse for the eighty-six people I saw rounded up today.

That begins with getting to the depot—and then back before the eleven o'clock curfew.

We board a bus. It had to be a bus. And my stomach turns over at the sight of a different driver. It's not as if *my* driver would've still been at the wheel this late in the day. He likely went to the federation after his last run to get medicine for that cough of his . . .

And now he'll never drive this route again.

I need to distract myself or else I know my emotions will eat me alive.

"Your girl," I say to Gabriel. "What's she like?"

Despite the mood, the environment, what lies ahead, Gabriel instantly smiles. It's not lost on me that I don't have a person who can instantaneously evoke that type of reaction. Makes me wonder if this is the wrong kind of diversion for my thoughts.

"Evie's a lot of things," Gabriel says. "Intelligent, funny, stubborn." He snorts at that last one. "Beautiful, selfless, fearless."

"Is that all?"

He laughs. "Took me a while to see it all, actually. We'd been friends for ages." He pauses, and I can see his mind working. He likely was raised with countless dinner parties with balanced conversations where one person asked a question and the other asked one in turn. Gabriel opens his mouth, and I shake my head.

"You don't have to ask me about my nonexistent love life," I say flatly and turn my attention to the buildings passing by outside the bus window. Instead, given how dark it is outside, all I see is the outline of my own reflection.

"Katherine, it doesn't have to be nonexistent. I feel like I've gotten to know you as best I can without actually knowing things like"—he lowers his voice so the few other bus-goers around us can't hear—"your actual name or who you were before all of this." He gives a half smile. "But I know you're someone who goes after what you want or you wouldn't be here. And that you don't let things like a little water stop you." My mouth opens and he quickly adds, "Yes, I saw you on that river and I cringed when I heard you came here in one of those little seadogs."

"Please don't remind me."

He laughs. "You're clearly funny. You're beautiful, spoken completely platonically."

I'm the one who laughs now.

Gabriel bumps my shoulder. "And I know you care a lot. And I know you can care a lot for someone one day if you give a man a chance to care for you. Unless he's a lying, cheating, married scumbag like that one guy you told me about. Don't judge all men from that one experience."

"I knew it was a mistake to open up to you. Now you're using it against me," I say, but in a tone where Gabriel knows I'm thankful for the pep talk and the not-half-bad distraction because . . . we're here.

In no time we're off the bus and have located Gaspar by the red tip of his cigarette.

"In, in," he demands, referring to a horse and cart waiting to take us the remainder of the way. "Under you go," Gaspar instructs.

Straw, he means.

It's damp and surprisingly heavy once I'm beneath it, joining a few resistants who are already in hiding. Warm, too, not entirely unwelcome. The trip to the depot is longer than ideal, but it'll be worth it, I remind myself.

Gabriel gives orders once we arrive, his words coming out as puffs in the dark, cold night. "One hour. In and out."

Gaspar's gruff voice contradicts. "Thirty minutes. No more. They say eleven for curfew, but they patrol well before that. Any reason to show us how big and bad they are."

The power struggle between Gabriel and Gaspar is palpable. Gabriel is our network leader, but technically Gaspar is part of no network. He's Maquis, with his own local guerrilla band to lead. We help them. They help us. Or at least we hope they do. That's as much of an agreement and of a structure that we have.

Gabriel's jaw is clenched, but he concedes, "Half hour. We each have our tasks. Any last questions for Théo about the lay of the land, ask them now."

I shake my head. The shed I'm targeting is actually the closest point of the depot, and Théo, our connection who works there, already went over with me the route I'll take.

I'm ready.

"No questions?" Gabriel remarks. "Good. Thirty minutes. Théo will set off his explosive three minutes till. Everyone else, delay your detonations to an hour. We'll rendezvous at the southwest entrance, where we'll cross our fingers and toes that we'll be able to sneak back out during the mayhem."

I nod, running my hands down my pant legs. From his lips to God's ears. But before we go, there's one last step I've been dreading: wolf urine.

I have to practically bathe in it. We all do. I only hope it doesn't expose us, as wolves have been eradicated from France in recent decades. The scent, if recognized, may be our undoing. But if it works, it could very well keep the guard dogs from mauling us to death, as the predator smell *should* make us seem big and scary.

One of Gaspar's men looks all too pleased to brandish the open bottle, the urine flying at me in unexpected splashes. I cover my face, doing my best not to gag at the overwhelming potent and sulfur-like odor, like the most rotten eggs mixed with spoiled cabbage.

Théo jokes how his wife won't touch him for a week.

Which, of course, results in crude comments about how others wouldn't have that problem.

Unsurprisingly, the urine tosser is none too pleased when it's his turn. "Not my face," he complains, leaping away from a slosh of the urine.

I can't breathe through my nose, only my mouth. Still, my eyes water and I very much want to hurt Gaspar for insisting on this portion of the plan.

Though he also suggested the next: testing the electric fence. And I watch, with perhaps a bit too much glee, as he grounds out his cigarette, then taps a stick against the fence. His body convulses for a blink of an eye. After a full body shake, to the amusement of his men, he says, "Electricity is on. I won't be able to pee straight for the rest of the night. We'll have to go up and over."

We already had this contingent plan worked out if we weren't able to use wire cutters on the fence. It's why we chose this heavily wooded section of the fifty acres.

Théo shinnies up a tree and shoots a grappling hook with an attached rope into a tree on the other side of the fence. He secures it on our side as well. "My kids are going to get a kick out of this story when they're older." He shakes his head in amusement, then, with a grip on either side of a metal tube, he zooms straight over the fence.

My turn.

I won't lie, I'd rather stay here on the ground.

But I'm also sure the eighty-six people who were rounded up today would prefer to be having dinner with their families or readying for bed.

I raise my right leg and put it on a low branch. With a grunt, I pull up my body, reaching for another branch. I make as quick of work of it as I can, knowing there are seven more men on my tail.

Dogs bark. Because that's what dogs do? Or because they

know we're here? Or better yet, they think a predator is nearby and they're warning one another to stay away? It matters little. In any case, I need to move—and quickly. I pull my own metal rod from a back sack, give myself a pep talk to keep my weight balanced, and kick off.

I'm in the air, my knees tucked toward my chest, for no more than a long-held breath. I let go of the tube a second before I reach the tree, like something out of *Tarzan the Ape Man*.

Théo's already gone.

I quickly drop to my knees and paw through the leaves for the metal tube. My hand hits it. I twist my bag from my back to my lap and pull out the barrel. I push it into the tube. I tighten the barrel nut. Then I slide the stock into place.

In seconds, my Sten gun is ready and I'm on my feet.

I set off toward the storage shed just as I hear a thump of another body landing on this side of the fence.

We're in.

Getting out will be harder, but we're banking on the commotion of our explosions to pull the guards away from the entrances and create an environment of chaos.

"Environment of chaos" being Gabriel's description of our ideal escape scenario.

I run as quickly and as quietly as I can. My chest burns from the need to cough and expel the rancid scent from my nose. At every little sound, I stop, silence my breathing, and raise my Sten gun. Each time I count to ten, then lower my gun and take off again. I find the shed that houses the spare train engines easily enough. It's tucked alongside train tracks, taking me only a few precious minutes to get here.

My breath puffs out in front of my face as I slip inside. It shouldn't be guarded, but I slowly, soundlessly close the door behind me.

It's dark. The chances of someone lying in wait in here seem slim. And if they are, they can certainly smell me. Still, I don't risk using a torch.

The intensity of the dogs' barking has increased. I curse under my breath, not knowing how exactly the dogs are reacting to us, then I lick my lips and edge into the room, keeping an arm outstretched. My hand hits the cold metal of an engine.

Bull's-eye.

I twist my bag into my lap again. In Ireland, we practiced during dewy mornings, at high noon, blindfolded, in the middle of the night—assembling guns, moving through the wilderness unseen, setting explosives.

Today I have three engines and three explosives to detonate.

Gaspar said to spend no more than ten minutes total, and the clock's ticking.

With the shed already dark, it seems like a silly thing to do, but I close my eyes and let my hands get to work. The primers need to be set up. The detonator is in a similar shape and size to a pencil, hence the name of a time pencil.

I connect the brass tube of the time pencil to a short length of safety fuse. My fingers grow stiff from the cold air. Sweat shouldn't be gathering on my brow, but there it is. I use my sleeve to wipe it away.

I slide up my sleeve to see my glowing wristwatch—thank you, science—and my nerves spike when I see that I should be further along.

I'm okay, I tell myself, and I refocus on the copper section at the one end. It contains a glass vial of liquid cupric chloride. Beneath the vial is a spring-loaded striker, held under tension and in place by a thin metal wire.

All I must do now is crush the copper section.

Only this is the step that is responsible for my less than acceptable success rate. There's a delicate balance to this stomp. Too hard and I'll crush the tube completely. Too light and it won't do a dang thing. The goal is to dent it, enough to break the glass vial and release the liquid.

I round my lips and let out a low, slow exhale. Then I replace my fingertips with the heel of my boot, stand, and bring my foot down, hoping the tube hasn't rolled and that I haven't missed my mark.

I visualize the cupric chloride beginning to slowly erode the wire holding back the striker. The end result: the striker propelling down the hollow middle of the detonator and hitting the percussion primer at the other end.

Is this what is happening?

All I hear is my own breath. The bombs don't make any noise. No fizz, no beeping, no countdown, like in a Hollywood spy film. It's all happening inside the bomb, silently.

Or at least it better be. If it is, in one hour's time, give or take a minute, it'll blow. I repeat the process again, and again, setting the three explosives, becoming increasingly tense that I didn't stomp with exactly the correct amount of force. And I won't know until this hour elapses. All I can do is get out of here. I brush my hands together and head toward the shed's door. I pause, listening for any sound outside. The dogs are barking—haven't stopped—but they don't sound any closer.

I check my watch again. I'll be over ten minutes, but I tell myself it's okay. I'll be at the southwest entrance in plenty of time.

I'm no more than two steps out the door when rain starts to fall, big drops that thunk against the fallen leaves. I wipe my eyes clear, my vision adjusting to the darkness outside better than in the shed. Still, trees look like guards. Bushes look like dogs. A fleeing squirrel or some other small creature nearly gives me a heart attack.

Slowly I make my way toward the rendezvous point. Théo said there'd be a row of pines near the guard tower. I mentally cast the map and directions in my head. I'm almost there. I press on, my nerves quickening my pace.

Every snap of a twig gives me pause. I hear a cough. One of ours? A guard? I can't tell what direction it originates from. The rain comes harder. My face should be free of urine now, but I rabidly wipe my face, afraid it'll run into my eyes.

I just about let out a hurrah when I see the outline of the pines ahead. At first, with the rain thudding down, I can't place a sudden sound. I listen, and it becomes devastatingly clear. Footsteps. From my right. From behind. And I know I'm only seconds away from being found.

CHAPTER 15

Violet

—

Ardleigh Red Cross Hospital, Essex
September 28, 1915

WAITING CAN BE EXCRUCIATING. IT'S SOMETHING I KNOW firsthand. As a school-age child in Argentina, my doctor advised my parents not to send me to school due to my lung ailments.

I begged and pleaded to go.

Finally, my parents agreed to less-taxing lessons with an English tutor. I relished her every word, every fact, every morsel of information.

When William and Philip began school, I still could not go, which was embarrassingly cruel for my younger brothers to attend school before me.

Eventually, when my doctor finally saw I had no plans for dying, he gave my parents the okay for me to attend classes.

My schooling began in earnest at the Escuela Normal. I couldn't have been more elated. I also couldn't be stopped. Each night, after my family was asleep, I crept to the kitchen to study, exhausting myself. Magically, I'd awaken in my bed each morning, my father likely moving me after waking early for work.

After we relocated to England, I continued my studies at the convent under the tutelage and watchful eyes of Breton nuns.

I could've easily qualified for an academic career or a vocation in medicine, specifically as a nurse. It's what the nuns said, what all my teachers said before them. But I never had the opportunity to sit for my examinations that would've completed my coursework. We know why—no need to rehash.

What's important is that it feels absolutely glorious to be learning again and to be working toward that exhilarating notion that I could be in the position to help make another human whole again. I showed up to my first day at the British Royal Red Cross Society's training facilities in London with a pencil behind each ear and another spare in my purse.

Turned out there wasn't much writing to be had. It was a more hands-on course with ten practical lectures and ten how-to instructions. First aid. Bed making. Performing a blanket bath. Feeding a patient. Keeping a ward clean.

It's uncanny how my work at sea translated so readily to my junior nurse training. With some of my more-demanding passengers, I all but washed and spoon-fed them.

However, there were skills to relearn, which brought me back to my childhood days learning from the doctor.

"If the skin is broken, cover the wound with gauze and collodion before dressing."

I smiled at the memory, at his praise after returning from that frostbitten man—who actually kept his leg, by the by—to tell me I'd done an exemplary job.

That's my intent now: exemplariness.

By the time my nurse schooling was complete, which took only a matter of weeks, I excitedly turned in all my powders, scents, earrings, and other jewelry for a handkerchief-style cap, a brassard, a gray dress, and a white apron with the bright red symbol of the Red Cross.

It's a uniform I am entrusted to keep clean at all times. This is often difficult. In fact, it's a challenge in this very moment as I sit at an injured soldier's bedside.

The man is squirting blood, an actual arc of fluids leaving his body. And he somehow has the wherewithal to look embarrassed by it. He also somehow has the ability to still be quite attractive, despite his washed-out skin and overall disheveled nature, no surprise after the ordeal of being shot.

I keep pressure on the wound with one hand and note his thankfully steady pulse with the other, and I peer over my shoulder for Dr. Lowndes. While I find myself a darn good junior nurse, the soldier tore open his fresh stitches and needs more than gauze, collodion, and a dressing.

Instead of the doctor, another nurse approaches. "Post for you, Miss Jessop."

Oblivious to the man's life in my hand, she mindlessly puts the envelope atop a small locker just out of my reach—not that I have a means to grab for it. Still keeping pressure on my patient's upper arm, I lean to see the return address.

Ealing.

Though it's not in the handwriting of my brothers or sister. Mother either.

"You'll be just fine," I say to the man absentmindedly, my practiced bedside manner kicking in.

He moans.

The mail is likely from my mother's nurse, but that realization shoots my own pulse higher.

"Just fine," I echo.

At that, Dr. Lowndes joins me at the man's bedside, assessing the injury site, questioning me, only semi-successfully questioning him, ultimately getting the soldier swiftly and artfully stitched back up.

A job well done.

With my hands bloodied, I can't yet handle the letter. Nor do I want to use my apron. I twist my lips just as the matron enters the ward, clapping, shouting, "We have men incoming! Both floors. Prepare to work late this evening, ladies."

I bite my lip. My shift was set to end within the hour.

Mrs. Ball goes on, "Do what you can to make them comfortable. You know what to do, girls." She claps again, just as footsteps begin to roar and men on stretchers are brought in.

Our hospital has only ten beds on this floor and eight on the one above us. At last count, we had eleven free, after losing a man this morning. Within heartbeats, all the beds are spoken for and I'm rushing to a new bedside. There's a fresh basin of water; I plunge in my hands to clean them. Then pour alcohol over my skin.

The poor lad is covered in filth. I do my best to clean him up for Dr. Lowndes.

After that, I'm instructed to go upstairs. The building—once upon a time a stable, before becoming the vicar's social hall—only has an external staircase. Out into the cool night I go. The perspiration that had gathered on my skin sends goose bumps up my arms.

Warmth is quick to return as I hastily go about my duties. Between moans and groans, I'm able to gather that the men were injured in Loos, France. There, a battle began a few days ago, these men falling early, stabilized quickly, and expeditiously brought across the English Channel to us and various other hospitals.

A high-pitched voice rises behind me. I know instantly it's Clara. She's being told no, something she explicitly does not like. It's happened before, when Clara wanted to perform a gruesome and rather advanced surgical dressing alone. Afterward, she sulked and I tried to console her—the very last time I'll ever attempt that.

I turn off my ears to her and focus on the man in front of me lying face down. I'm doing my very best not to gag. *Dios mios.* By the looks of his dressings, a portion of his back has been blown off. The rest of him twitches, no doubt in extreme bouts of pain.

"Shh," I tell him in my calmest of voices. I say a prayer over him, encourage him to drink from a straw, administer an appropriate dosage of drugs, and make him as comfortable as possible.

I regret leaving him, but I still have more beds to see to. I turn, bumping into another nurse, both of us chuckling at the ward's chaos. Sidestepping, I approach the new bed. "Welcome, welcome," I say in a singsong voice. It's how we've been taught to greet them.

Make them feel at home.

Talk to them as if they're friends.

This one is sleeping—or unconscious—but I continue as if he's awake. "It's my pleasure to meet you." I bend toward him, to gently wipe dark hair from his eyes, when I go still. Mere inches from the lad's face, my hand begins to tremble.

Henry.

My well-informed *amigo*. The last I saw him was when we disembarked from *Olympic*, Henry fired up about joining up.

And now he lies before me. I take in his smaller frame, only a few short years out of puberty. There's a dressing on his arm, but otherwise he looks unscathed, save for a stray cut and bruise.

"I'm going to take care of you," I whisper into his ear. Whatever that entails. "Miss Violet is here."

"So is Dr. Lowndes," I hear.

I chuckle. I like him.

"Why's he here?" I ask the doctor. "Was he part of Loos too?"

"His injury predates the battle, I'd say. He has a badly suppurating arm. It's probably been a bother for quite some time."

I search my memory for the term, unsure if it was something we covered during our lectures.

"He has lumps, large ones, along his lymph nodes. They'll need to be drained and dressed every two hours. Day and night. This one is sure to keep you and the other nurses busy, Miss Violet."

"It's no bother. I know him," I say, my voice catching. "He'll be fine afterward?"

"Should be. Just very painful until then. The drugs he's on appear to be doing the trick. Want first stabs at draining him?"

I shake my head at Dr. Lowndes's sense of humor. It can be hard to take him seriously. The spectacles he wears magnify his eyes, making him resemble an insect. I put it out of mind, and more seriously I say, "Show me how."

It's not an enjoyable process, for anyone involved.

Henry's eyes flutter open and he calls out in pain. I see the confusion when recognition strikes him.

"*Sí*, Henry, it's me," I say. "I'm caring for you now."

He calms, and I'm filled with such a sense of love, of duty, and relief that I'm here for him.

When it's done, he sleeps. I want nothing more than the same for myself. Besides coffee. Coffee would be heavenly.

I tiptoe from the now quiet room outside to return to the first floor. I pour myself a hot coffee, silently thanking the kind soul from the night shift who recently brewed a pot.

The first floor is livelier, but the noise level is noticeably lesser than during the day, as if whispering is the unspoken preferred means of speaking at night. I check on a few patients until, from across the room, the matron gives me the universal shoo sign.

I motion back, grateful to go. I'm two steps toward the door when I remember my post. I'd left it earlier on a patient's locker. A nervousness that I'm glad hasn't lingered with me all evening promptly settles on me.

I lick my lips, my sight set on the small white envelope.

"Hello."

I all but jump out of my uniform. My hand goes over my heart.

"Sorry," he whispers. It's my patient with the squirting artery, who fortunately looks like he's been recovering just fine. He says, "I wanted to thank you for giving me a hand before." There's cheekiness in his voice. And I know for certain his word choice was intentional when he adds, "Literally."

I smile warmly, but there's no way to hide the exhaustion from my voice as I whisper, "Just doing my job."

"One you do with both calm and grace, I've gathered from my horizontal position."

"Where you'll remain," I chastise. "We can't have you pulling your stitches a second time."

"If I do, will I see more of your beauty?"

He hasn't lost the humor in his voice. But now, the way he looks at me also feels intimate. I turn my head, an attempt to hide the red I know is blooming on my cheeks. The men flirt with the nurses . . . often. I've used this line before, but I say it again: "It appears you've bumped your noggin too."

He shakes his head. "You intrigue me. Impress me."

I find myself setting my gaze back on him and shaking my head, too, but for an entirely different reason. "Time for me to go."

"Must you? I think something hurts."

"You're trouble," I point out. And my earlier observation wasn't wrong; he's quite handsome, even more so with the color returning to his cheeks. High cheekbones, at that. A strong-looking chin. Green eyes that defy the darkness of the room. I'm sure he'll make a woman very happy after this war.

"I'm actually Leo. And you're Violet. I may've asked."

"Is that so?" I respond, not actually looking for him to answer as I take my mail and retreat a step. Friendly banter is fine. Harmless flirting can be momentarily entertaining. But that's as far as I ever let it go, prepared to nip this in the bud as I'm thoroughly uninterested in attaching my heart to anyone.

It's been relatively easy thus far in my career. At sea, passengers reach their destination, most never to be seen again. My crewmates will eventually switch lines or tire of a life at sea, displacing them from my daily life.

It's for the best. Any romantic entanglement could never be more important than the six people back home. The letter in my hand all but sings to be read. I tap it nervously against my palm and give Leo a parting dip of my head. Then I rush toward my room in the vicarage. There are seventeen rooms there, for the nurses, a cook, housemaids, the clergymen, the matron, and the commandant. I regrettably share a room with Clara. She's sound asleep upon my return, a blessing.

I do not open my letter until I've readied for bed, climbed into my bunk, and my blankets are tucked neatly beneath my arms. The night's nearly full moon provides just enough light to read.

I'm right. I verify presently that the letter is from Mother's nurse. I let out a sigh of relief when I see the first line has nothing to do with my mother's health. But my grip tightens and tightens as I read and as she informs me my brothers—all four of them— have been called to the trenches.

> *I wanted you to be made aware.*
> *Pray for them.*
> *So great of you to volunteer as you do.*

I close my eyes.

I'm not naive; I knew my brothers would serve—*are* serving. However, I didn't allow myself to think about them being called to the front line. To the trenches. To where enemy fire rips through arms, bodies, and legs. Where injuries happen that put men like Leo on my hospital beds.

At sea, I love, worry over, and care for my brothers from afar. But this war has squashed that separation and has put them in a position where they could very well be at my doorstep at the pull of a trigger. Earlier, I would have given anything to lie down on the floor and sleep. But now that I should be sleeping, I lie wide-eyed.

CHAPTER 16

Daphne

CODE NAME KATHERINE
Alias Madame Irene du Tertre

Lyon, France
November 16, 1942

FEAR GRIPS ME. I WIPE RAIN FROM MY EYES IN AN ATTEMPT to keep my vision clear. How to save myself rushes through my head. I can run. I can hide, though my wolf-urine smell could give me away. I can fight. Better yet, I can shoot. Prepared to do what's necessary, I raise my Sten gun and aim where I heard the first sounds of footsteps.

But there are two sets of them.

And only one of me.

I don't like the odds.

The footsteps grow louder, outlines appearing. If I can see them, they can see me. Or at least the human shape of me.

"Who's there?" I say in German as gruff as I can make my voice. Perhaps they'll mistake me for another guard.

One of the approaching men stops advancing, but the other one keeps coming. "Harry Baur," he says in a muted voice.

I let my arms fall in relief. Harry Baur is a famous French

actor, his name a code word to use if needed that aligns with the theme of our network of FAME. "Gabriel?" I whisper.

"And Gaspar's with me," he says back.

"You two scared me half to death."

"But you'll live," Gaspar says.

For now.

We still have to get out of this depot. We hurry toward the pines, finding five of Gaspar's men already there.

His French comes out rushed, asking them if they've set their bombs. They have, targeting various buildings that house ammunition. Gaspar put explosives on the tracks. Gabriel laid them inside another storage shed. Only Théo is still missing, but that's how it's supposed to be. He's to set the explosion that creates the diversion for all of us to escape. Then, while we're getting as far from this depot as we can, the rest of our bombs *should* detonate, allowing for Théo's escape.

A brilliant plan.

I take in a big breath through my mouth, wanting to spit; our aroma is heightened with all of us together. One of Gaspar's men remarks, "We all smell like—"

Gaspar silences him with an elbow. His attention is intent on the guard station on the other side of the pines.

In total, there appear to be six guards and a very unsettled dog that's pacing and howling every few steps. He's on a lead held by one of the guards; otherwise I'm not sure what the dog would do. The German shepherd's behavior has caught the attention of the guards, though.

The thing is, they're searching out, not in, and it gives me a jolt of pure satisfaction to see the buffoons peering the wrong way.

It also helps that we have them outnumbered. We have our guns. But reinforcements are bound to be nearby. Other dogs too.

I quickly grow impatient, even while knowing the blast should be coming any moment now. Théo was supposed to set off his explosion at three minutes till. A half hour has come and gone.

"Something's wrong," I mouth in English to Gabriel.

The way he regrips his gun is all the answer I need. He's worried as well.

Then, suddenly, there's an explosion.

Théo's done it.

The shepherd dog becomes frenzied, jumping on his lead, barking, snarling. The handler lets it go and the dog tears up the ground toward the blast site.

Shouts are exchanged between the remaining guards. Four immediately set off running toward the explosion. Two stay behind.

Gaspar gestures for us to go. At a crouch we begin winding around and through the pines. With the shepherd dog gone, I tell myself we have a chance. The remaining guards are distracted, more concerned with what's going on inside the depot now.

Once I'm beyond the pine trees, I look in the direction of Théo's explosion. The orange and red glow of the fire licks at the surrounding trees. The smoke blackens the already-dark sky.

If shots need to be fired, Gaspar demanded to be the one to take them. This is personal for him, with so many of his friends being forced to labor at the depot. He keeps his gun trained on the one guard, then the other, and back again as we creep toward the gated entry. It's two chain-link gates, latched together. With the entrance guarded, there doesn't appear to be a lock of any type, just as Théo said.

"They let us in and out each day, just a quick flip of the latch to open the doors. Once we're in, they do roll call. If we aren't there, they go after our families. Only reason I go each day."

He'd said it with such anger. I can only imagine the justice he's feeling at this very moment after setting off his bombs.

As we creep, it feels as though ages have passed, but no more than ten or fifteen seconds actually have. The guards are both turned toward the flames.

I smile to myself as Gabriel lifts the latch, waggling his brows as he does so. Because this feels easy. Too easy. But I will enjoy the feeling for as long as it lasts.

One by one, we each slip out of the depot and run under the cover of night toward where we left Gaspar's wagon.

I don't stop running until my two hands hit the bed. A laugh bubbles up in me. I could float. Better yet, I could fly.

We've done it, and I want this feeling to live on in me forever.

Gaspar's men pat each other on the back. Gabriel and Gaspar shake hands. I smile at them all like a goon.

In another few moments, the remainder of our bombs should be going off. Not only will they decimate their supplies, but they'll also create that diversion for Théo to make his exit.

If I stomped correctly . . .

All that's left to do now is wait, continue to relish in our successful escape, while hoping the Germans don't wise up to us out here and set a dog on our scents.

The next bomb goes off and one of Gaspar's men lets out a silent cheer, raising a fist into the air. I tap a hand over my heart, feeling the rush there, hopeful that bomb was mine. Or it could be the next. Another of Gaspar's men begins a countdown with his fingers, getting to zero, letting his head droop in mock shame, then raising his hands to count again. He has two fingers left to go when another blast fills the night.

Then another. Then so many at once it's like the finale of a fireworks show. I cover my ears, still grinning, imagining the engines and ammo and buildings being destroyed. My success rate just went up.

Once it's done, nerves promptly set in again. Théo should be arriving any minute. And now that minute passes, and another. Gaspar rotates a finger in the air, a sign for us all to get in the wagon.

I'm reluctant, but reason with myself that we'll be ready to hightail it out of here once Théo emerges through the trees. The last glimpse I have of Gaspar before concealing myself under the straw is him throwing down his hat. Angrily, he picks it up from the ground and slams it back onto his head.

My heart continues to pound, waiting to feel the start of the wagon. Our scent is overwhelming beneath the straw and my eyes tear. Someone lets out a muffled cough. But I hear nothing else.

The ride is long, bumpy, and wet, the rain seeping through the heavy straw.

I couldn't be happier to arrive at Gaspar's farm. But as I begin counting bodies in the moonlight, my heart sinks.

Théo is not among us.

★ ★ ★

A BOTTLE IS PROMPTLY PROCURED AND PASSED AROUND. WE celebrate tonight's success. We mourn Théo and whatever has become of him.

We don't know.

He could've been caught. Or he could've escaped, and for this reason or that reason he didn't rendezvous with us as planned.

All I know is he's not here, and that guts me. I've known the man for a matter of hours, but I can paint a picture of him in my head. A family man who's been forced to help the Germans or else his wife and children pay the consequence. But who was willing to risk it all and help us.

And . . . a cold bucket of water could've been thrown in my face with that realization. We're sitting in Gaspar's barn in a circle, the windows boarded up and a fire roaring. Meanwhile, the Germans could be retaliating against Théo's loved ones for what we accomplished tonight. My skin prickles with unease as I ask, "Théo's wife? His family? Are they safe?"

My answer comes from the men in the form of another deep swallow of the bottle, an aversion of eyes, a distraught expression, and I know they're in danger.

I insist, "We must help them. Hide them."

Gaspar expels a deep breath. "It's nearly curfew. It's a death sentence. Camille has her wits about her. If Théo doesn't return, she'll go somewhere safe."

I'm not willing to accept this answer. The fact he knows her first name means he shouldn't accept it either. But part of me gets this heartless response; hard decisions need to be made. Gaspar is head of the resistance group. If he gets caught, it'll go under.

But I am not Gaspar. The location of tonight's sabotage was my idea, my doing. And now I can help. I will help. I stand. "Where do they live?"

Lines form on Gabriel's forehead. "No, Katherine, you're not going anywhere tonight."

I ignore him, locking my gaze on Gaspar. "Where do they live?"

It's not Gaspar who responds but one of his men. He says an address in Lyon. When Gaspar shoots him an angry look, he shrugs and says, "What? The guy has young kids. If Katherine wants to help them, I'm not going to stop her. You know if something happens to them, Théo will haunt us from the grave."

"Thank you," I say.

Gabriel stands too. "Then I'll go with you."

I shake my head. "I'll take a bike. Women ride bikes all over. We blend right in. You'll only bring more notice to us."

"But your bike's back at the safe house," Gabriel points out.

Gaspar's gruff voice cuts in. "I have one she can use."

So the man does have a heart. That or I'm dispensable to him. Either way, I'm doing this. I can't stand by and do nothing while the Germans round up more innocent people, especially children. As a child, I was saved. It's why I'm here today.

* * *

THÉO AND CAMILLE'S APARTMENT IS PART OF A LARGER building.

I'm nearly breathless by the time I arrive across the street, my throat and fingers numb from the cold. The rain continued just long enough to soak me through, leaving me shivering now.

I remain in the shadows, making sure I'm not the only one here interested in this family.

I'd like the luxury of being completely sure, but time is not on my side. There's less than an hour to curfew. I'd be doing more harm than good if I pull them from their home and they're caught breaking the rules.

Now's not the time to worry about ifs. I leave the bike propped against the wall and hurry across the narrow street, eyeing the third floor as I go.

At the entryway, I pull a handle on a panel, a buzz I can't hear signaling in the apartment upstairs. I quickly backstep, allowing myself to be seen from the third-floor window. When no one appears, I pull the handle again. Twice, for good measure.

This time someone comes to the window. The woman has curly hair, just like I was told Camille would have. I motion for her to come to the door. She doesn't move. I motion again. When she disappears, I'm relieved. Eagerly, I wait by the door.

But she doesn't come.

Anxiety crashes into me. Curfew is yet another minute closer.

I pull the handle a fourth time, then make myself visible once more from their window. She appears again, annoyance but also fear clear on her face.

And I decide I must lie. "Théo sent me," I call out.

Surely if the Germans are here watching, monitoring, that would've done me in. I'm still as a statue, waiting for Camille to react. Waiting for the Germans to seize me.

Fortunately, it is Camille who nods, tucking a curl behind her ear. She disappears from the window. This time she opens the entryway door a crack.

"What is it? Who are you? Where's Théo?"

Her barrage of questions isn't unexpected. On the ride here, I prepared a response. "I am not sure where he is—"

"But you said he sent you?"

I bobble a nod, not denying, not confirming. Instead I say, "I want to make sure you and your children are safe. You cannot stay here. Not tonight, at least."

Camille's expression is stoic. I have the mind to repeat myself. But then . . .

"The children are sleeping. Step inside. I'll go get them."

Each second feels like an eternity, but she returns no more than three minutes later with a bag slung over her shoulder, a child in her arms, and one sleepily holding her hand. The little boy by her side hugs a stuffed bear and is bundled under at least three layers of clothing.

His nose scrunches. "You smell."

I changed into new clothing at the farm, but I have a feeling I'll smell until I've had a thorough washing. What's there to do but shrug?

The little boy chuckles, and the infant in Camille's arms wriggles. She can't be more than a few weeks old, just as bundled as her brother.

The sight of the baby, nestled in the safety of loving arms, triggers a longing in me. A gratefulness. It always does. "I'll make sure you're safe," I say. "This way."

My safe house isn't far, a good thing as we have to walk, me pushing my bike. But I get a prickling sensation as we draw near. I can't place the feeling, other than an extreme sense of unease, until . . . I place the men.

They're at the far corner of the street. Not in uniform, but neither were the ones involved in the roundup at the federation. Their concentration is on the bar. No, on the windows above it, on the windows of my safe house.

I push Camille backward and nearly lose the grip on my bike as I awkwardly one-arm pick up the little boy to hurry the process along. Once back around the corner, he slips free, laughing. "Shh," his mother chastises.

Every part of me wants to toss the bike against the wall, putting my full anger and frustration on display. Somehow I manage to place it carefully.

"What is it?" Camille demands. I can tell she's trying to keep her voice as normal as possible. There's no hiding the concern in her eyes, though. "I need to know what is going on. My actions affect more than me. So did his, now here we are."

I don't know what to say other than, "I'm sorry."

"Don't be," she whispers. "I understand why. I didn't try to stop him either. It's important to him, which makes it important to me. No questions asked. Please tell me, though, is he *S-A-F-E*?"

"I'd like to say yes, but I do not know."

I see some of the fight and strength drain from her face. Her son clings to her leg. Her baby sleeps soundly, unaware of the situation they are in. I realize . . . that I'm putting them in. The Germans weren't outside her apartment, but they are outside of mine. It makes me think they didn't know Théo was involved. Or maybe they've tortured him and he's revealed who his accomplices are. There's also the possibility this has nothing to do with Théo at all. Have I been sloppy? Has Gabriel? Louis? My bus driver knew I'd wanted to evade the Germans. Had he suspected me of helping the Resistance? Did the man down the hall, who noticed the odd hours I keep, suspect as well? Perhaps he said something to the wrong person. There's no way to tell for sure.

I turn away, pressing my cold fingertips to my temples. Then I dig my compact from Colonel Buckmaster out of my bag, positioning just right so the mirror shows what's around the corner. I need to see if the men are still there. They are.

The Old Town clock begins to strike eleven.

I curse under my breath.

We need to hide. But where? Should we go back to Théo's apartment? Every ounce of me wants to scream. The situation seems impossible. My hatred for the Germans is so strong that I have the urge to spit. No, I have the urge to do a lot more. I loathe the day they marched into Paris, the day they marched into Lyon.

And then I think . . . the traboule, the secret passageway, the one I slipped into that day Klaus Barbie paraded by. The woman who had piles and piles of food and clothing, which I'm telling myself she'd been gathering to help refugees or the Resistance.

"Let's go. We can't be seen," I say.

Camille doesn't ask where. She only pushes her son forward to follow me.

I hope I'm not leading them astray again.

The streets are eerily quiet. We see no one. No Lyonnais. No one risks being out after curfew. Except us. Though, we're having an unbelievable stroke of good luck. I see no Germans, either.

Still we move more swiftly, Camille's son struggling to keep up. I sweep him into my arms again. At the wall where I entered through the traboule before, I hastily run my free hand down the ivy, finding the knob. I usher Camille into the courtyard, unable to stop myself from looking over my shoulder before also slipping inside. We could stay here, the courtyard feeling exponentially less dangerous than the streets or the safe house. But it's cold. We'd freeze. Already, the little boy's nose and cheeks are red.

And the woman who helped me before still has a light on.

It's well worth the risk. I knock.

There's shuffling around inside, but no answer. I pull my bottom lip between my teeth and eye Camille. She's bouncing her baby in her arms, singing a soft melody, the words coming out as visible puffs.

I knock again.

This time the door opens.

"I'm sorry to bother you so late," I begin.

The woman's forehead creases. Recognition dawns on her face. "You again," she says, not unkindly.

I let out a soft laugh. I'm now glad I was brazen about my disgust toward the Germans.

The woman eyes Camille and her children.

"Just for one night," I plead.

The woman steps aside.

* * *

MADAME LEROY IS A PURE DELIGHT. NOT ONLY WERE MY instincts correct that she's dispersing food and clothing when she can, but she offers for Camille and her children to stay as long as they need.

Me, on the other hand, I'm eager to return to the farm.

"After you wash that stink from yourself," Madame Leroy insists.

Who am I to fight her on that?

Once clean and once curfew has lifted, I wait for Madame Leroy to give me an all-clear from her second-floor window. Before she can, Camille clutches my arm. "If he was captured . . ." She needs to compose herself, pressing a hand over her chest. The love she feels for her husband all but radiates from her, to the point it's palpable. She tries again, saying, "If he was captured, he wouldn't have spoken a word about you or anyone else being involved. That's who Théo is. I know it in my heart."

I don't know what to say. Nor do I know what to believe. Of the two of us, Camille knows Théo a thousand times better than I do. I'm saved from a response when Madame Leroy's signal comes, and I covertly melt into the foot traffic on the street.

My bike is where I left it across the street from the safe house above the bar, which is no longer safe, and which no longer looks to be under surveillance. Did they watch all night? Did they go inside? They would've found nothing, including Louis. He's at the safe house by the Hôtel Terminus.

Rather, he's at Gaspar's farm. I'm relieved and surprised to see him as I enter the attic of one of the outbuildings.

"Time for you to move?" I ask him.

He nods, his focus on his handkerchief with a substitution

grid printed on it. With it, he has a one-time pad that has random keys in groups of five letters. Together, he uses them to code his messages.

I sit quietly beside him for the first minute, but when he pauses, scratching at his beard, I fill him in on how the bar safe house has been compromised.

He grumbles a response just as Gabriel comes in. "You're back," he says to me and tousles my hair like I'm Camille's son.

I swat him away. Better yet, I take the coffee he's holding.

He frowns but only says, "You did what you needed to do?"

"They're safe," I say simply.

"Good. So I overheard walking up that we lost the bar safe house. Think you can find us a new one today?"

I sip the coffee, eager for the magical beans to do their work. I'm exhausted, yet, I realize, already feeling wired. "Mm-hmm. I'll check with one of Gaspar's railwaymen. I heard through the grapevine one of them may have a ground floor available somewhere."

"Brilliant," Gabriel says, trying to steal back his coffee. It's a wonderful blend of honey and citrus, and frankly, I'm not sure how Gabriel got his hands on it. All I know is I'm not letting it out of *my* hands. I body-block Gabriel. Behind me, I hear him chuckle and then his footsteps thump toward the attic window. My own chuckle slips out. Today feels good. Théo's fate is still unknown, but I'm riding high on the knowledge that I likely saved his wife and children from the Gestapo. Then there's the whole successful raid of the depot.

Picturing the Germans running around chasing their tails and cursing their saboteurs as they put out fires is something I would've given anything to see. I'll settle for knowing it happened—and soon for London to know it too.

"I'm ready to start tapping," Louis says. He tears the group of used keys from the one-time pad, passing it to me to burn, and slides the silk handkerchief into the lining of his briefcase. "Got one minute until they'll be expecting me."

And here we go. I light the match and set it to the torn paper, dropping it into a rubbish bin. I check my watch. He's got twenty minutes, never longer. "I'll keep an eye on the time."

"Thanks," he says, then begins with his Morse code.

The tapping of it is rhythmic. I always enjoy the sound of it. Gabriel sits by the window, his legs stretched out and crossed at the ankles.

Suddenly his feet stomp to the ground. He lets out a string of profanities. His voice is urgent. "We've got company."

"What does that mean?" I ask. But I know. I run to the window, needing to see for myself. It's exactly like we were told in training.

There're two caravans. Men get out. One of them is a German policeman. But the others are clearly direction finders. They have the telltale long coats, the oversized watches.

"How'd they find us?" I ask. "Louis, I thought you could switch to battery so they couldn't trace you?"

"Batteries only last so long. I thought I was being careful. Which answer do you want, Katherine? Either way, they're here."

I could scream. But that'd be the absolute wrong response in this very moment. I grab my gun, tucking it into the back of my waistband.

Gabriel runs a hand through his hair. "We need to hide what we can."

"The basement," I suggest.

We all but tumble down the flights of steps and onto the soft sand there. Behind the lift shaft, Louis starts digging. He drops his briefcase into the hole and we kick the sand over it.

"Our guns?" I ask.

"Keep it," Gabriel says. "We may need them. Just don't get caught with it."

At that, we climb the stairs and hurry to exit through the door to the back garden—and straight into a German officer.

Gabriel uses the butt of his gun against his head, the man dropping to the ground. "Go, go," he says to us.

I'm running.

The fields have been harvested, nothing to conceal us. But the fields are the only direction to go, a cropping of trees that leads to a denser forest on the other side. I don't see how this doesn't end in us being caught unless we can get to the coverage of those trees.

Angry voices carry through the cold air. My breath is labored, my lungs on fire within steps, fear pushing my heart rate faster than I ever thought possible.

I must do something.

When Adele lost her footing and was swept up in the river, I did nothing. Absolutely nothing. The fact the danger involved water doesn't lessen my culpability.

This time I'll do whatever it takes. This moment is larger than the three of us. "Gabriel," I say between strained inhales. "You have"—I search for her name in my head—"Evelyn waiting for you after this war. And Louis, your daughter. Whereas I have . . . to do this."

I stop running.

Gabriel skids to a stop. Louis keeps going, faster than I ever figured him to be. The trees aren't far off for him.

I shake my head. "No, go. All those letters you wrote won't be lies," I say. "You two need to make it."

"Katherine, no. Come on," he demands.

I discreetly drop my gun, then distance myself from it. Being caught with a banned firearm is a clear sign of being against the Germans.

I meet his eyes. "Go. Now. Please."

Gabriel curses again. "My God, Katherine, you really are stubborn. Do whatever you need to do, say, or become to save yourself. You matter, Katherine. Please know that. You matter." Then he turns and runs.

I hear his words, but I don't have time to process them. Two Germans have rounded the outbuilding and are now coming my way. I don't move. I'm a sitting duck. My mind races. I will away the tears that want to form in my eyes.

As the first officer reaches me, I pretend to faint.

CHAPTER 17

Violet

—

Ardleigh Red Cross Hospital, Essex
September 29, 1915

REALITY AND MY IMAGINATION MIX IN MY SUBCONSCIOUS. I
dream so intensely that when I wake, I truly feel as if I've been
beside my brothers in the trenches. Dirt walls, dirt floors. Living,
eating, sleeping in the constant threat of gunfire. Unable to light
a cigarette for fear of the red glow creating a target.

I'm instantly relieved that I am in the safety of my room in
the vicarage while simultaneously agonizing that what I dreamt
is my brothers' reality.

I try to shake the lingering tentacles of fear. Ironically enough,
I'd take the trenches over the alternative: having them on one of
my beds because they've been gravely injured.

Clara has already begun her shift, leaving behind a trail of
everything she's touched. Pajamas on the floor. A wardrobe open.
Even the scent of her perfume, though we've been instructed not
to spritz any.

As I approach the hospital, I hear her through the second-
floor windows even before I see her. She's hollering. A patient is
screaming. And my heart sinks at the recognition of the voice.

I take the outside steps two at a time. I rush to Henry's bedside.

"Don't you touch me," he growls.

"Clara!" I scream, reaching for her arm. She has the same equipment I used last night to drain Henry's wound.

"This boy is a delinquent. Doesn't know I'm trying to *help* him." She emphasizes the last part while glaring at Henry.

He shakes his head frantically. "I don't want her help, Miss Violet. Yours. Only yours."

I blow out a slow breath. "It's okay, Henry. It'll be okay." I lower my voice. "I can take over, Clara."

"Like hell you will. This patient is part of my morning rounds."

"I understand," I say in a soothing voice. It's a voice that's worked on Lady Duff Gordon, Miss Anderson . . .

I fear it won't work on Clara with how she's glowering at me. She snaps, "Do you? This boy is currently *my* patient."

I nod. "He is, but Dr. Lowndes needs him drained every two hours, correct? We're wasting time, and you know he likes to keep a strict schedule."

Clara rolls her eyes. But the rationale lands. Despite her insubordination in doing things such as wearing perfume, she doesn't want to be the reason for unruliness at the hospital. Neither of us do. But even more important to me than the hospital running smoothly is Henry's well-being.

With a huff, Clara concedes, shoving the draining apparatus at me. I smile politely.

Then I get to work, Henry not making a peep until I'm done. "Sorry for making a scene, Miss Violet."

"None of that," I say. "I told you I'd take care of you and that's exactly what I intend to do." I wink. "Every two hours. I promise."

I cup his chin before telling him I'll be back soon.

As I turn, I bump his locker, his cap falling to the floor. When I retrieve it, I notice for the first time the regiment badge attached to it.

It's not one I recognize, nor did I pay attention to a man's regiment before. There's only one badge I know by heart. The London Irish Rifles. A harp with the royal crown atop.

Could that badge be in this very room? If it is . . .

My heart rate quickens as I rush to the bedside of one of the men brought in yesterday from Loos. A shaky but relieved breath rushes out of me.

Still, various battalions could've been in the fight. I hasten from one bed to the next, ignoring the patient and looking only at his cap.

If I find my brothers' regiment crest, it means they're not only in the trenches but in an active battle.

But I do not see theirs.

My chest rises and falls as I fight to regain composure. I'm okay. They're okay. It's the man from yesterday with his back all but torn off who needs my attention.

And my attention is what he gets.

Then I'm back with Henry.

Afterward I continue my rounds, until somehow the hour hand has rounded my wristwatch two more times. If it were possible for time to quicken to double speed, it's happening this very day.

I barely have time to eat, to pour myself coffee, to step outside for the autumn air to refresh my senses before the poor lad's arm needs draining again. And again.

Not that I'm to make a fuss. He needs me.

At the day's end, Matron stops me. "The night duty nurses will see to your friend. Why don't you get some rest?"

I'm shaking my head before words can formulate. But they do and I say, "No, I'm fine. A catnap, then I'll be with him through the night."

Matron presses her lips together.

"At least these first few days and nights," I insist. "He's so young."

Mrs. Bell sighs. "That he is. As long as you don't wear yourself too thin."

"I won't."

I think we both know it's a lie, but she allows it. And I have faith I'll survive. I've gone on little sleep before. With each new baby Mother had, I was there, bringing my brothers and sisters to her breast day and night, removing them when they'd had their fill and Mother had fallen asleep.

I'd tell myself they wouldn't be newborns forever. They'd need to nurse less. They'd sleep more.

I tell myself now Henry won't be injured forever. He'll need to be drained less as he improves. I'll help him heal completely in time.

In the meantime, I know how to function catching pockets of sleep.

"Miss Violet."

Lost in my thoughts, I startle at my name.

Two beds over, Leo smiles at me.

It's contagious. "Do you need something?" I ask him.

"Your attention."

I snort, though I really shouldn't give him that reaction, or even my response of "Is that so?"

He lowers his voice conspiratorially. "Yes, you've stuck me all day with Clara."

This time I laugh in earnest. "Well, it wasn't my doing."

Leo tries to sit up, but I *tsk* him. He chuckles, closing his eyes and shaking his head at my admonishment. "I feel like an invalid lying here unable to talk to you properly."

"You *are* an invalid, Leo. Temporarily, at least."

He lays a hand over his heart, his head rolling to the side. But he's smiling. Leo has a nice smile, contagious, I thought only moments ago. The kind that makes my own lips quirk up involuntarily.

And he relaxes that enticing grin of his just enough to say, "I love hearing you say my name. An Irish accent. Yet I heard you speak Spanish earlier. An enigma of a woman."

"You're talking silly."

"Nah. Never."

I roll my eyes, but my own smile gives away how much I'm enjoying our lighthearted exchange.

"How about this . . . how about after I get better, we have a proper, upright conversation?"

I huff a quick laugh. "So hopeful of you."

"What? I won't live?"

"No, no," I correct quickly. "You'll be just fine. It's that I simply do not live based on hope."

"You speak of hope like it's a bad thing." I shrug, and his finger twitches toward me, though he stops short. "I'll make you see otherwise."

"You're most certainly silly. I wager after you heal you'll be off"—I flap my hand, trying to be casual when I'm actually quite curious where that'll be—"back to your regiment? Back home? What *is* next for you?"

It's not a question I've asked any of the men I've helped nurse back to health. Their futures won't affect my own. But there's something about Leo, about this effortless banter between us, that I don't want to walk away from so quickly.

"What's next is going back to fight," Leo says, "to see to this war's end. After that, a future, a small family of my own, a roof over our heads, a piece of myself that'll go on even after I'm nothing but dust and bones. That's my *hope*, anyway."

I fight the urge to swat his arm. That wouldn't be good. Instead, I perch a hip onto Leo's bed. I tell myself it's only because my feet hurt. And I remark in earnest, "That sounds very nice for you."

"It's time. I'm nearly thirty. My baby sister is married with kids. I thought I'd have those things by now too. But with the war . . . it's all been delayed. I have some catching up to do." He gives me a suggestive expression that I choose not to decipher. "What about for you? What will you do after Germany's defeated?"

"Well," I begin, "it's rather more straightforward for me." As much as I'd like to continue on as a nurse, the wages pale in comparison. So this is it. My one hoorah in medicine. I sigh. "I'll go back to sea. It's always the sea." I can detect his forming question in the movement of his brows. "I've worked as a stewardess for years, and after the war I'll be doing it for many more to come."

"The sea, huh? But where's home?"

I'm glad I'm sitting because his question affects me in this moment more than it should. At the mention of *home*, it's the sights, the sounds, the memories of the Andes I think of. It's that perfect night around the table. I'm forced to clear my thickening throat. "My family has a house in London, but I'm only there between voyages. Mostly it's the sea for me."

"Sounds exciting."

"It can be."

It can also feel like chains. But even allowing the thought to filter through my head brings about a surge of guilt as I think of my family being an obligation. But they are. They're my duty, my responsibility—perhaps one of those word choices more sparing.

And right now I have the added responsibility of fixing up these men who could very well be any of my brothers.

I haven't yet taken notice of Leo's regiment crest. I do so now, but it's not one I recognize. I ask him, "Have you come across anyone from the London Irish Rifles?"

Leo licks his lips, then nods.

"Any Jessops?"

He scratches his cheek, where stubble is closing in on a beard. "Philip. Yes, I believe he was a Jessop. Cursed in Spanish, now that I think about it."

My back stiffens and I have to choke out the question, "*Was* a Jessop?"

Leo jerks up an arm, his face scrunching in pain. "Is. Is. My God, sorry. He *is* a Jessop. That battle's past tense for me now. I have to put them behind me. Each one of them."

My heart's still racing, but I let out a slow breath. "Philip's my brother. All the Jessops. Jack. Patrick. Philip. William."

"Violet Jessop," he says slowly, trying out my full name. "Pretty." He huffs. "Now, your brothers . . . last I heard, all the Jessop brothers are doing just fine. Philip made a name for himself because he won the high jump in the battalion sports. He's a fine sport."

"Philip did? Patrick's always been the sporty one. I do suppose Philip's got the height, though." And my insides warm at him spreading his wings. Philip's always been more serious, more practical, in need of a solid plan. My brothers want to open a construction business together one day. Jessop Brothers is what they'll call it. It's why it's so important they finish school, so they know how to do all the books and numbers. It's why I need them to finish this war. Out of all of them, Philip's the one who doesn't take risks. To think of him launching his body over a high jump . . . and winning. Now, that's something.

"I can see by your face how much you care about them."

I nod. And while there's nothing embarrassing about it, I also avert my gaze, needing a moment after this glimpse into my brothers' current lives.

Leo touches my hand, and I shoot my eyes back to him. It's the first time we've touched in a nonmedical capacity and I feel the tips of my ears heat. "They're lucky to have you as a younger sister."

"Older," I correct.

"I know." And he smiles devilishly.

★ ★ ★

THAT SMILE AND THE NEWS THAT MY BROTHERS ARE DOING well adds a pep to my very tired step.

The next day Leo feigns a fever for attention. It's only when I lay a hand on his forehead that he erupts with laugher.

Lord help me, I walk away laughing too.

It's a busy day, a handful of men being moved into the hospital and another handful moved out. I suppose, I realize, rubbing a hand along my neck, that Leo will be among the ones leaving soon.

I also realize that none of those arriving have the London Irish Rifles crest.

By nightfall, I've yawned so many times it's become an inside joke of sorts. I'm the Medusa of nurses. Make eye contact with me while I'm mid-yawn and your fate is sealed. Why does that happen, with yawns being passed from person to person?

My tired brain ponders it as I sit at Henry's bedside, readying the draining tubes. I'm five minutes behind the schedule I've set for myself, and I do not like being behind.

I fumble a needle, and it clamors to the floor. As I pick it up, I yawn. The nurse a bed over happens to be watching me. Immediately she yawns.

"Sorry," I whisper as she playfully shakes her head.

Back to work, I set to sterilizing the needle. In doing so, I prick myself, nearly dropping it a second time. Annoyed, I blow out a sharp breath, then suck on the small drop of red.

I'm glad Henry's sound asleep, not witness to my sloppy nursing skills. "See you in two hours," I whisper before dragging myself to my room for a quick nap.

I say it again and again, the number of days blurring together. The only sign of a new day being the arrival of a new group of wounded men.

Then, one day, it happens. At first I think my brain is playing tricks on me. But no, there's the harp. There's the crown.

These men are from the London Irish Rifles.

I trail one of the men as he's transferred to a bed. He's clearly in pain. Bleeding. Moaning. Not in any shape for an inquisition. Still, I have the urge to shake him and demand, "The Jessop brothers. What do you know?"

Somehow I refrain, clenching my jaws. They feel tight. All my muscles and bones are too stiff.

The other two men from their regiment aren't faring much better than the man I followed. I care for the London Irish Rifles men with added discipline, convinced if I use a softer voice, a lighter touch, a renewed devotion, maybe even a higher dose of pain medications, that they'll be more quickly in a state to be able to answer my questions.

Finally, one of the men has enough capacity to ask, "Where am I, Nurse?"

"Where were you?" I ask him instead.

His head rolls. "Loos."

I nod. "You're okay. You're in a hospital in Essex. Back in England," I assure him. "But tell me, please. William Jessop. Philip Jessop. Patrick Jessop. Jack Jessop. Do you have any news of them?"

The man's mouth opens, silently mouthing, "What?"

"Please," I say as a painful spasm rolls up my arm. "Think. The Jessop brothers."

His eyes flutter, but he's able to mutter, "Jack. A signaler. He went over."

"Went over?" I try to swallow, but my throat feels too thick.

"Went over," he repeats. "Hasn't come back. Been days."

There's not enough air. My breathing's never been the best, not with a portion of my lung being removed as a child. But right now it feels as if I've not a single airway.

My fingers wind into his bedsheets, holding on. Holding on, but I feel myself slipping. I fight to stay here, to stay upright, to remain strong. The darkness is stronger.

CHAPTER 18

Daphne

CODE NAME KATHERINE
Alias Madame Irene du Tertre

Oullins prison, France
November 16, 1942

I'VE GONE SLACK. THE GERMAN OFFICER HAS CAUGHT ME. I do nothing to hold on to him or lessen my body weight. Every bit of me is trying to sell the fact I've fainted.

I'm lowered to the ground.

It's cold, hard. I'm without a coat, and I do my best not to release a shiver.

I hope to accomplish three things by this display.

The first, to give Gabriel and Louis a chance to get to the trees.

Second, to distract the Germans—and it sounds like there are two of them here with me—from noticing the gun I've tossed in the cut-down crops.

And third, to begin to spin my story.

"Just pick her up," one of the officers says in German. "He's long gone."

He. Singular? Did Louis make it unnoticed to the trees? Then a sobering realization hits me: Could we all have? If I hadn't stopped to sacrifice myself?

Little good that'll do me now. I've made my bed.

The German grunts as he hefts me into his arms. With each step, I begin formulating the ins and outs of why Madame Irene du Tertre has been caught running.

* * *

I'LL SAY NOTHING UNTIL I HAVE TO. AN INTERROGATION IS coming, this I'm certain of. The question is . . . when?

I continue with my act, having only moments ago "startled awake." Now I'm distressed, overwhelmed, scared.

It's not difficult to play that part.

I'm brought to a prison. I'm placed in a holding cell. I'm the only woman in here.

The fact I'm the only woman triggers my next thought: I'm also the first woman . . . the first woman of the Special Operations Executive to be captured, that I know of.

Way to go, Daphne. The honor is all yours.

There's shame in that realization. There's also a very real fear. I do not know what will happen to me.

What had Young Allan Jeayes said?

"You're to be within our first group of women to officially be trained and dropped in. There's no telling if you'd be treated more humanely than the men have been."

And the men hadn't been treated well. Cold bath, electric shock treatment, sleep deprivation . . . all have been methods that've been used to get them to talk.

After, some were shot. Others went to detention camps. Some have likely since been taken to killing camps.

Never were they released.

I drop my head into my hands, squeezing my fingertips into my scalp. I look guilty as sin. And they know I've done something. I ran, didn't I? The trick will be convincing them of my narrative.

Hours later, I'm relieved when it's the French police who

approaches my holding cell. I launch right in. "Please don't tell her." My voice wavers. The emotion is pure. The plea is part of my plan.

"Tell who?" one of the officers asks.

I stand from the bench where I've been seated and wrap my hands around two of the cell's bars. Handcuffs dangle between my wrists. "Liam's wife. She cannot know." I avert my eyes. "I'm ashamed of my behavior."

The officer grunts and begins to open my cell. "This way," he demands, taking my arm roughly.

Why? I wonder. Why do Frenchmen exist who collaborate with and support what the Germans are doing here? I will never understand.

I purposely struggle to keep up with the officer, allowing myself to appear helpless. "Sit," he barks when we reach a small room with a table and chairs.

At least I am not standing *on* the table this time. I take one of the chairs and rest my clenched hands on the wood top.

It's just the two of us.

I remind myself I've been trained for this very moment.

Don't ask questions.

Remain stoic.

Retain eye contact.

Avoid the use of um.

No unnecessary details.

The officer takes the chair across from me. I meet his eyes. For a heartbeat, I wonder if I appear too defiant, when I want him to see me as a timid, maybe even weak-willed woman. My heart beats so strongly I'm surprised there isn't an echo of it in the room.

But no, a dropped pin could be heard. Finally, after likely assuring himself he's made me an ample degree of nervous, he asks in a booming voice, "What is your name?"

He cannot know me as Daphne, nor as Katherine. I can only

be Madame Irene du Tertre. Irene has a chance to survive this. Daphne and Katherine do not.

I answer accordingly.

He stares at me. I stare back. If he expects me to crack on the most basic of questions, he'll be sorely disappointed. "What were you doing at the farm, Madame du Tertre?"

I stick with words I've already spoken, only rearranged, and while I should remain stoic, I let a hint of hysteria slip into my response. "I'm ashamed of my behavior. Please don't tell Liam's wife."

"I'll bite," he says. "Don't tell her what?"

I release a shaky breath. Again, part of it is genuine; I'm about to spin a story. My hope is I don't include any details that can trip me up later. "About the affair," I begin. "My husband was part of the German Wehrmacht."

"Was?" he asks.

Inwardly, I'm smiling. Young Allan Jeayes said we could make me a widow in time. That time has come. "He recently died."

I don't say how. I won't, unless asked.

"I see." It's not followed by any condolences. He only asks with an edge of contempt, "And you comforted yourself in the bed of another man? A married man?"

I drop my head. "Liam, yes. I didn't know he was married at first. I'm ashamed of my behavior."

"So why did you run?"

"I was startled. Then I was being chased."

"You ran with this Liam?"

I weigh how to answer that question. During my capture, they had said *he's long gone*. They know about Gabriel. "Yes," I say.

"Do you know where he could have gone?"

I shake my head. Again, inwardly, I'm smiling. Gabriel and Louis got away.

"You have no idea at all where he would have gone? I find that highly suspicious."

"Home, maybe? We met for our . . . we saw each other at the farm. A friend of a friend's place, I believe. I really don't know. Only that it was available to us."

"So you could sleep with another woman's husband?"

He's enjoying this. "Yes," I say.

"Let me ask you this, though." He taps his fingertips against the tabletop. "Do you always run with a gun?"

"A gun?" I parrot, buying myself time. Warning bells are going off in my head. I scrunch my brows. "I don't own a gun."

"Yet you had one."

Deny, deny, deny. "I apologize, but I don't know what you're talking about."

"You're saying the gun we found only feet from where you were arrested wasn't yours?"

I open my mouth.

The officer presses, "Are you saying it's Liam's? What is this Liam's full name?"

Ah, this fictitious Liam is a much bigger fish to fry than a lonely widow. I lean closer. I supply a full name, noting it to memory. But in response to the gun's owner, I say, "I don't know. I've never seen Liam with a gun. Maybe, though?"

"Hmm," he says. He taps his fingertips some more.

"And what about the wireless?"

No, I want to scream. Every ounce of me wants to close my eyes and let an honest reaction roll over me. The discovery of Louis's wireless means one thing: our network is kaput. FAME is compromised, over as we were just hitting our stride, completing only our first small act of sabotage when we had enough guns and explosives for many more attacks on a larger scale. Louis's handkerchief will be found in the lining of the briefcase. They'll know how to decode his messages. But I have to hide my utter disappointment. Instead, I feign ignorance like I had with the gun.

The officer asks, "Is Liam the owner of the wireless too?"

"We only visited the outbuilding once a week. I don't know who may be there the other days of—"

"Yet," he cuts me off, "you've been seen boarding a bus daily, headed in the very direction of the farm."

I lick my lips. My mouth is suddenly dry. I've been caught in my first lie, saying the farm was a friend of a friend's. What to do . . . what to say . . . I decide not to abandon my story but to build on it. "I've since taken a job at the farm."

"You're a busy one, aren't you, Madame du Tertre?"

"I'm not sure what you mean."

He smirks. "A widow. A mistress." He waves his hand. "A farmhand. Oh, and also a caregiver of an ill relative."

Lord help me. "Yes, that's why I came to Lyon."

"I see."

Please let that be true.

When he stands, I reposition in my chair, ready to do the same.

"So I'm free to go?" I ask, holding up my cuffed hands, trying to hide the eagerness from my voice.

The officer laughs. Actually laughs at me. Then he slams the door as he leaves the room.

* * *

OVER THE NEXT FEW DAYS, I'M QUESTIONED AGAIN AND again, during which I receive a gauntlet of reactions, ranging from distrust to incredulousness to one officer who surprisingly believes me.

The worst I receive, though, is a backhand across the face, his knuckles connecting with my cheekbone like no other.

I almost earned a second pummeling when I raised my chin in response.

In between interrogations, I'm imprisoned in a cell on the women's floor. It's a gaggle of Madame Leroys. But no actual Madame Leroy. Or Camille. I hid Théo's family well. It's a relief, and at least I have that small win to lift my spirits.

My morale certainly suffers when I'm turned out into the courtyard for the daily thirty-minute exercise period and I recognize Théo being escorted back inside. Rather, he's all but being carried, his left leg appearing to be broken. Or at the very least badly injured.

I quickly turn my attention elsewhere. It'd get me a lot more than a swollen cheekbone if the two of us are connected.

I had hoped he'd gotten away. That he simply arrived too late to the wagon but was able to find his way to safety. And then somehow made it back to his family.

But no, it hasn't gone that way. He's here, with me. And I believe, even without any evidence to the contrary, what Camille told me. Her husband has had no part in my capture.

I picture the Gestapo rifling through the safe house above the bar. Is there anything incriminating to find there? I can't recall what I'd left behind that'd be worse than what they've already found at the farm. I know what they certainly won't find, though: a sick aunt or any medicine.

I roll my head in a circle, feeling the pull of my stiff muscles all the way down my back. I still haven't worked out how I'll answer that question. Days pass, and I still don't know.

She worsened and I had to move her to a hospital? To which they'd check to see if she's there.

She's recovering in the mountains . . . that fresher air . . .

She died . . .

How morbid. Although my storytelling has also killed my fictional husband as well. The officers could grow even more suspicious with me if I say someone else is dead—that is, if I'm questioned further. Not knowing if they'll interrogate me again is its own kind of torture.

More days pass. A week, then two. It's now the third. I think. All I know is that it's been a cumulation of nearly identical days where I wonder if this'll be the hour they come back for me,

demanding I tell them more, something new, something impli-
cating myself or someone else.

Each day I become more ashamed of how I've landed myself
in prison. The American agent would be disappointed in me. Denise would find me pathetic. She never would've allowed herself
to be caught, let alone be the first woman captured. Colonel Buckmaster must see me as a waste of their time, effort, and resources.

I find little things to distract myself and preoccupy my mind.
I notice the Germans never come to the prison. The black bread
we get with our dinner is supposed to hold us over until lunch
the next day, as we only receive boiled water with a grain-based
coffee substitute in the morning. I'm 99 percent sure one of the
three women in my cell, a young French girl, is a stool pigeon.
The guards don't treat her as roughly. She's also always first to
start a conversation. I wonder what led to her arrest. Even more,
I wonder what they've promised her for spying.

"What'd you do to land yourself in here?" she's asked me multiple times.

She's either losing her mind or determined to get an answer
out of me. Each time I stick with my story. "I got scared and ran."

Every night a man comes by rhythmically pushing a broom.
He wears the same prison garb as the rest of us, but he must have
done something to earn this freedom to leave his cell, if only to
clean.

Seeing him is my favorite part of the day, because as he's
sweeping, he sings softly to himself. The language isn't one I
know, but the sound of it is lovely, something beautiful in an otherwise ugly place. Soon I begin to recognize the repeated words,
even if I don't know their meanings.

In time, as he—the custodian, as I begin to call him—goes
by, I join in, singing the unknown-to-me words in tune with him.
One evening after he passes, I catch the slightest of grins on his
face, and I turn to the older French woman in my cell. There are

two others in addition to her: the French girl, who I think is the informant, and another older woman, who I guess to be of Slavic descent and who hasn't yet spoken, not in all this time. I say in French, "Do you know what language he speaks? What I'm singing?" That second question stirs the first laugh out of me in God knows how long.

The French woman shakes her head. The French girl tells me no. For the Slavic woman, I try the question in Russian, then in Arabic. I don't dare speak English. I try Spanish, Italian. It's not until I repeat myself in German that the Slavic woman reacts. "It's Croatian he speaks," she says back in German. "He's Yugoslavian, like me. You're singing about how if you look at your forehead, there won't be any wrinkles there and how you'll hide your true face. And if I were to look into your eyes, I won't know anything about you because your eyes won't give you away. But to look at your shoes because they'll tell everything about you, that you've searched for a love for all these years."

I retain a stoic expression, the lyrics making me oddly uncomfortable, more than I want my forehead and eyes to let on. "Interesting," I say, pushing the idea of searching for love from my head. Instead, I ask in German, "Will you teach me your language?"

"No French," she says. "Only German. I no trust that other girl."

Great instincts. Also a marvelous tutor, Ivana is.

Three weeks turns to four. With it, I gain an understanding of the custodian's language, enough to whisper to him during his nightly serenades, asking if he could let me know if a friend, Théo, is still in the prison. Although I look for him during the daily exercise, I never see him.

But he could still be here. Ivana also mentions how she's been at the prison for months. How many, she's uncertain, but she whispers one evening how we're all just waiting to be shot. The prison is nothing more than a holding ground for anyone who has made an attack against the Germans.

"Every once in a while they question me," Ivana supplies in Croatian, me doing my best to decipher. I surmise she's saying, "I think they hope I will give up someone important." Ivana shrugs. "So I keep my head down. I hope they forget I exist. Before, a woman wasn't as fortunate. They said they had evidence . . ."

That's all she says. But honestly, it's enough. Isn't that the boat I'm in? Waiting to see if they are able to gather any real evidence against me? If so, I'll be shot.

Has Théo already suffered the same fate? If they captured him, they likely caught him red-handed. They've likely already tortured him. Or maybe his leg was hurt trying to escape.

The next night the swish of the custodian's broom raises my pulse. His sweeping sounds especially loud, and for the first time I notice how the night is void of the other usual noises I hear throughout the day: the cough of the guards, their too-loud guffaws, their inappropriate jokes. As the custodian passes my cell, he gives me a discreet nod.

Théo's alive.

But for how long? It kills me to think of his children without him. I know what it feels like to go through life without a parent. Hell, two parents.

I breathe heavily, offering a quiet "thank you" in Croatian to him. He startles at my use of his language. Then, to the same rhythm he uses nightly he changes the words and sings, "But I sense time is running out. For him. For all of us maybe."

It's my turn to startle. I'm not sure I've translated correctly. But when I look at Ivana, her sour expression confirms his secret message.

I face him again. He's eyeing me with interest. Then he moves as close to the cell as he can, his cheek pressed into a bar. I move closer to meet him and he whispers, "Katherine? The one the guards speak of?"

Not Irene du Tertre. But Katherine. My knees buckle, and he covers his hand over mine. He squeezes—such a paternal gesture—then he's on his way, once more singing softly to himself.

I lower my forehead to the cool metal. They know my code name. They know with certainty I'm lying.

"Time is running out," the custodian just said.

And he couldn't be more right. I don't know how, but I need to find a way out of here, taking as many with me as possible.

CHAPTER 19

Violet

—

Ardleigh Red Cross Hospital, Essex
October 9, 1915

I HEAR THEIR VOICES. I RECOGNIZE THEIR VOICES, EVEN.
Dr. Lowndes, Mrs. Ball . . .

I recognize their words, but they don't fully arrange in my conscious brain . . .

"Exhaustion."

"Poisoned hand."

"Delirium."

"Fever."

I smell the same bitter and sour odors, the same sounds of coughing and moans of the ward I'm familiar with, yet it's hotter than it's ever been before. Faces pass over mine. Suddenly, Leo is above me. Standing, not lying down.

"No," I mutter, his face dancing across my vision. "Shouldn't be."

I blink and his high cheekbones morph to soft freckled cheeks, the face of my brother Jack. He went over enemy lines. He hasn't returned.

"J-Jack?" I stammer.

"Jack is fine," Dr. Lowndes says. Then he's gone and these same words are re-spoken, but in the voice of our matron.

Then Leo's.

Each time the darkness around me recedes, the heat abates, the poison dissipates.

Until I surface from what feels like years of slumber.

Clara's hand is on my forehead. "Cool as a cucumber," she says. "About time."

"About time," I parrot, a slog to my brain. I blink. Clara's still there. Why is it she who remains, yet the others always flickered away?

"Undersupplied. Understaffed," Clara murmurs to herself.

"Miss Clara," Mrs. Ball says flatly. "I'll take it from here."

"Yes, Matron."

Then: "Violet, welcome back, dear. You put us all through a scare."

"How long?" I cough some of the hoarseness from my voice. I turn my head, seeing nothing but white curtains cornering me off from the rest of the room. "How long have I been sick?"

"Just shy of a week."

And all that time . . . "My brother Jack—"

"Is fine. Some more men from Loos have been brought in. They told us Jack was able to find his way back. Our troops used some sort of gas on the Germans, but the weather hampered things, blew the gas back into our trenches and made it linger in no-man's-land. But your brother made it back, with nothing more than a cough and blisters. He's very lucky. You're very lucky, Violet. All we could surmise was you pricked yourself while caring for Henry and intoxication set in, further complicating your preexisting fatigue."

I try to swallow, but I cannot. Mrs. Ball is quick to offer me water. It helps soothe my throat but does nothing to alleviate the weight I feel at not being there for Henry the past week.

"I know what you're thinking, Violet, but Henry is also fine." She chuckles. "He and Clara bumped heads quite a few times, but I actually think it improved his spirits. Gave him more incentive to heal, at the very least. He was discharged yesterday."

"He's gone?"

"That's right. Just as we hoped."

"Okay."

I close my eyes. I'm tired. But as soon as I do, I think of Leo. Through a gap in the curtains, I can make out a portion of the other beds. Leo's bed is by the door, where he'd catch me as I tried to tiptoe out each night, as he said hello each morning when I came in. Where we'd have exchanges in between, his laugher, his smile, his hopefulness chipping away at a wall I routinely place between me and others. But now, in his hospital bed, the shape of the body looks smaller. The hair is lighter. I take in a deep breath. He's gone, also discharged, without a goodbye.

* * *

ONCE I'M ON MY FEET AND BACK TO WORK, I SLOG THROUGH blanket baths, temperature checks, dressings and redressing, tidying the ward, and the other odds and ends of my day.

Henry is back fighting. Leo is back fighting. My brothers are still fighting. Where, I don't know. The Battle of Loos is over, though soldiers are already fighting elsewhere up and down the Western Front.

And while I know Henry is alive and well, I wasn't able to keep *my* promise to him. It's an uncomfortable emotion. Yet there's another feeling I'm left with too. This one is unsettling, not unlike that pit in my stomach when I've left the house but I'm uncertain if I've turned off the iron.

It's Leo who is spurring that unease. I let him in, more than I have any other patient, knowing full well he'd leave. That in itself shouldn't be causing me distress. But I feel it, all because I didn't see him before he left the hospital. And that right there is a startling realization. Missing a goodbye with a patient has never had me blankly staring at the wall before.

"You all right, miss?" a soldier asks me. I look down at him in his hospital bed. His blisters are improving.

I ignore his question, instead asking my own, "What was the gas like?"

I don't know why I asked. I don't want to hear it.

"Scary as hell," he says. "The Germans have been using gas for months, but it was the first we have. I couldn't see more than ten yards ahead of me. I looked for landmarks but couldn't find a dang thing. Thought my heart was going to burst free from my chest. We made progress, though. Pushed the Germans a bit. Shame they took the ground right back. Shame my mask didn't hold up and now I'm here."

"Then what was the point of it all?" The question's out before I can stop myself. It's very American of me, but I'm British through and through. "I'm sorry, I . . ."

The man flicks a wrist to stop me. "It shows we can push them, miss. It shows that we need heavier artillery if we want to win next time."

I nod. But the patriotic fervor I felt months ago no longer zings through me.

Fight, retreat, advance; fight, retreat, advance. And all for the gain of pushing the front line a few miles. Really, it's nothing more than a bloody stalemate.

And that's how things continue to go, as days turn to weeks turn to months.

"Home by Christmas" becomes something all of England once said, but says no longer.

*　*　*

ONE DAY AFTER A LONG SHIFT, I'M DESCENDING THE OUTSIDE staircase when Dr. Lowndes honks his automobile and motions for me to get in.

"How are you feeling?" he asks me, the engine roaring.

"I'm well."

He dips his head forward, his spectacles shifting down his nose. He looks overtop them at me. "I mean no disrespect, Miss

Violet, but you're still weak from your poisoning and you've had a listless disposition."

"I'm sorry. Truly. I'll do better."

He shakes his head. We still haven't moved. "Violet, you're a wonderful nurse. How about a quick field trip?"

I quirk a brow.

"Humor me," he says, finally accelerating forward.

We drive, the windows down. The springtime air funnels in through the windows and I hold my cap in place. Suddenly the air changes, as it does at sea when we approach land. Only this is the opposite. I smell the transition from land to sea. In the darkening sky, gulls fly.

I relax into my seat. It's been months since I've been to the water, an especially odd thing as the hospital can't be more than ten miles from the port. But any time off I've had has meant trips to London to see my mother. She's much the same, not worse, not better. Almost as if she's stuck in time.

We're at the water within minutes. A handful of ships— destroyers, light cruisers, and submarines—are in port.

"I hesitate to suggest this," Dr. Lowndes says as he parks, "because I don't wish to lose such a dependable nurse, but I wonder how you'd fare back at sea, Miss Violet."

"Excuse me?"

"The salt air. As you may know, it has restorative particles. Salt, iodine, magnesium. More modern research even says the sound of lapping waves can alter brain patterns in a positive manner. Very interesting science, indeed. A change of scenery from land to sea may be what you need to get back your strength and zest."

Return to the sea, on my own accord? For my own well-being? They're such foreign thoughts that I chuckle.

It earns me a peculiar look from Dr. Lowndes. "Are you opposed?"

I shake my head. "No, I suppose not."

The lapping sounds wash over me, and I'm stuck in an in-between. Hadn't I told Leo I'd go back to sea? I'd known working as a nurse was a momentary respite, a fleeting opportunity to sink into something I've long desired.

But this is sooner than expected.

The sea has called me. And, regretfully, I continue to need it, this time for my own welfare and survival.

CHAPTER 20

Daphne

CODE NAME KATHERINE
Alias Madame Irene du Tertre

Oullins prison, France
December 1942

HOW TO COORDINATE OUR SURVIVAL IS THE QUESTION OF the day. Hell, the year. Nightly, the custodian comes. I notice how he's grown thinner. I likely have, too, my clothing hanging looser. Still, I give him half my daily bread. I want him healthy. I want him to like me.

I want him to help me.

And, to the rhythm of his songs, we exchange messages.

I soon gather there are eighty-six prisoners in all.

Ironic, really. Eighty-six, the exact number of people I watched being rounded up at the federation building.

I learn that the guards take a smoke break each evening, the quiet I've come to recognize. No coughs. No laughter. No voices. Only the custodian sweeping the floor and singing his songs.

I confirm this the next two nights, the sounds of the custodian and me singing, our soft conspiring the only noise.

I have to wipe the smile from my face when I turn toward my other cellmates, in particular the young French girl.

If she notices anything peculiar in my exchanges with the custodian, she doesn't let on. But why would she? I'm not letting on that I suspect her of working with the Germans.

But at this point, I'm 100 percent certain.

Last night we had a new woman in our cells. At first, when she was thrown in, landing on her knees, I thought she was Camille. The likeness of her hair color, her curls, her small size was uncanny. But when she raised her head, tears in her eyes, and wiped the hair from her face, I realized it wasn't her.

The young French girl did as I thought she'd do: she peppered her with questions, feigning sympathy and solidarity. How maddening to see her "work."

I tried to silence the new woman, letting out a *shh* sound I hoped the young French girl would decipher as me trying to comfort the woman, whereas the woman would see my *shhs* as a warning not to implicate herself. The French girl was so obvious to me, to Ivana. Yet somehow not to the new woman. She has yet to return from our earlier daily exercise.

Tonight the custodian sings how the mood is different, heightened, an electricity in the air. He feels like something is bound to happen soon.

The new arrival's execution? Théo's? Mine?

Maybe all three of us at once? A firing squad. Ten of them, three of us, saving them from the guilt of knowing if their bullet is the one that takes our lives. How nice for them.

I may retch from nerves. But I need to focus, to think.

"How long until the guards are back?" I sing in Croatian.

"An hour. More. They've taken to the bottle. A celebration."

I concentrate on his every word, my knowledge of his language still in its infancy.

"Tonight." It has to be tonight. "Keys?" I begin, pantomiming discreetly at the cell's lock.

He understands what I mean: Can he get them?

His sweeping stops. His dark brown eyes stare into mine. "I will try."

He resumes sweeping and we resume singing his normal song, of foreheads without any wrinkles and eyes that give nothing away.

When he turns the corner, making his way toward the guard station, I begin to count every second that passes.

I'm at four hundred twenty when I hear the faint sound of his sweeping again. Miraculously, I hear the jingle of keys.

"We must hurry," the custodian tells me.

He certainly doesn't need to tell me twice.

While the guards are partaking in their revelry, the custodian unlocks the cell.

"*Idemo*," I say to Ivana. She also doesn't need to be told twice for us to go. Neither do the other two women, including the French traitor, even if they didn't understand our exchange. An open cell door is clear enough. Though, once free, they're reminiscent of lost sheep, following on my heels as the custodian leads me to the men's wing, where I unlock the first cell.

No Théo.

But at the second, there he is. I call his name. It takes three more tries, as I work the lock, before his head lifts.

I see his recognition of me. I want to run in and drag him out, but there are still more cells to open.

I'm on third when I hear the first sounds of the guards realizing what's happening.

At the fourth cell, I mumble an apology and toss the keys inside.

I circle back to Théo, slinging one of his arms over my shoulder, helping him walk-jog out a side door the custodian uses to take out the rubbish.

In total, I have to imagine over thirty of the eighty-six have been freed, including Ivana. But most importantly, the custodian.

Bless him and his courage, his cleverness. I kiss his cheek before we go our separate ways, Ivana at his side.

"An angel you are," Théo says to me as we escape under the cover of night.

I push aside a low branch, trying to get a sense of how he's been treated. Shadows or bruises? Maybe both. I ask him, "How's your leg?"

"As if the pain matters," he says, though the discomfort is as clear as day in his voice.

I search through the darkness with my eyes, but also my ears. I don't know where I'm going exactly, the darkness impeding my sense of direction. My main objective is away from the prison. But also . . . "We need a river. A stream."

Something ankle-deep preferably.

Sounds of the others fleeing are a constant around us. A gunshot. Thankfully, no barking dogs. Not yet. But the canines could be coming, and we need water to lose our scent.

Théo's weight is growing heavy. Our pace is slowing.

"I told them nothing," he says, his voice sudden, urgent—desperate-sounding, even.

"Camille said you wouldn't."

"Camille?" he gasps. "You saw her?" He stops so quickly he almost brings me to my knees. "We must go back for her."

"No," I say, dragging him into a run again, my teeth gritted at his heaviness, "not in the prison." I tell him of my night with his family.

Never before have I heard a grown man sob like Théo does, his words—"They're safe"—barely decipherable as his body racks with emotion. My eyes blur with tears. It's a love I've never witnessed from a man before. A love I didn't know I ached to have until Théo and Camille taught me it could be possible to care about and stand by someone that intensely.

We crash into a river, the bank suddenly upon us. As I fall, I go under. But my feet hit the bottom, the water blessedly below my knees. I can do this. We bound downstream, the noise we're creating so loud I cringe with every step.

"That's far enough," I say after a while. I take hold of a tree limb to pull myself from the river, then offer Théo my hand. Onshore, he grabs my shoulders. "Where can I find them?"

"I'll take you there as soon as it's safe for us to go."

He shakes his head. "I'm only slowing us down. You need to go. Save yourself."

"Oh, believe me," I say, "that's the plan."

It gets a smile out of him, barely visible in the moonlight. He looks up. "I'm going to take my chances up there, hide out until the coast is clear."

"In the tree?" I ask.

He nods. "Where's my family, Katherine?"

As soon as I tell him, he begins walking to the river, then at the water's edge he retraces his footsteps, doubling back. If I didn't know any better, I'd think the man has spent some time in the wilds of Ireland too. Anyone tracking him will think he went into the water again, when instead . . . he's already up the tree.

"Good luck," I say, barely more than a whisper, the sentiment meant for us both.

★ ★ ★

I'M TIRED, HUNGRY, AND COLD. MY EXHAUSTION IS SO SEVERE that for long stretches it's as if my left foot has forgotten how to move. With each stride, it takes an unreasonable level of concentration to keep my knee and ankle straight and to land properly against the hard ground. At any moment, it feels like my leg will buckle.

When I inevitably fall, my hands hit the ground, unfeeling. They've grown numb. It's tempting to crawl into a ball, to preserve the little body heat I have left.

I need food and rest, rest and food.

But I somehow stand. I didn't escape a firing squad to die in the woods like an animal.

When the sun is high enough that I reckon curfew has lifted, I dare to approach a village. As I draw nearer, I realize it's more than a village; it's a monastery.

It's a gift—if they'll allow me inside. Women are not always accepted. And now I'm a wanted woman, for all the wrong reasons.

I stumble down a path within a browned lavender field, a coating of frost on the dead plants.

At a tall stone wall, I ring the bell.

And that is that. All I can recall.

I wake in a sparse room on a narrow bed. There's a steaming bowl of soup at my bedside, the aroma the likely culprit for bringing me back to consciousness. My first emotion is gratitude; I've been allowed in. This relief is only amplified when I'm told the Benedictines will make arrangements to contact London on my behalf.

While the black monks prefer to remain separate from the world outside their hamlets, news reaches us that four of the escaped prisoners have already been recaptured. They do not know who, nor do they want to be involved. As such, they are prepared to move heaven and earth to have me on my way.

It dawns on me: I'm not sure where I'll land. I've long been without a place to call home, and being in a prison only intensified that sensation. Ivana had cried one night, saying how she'd longed for home, a small seaside town where each hour is marked by the bell tower of the Cathedral of St. Anastasia. Would I ever have such a place where I feel at home?

It takes nearly two months for messages to be exchanged through the Catholic networks. I use the time to recover, to continue to reflect. But mostly I'm quiet, respecting the monastery's periods of silence where I practice sitting meditation, rest, relaxation.

It likely saves me from anxiety eating me alive. I'm certain when my orders come in I'll be called back to London. That'll be it, the end of my great adventure. Though calling it such now feels minimizing and only scratches the surface of what I'm doing has become to me. Still, it will be the end of my time as an agent and the start of . . . I do not know what.

I'm astonished—*astonished*—when that is not what happens.

I'm in the midst of joining in on an hours-long service that began well before dawn. The seats are quite ingenious yet incriminating. You see, the armrests work only when there is resistance. When I'm sitting properly, with my arms where they should be, the chair's armrests remain down. But when I drift off to sleep—as I've just done—the weight of my arms shift, the tension lifts, and the armrests snap up. The result is a great, embarrassing bang.

I cringe and focus intently, pretending as if none of this has happened. But a monk approaches me, silently motioning for me to follow him.

"We pray the Lord bless you and keep you," he says and passes me a sealed envelope. His smile is warm before he leaves, the rustling of his black habit the only sound in the hall.

With trembling hands, I tear open the envelope, unfold the letter. My mouth falls open.

I'm not being called back to London. It's quite the opposite. I'm being sent north, to the HOLIDAY network.

I'm told of my new mission: to help build and execute an escape route.

I'm no longer Katherine or Madame Irene du Tertre.

I'm code name Claire.

I have an alias of Madame Claire Fondeu, a seamstress, married—at least this one not involved with the Germans—to a butcher named Evan Fondeu.

And I'm to leave immediately.

* * *

MY FIRST DESTINATION IS A SAFE HOUSE IN THE SOUTH OF
France, where a woman code-named Marie will supply me with
new identity papers, a refreshing of belongings—as all mine are
long gone—and directions to my next destination.

I arrive via a bus, and my mouth falls open a second time
at who greets me. "You're everywhere," I say to the American
woman.

"And you are miraculously not dead."

"I'm surprised you aren't chastising me for buggering things."

Marie smirks. "I'd say having a hand in a string of explosions
at the depot and breaking yourself out of a jail doesn't qualify as
buggering."

Once at the safe house, she pushes me down into a chair, just
as a man with a camera enters the room. "Introductions aren't
necessary."

Marie motions toward me and I barely have time to square
my shoulders before the photo is snapped.

At that, he leaves again.

"Coffee?" Marie asks me.

"Please," I say, a bit too enthusiastically. I moan at the first
non-grain-based sip. The monks had gone without, not for pious
reasons but to allow others greater access during rationing.

"I'll just give you a moment," Marie says coyly.

"No," I say, though I don't dare release the grip I have on the
mug. "What do you know of the other prison escapees? I heard a
few were captured."

"Sorry. I only know that you got out. And that Gabriel and
Louis have been reassigned elsewhere. Gaspar will continue,
though in what ways I don't know."

"And Théo?"

Marie clears her throat. "A small fish I don't recognize."

Which means asking, "The custodian?" would be the longest
of long shots.

"Okay," I say. "Okay. What about the war?"

She makes a clucking sound. "I dare say things are on the up-and-up. Momentarily, at least. We have Germans trapped in Africa, Germans surrounded at Stalingrad, and the Japanese are getting closer to abandoning Guadalcanal."

"Is that all?"

She smiles. "Not the worst update, no."

Marie stands, crosses the room, her limp once again noticeable, and knocks on a door down a hallway.

"Five more minutes," I hear called back.

I slump into the chair and make quick work of the remainder of my coffee. Not a drop will be left behind. No sooner have I finished my mug than Marie reenters the room at a rush, saying, "Shall we get you on your way, then?" She begins moving about the room, attaching my new photo to my identity papers, collecting odds and ends, concealing some of those odds beneath my clothing, shoving some of the ends in a sewing bag, complete with sewing apparatuses, then into a suitcase.

"If anyone actually asks me how to use any of this," I say of the sewing doodads, "I'll be cooked."

I get my first genuine laugh from Marie. "You and me both, sister. Also, you should know, this may be the last you'll see of me."

"Oh?"

"They're pulling me out of France. Things are too hot for me. The Limping Lady, it's what the Germans call me. A lot of them, which is the problem. But if I have my way, I'll be back once the smoke clears."

"Well," I say, "I hope it's over before you get the chance."

"I'll take that too." She checks her watch. "The train is leaving soon. So . . . chop, chop."

CHAPTER 21

Violet

—

Aboard *Britannic*
November 12, 1916

THERE'S BEEN AN URGENCY WITHIN ME, ONCE I'VE MADE the decision to return to sea. As if I'll change my mind, putting my life in further jeopardy, if I don't commit straightaway. Yet it's the sea that's tried to take my life on more than one occasion.

It's not a healthy relationship, the sea and I. But it's the only way forward I know, and I'm most anxious to feel like myself again, a part of me afraid my languid and phlegmatic state is too similar to my mother's.

I don't tell her of these new plans. Funny how this makes me feel like a wayward teenage girl and not a nearly thirty-year-old woman.

After Dr. Lowndes suggested I return to sea, I reached out to the White Star Line, explaining everything and asking to be allowed to make a trip somewhere. Anywhere. They replied most agreeably, promising me the first vacancy on one of their recommissioned ships. It took time, many months, in fact, where I wasn't bringing in an income, but here I am aboard the HMHS *Britannic*, which happens to be yet another sister ship to *Titanic*.

While she was intended to be another grand transatlantic passenger line, she's now a hospital ship, the largest in the world. Like most things, the war changed its plans.

My own included, bringing me to unpredictable wartime waters. Waters I've already seen sink a ship with a single mine. And it's on these waters where I won't be working as a nurse but as a stewardess to the crew. Am I disappointed? *Sí.*

However, a silver lining: While boarding, I'd crossed paths with the ship's surgeon, a Dr. Beaumont. A very agreeable man, quick to smile, who says he's always thankful for an extra hand. He went as far as to give me an open invitation to assist him based on my previous, albeit brief, nursing experience. He called *Britannic* the most wonderful hospital ship that ever sailed the seas.

I joked back that I'd rather have the safest.

"You can thank the Geneva Convention then, miss."

What he means is that hospital ships are protected from attack. To my additional relief, improvements have been made to *Britannic* after that disastrous April night four years ago. She's eighteen inches wider, on account of a watertight inner skin. There's now a double hold along the engine and boiler rooms. A pneumatic tube that links the bridge to the radio room has been added to more quickly send out a distress call. Five or six of the sixteen watertight bulkheads have been extended as high as the bridge deck forty feet above the waterline. To be truthful, I'd fail an examination if asked to explain any of those. But I am completely and utterly aware of the necessity of lifeboats, and this one has forty-eight versus *Titanic*'s twenty.

I know it for a fact, as I've only just now finished counting them. Now I turn slowly, sucking in each and every salt-filled water droplet that mists onto the boat deck, glad for my coat to keep the chill at bay.

The ship itself is white. Very white. Such a change from *Olympic*'s and *Titanic*'s bold black exterior. Here, only a thick green strip runs from bow to stern, interrupted three times by a large red cross. Otherwise, the only other splash of color is a line of green lights along the decks, illuminated at night.

I've been instructed to familiarize myself with the ship and I get to it.

The promenade decks are crowded with hospital beds.

Her first-class dining room is the intensive care ward.

The operating theater is next door, formerly the grand reception room.

The public rooms on the upper decks are where many of the wounded will be.

The first-class staterooms are for the hospital elite, the doctors, Matron, the medical corps officers, the chaplains.

Then there are the lower-class cabins, where I'll be staying. It's fine, an upgrade really from my previous teeny tiny staff staterooms.

There's time to wander like this, to get acquainted with a ship that is both familiar and foreign. Currently only the crew and medical staff are on board. Soon we'll be brimming with thousands of patients.

For now, though, all that's to do is prepare. Nurse Macbeth, who'd been serving on *Britannic* for quite some time already, was nice enough to make the beds this morning, saving me from having to do so upon my arrival. On the bulletin, I see she'll be giving a morning gymnastics class and there'll be an afternoon game of cricket, followed by tea, along with an afternoon swim.

I'll pass on the latter.

In fact, I plan to do nothing but sit up on the deck until I'm needed. I think I may enjoy this interlude.

I pass a nurse in VAD uniform. We exchange smiles and she says, "Welcome, I'm Florence."

I chuckle. "I'm Violet, and you happen to be the fourth Florence to introduce herself."

"Well then, Violet," she says in a friendly manner, "if ever in doubt, you'll know which name to call out."

"How true," I muse. I continue on, my spirits already feeling lifted with this change in scenery, with the salt air, with the rocking motion. And look—there's Sheila, a stewardess I served with on *Olympic*.

"There you are, Violet," she says in greeting. Quite the straightforward woman, warm and fuzzy never her thing. As it was never mine either, except with those select few, it was simple to keep her as a mere acquaintance.

"Hi, Sheila," I say, prepared to continue as such.

"A post came in for you. I said I'd deliver it since I recognized your name."

"How kind of you."

And that's that. It may be the most we've ever spoken.

I breathe in the cool air, then see to my mail. It's addressed from Mother's nurse again, not uncommon at this point.

She often writes for reminders of Mother's favorite recipe: shepherd's pie.

With news that my sister Eileen is excelling at school despite being mostly deaf now. She's a wonder at reading lips.

And also little things, like how Mother likes the new parish priest and how they've taken to feeding a stray kitten.

But this letter isn't filled with feel-good updates. She cuts straight to the quick. My brother William has malaria. He contracted it in Malta, a location I didn't even know he was in.

Why? I don't understand why so many afflictions have come upon my family. Ray died of scarlatina. William survived diphtheria. Philip too. Denis died as an infant, unexpectedly, for reasons I still can't comprehend. Meningitis took Molly. There's Eileen, who had rheumatic fever. Mother's psychosis. Then me, having survived too many illnesses to bother listing them all, not that my brain would properly cooperate. It's spinning.

I press the heels of my palms into my temples.

It does little to help. The white walls of the ship swirl around me. Footsteps pound, growing louder. A hand grips my elbow. A face begins as three and narrows to two, then one. Somehow it's Leo's.

My Leo.

His presence causes even more confusion.

"Oh, no you don't," he says in a soothing voice. "I've seen that expression of yours before. Took a nice long nap last time. Hated seeing you like that. Now, Violet, take deep breaths."

"My brother . . . ," I begin.

He finishes, "Was fine last time. Now, I don't know if this is the same brother—you have a slew of them—but this one'll be fine as well. Here, let's have a sit-down."

I end up on a yet-to-be-occupied patient bed, my back ramrod straight, a hand pressing firmly on either knee.

"That a girl," Leo says, squatting in front of me. "Violet," he says, shaking his head. "I was more than shocked when I looked up and saw you." He lets out a huff, then points to my letter, wrinkled beneath my hand. "May I?"

I bobble my head.

"All right, let's see." He reads, then comments, "Okay. It's likely William is already on a regiment of quinine. He'll be getting plenty of rest. He's young, healthy. He could even be recovered by now, with how long the posts take to reach us."

I take a shaky breath. "Do you think so? I've had it."

"And here you are," Leo insists.

Yes, here I am. I've survived the very same illness that now inflicts my brother. I can only trust he's receiving the proper medication to pull through the fevers, but nothing is guaranteed in this world. What if he does not? I'll always wonder why him . . . and not me. I shake my head, dismayed over my brother, in shock that Leo is before me, reassuring me. "How do you know all of this? How are you even here?"

"I'm in the medical corps. This is a hospital ship. It's you I'm surprised to see. Are you with the VAD?"

"Stewardess," I say.

"Ah, back at it. So it's you I should go to if I'm in the need of an extra pillow?"

I raise a brow. He laughs. "There, I've succeeded at distract-ing you. Your breathing is back to normal."

It is, and my head no longer feels like it'll roll clear off my neck. "Thank you."

"My pleasure." He leans back on his heels. "I sure didn't think I'd see you again. I said goodbye, but I wager you didn't hear me."

I shake my head.

"Yeah, thought so. But I did. Told you I hoped to see you again."

His bright green eyes are nothing but sincere, but still I ask, "You did?"

"Of course. You were a much better alternative than hoping to see Clara again."

I laugh weakly at that. "She's not exactly the epitome for com-parison."

He shrugs, but then he lifts his hand toward my face. He stops just shy of my cheek. "The freckles here resemble a constellation. Aries, if my memory doesn't fail me."

His comment is like a weight, both anchoring me yet making me feel heavy. "My father used to say a face without freckles is like a sky without stars."

I trace my cheek, knowing exactly where each dot appears on my skin. Leo watches me as a silence stretches between us. Eventually I fold my hands in my lap. "So, you're a doctor of some sort?"

Leo watches me a heartbeat longer before he answers, "No, nothing like that. I've picked up some medical knowledge along the way, but I was an ambulance driver before. After I took that bullet, I wasn't quite cut out for the job anymore. I'm an embarka-tion medical officer now. Basically, I'm told every day how many patients are awaiting shipment. How many are lying cases or walking cases. Hospitals give me an idea of how many they can accommodate, and I figure out who is going where."

"And you like it?"

He nods. "Not how I saw myself finishing the war, but someone did all this for me. I like knowing I'm doing it for others now. Last time we ported in Southampton, it took fifteen hospital trains. Hate that number being so large, but also satisfying to know we helped thousands get the help they need." He smiles. "But you—how'd you end up back as a stewardess so soon?"

I'm too embarrassed to be honest that my body was too weak to stay away a minute longer. Instead, I sweep my arm, drawing Leo's gaze to the expansive sea.

He muses, "It's like it goes on and on, huh?"

"And on," I say, Leo seeming to miss the melancholy in my voice.

"And on, until we hit Naples for fueling." He checks his watch, more for theatrics than anything, because he says, "That's five days to Italy, and another two days sailing to Mudros to pick up our patients. Seven days, Violet. Uninterrupted, mostly. And I want to spend them with you."

"That's not necessary," I retort.

"Whyever not?" But he asks with a twinkle in his eye, as if he's prepared to wear me down.

I look toward the horizon. "I don't see the point."

"The point," he reasons, tipping his head toward mine, pulling my attention back, "is you are here. So am I. Did we ever think that'd happen again?"

"No," I say, this time in a different tone. One we both read as me acquiescing to the idea of spending time together.

He claps his hands. "Fabulous. I have big plans."

I raise a brow. "Already?"

"Fine. I *will* have big plans."

"Doing what?" I ask.

"Oh, you'll see."

CHAPTER 22

Daphne

___

CODE NAME CLAIRE
Alias Madame Claire Fondeu

La Ferté-Imbault train station
February 2, 1943

I SHOULD'VE ASKED MORE QUESTIONS. I SHOULD'VE ASKED Marie where exactly I was meant to ride in the train.

"Your chariot awaits," she says to me in a low voice, her bike leaning against her hip.

I sigh.

We stand off the platform, at the corner of a building. There's one passenger car after another. Plenty of room for little old me. Yet I'm meant to climb inside the coal bunker.

We have to get you discreetly over the demarcation line, Marie had told me on the way here.

"It's easier. It's cleaner," she says now, smirking at the double meaning, considering coal is the opposite of clean. "It's safer."

It'll be a lot less comfortable. But I reckon it can't be worse than riding beneath wet, heavy straw, inhaling my already breathed air that smelled of wolf urine.

The train whistle sounds.

The platform agent has his back to the fuel car. Marie pushes me. I take off at a sprint, holding my suitcase tightly against my chest.

At the coal bunker, I chuck in my suitcase, then hoist myself up, finding a foothold on an oversized bolt.

If the fireman standing on the footplate outside the coal bunker is surprised to see me, he doesn't let on. But of course he knows I'm a stowaway. This is all prearranged.

I offer him a smile and an awkward wave.

Half his mouth quirks into his own smile. Then he digs his shovel into the coal and turns to feed the boiler.

There's also another man on the footplate. My guess is he's the engineer, but if he sees me, he gives no indication of it.

I steady myself against the coal as the train begins to rattle down the track. When I reposition my hand, I see it's already blackened. I wipe it against my black coat, but there's no getting the grime out of the creases of my palms.

Every fifteen or twenty seconds, the fireman is back, digging his shovel into the coal. I find the coal shifting beneath me. I find myself having to move about the bunker, trying to dodge where he'll go digging for coal next.

And . . . I think the fireman is purposely shoveling coal from near me, making a game of it. I'm sure of it after I catch a grin on his face as he turns away toward the boiler to make his deposit.

He's younger than me. Perhaps even a decade younger. Attractive, too, I'll admit that.

I'll also admit to enjoying whatever it is that we're doing. Flirtation is so out of practice for me that I can't be sure it's what he's doing, even after he catches my eye, a full-blown smile forming on his sweat-streaked face.

The fireman feigns digging one way, I begin to shift, and he goes the other. I let out a laugh, the sound of it eaten up by the roar of the train.

It feels good to laugh. It feels good to let myself enjoy this man's antics for this moment in time.

During my last evasive maneuver, a strand of hair freed itself. Upon returning from the firebox, the fireman removes his glove. Slowly, a bit timidly, he tucks the strand behind my ear. His hand lingers there.

For a moment, I cannot breathe. When's the last time a man has touched me in a way that wasn't playful, professional, fatherly?

I can't recall.

Nor can I recall when exactly we crossed the demarcation line. With the free zone no longer existent, I don't see why this borderline still exists. But it still does and we make various stops, the checkpoint at Vierzon one of them. The Germans would've come on board to check identity papers and passes.

These passes are nearly impossible to get. All requests have to be accompanied by a full set of documents, including a reason for crossing. The majority of the time they are granted only for urgent needs, such as births, burials, serious illnesses—and only for close relations.

Then there's the fact foreigners are not allowed to travel. Jews are not allowed to travel north, though why would they want to? It's hardly safe. In addition to what I witnessed at the federation building, about six months ago, over ten thousand Jewish people—men, women, and children—were ripped from their homes, the streets, their places of work and sent to camps.

The thought makes me sick.

The thought makes me realize how fortunate I am that we could've forged a pass for me, if we had wanted. But as it turned out, London preferred this more unconventional way for me to travel.

I suppose it hasn't turned out half bad. Too soon, my time with the fireman is up. Hours have passed. Five, six, maybe more. Yet with my fireman it felt like a snap.

As the train slows, he takes my hand to help me from the coal bunker, the coal nearly gone. Even after my feet hit the footplate, he doesn't let go. Then he kisses my hand, like the train has transported us back to Regency days and he's about to put his name on my dancing card.

I snort at myself. I don't know what's gotten into me. It must be the heat of the boiler, the unfamiliar heat of a man's interest. Either way, I don't mind it.

⋆ ⋆ ⋆

THE NEXT LEG OF MY TRIP WILL CONTINUE BY TRAIN AS well. However, this time I'll travel in a passenger car, no need for a travel pass, only my new identity papers.

Next stop: Paris.

I'm not sure how I'll feel about being back. The idea of home is something I pondered during the quietness of the monastery, and I suppose Paris is the closest I have to it.

It's my last connection to my mother. It's where I worked and lived happily before the war. But it's also where I felt such shame for how France reacted to the Germans.

Not all Parisians folded, though. Not me. Not various clandestine groups and networks. Anti-German slogans have been left on walls; an underground press has been created; German officers suffer the same attacks they impose. It's all so dangerous, and any retribution by the Germans is quick-handed and severe.

It was also at the monastery where I internalized how much worse it could've been for me in prison. The fact I was not tortured makes me fear being caught and tortured even more.

I can liken the fear to a childhood memory. Something silly, nonsensical in the grand scheme of things, but my best course of comparison. I was at boarding school with Josette. The kids were playing pinfinger. Truly, an asinine and harebrained game, if it can even be called a game. I prefer my games to be time well spent.

Nevertheless, Josette and I had been wheedled into playing, both having been accused of being too hoity-toity to join in the "fun."

So there I was, my fingers splayed on the tabletop. Then one of the girls brought down a knife between each of my fingers.

Faster and faster she went. I didn't blink. I stared at my hand, willing the knife to *thud, thud, thud* on the tabletop and not into my flesh and bone.

With laughter, she stopped, declaring it was Josette's turn.

And while Josette suffered through the same experience, I realized I could never partake in such a thing again.

I wasn't stabbed. And so I don't know what it feels like for the blade to pierce my skin. Granted, I'm glad I don't. I know it'd be painful. But how badly would it hurt? Would it leave a scar? Could I lose the finger entirely?

I was more scared after than I was before.

And that is how I feel about the idea of one day being tortured.

It's a thought I ponder as I board my second train. It's crowded, and I immediately sense an uneasiness in the air.

There are Germans, many of them, and their scowls are more hardened than usual.

What have I missed while stowed away in the coal bunker for hours?

Regrettably, the only available seat nearly puts me on the lap of a German officer. I offer him a congenial smile, so different from the one I'd given to my fireman. Truth be told, I'd much rather be back in the dirty bunker than giving this artificial greeting. But if I do not, it'd seem like a personal affront.

His expression changes little, perhaps the slightest hint of a smile.

That out of the way, I position my suitcase between my knees. My suitcase with a slew of incriminating items, like a revolver and ammunition and replacement quartz crystals for a wireless. There'd be no confusing the crystals for gemstones. They look more like something you'd plug into an electrical outlet, encased in a hard black plastic.

On my body is even more he cannot know about. Wrapped

securely under my black cloth belt, Marie and I have hidden
banknotes and blank identity and ration cards.

Even with the warmth of the train car, I'd prefer to keep my
coat on as another layer between my contraband and the officer,
but the wool is covered in coal dust and I'm afraid it'll rub off on
him, inciting unwanted questions and conversation.

He already seems excitable, in all the wrong ways, folding
and refolding his coat, his foot tapping excessively. Seeing his feet
pulls my attention to my own, where I've left a residue on the
train floor. I won't move them again.

Shifting only my eyes, I gauge the others in the train car,
hoping to overhear something that could clue me in as to what's
happened.

I learn soon enough.

Marie had said the Germans were surrounded at Stalingrad.
Now they've surrendered. Victory goes to the Soviets. And nearly
a hundred thousand Germans have gone to prison.

"Including twenty-two generals," a German officer says under his breath in German from the next row of seats. "Paulus too."

The German beside me goes rigid.

Another responds, "The Führer is furious."

"No wonder. He gave direct orders not to surrender, but Paulus didn't listen."

And with all of Germany's ridiculous propaganda, I bet
these Germans don't know how bad it was for their comrades
in Russia's winter. I'm speculating myself. But I know with zero
speculation that an angry Hitler is an even more dangerous Hitler. A ticking time bomb. I keep my expression blank. I know
this loss is gigantic for the Germans. The battle had been raging
in Stalingrad for over five months. But an even bigger compo-
nent of the defeat is how this is the first of Hitler's field armies
to surrender.

I reposition in my seat, the officer's folded coat jostling with
my movement, and I've done it; I've stirred his attention.

I avert my eyes. The German focuses more intently on me; I can feel it.

"And what brings you here today?" he asks, not unkindly, yet there's still an edge to his voice, like he could become cruel if provoked. His question comes in German, giving me a decision to make. Do I feign not understanding his question? Or do I respond in German, which may make me appear accepting of his presence in France?

I respond, "Returning home to Paris."

"And what brought you down this way?"

"I'm a seamstress," I say. "My cousin is getting married and asked me to visit to create her dress."

This lie seems plausible and the need large enough. There's a shortage of many things, clothing included.

I smile politely once more, an attempted punctuation mark to our exchange. If he says, "And what," a third time, I'll scream. There's a pompousness to his wording.

Unfortunately, this is not the end. Even more unfortunate, he says, "It appears I am in luck on this very unlucky day as I am in the need of a seamstress."

His coat is draped across his lap and onto mine, no care for my personal space. He turns it until he finds where a button has gone missing. He points at it, not even bothering to ask me nicely to aid him in sewing it back on. He just assumes I'll do his bidding.

"Of course," I say calmly, while internally I'm panicking. "Do you have the missing button? I'm afraid I don't have one that would match."

"You know this without even looking?"

I release a small laugh. "I'm a bit meticulous."

"This time you are the one in luck." He turns the coat until he finds the coat's pocket and produces the missing button.

My neck prickles with heat. "Wonderful," I lie.

What to do now?

Do I attempt to sew it? How hard could reattaching a button be? I can detonate a bomb, for pity's sake.

But that would require me to open my suitcase. My sewing bag is at the top. There's a chance that is all he'd see. But if he decides to look beneath . . . then I'm in a world of trouble.

It truly would be his lucky day.

And while I've deliberated, he's been holding the button out to me, annoyance building on his sharp features.

I begin to offer him my palm, then realize that even after wiping my hands, I wasn't able to remove all traces of the coal. Instead, I try to pinch the button from his fingers.

It's a failed attempt at trying to hide the coal. There's coal dust under my nails.

He regards me with disgust. Germans like their cleanliness.

My cheeks heat, despite the fact I don't care if he likes me or not. Though perhaps my reaction is endearing to him. Or maybe he enjoys seeing me embarrassed. Or maybe he simply wants his button reattached as it unsettles him severely to have it missing.

He releases the button and gestures to my suitcase.

Heart racing, I unclip the snaps and begin to open it just enough to reach my hand into my sewing bag for a needle and thread. The spool and needle case should be easy enough to blindly find.

But no, this is not how it goes. The officer kicks the lid of my suitcase, causing it to fly open and bang against the linoleum flooring.

"And what else do you have in here?"

I want to growl, while also throttling this arrogant, haughty man. German or not, I'd despise him. The fact he's German, though, also makes me fear him.

Within view is my toothbrush case, a sewing bag, and a box of sanitary napkins. Inside are the crystals. Beneath all the visible items, wrapped in spare clothing, are the gun and ammo.

If that gun is found, I'll be arrested. If I'm arrested, I'll be searched. The blank identity papers, the blank passes, the banknotes will all be found.

They'd question me aggressively to learn what I know and why I have such items. There's no way I wouldn't be tortured this time.

I ignore his inquisitive question and hastily reach for my sewing bag. "Let me just get the needle and—"

"I said, what else do you have in here?"

The audacity . . . In what other world would it be okay for a full-blown stranger to snoop around in my belongings? But this is what Occupation looks like. They can do whatever they want.

And I'd be a fool to try to tell him no right now.

"My toothbrush. I never go anywhere without one." I force a smile.

He shakes his head dismissively and points toward the Kotex box. "What's in there?"

A woman would never ask that question. But perhaps this is my chance to make him so uncomfortable that he abandons his investigation. "They are sanitary napkins to collect and dispose of my monthly bleeding."

Each word of my sentence hits him harder than the last. By the time I reach *bleeding* he's paled in color. I'll be a monkey's uncle if he asks to see what's inside the box now.

I hear, but don't dare acknowledge, a few chuckles from surrounding men.

From the officer's throat comes a low rumble. He snaps, "And what's beneath it all?"

I startle, a very true reaction, and in doing so his button slips from my fingertips and rolls beneath another seat.

"Oh!" I say. "I'm sorry. I'll get it."

Though I have no intention of actually finding the button. I begin to drop to all fours, but the officer says in the most demeaning of voices, "Have you no self-respect, woman? You'd go crawling about the floor like some dog? All for a button?"

My cheeks flush again. I close my suitcase and then sit back in my seat, folding my hands in my lap. My dirty hands. He eyes them, perhaps thinking he was a fool to ask me to touch his belongings. I think he's had enough of me. There's little room to inch away, but I can feel him trying.

I have a mind to start coughing, a real phlegmy-sounding one, to make him fear I'll infect him with an illness. But no, I won't press my luck. So I take a deep breath and allow my racing heart to slowly, slowly return to normal.

CHAPTER 23

Violet

—

Aboard *Britannic*
November 17, 1916

HOW WILL I EVER RETURN TO NORMAL AFTER FIVE DAYS traipsing around the ship with Leo? It turns out to be the happiest five days I've spent in a long, long time.

How quickly he becomes familiar. We joke, we laugh, I lose at cricket, we walk, we skip like children, we share stories. I speak of *Titanic*, the first I ever have. He animatedly recounts how he ran with the bulls in Pamplona.

I feel things I've never felt before. Things I thought would only ever be a luxury. Things I know can only be fleeting.

Still, Leo is intoxicating. Persistent. Hopeful. Impulsive. Playful. And so I allow myself this second respite from real life.

We drink, we eat, we kiss, we play cards, and we talk of the future.

Well, Leo does. I *uh-huh* him when he says how the war's changed him, has created a sort of desperation in him to go after what he wants. He says we'll see out this war *together* on *Britannic*, and then *together* we'll both find vocations we're passionate about.

"Uh-huh."

"Still at sea, you think?" he asks me.

"I don't know."

"If you could do anything, something you've never done before, what would it be?"

I pull my bottom lip between my teeth. Well, besides nursing, doing *anything* isn't something I've ever been able to consider. My honest answer is still "I don't know."

Eventually he insists that we'll retire in a country cottage— Suffolk is an option—as close to the water as possible so I can still smell the salt air. We'll collect chicken eggs and tend to a garden. "If you want to, that is."

I shrug, which feels insufficient to Leo's glowing face. It sounds beautiful, and fitting for him. I wouldn't mind it too. Playing house with him between my ship duties has been fun. Leo even helps me make up the beds one morning, remarking about how it's a glimpse into our future.

"Uh-huh," I tell him.

Now on the boat deck, I peer blankly over the water, a break in my day. Leo is on the promenade, doing a final check of hospital beds. A mere deck below me, though I wish I could see through to see him, so smart in his uniform.

This isn't the first time I have to remind myself that I'm taking these days for what they are: a holiday before the ship fills with patients, before the war ends and Leo and I go our separate ways. Leo to a future that's as exciting and vibrant and spontaneous as he is. And me . . . back to my mother, who I pray doesn't know about William's illness. Back to my sister, whose future is as uncertain to me as the ocean's depths. Will she be able to find work being unable to hear? Will she ever have the opportunity to find love? Will I?

Have I?

Am I squandering it away because my life is too complicated to unload on another human being? Or maybe because my life doesn't feel like my own to begin with. Or even that my heart seizes at the notion of losing myself to Leo, only for him to be ripped away in some way. The war. Illness. Another woman.

I grip the railing, Naples just coming into view. Right now

there are too many maybes for *one day* . . . *someday* to ever feel like a reality.

"Found you," Leo says, his arms wrapping around me where I stand at the railing, his chin perching on my shoulder. It can't be a comfortable position, nearly bent in half. I'm a full two heads shorter than him.

"Here I am," I say. "And here comes Naples."

I feel his smile, his chin rounding into me. I ask him, "How long does refueling generally take?"

"All day."

I tilt my head toward him, trying to see his expression. I sensed a hint of mischievousness in his voice and it's matched on his face.

"All day for those big plans you've spoken of but haven't yet delivered on?"

He spins me, facing us toward each other. "What? These past few days haven't been enough?"

More than you'll ever know, Leo.

But of course I don't say that.

His gaze trains on my face. Then he runs a thumb down my forehead, right over a worry line I know that's there, stopping at the bridge of my nose.

★ ★ ★

THERE'S A CAR WAITING FOR US AS WE DISEMBARK.

"You arranged this?" I ask him, cupping my eyes against the late morning sun.

"O ye of little faith." He takes my hand, bringing us from a walk to a jog. "It's ours for the day."

I point back at the ship that we've both been on for days. "How?"

"When there's a will, there's a way."

The roads are windy, our driver barefooted, my grip firm on Leo's leg, but I can't wipe the grin from my face.

Charming. All of it. The scenery. The hillsides. The fountains. The churches. The castles and palaces. My company. A spaghetti lunch at a quaint country inn.

Afterward, we walk hand in hand through a marketplace. Leo plucks a small figurine from a table. "My sister would love this. Has these types of knickknacks all over her home." He asks the vendor how much, haggles, then finalizes the transaction with a winning smile. "Now I only have my nieces and nephew left to shop for."

Which he quickly accomplishes.

"There," Leo says. He doesn't actually do it, but I imagine him dusting off his hands. "My work here as a brother and uncle is done."

I laugh. "How nice for you." But I could also say, "How simple for you."

"How about you, Vi? Want to make any purchases for Christmas? Now's the time, and I reckon your shopping list is a mile long."

"My mother, four brothers, and a sister."

"Oh, a sister too? You haven't yet mentioned her."

"*Sí*, Eileen." I leave it at that, focusing instead on a bracelet lined with small rhinestones. She'll love it.

I add a bluebird pin—which the vendor says is for happiness—and four sets of cuff links to my holiday trove. A successful shopping trip. A successful day in general.

All thanks to Leo. I'm giddy and full of spunk and saddened to return to the ship and leave Naples and this whimsical existence with Leo behind.

I wish this day could go on and on. Dr. Lowndes had said that a change of scenery from land to sea may be what I needed to get back my strength and zest. But I think I needed a Leo.

If only he could last. Leo's begun to take up such a large part of my mind and heart that I'd even risk a life with him. If that were possible. But Leo's vision of what my life could be and the reality of all my life can become are vastly different.

We are just climbing the gangplank to *Britannic* when a fat raindrop hits the tip of my nose. A step later, the sky opens.

Leo takes my hand, leading me toward the ship's overhang. A squeal leaves my lips. Finally undercover, I find myself out of breath, laughing, hair plastered to my forehead and cheeks.

Leo brushes the hair away from my face. "Well, that was something."

I peer around him at the dark sky, growing more sinister by the second. The grand ship rocks beneath us. "It'll continue to be something is my guess."

Leo looks caught between the realization that the ship likely won't be going anywhere tonight, giving us more time together before picking up patients, and the knowledge that those patients are awaiting our help.

"We'll be there as soon as we can," I reassure him.

He nods and dips to my height. "How is it that you can read my mind already? I bet you'll be doing it until we're old and gray, Vi."

I look into his brilliant green eyes, nothing but sincerity and newfound adoration there. The weight of my family's Christmas gifts hangs across my chest.

"Uh-huh," I say, and I kiss him.

CHAPTER 24

Daphne

CODE NAME CLAIRE
Alias Madame Claire Fondeu

La Ferté-Imbault train station
February 2, 1943

I COULDN'T ARRIVE IN PARIS QUICKLY ENOUGH, JUST NOW stepping to the train platform. It's here I'm to meet my husband.

The note from London didn't include the intricacy or details of our ruse. I find it interesting that my cover name and code name are one and the same. There must be a story there.

I wonder if I'm to live in his residence? That could be quite awkward, though I did share a space with Gabriel and Louis just fine. I also wonder if the appearance of a sudden wife will raise questions.

All will be revealed soon.

I peer left and right through the many bodies on the platform.

It's comical, really. I'm searching for a man, yet I have no clue what he looks like. In one of my father's films, his love interest donned a specific flower in order to be identified upon their first meeting.

Perhaps he's been told to look for the tired, grimy woman covered in coal. I'm a dead ringer.

I walk on, lugging my suitcase at my side. He'll find me. The crowd is thinning and still no Evan Fondeu.

"Claire," I hear in a deep voice from behind. It's not spoken as a question. There's confidence in how he says the name, as if he's been doing it for years.

I begin to turn, already saying, *"Bonjour."*

Hello, I repeat in my head, a bit taken aback by his attractiveness. Tall, dark, and handsome, a very strong likeness to Rudolph Valentino, for whom the cliché was popularized.

I had meant to include Evan's name upon greeting him, to showcase my own familiarity, but before I can get another word in, his mouth touches mine.

I'm more than a little surprised. But it's over so quickly, just the briefest of pecks, that I've little time to react. He chases the kiss with a tight embrace.

I'm once again trying to play catch-up to his acting abilities, my arms pinned at my sides, yet fully aware of how hard my heart is pounding against him. When there's space between us again, he snatches the suitcase from my hand. "On our way, then, darling?"

I almost ask the man to give me a moment, for Pete's sake. "Yes," I say, a soft titter escaping me as our hello finally registers in my brain as comical. "Of course, honey. Oh, how I've missed you."

I almost add "husband," but it feels a bit too on the nose. Though not a bad gig, to have to playact as this man's wife. Certainly an improvement over my last one, whom I fictionalized as an ogre in my head. Evan wears a black work cap over his nearly black hair. His coat is long and black. Very coordinated. He's older than me, I'd guess, but I'm not certain of his age. I'd put him at no more than forty, though. What I like most is his height. Being a woman of considerable height, I enjoy looking up, not down.

Short in height, short in morals.

An unfair generalization, I realize as soon as I think it. I'm projecting from the man I dated who turned out to be, unbeknownst to me, married. Apparently I haven't fully put that behind me.

Evan's strides are twice the length of mine, and my heels *click-clack* against the platform to keep up. Outside the station, I get my first real look at Paris since I left.

Remarkably, it looks much the same. No clear destruction. Fewer people, yes, but it's still a major city with major foot traffic. The people who walk about, however, seem cold with one another. Parisians are generally very friendly, especially those they are familiar with. But so many are walking by each other without a raise of their head or hand.

Has the Occupation created a general sense of mistrust here, not knowing in whom you can confide?

And here I am, about to hop into a total stranger's lorry. He motions toward it.

"Evan?" I ask. If nothing else, I can at least confirm his name.

His head cocks. "Yes?"

"Just making sure."

Amusement crosses his face. His smile deepens the cleft in his chin. It's something we have in common, a rare trait, and somehow makes him instantly more familiar.

I climb into the passenger side of the lorry's bench seat, watching as he rounds to his side, dropping my suitcase into the bed.

Wordlessly he joins me, starts the engine, and off we go. I pick at the grime beneath my nails. Now that my fear has fully abated, I can fondly remember how uncomfortable I made the German officer.

I sense Evan's eyes on me a moment before he says, "You're smiling."

I snort. "Just remembering something."

He doesn't ask what, but he does say, "I take it Claire's not your real name? That'd be too much of a coincidence."

I waggle my brows. It's not something I've ever done before. But I think of my fireman flirting with me. It felt good.

Evan's brows crease. "What on earth does that mean?"

I slap a hand over my face. "Nothing. Just nothing." Flirting with my faux husband is likely a bad idea. I think I waggled all wrong anyway. "Just please think of me as Claire Fondeu."

He sighs.

"You're sighing."

"I am."

But that's all he says.

And he continues not to say much until we've left Paris. On a winding road, he stops and gets out. A moment later he returns with my suitcase. "Mind hopping up a second?"

"Um, sure." I comply, and he lifts the bench to expose a cavity beneath. My suitcase barely fits, but it's in. He plops the bench closed, gives me a wink, then settles back into the driver's side.

"How clandestine of you," I remark.

That earns me a second wink and promptly makes my stomach do a weird thing. For some reason, there are few things sexier than doing something surreptitious with a scrumptious-looking man.

And, okay, I cannot be having these thoughts.

Minutes, then hours tick by, neither of us saying another word. I don't even ask where we're headed. I assume Plouha, which is in the coastal region of Brittany about four hours from Paris. It's listed as my place of residence on my new identity papers.

My new home with my new husband.

Now that's not something I ever saw myself saying. Or at least not anytime soon.

Every once in a while, Evan glances at me. It makes me even more nervous, as if he's working something he wants to say around in his brain.

Well, I have my own questions. The next time he sneaks a peek at me, I start with an icebreaker. "You kissed me."

A hint of red rises in his cheeks. "I'm supposed to be your husband. I wanted to sell it."

"A job well done." I'm smirking. "And who is my husband?"

"A butcher."

"They told me that. I mean, who are you to France, in this war?"

He taps the wheel, his gaze remaining on the road. "I'm picking you up. I'm pretending you're my wife. I'm allowing you to stay in my home, fully knowing who you work for. That should answer your question, no?"

So a Théo, maybe even a Gaspar. "Do you take orders or give them?"

This gets a hint of a smile from him. "I work with a cleaver. Not many people tell me what to do."

I laugh. So the Gaspar of this area.

"Though Francis—or whatever his real name is—likes to think he's in charge."

Francis, my new network leader.

"Well, I hope you two are able to play nice for the sake of France."

Evan looks at me again. "You don't seem British," he says. There's a question in there. I can tell he's curious about my story.

I smile. "Good."

He nods. "Yeah, I guess it is."

The situation we are in is an odd one. When I became Irene du Tertre, it was very black and white. This is who you are. This is your backstory. I had the flexibility to develop it from there. But this time is different, with Claire Fondeu being a real person, the real wife of the man beside me . . . a woman who is no longer here, who is no longer his wife.

Why is that? How is that?

I should know why. I *have* to know why. And I know my next question may be uncomfortable—for the both of us—but it feels important if I'm to play my part. "So the real Claire Fondeu, who is she?"

"You are now, apparently."

"Okay, yes." I pause. I scratch the side of my neck. "But before me?"

"My wife."

I nod. Twice. Three times, working up courage. "Where is she now?

"Gone."

As in . . . dead, missing, imprisoned?

His tone doesn't invite further questioning on the topic, so I pivot, asking, "Who is she? So I can better play the part. And please don't say 'a seamstress.'"

"Claire Fondeu"—he clears his throat—"isn't someone I thought would be in my life ever again. But her identity was for the taking, and so . . ."

"London took it and gave it to me?" I feel as if I should apologize.

"It was my idea. So I can't be mad. It's just strange." He runs a hand over the stubble on his cheeks and chin.

"I get that."

But . . .

I clear my own throat. The day has turned to night, shrouding us both in a growing darkness. It helps, with the present awkwardness. I have to ask, "Do I look like her?"

"No."

I lick my lips. "Will that be a problem?"

"Not for the Germans."

But for him?

Evan adds, "They've never seen her before."

"Claire's friends, though? I should know who they are, right? I should know about her life."

Like how she died. Or where she is now. And how it's possible for me to use her identity . . .

He snorts. "Claire wasn't much for people, which is comical because we worked and lived at my shop. She always pretended to be friendly to help the business, hers and mine, which got her invited everywhere and got her caught inviting women up for tea. Always people coming and going."

"I can use that," I say. "In case we're bringing people in and out."

He nods.

I twist my lips. "Is there a story for where I've been or won't it be strange that I'm suddenly here?"

"Lots of people here are involved with what we're doing. They know about Claire, about you."

"And we can trust them?"

I can sense the tension even without fully seeing his face. "I've known these people my entire life. As far as the Germans, we'll say you were stuck south of the demarcation line and have just now been able to come north."

"Okay," I say. "That's sound." That part at least. And because this moment feels like it calls for it, I make a joke, adding, "Though we'll leave off how that crossing took place in a coal bunker."

He raises his brow at that.

I could explain, but I press on. I have another question I need to work up the courage to ask. I swallow. "So I've been gone. For how long?"

I think he'll clear his throat again, except, no, this time he lets out a long breath. "Two years."

I want to ask him if he's okay, if his heart is okay. It feels too personal. I won't ask. Besides, it's not the right time; we're slowing, a checkpoint ahead.

There's a paper on the dash. He slides it off and into his lap. He rolls down his window.

"Pass and identity papers?" we're asked.

I take mine from my coat pocket and hand it to Evan. Without a word, he lets the officer review them. I consider reaching over and holding Evan's hand or perhaps squeezing his knee. Something a married couple would do? Before I can decide, the check-point officer dips to see me better, shining a light in my face. I'm left seeing stars when the beam of light moves to Evan's face.

Then the officer hands back the papers and motions us on.

"A pass to get into Brittany?" I ask.

"Yep," Evan says, accelerating us away from the checkpoint. He checks his mirrors. "Only people from here are allowed in and out. The Germans have declared us a forbidden zone. Hitler is building what's being called his Atlantic Wall. Basically barbed wire, mines, machine-gun towers all along the coast. A series of defenses with us being so close to the Channel and Britain."

What he says makes sense. Still, I scrunch my brows. I'd been waiting to talk to Francis about my official role in our mission. All my orders from London said was that I'd be there to help with an escape line. "This escape line of ours, will we need to get people into Brittany?"

"That's right."

"So we'll need to forge passes?"

"Or smuggle them in."

"Right. Then . . . from there, what's this escape line of ours? The other escape lines I've heard of take people over the Pyrenees to Spain."

"This is *Breizh*."

"*Breizh*?"

"Breton for Brittany."

"Of course. I knew this region had its own language." I shake my head at forgetting that detail from my studies. "Say something else in Breton."

His head ticks my way. "Excuse me?"

"Anything," I say.

"*N'eus mounnoù Pyrenees ebet amañ.*"

I twist my lips. "Something about the Pyrenees?"

"I said those mountains are not here."

"Well, okay, yes, I know that—"

"But we have lots of water."

Something sinks in me as realization strikes. "We're to help people escape by ship?"

He eyes me as he makes a sharp turn. "Not a fan of the water?"

"You could say that."

"Fitting. Claire wasn't either."

I try to read the tone of his voice, but I can't gather much. "Well, it's fine," I eventually say. "I'm not the one escaping."

It'll be downed pilots and refugees I'll be sending off on those steel behemoths. Hopefully hundreds of them. Important work. Crucial, in fact. London would much rather recover an experienced pilot than train a new one. Just the thought of getting started on this new mission gets my knee bouncing.

Evan turns off the lorry, then drops his hands from the wheel. "We're here. *Degemer da Breizh.*"

"You spoke more Breton." I smile, debating if I should tell him languages are one of my most favorite things. "Okay, don't translate yet." I hold up my pointer finger as I try to reason out what he said.

He watches me, the same amusement I saw at the train station blooming on his face again.

For the fun of it, I flex my own language muscles. "*Da* in Russian is 'yes.' Not a word in English. In French it's 'there.' Same with German. In Italian it's 'from.' 'Gives' in Spanish. 'That' in Croatian." I close one eye, as if that'll help.

"I can just tell you," he offers.

I make an intelligible sound and wave a hand at him. "*Da* in Arabic is 'this.'"

"Arabic? Come on."

"Mm-hmm. I think *da* can also mean 'good.'"

I'm not sure. I think Breton is closest to Cornish, which I absolutely do not know. "Fine," I say, "tell me."

"You're sure? Not any other languages you'd like to sort through? I could really see your mind working there."

I narrow my eyes, which pulls a laugh from him. "It means 'Welcome to Brittany.'"

"Oh. Well, thank you," I say, committing the words to my memory, eager to add more. "I'm very happy to be in *Breizh*."

The darkness steals Evan's expression, but the silence that stretches between us makes my stomach begin to flutter.

Twice I think he'll say something. When he finally does, it comes in a gruff voice. "Let's get you inside."

He doesn't flick on any lights as we enter his butcher shop. As my eyes adjust, I make out a long counter that stretches the length of the room. He lifts a portion of it and we cross beneath.

"Back through that door," he says in a soft voice, "are the freezers, fridge, the grinder, a kitchen, and such. This place has been in my family for generations. We're going to go this way." Evan guides me through another door that leads up steep stairs. My suitcase bangs against the step a few times.

"Careful," I say. "I have crystals in there for my wireless op."

"Zacharie."

"Thank you. I didn't yet know his name. I'm assuming I'll be meeting Francis and Zacharie—"

"Tomorrow." At the top of the stairs, there's a second door. Evan pauses. "I'm sure it's not what you're used to back in London."

"You know nothing about me." I smile. "You could have a palace up here."

He laughs. "I wouldn't get your hopes up. It's not much, but it's everything."

What a touching sentiment.

Though the man's not lying. As soon as he turns on the lights, I see pretty much the entirety of his home in one shot. The only part I cannot see is behind a small privacy screen off in a corner.

All the windows are covered, keeping our light inside.

Immediately I notice the elephant in the room.

"There's only one bed," I point out, as if this is news to him.

He runs a hand through his hair. "Yeah . . ."

"Is there a couch or . . . anything besides a table and piano?"

Truly, that's all there is. I'm tempted to peek beneath the tablecloth. All I can think to do next is ask a lighthearted yet leading question. "Um, how long have we been married?"

He snorts. "Nine years."

"Wow, okay. That's longer than I expected. And we're adults. You stay on your side of the bed. I'll stay on mine."

Evan points awkwardly to the floor. "I can sleep—"

"Don't be ridiculous." I do my own pointing, to a door. "Is that the toilet?"

With confirmation, I escape inside.

When I emerge, my fingernails free of coal, all the lights are off other than a lamp on the bedside table. Evan is sitting up in the bed, no doubt trying to appear casual.

If I didn't press my lips together, I wouldn't be able to stop a laugh at how uncomfortable this is for him too. I'm cognizant of every movement I make as I get into my side of the bed, trying to do so without flopping in like a walrus.

Evan's throat bobs on a swallow. "You know," he begins, "this would be a lot less awkward if I knew your real name. It's only fair since you know mine."

"Nice try, buckaroo."

Fair or not, Evan and I will only exist as Evan and Claire, and only for the duration of my time here. Besides the obvious risks of blowing my cover—though I don't doubt being able to trust Evan—there's no need for him to know about my past. Or my future, for that matter.

"Buckaroo?"

I fold over my covers neatly, busying my hands. "You apparently have never seen an American western."

"British." Evan taps a finger. "American westerns." He taps

another. "Russian, German, Arabic, for crying out loud." He runs out of fingers. "Yet fluent, pure French. You may be the perfect agent."

I waggle a brow. This time it lands better, Evan laughing.

"Okay, *Claire*," he says, emphasizing the name. "You win. For now."

I shimmy lower into the sheets. "Good night, Evan."

I'm hyperaware of how close he is to me. I could stretch out my pinky finger and touch him. But I won't. I can't. Again, I blame the fireman from earlier. He's put me in a flirting mindset, primed to meet this new handsome husband of mine.

"Night, you," he says, then the light goes off.

In the morning, there he is, Evan sprawled out beside me. And because it'd be completely weird to wander about his home in search of coffee beans, I don't move.

Instead, I decide to watch him, exponentially weirder.

Who is this man, who was married and shared his life with someone for almost a decade, who has a long history here in *Breizh*, who is willing to risk his life to defy the Germans?

Besides the last point, we couldn't be more different.

Boarding schools were not homes. Schools existed for a finite number of years. Visits with my father at one of our various houses had an extremely abbreviated expiration date. My relationships were all short-lived.

Evan seems like the type that sticks around.

He stirs and I press my eyes closed. The bed shifts as he gets up. I lie there, motionless, pretending to be asleep as he opens drawers, goes in and out of the toilet.

Eventually I hear his footsteps going down the stairs.

I peek an eye open. Then two, my gaze falling on the privacy screen across the room. Curious, the rest of the space an open book, I make my way in that direction.

What I find feels like it's been frozen in time.

A table with a sewing machine. Various rolls of fabric leaning against the table. Scraps of cloth, a measuring tape, scissors, chalk . . . all strewn about on the tabletop.

"It's all exactly as she left it," I hear.

I twist to find Evan standing behind me, a hand on the privacy screen, a long apron down to his knees.

"Dust excluded." He tries for a smile.

"I'm sorry."

"Me too."

I want to clarify that yes, I'm sorry she's no longer here, but that I'm also sorry because it feels like I'm intruding.

But then he says, "She was very talented. We met in Paris. I'm there from time to time, some bigger buyers. I practically ran her over. Not with my truck"—he smiles—"On a footpath, but I completely upended her sewing bag. You like films, it seems. And our connection seemed straight from one, not that I've seen many. In a matter of days, we were married, madly in love. She came back to *Breizh* with me. I was so proud to show her off. This put-together, charismatic, beautiful Parisian who had chosen me, a butcher." He puffs. "It was an adjustment for her, for sure. Little town, everybody knowing everybody. But she adjusted. She began making clothes for people. I think she brought more people into the shop than the meat and fish at times." He smiles at this. "Then one day . . ." He twists his nose, sniffs. "Well, one day it was all over."

My mouth parts. I do not know what to say, other than I'm sorry, but I've already said that. It feels worth saying again, though. I repeat the words just as someone else says, "Knock, knock."

As Evan turns, he wipes the emotion from his eyes. "Francis," he says. "Look who's arrived."

I step out from behind the privacy screen and give an arching wave with my hand. "Hello."

"Claire, wonderful," Francis begins. "There's much to do."

I glance at Evan. If I hadn't been here for our conversation, I never would've known this man had just been spilling out his

heart. The real Claire Fondeu stole this man's heart and subsequently broke him. And here I am, throwing her—if only in
name—back into his life. This isn't going to be easy, for either of
us. But I know it'll be significantly easier if I tread lightly and keep
from pressing on that bruise.

★ ★ ★

FRANCIS WAS NOT DOWNPLAYING THAT THERE'S LOTS TO DO.

I begin with giving Francis his new blank identity papers,
which he snatches up, and Zacharie his replacement crystals. He
snatches as well.

Fortunately, because of Evan's extensive network in *Breizh*—
aka his twenty-some local friends—Zacharie has seemingly
endless places to stay as he transmits with London.

It saves me the trouble of having to find locations here for him
or eventually for our escapees.

That leaves me with hunting only in Paris, where we'll hide
the pilots and refugees until we slowly but surely relocate them
into Brittany's forbidden zone. But the city—*kêr* in Breton, Evan
translates for me—will be ripe with apartments to rent, resistants
with attics to use, and unfortunately many abandoned proper-
ties from Parisians who have fled. Then there's the surrounding
provinces and their farms and barns.

Francis tells me that our first round of pilots and refugees to
escape via ship—those poor souls—will be arriving in May, three
months from now.

"How many?" I ask him.

He shrugs. "As many as we can get out."

"Hundred? More?"

"Ambitious of you," he says.

"Less, then?"

"We'll shoot for a hundred. How about that?"

A hundred it is. I create a mental checklist . . .

Forged identity cards.

Clothing.

Food.

Passes for Brittany's forbidden zone.

Or, for those we smuggle in, moonless nights.

Three months to accomplish all of this.

But first: "Evan," I say, "will you introduce me to the local printing press? Or . . . will this be more of a reintroduction?"

"You already know him."

I nod. "Okay, then, let's go have a talk with . . ."

"Ronan," Evan supplies.

We find him outside his press, about to head inside. He sees me. He sees Evan. His eyes come back to me. Evan nods. There must have been a prior conversation about my arrival and the part I'm to play. Understanding blooms on Ronan's face, and before I know it, he's kissing both my cheeks and talking speedily in Breton.

A group of Germans sit at a table, bundled in their hats and scarves, in the midst of a late breakfast from the bistro next door. The downtown—*kreiz kêr*—is picturesque, plucked from a postcard, with fountains, though dry for the winter, stoned roads, various parks, half-timbered homes, shops, and cafés, most with wood statues and other ornate features carved into their sides.

I muse it'd be even more beautiful without the men in greenish-gray uniforms.

I return my focus to Evan. He's responding in Breton, his sentence ending in laughter. "You know Claire hasn't fully tackled the language yet. Let's continue in French, yes?"

"Please," I say. "But I wouldn't mind the translation of a word here and there. I'd like to continue to learn."

Ronan arches a brow. He's an older man, those brows resembling caterpillars. Something passes between him and Evan. Something about Claire?

But no, I chastise myself. After Francis interrupted Evan and me, I told myself I wouldn't push again on the bruise that is Claire no longer being here. Her departure from Evan, however that took form, isn't a part of my current narrative.

And when my curiosity undoubtedly gets the better of me again, I'll need to remind myself of that once more. For now, I'm content to follow Ronan inside. It's his help I need. Actually, it's his paper.

Paper that'll work for the identity cards and forbidden-zone passes.

As we leave, I call out, "I'll be back next week, then, to measure you for those pants."

I'm certain the Germans—still enjoying their leisurely non-rationed meal—have heard me. Brilliant. When I return, they shouldn't bat an eyelash at me being here.

I spend that week familiarizing myself with Plouha. Like I did in Lyon, I bike, I bus, and I make myself a commonplace rosy-cheeked figure as I move about the charming thirteenth-century abbey and gardens at Beauport, the harbor at Paimpol, the quaint buildings and washhouse along the canal in Pontrieux, the village at La Roche-Derrien, the basilica in Guingamp, and the Pointe du Roselier, with its stunning view of the cliffs and beaches. Though less stunning with its current fortifications, on account of Hitler's Atlantic Wall.

I'm just turning from the cliffside, taking in one last deep in-hale of the crisp, clean air, when an abrupt voice stops me.

"Pardon?" I say, a hand shooting to my chest. The landscape here is an expanse of grass, a walking path. Very few other people. I hadn't been expecting . . .

"I said, I need to see your papers."

"Oh." I dig in my bag. "Of course. Apologies. I was lost in the view and—" I shrug, smiling, trying to give off the impression *yet again* of a feeble woman.

He snatches my papers. His regard dances between me, my photograph, me, my photograph.

Compare all you want. It's truly me. But even with that knowledge, my neck prickles with fear. Any wrong step with a German officer would be the equivalent of throwing myself off this cliffside.

"This is you?" he barks, eyeing me from head to toe. "I haven't seen you before. I would have remembered."

There are thousands in Plouha, but it'll do me no good to point out this detail. I steady my breathing, though would it be strange even if it did come out a bit ragged when questioned, when roved by someone's eyes? I think not. "I was visiting family and became stuck south of the demarcation line. I've only just now been able to come home."

His regard remains pinned on me. "Claire Fondeu."

"Yes."

"Claire Fondeu," he repeats, skepticism in his voice.

"Yes."

"Claire!" another voice chimes in. This one a woman's. Where had she come from? And when will this game of saying my name end?

"How wonderful to see you again," the woman gushes. I've never seen her before. "I've been so jealous of my father. He said you'd stopped by his printers . . ." She pauses, as if wanting me to fill in the blank, wanting me to speak next.

I jump at the chance. "Ah, yes, fitting Ronan for pants."

"Claire, here," the woman says to the German officer, "is the town's best seamstress. Though"—she runs her gaze up and down the man's uniform—"you're dressed impeccably. No need for her services, sadly." She turns to me, taking my hands. I clasp them back. "I'm so thrilled you're home. I planned to stop by the shop to say hello."

"But you caught me during your morning walk."

"Doctor's orders."

And as if we both rehearsed this very moment, we offer the officer twinning, winning smiles.

In no time, he returns my papers and is on his way.

"Thank you," I whisper to the woman. "You're a savior."

"Enola," she offers. "And I'm glad I saw you when I did. Evan mentioned you'd be coming. Riog, Bernez, Yannick, Abram, Glenn—the whole lot of them are more than happy to lend a hand to get the Germans out of our home."

I recognize some of the names. I've met Bernez, a fisherman. The others I haven't had the pleasure of meeting yet. I'm certainly pleased to have met Enola, though.

"So, Evan," she says. "He's very handsome, isn't he?"

I laugh, caught off guard. "You'd make an excellent agent. Wonderful actress. Probing questions."

"It's true, then." She links her arm in mine as if we've been friends for ages, and we begin down the walking path. "You do find him handsome. Not the only one. All the girls here do. Then he met Claire, dashing all our hopes. But don't worry, I'm not interested in your husband." She rocks into me. "Nor would he be interested in me. Or anyone, for that matter."

That last bit shouldn't stay with me, but it does. I'm later than usual when I return to Evan's shop. I've taken to cooking for us, not something I'm especially skilled at, but I smell the aroma of dinner before I've even reached the kitchen. I peek in—empty, save for a smattering of dirty pots. I climb the stairs, finding Evan bringing two plates to the table.

"There you are," he says, not looking up from his task.

"He cooks?" I say, joining him, rubbing my cold hands together from today's excursions.

"Not well, I'm afraid. But enough about me. What'd you see today?"

"I actually visited Bonaparte Beach."

"Did you now? I'm surprised."

It's where we'll ship off our first escapees. "No boats there today to spook me," I say with a playful shiver. "But I did get questioned by an officer. A friend of yours saved me. Enola."

He raises a brow. "Bet she talked your ear off."

"She had some things to say," I respond vaguely.

Evan pulls out a chair for me. "I think you've seen more in a week than . . ." I take my seat, the scraping of my chair as I pull it in a welcomed noise to fill what Evan likely was about to say. "Let's just say you've seen a lot."

"Sadly, my *tro Breizh* is coming to a close. I'm back to Ronan's tomorrow. By the by, did I say that correctly?"

Evan smiles. He's been doing it more and more, the type of smile a leading man would flash on-screen. "'Tour of Brittany.' You said it perfectly."

I swell inside at his praise, us falling into a companionable silence, just the clinking of our forks and the slicing of our knives.

How cozy this feels.

Evan sips from his water. "I must ask. I've been dying of curiosity."

"Uh-oh," I tease.

"I know, I know. You're a closed book. Very secretive," he says, wiggling his fingers.

"Is that what this means?" I pantomime him. "Secretive?"

"Anyway," he says, ignoring me, "you're here for a reason. This isn't a holiday."

"No," I say, and decide to share, "but ironically enough, that's my network's code name."

"I'm aware of that. It's you who is still the mystery."

"You want to know about me?"

"I do."

I lick my lips. The thing is, I *want* to tell him. It wasn't hard not to share with Adele or Suzanne. Certainly not Denise. But I ended up giving them a partial truth about why I'm in France. Gabriel eked more out of me, telling him about my failed relationships.

But . . . being here with Evan feels more intimate and personal. He's allowing me to live in his house. To sleep in his bed.

I almost palm my face at that thought. To use the identity of his wife. That's huge. To trust me with his friends. To trust him.

"Why I'm here has changed," I begin. "Grown," I correct. "I came here for France, for what I saw happening in Paris."

"You lived in Paris?"

His question has a note of something, though I can't tell what.

I nod. "For a few years. My mother was from Paris. My father's English. We have a place in London too. Not a palace. But it's not as if I live there with my father. Never have. I've lived all over. One school after another. My father was only concerned with making sure the bills were paid so I'd have someone to care for me."

Evan has pushed aside his plate. He has both elbows on the table, leaning closer. "And your mother?"

"She died at sea when I was a baby."

"I'm sorry."

"I am too. It was just me and my father after that. But like I said, it was really just me. Whenever I did something big, like a significant accomplishment, he'd invite me to wherever he was at the time. His château, the London house, some destination." I wave my hands. "A film festival, an awards ceremony."

I almost didn't add those last two. I'm not supposed to reveal anything personal, anything that could give away my true identity. But I want Evan to know me as someone other than *Claire*.

Evan's eyebrows scrunch. "Is your father famous?"

I half smile. "He's Charles Labine. Actor. Director. Filmmaker extraordinaire."

"I am being nothing but genuinely honest when I say I have no clue who that is."

A full smile blooms at that. "What's sad is that no one has any clue that I'm his daughter. Well, besides the London office, my friend Josette, and now you."

He lays a hand over his heart. "I'm honored."

I laugh. "But to answer your question, because, wow, I've gone in a circle here. Charles Labine was the original reason why

I came. I wanted to do something so grand, so impactful, so brave and daring that he'd be so immensely proud of me that he'd say, 'Just remarkable, Kitty,' and want to be a greater part of my life. It's shallow, I know."

Evan reaches across the table and covers my hand with his. "It's not. It's human. Also, I don't know if you realize it, but you just told me your name."

I raise a brow. "Think so, do you? It's actually not my real name. It's just what he calls me when he's feeling like my father."

Evans snaps in defeat.

I chuckle, and that companionable silence falls between us again as we finish our meals.

The next day I stop by Ronan's, returning to Evan's with a roll of paper wrapped in cloth. Evan's not in the shop so I go straight upstairs, a realization hitting me that I'm disappointed he's out. Though part of me is also relieved. Our conversation last night was a lot, and I can't help feeling a bit self-conscious about all I told him. Not scared he'll blow my cover. Just vulnerable.

Upstairs, I arrange myself at his table and get to work, humming to myself as I meticulously measure and cut the correct sizes for identity papers and forbidden-zone passes.

Evan appears on the stairs, pulling his apron from over his head. "You're back."

The way he says it instantly makes my insides do a dance.

"And hard at work, I see. Need any help?"

"Thanks, but I've a routine."

He shrugs and makes his way to the piano.

I still my work, content to hear him play for a moment. It's beautiful. He's beautiful, the way he has his eyes closed, his fingers effortlessly moving over the keys.

Evan begins talking, his fingers still moving, his lids still closed. "This piano has been in the family for years. My *grand-père* discovered it on the beach, of all places. He used to make up bedtime stories of how it got there. Pirates. Mermaids. Traveling circuses. A king visiting from afar. It took some work, but my *grand-père* got it working again. It's sat in this very location ever since, passed down from my *grand-père* to my father, to me, and to my children one day."

Evan swallows hard, opening his eyes.

"It's so special."

He nods. "The Germans have taken so many homes here. They just walk in and declare it's theirs. I think the only reason they haven't bothered me is because the butcher is a necessity here."

"And that giant cleaver you wield."

"That too. It's why I'm risking it all. This town, this shop, this place means the world to me. It's literally my world. I won't have it taken from me. And I'll do whatever I need to do to give France back to France."

"I can tell it's important to you."

He plays a few more notes on the piano. "It is." Then he taps the bench beside him, to which I vigorously shake my head. "No, I couldn't."

"You've never played at all those fancy schools of yours?"

"No, I have. The piano is just not one of my hidden talents."

"Ah, come on," he prods. "Surely you still remember a little of Beethoven. Here, come do the left hand of 'Für Elise.' I'll do the right. Do you know it?"

"Not well. I'm warning you."

My shoulders rise and fall as I sit beside him. This won't be pretty.

Evan begins, the first few notes only him. When he hits the A note, I do too. From the corner of his eye, I see him appraising me, a grin on his face.

My part truly is simple, more or less just going back and forth between A and E. When I have to add in the C and G, while still remembering the A and E, things start to go south. I cringe at hitting a wrong note. Evan chuckles and bumps me with his shoulder.

Fortunately, there's a short break, during which I realize my heart is pounding. Such an odd thing to happen while playing the piano. It only pounds harder when Evan puts his left hand over mine, bringing my finger down on the A key, the A again, the E, the C, the G.

All I know is the pressure of his fingers on mine. We hold the E key so long—the length at least seven seconds—that I'm nearly out of breath, and the charge between us feels too large for the room.

I pull my hand away, motioning for him to continue on his own. "Show-off," I say at one point, though my voice is breathier than I had intended.

When he finishes, he drops his hands into his lap. "I must apologize, for you did warn me."

I widen my eyes, raising a hand to playfully smack him. Evan twists, squaring his shoulders to me, and catches my hand.

We're inches apart.

I think he may kiss me.

I think I want him to.

But then Evan clears his throat, mumbles something about checking on tomorrow's ration numbers—though they don't ever change—and the moment between us snaps.

* * *

IN THE MORNING, I'M OFF TO PARIS VIA TRAIN. JUST ME, four memorized addresses, and my sewing bag.

I hope no one will actually make me use it. Rolled in my fabrics, I arranged rows and rows of paper, cut to the size of identity cards.

It'd be easier if we could telephone or telegraph instead of me making the hours-long trip, but the Germans have prohibited these types of communications in and out of Brittany. Even if they hadn't, they'd be listening to anything we try to say. That makes me the messenger.

My first contact is a forger, who'll fill in the necessary details for our escapees as they need them.

My second contact is someone from the underground press, to which I relay the details of our first relocation into the forbidden zone, which he'll print in code.

My third contact helps me secure housing. I'll need to return to secure more, especially with my goal of a hundred escapees.

My fourth contact is a local resistant who agrees to help find clothes, as we can't have our pilots arriving as pilots.

After all that, I return to Evan's home, exhausted, my feet hurting, my body chilled through, my mind still stuck on yesterday's moment with Evan.

The *almost* moment with Evan that's left me feeling all jumbled up inside. My track record with men isn't good. Romantically, and also with my father. In either scenario, I'm wanted only for a finite amount of time. Is that how this'll be with Evan?

When I enter the upstairs, he's not alone. The German officer from the cliffside is at the table, casually sipping from a coffee.

"Claire." Evan stands. "How was Enola's?"

"Wonderful," I say. Then I kiss his lips. Just a wife greeting her husband, never mind the surge of heat that courses through me. I'm certain it shows on my cheeks as I turn toward the officer. "Hello again."

The first thing I notice, besides the obvious, unwanted interloper, is how the privacy screen in the corner is gone and it looks like Claire's desk has been tidied. Evan's doing, I assume. For me? He's left the sewing machine, which acts as part of my cover, but the scraps of Claire that were left behind have been cleared away. I cross to it, my throat thick with emotion, acting as if this is my usual first stop upon returning home, and set down my bag.

I turn back to the officer. "I see you already have coffee. Can I get you anything else?"

He clears his throat. "All appears to be in order here. I was just leaving."

"So soon," I want to say. I do not. I'll need to be careful. I can't blow my cover a second time. There won't be a third—a thought so rattling I immediately begin shaking my hands at my sides after Evan sees him out.

When Evan returns, his face is unreadable.

I have an overwhelming desire to touch him. His arm. His hand. It doesn't matter where—just to have that connection with him. But then he walks toward me with such force I almost backstep. Evan stops, mere inches from me, and begins to unwind the scarf from around my neck, still not uttering a word. I feel the heat of the wool even after it's gone.

Evan steps closer still, our bodies nearly touching. "You kissed me," he says.

"You kissed me first," I counter, unsure how to act, feeling the need to shake out my hands again but for a completely different reason. Something passed between us yesterday. Something is passing between us now. I just don't know what it is.

I need him to tell me.

To show me.

I'm too scared to put my own words to it.

All I have are Enola's, that Evan will never be interested in anyone again.

And all he does now is retreat a step and pose a question neither of us are able to answer: "What will happen between us after this war?"

CHAPTER 25

Violet

—

Aboard *Britannic*
November 21, 1916

THE STORM'S WRATH KEPT US AT PORT IN NAPLES FOR TWO days. I'm relieved when the rain, wind, waves—and my stomach—calm and the sun proves its existence again, as perfect a day as November in the Mediterranean can ever be, allowing us to set off for Mudros. With *Britannic*'s stokeholds full of coal, we'll be able to make a nonstop dash to England after we pick up our cargo of wounded soldiers.

The sun continues to shine as I go to morning Mass, the rays cascading through the windows of the lounge.

Kneeled beside me, Leo looks as handsome as ever in his khaki uniform. His stomach growls, and I stifle a laugh.

"I can't help it," he whispers.

It only makes the laughter bubble harder. I elbow him.

He says, "Finally," as the chaplain concludes the service.

There's a scramble toward the saloon. If I weren't walking at a slower pace, shaking my head at their zest for breakfast, Leo would be leading the charge. But he stays at my side, silently coaxing me on.

Impishly, I slow more, which makes my laughter finally rise to the surface.

"You're cruel," he says.

"My apologies," I say with a smirk and resume a normal pace. In the saloon, the men are like wolves, Leo included. You'd think they hadn't eaten in days. I know they're fueling, though. By this afternoon we'll begin to board the injured soldiers. It'll be all hands on deck.

Leo says something undecipherable around a mouthful of porridge he's shoveled into his mouth, not bothering to find a table before he begins eating.

"Was that another language?" I say, amused.

He swallows. "Don't worry, Vi. I'll have years to pull my own hijinks on you."

"Uh-huh."

He pauses, catching my hand. "You don't believe me?"

I lick my lips; how to say this? "It's not that I don't believe you, Leo. It's that you make me think and want things that I cannot have."

His eyebrows scrunch. "What does that mean?"

"It means," I begin, and I can't believe I'm doing this here, in the middle of the saloon, but they are words that'll eventually need to be said. "It means you want a small family of your own, a home, a piece of yourself that'll go on even after you're dust and bones."

"And you don't want those things?"

I pull my hand from his and begin filling my plate. "Like I said, you make me want things I cannot have. Not when I have a responsibility to my family. To care for them. To provide for them. That won't be ending anytime soon."

"And I can't be a part of that?"

"You are a very good man, Leo Jenkins, but you don't know what you're saying." I sigh. "I need to take a plate to Sheila. She's in the sick bay, and I don't want to keep her waiting. Go," I say. "Sit down and eat. I'll find you later. There's no reason why we shouldn't enjoy whatever time we have left together at sea."

I don't let him respond; I continue on to the pantry in search of tea. I've only just picked up the teapot when *Britannic* gives a shiver, a long, drawn-out shudder that runs down the length of her from stern to bow.

On the serving table, the crockery rattles. Dishes crash to the floor. Windows shatter. Shouts call out. I stumble forward a few paces, then back again.

When I regain my balance, I realize the ship is still moving. Her engines haven't stopped. But I know without a single doubt we've struck something.

My veins run cold. My first thought is an iceberg. It's happened again. How has it happened again?

On unsteady legs, I leave the pantry, headed for the saloon.

The men have transformed from wolves to graceful deer, leaping from their chairs, jumping over tables. Within seconds, all the khaki-clad men are gone. Leo included.

It's so different from my experience with *Titanic* that alarm pounds even greater in my chest. Then, everyone was unhurried and calm after we struck the iceberg. There was no panic. Now, the men leapt so quickly into action that my head spins.

This is no iceberg. We're at war. Have we struck a mine?

I've borne witness to what a mine can do to a ship.

Lifeboats, I think. I must get there. But then I remember Sheila in the sick bay. Heart pounding, I set off in that direction.

The ship's alarm is sounded. Doors are left ajar. Sisters and nurses hurry this way and that way, collecting belongings and supplies. One comments how it's a blessing we do not yet have any wounded on board.

I've only just torn my attention away from their conversation when I hear "Miss Violet" over the high-pitched alarm, from a young army medic Leo is friendly with. "Thank you!" he shouts. "If you didn't encourage Mass this morning, I'd still be in my pajamas."

I can tell from his forced smile he's trying to bring levity to the mad dashes we are both making. "Welcome," I tell him. Then abruptly I holler, "And don't forget a toothbrush!"

He gives me a puzzled expression. It's not an unreasonable response.

"Please just don't undertake another disaster without first making sure of your toothbrush," I remember my brother recommending to me after *Titanic*.

In my panicked state, I regurgitated his words—and confused the lad. I rub my forehead as I hurry toward Sheila. I find her by an open porthole, trying to peer out while simultaneously trying to dress herself, fingers shaking, dropping her dress.

"It'll do no good on the floor," I jest, trying to ease the tension I know we're both feeling. "Here, let me help you."

In no time—but in what feels like forever—I have her dressed and her toilet completed. As we leave the sick bay, I flag a passing medic. "Will you see her to the boat deck?"

"You're not coming?" Sheila yells, panic in her voice.

The blaring ceases, both of us looking at the ceiling. I assure her, "I'll be right along," before scurrying through the mostly deserted alleyways to my cabin.

My roommate's gone, leaving her unfinished breakfast in her wake. Manners aside, I grab a roll, ripping off a large chunk as I survey the room. I've no tips to grab, not as this type of stewardess.

But my prayer book.

My toothbrush.

The Christmas gifts for my family.

Stanley's watch.

The remainder of the roll.

Each gets shoved into the pockets of my uniform apron. Then I fold over the sagging garment, tucking it into my waistband.

On the way out of my room, I grab my coat and life belt—then run straight into Leo.

"There you are," he breathes. "I couldn't find you." He waves himself off, instead saying, "They're already loading the lifeboats."

"Sorry," I say. "I was in the pantry first, then—"

"The pantry?" He scratches his chin, a nervous tick I seldom see. "I thought you were going to the sick bay."

"I did. But after the pantry."

"I must have missed you. When you weren't there, I came here. Then went there. Back here."

"And I must have just missed *you*."

He shakes his head. "Well, now that that's all sorted out . . ."

"Lifeboats," I say, as if it's its own punctuation mark. We'll get to the lifeboats and we'll be safe.

The boat deck is crowded and chaotic and cold.

I know the proper procedure: life belt beneath a coat. But I also know the discomfort of having the stiff, hard life belt against my body for hours. There's no telling how long we'll be in the lifeboats until we're picked up. So my coat goes on first, creating a comfortable barrier between me and the cork.

Two lifeboats are already very slowly drawing away from the ship.

"Why are our engines still going?" I ask Leo.

"Captain is trying to get to shallower waters."

I let out a huff. "Shouldn't we wait until the engines are off, though? Us moving is not making the lowering of lifeboats very easy."

Nor does it make me want to climb aboard one of those tiny boats anytime soon as they rock and bang against the ship. However, I know I must. I know it's a lifeboat that saved my life before. I take a deep breath. "Okay, then."

"Miss," an officer says, approaching. "Are you ready to board?"

I nod. "I'm going. This boat here?" I ask, pointing to one marked with a number 4 that's about to be lowered.

I notice how it's nicely toward the front of the ship—far, far away from the churning water caused by the propeller.

I look that way, and a hand flies to my mouth. A lifeboat, despite the very best and hardest efforts of the oarsmen, is being pulled directly toward the propeller blades.

"No," I utter. "No, no."

The men in the boat continue to scramble. The ones with oars paddle harder. The ones without oars thrust their hands in the water. One man jumps overboard. None of it does any good.

There's a cacophony of noise, screams, all pleading for the men to distance themselves from the propeller. I watch in horror as one moment there is a lifeboat full of men and in the next breath there is debris and red-streaked water.

I turn into Leo's chest, a sob choking me.

His hand circles the back of my head, dislodging my uniform cap.

I'd give anything to unsee what I just saw. Anything.

"Miss." An officer tugs on my arm. "We must disembark."

"Are you mad?" I shake my head fiercely into Leo's stiff chest. "I cannot."

"The boat's sinking," Leo says in a calm voice. "What other choice do we have?" Next thing I know, he takes my hand and is leading me the final steps to the lifeboat, where a handful of men and a young lad are waiting.

Another lifeboat closer to the aft lingers halfway down the side of *Britannic*, with men holding on to the falls that lift and lower the small boats.

To make matters worse, *Britannic* begins to list to starboard.

"Lower! Quickly!" someone yells.

The boat halfway down the ship continues its journey to the sea.

"In you go," Leo encourages.

I swallow, breathe, and clamber inside. Leo's next, though he positions a lad ahead of him. He's a sea scout, if I have to guess. But no speculations need to be made about how he's feeling. The poor child quivers.

Seeing his fear is enough to stifle my own.

"It's going to be okay," I tell the lad. "Our oarsmen will know what to do. The worst is behind us."

He does not look convinced.

"Listen," I try. "My father told me a many great things, one of which is that it's better to be a coward for a minute than dead the rest of your life. You've had your minute. I've had mine. Now shall we get on with it?"

I think my words may've done more harm than good, but then, ever so slightly, his head bobs.

"That's a good lad."

He climbs in, then Leo settles beside me, pulling me into his side. He kisses my temple, hard, long. "You never cease to amaze me."

"There you go talking silly again—"

We begin to lower jerkily. My breath hitches. The next breath I hold, releasing it as a gasp when our lifeboat tilts to such a degree that Leo lunges forward to hold both me and the sea scout inside our tiny boat.

"Hooked on an open porthole," an officer explains. "That's all."

That's all, I think incredulously.

But we've righted and we're lowering again, scraping against the ship's side. The fall rope is within reach of the young sea scout, who lets the rope pass through his hands as we go, as if he's ready to grip tightly to it if we're rocked a second time.

Another lifeboat is in the water. I turn away, unable to look. But by the way Leo positions his body, shielding me if I had any inclination to look, this boat is also struggling to fight against the propeller.

I hear a splash. And another splash. A third. Fourth.

I must look.

The men are abandoning the lifeboat and are trying their luck at swimming in the lapping waves. *Por Dios*, it appears to be working. They're gaining ground better as individuals than they did as a larger and heavier boat. Other men—from the lifeboats out of the propeller's pull—shout and encourage them on.

I'd do the same, if the impact of us hitting the water didn't smack my teeth together. And if my next question to Leo didn't feel so pressing. "What now?" I ask, panicked. "Can't the engines be turned off?"

But he's not looking at me. His attention is up, where the young lad now dangles from the fall rope like a jungle monkey.

"Let go!" Leo encourages.

The lad shakes his head. "You'll tire," Leo tries to reason. "You need your strength."

It's very sound reasoning, and I think it'll help, but the sea scout shakes his head again.

"Come now," I try, gathering my own courage. "Those men swimming are nearly to safety. We'll do exactly as they're doing if we need to."

The others in my boat shout their own persuasions. Finally, the lad lets go.

I let out a long, slow breath. "There you are," I say to him. "That's better."

"Push," I hear. "Pull."

The struggles of our oarsmen are loud and clear. I count thirty seconds and we're still no farther away from the ship. We are, however, closer to the propellers.

"Leo . . ."

"I know," he says, his head pivoting left and right, evaluating, thinking—making a decision. "We need to jump."

"And swim?" I screech.

"Yes."

I want to scream how I cannot. I don't know how. But doing so will only frighten the young lad even further, especially as I lured him back into the boat by suggesting we swim.

"Are you ready?" Leo asks me.

I shake my head.

"This'll be a story to tell, Vi."

I close my eyes. The boat rocks with each man who flees our lifeboat. I open my eyes to see them struggling, arms pounding in and out of the water. But their life belts . . . they hold them up. Buoyant. Allowing them to better fight against the current.

"You first," I tell Leo.

He angles the young sea scout toward the boat's edge. "Go on," he tells him.

The lad raises his chin, then he slips into the water like a duckling into a pond. He lets out a whooping sound, the water undoubtably cold this time of year.

Leaning over the lifeboat, Leo gives him a strong push in the right direction, using our boat as a shield from the current.

I decide I need to get into the water before Leo turns back. I need to be brave.

I jump overboard.

I hit the surface.

I go down and down, thinking at any moment I'll pause, then bounce toward the surface. But I do not.

With my life belt atop my coat, it doesn't fit snugly. The water forces the cork up, and it presses against my chin, pushing my head back, straining my neck.

I curse myself for not wearing the life belt properly, making it impossible to discard my jacket. The heaviness of it pulls me deeper.

Breath already waning, this is the very first time I've ever been underwater. I fear it'll also be my last.

Instinctively, I kick. I reach up with my arms, then thrust them down. I do it again and again and again. I look for a hand— Leo's—searching for me beneath the water, but I see nothing.

Miraculously, I feel myself rising. But I also feel myself twisting and turning. I kick, unsure if I am exerting my efforts in the correct direction. I thrust my arms, praying I'm going toward the water's surface.

My chest begins to burn.

The water roars, a noise so loud I have the instinct to cover my ears.

I'm whipped around once more and then—*¡Ay, caramba!*—my head hits something so roughly, so violently that stars erupt behind my eyes. I have only the cognition for a mere moment, a single tick of a watch, to know I've struck *Britannic*'s hull before everything goes black.

CHAPTER 26

Daphne

CODE NAME CLAIRE
Alias Madame Claire Fondeu

Plouha, Brittany, France
May 16, 1943

I DIDN'T COME TO FRANCE OR *Breizh* TO FIND MY SO-CALLED better half. I'm not even certain if Evan wants to fill that role. While I'd read between the lines of his what-comes-next question, I could have read wrong.

All those months ago when I sacrificed myself for Gabriel and Louis, Gabriel had told me I mattered. I . . . I'm not sure I've ever seen myself that way, as someone who matters without conditions. But Evan makes me feel like I matter unconditionally, a colossally new emotion for me. I've never been on the receiving end of genuine, selfless love. But I can see it with Evan, like how he always insists on walking on the street side. Or how he knows I strongly loathe any garlic on my food. Or how when we pass a park, he always remarks about it being another perfect place to play fetch with the dog I've always wanted but could never have.

During our short time together, it feels as if we've begun playing house. And more and more, Evan's home feels like my own. I have my belongings in the toilet, in a drawer, and admittedly strewn about in places my belongings should not be. I can be messy. I've acquired more than the measly change of clothes I came with. I have a book beside our bed. A banned book, at that. We read side by side every evening, the space between us no longer existent with my head so often on his shoulder.

It'd be so easy to uplift my chin and for my mouth to find his, a real kiss.

But that feels like a line, one we shouldn't cross.

Weeks have passed, and we both pretend like Evan's question was never asked.

There are other, bigger things to focus on, like our first evacuation.

It could've happened yesterday, though it did not. It could happen tonight. Tomorrow. Or the day thereafter. It could happen a week from now. Every night we listen to a nine o'clock broadcast from London, hoping for the secret phrase that means we're a go.

Over the past three months, I've taken at least ten more trips to Paris, all under the guise of seamstress work, and we've brought close to sixty evacuees to *Breizh*, a few with passes, but many of them smuggled in car boots, open-backed baker's vans, lorry beds, and the oh-so-familiar train coal bunker. They'd then stand in the food queue at Evan's shop. Along with their allotted package of meat, they received an address at which they'll be hidden until it's time.

Our first evacuation cannot come soon enough, yet I often find myself pacing, feeling the weight of not bringing a full hundred to Brittany as I had hoped.

Daily, there seems to be a laundry list of happenings all across Europe, some positive and others negative to this war ending in our favor. Perhaps, as May progresses, I've been focusing more closely on the negative ones on account of how tightly wound my nerves are.

The first of May brought the death of an assumed eight hundred British soldiers and sailors when the Germans bombed the troopship *Erinpura* in the Mediterranean.

Two weeks later, an Austrian hospital ship, *Centaur*, was sunk by the Japanese.

A day later, a German submarine torpedoed and sunk the steamship *Irish Oak* off the coast of Ireland.

Earlier today, news reached us about the Germans' latest announcement: the final eradication of Warsaw's Jewish quarter.

Francis had rubbed his brow and mumbled how that had to be more than fifty thousand innocents.

We need to get our refugees to safety. We need our pilots back in the skies. But I won't lie, the recent ship-related happenings have fully sent the wind up me, especially because *Centaur* was a hospital ship and *Irish Oak* was marked as a neutral vessel. That should've meant those ships weren't to be targeted.

But they were, and it reminds me of *Britannic* from the first war.

Part of me wonders if she was doomed from the start, the third and final vessel of the White Star Line's sister ships to launch and, subsequently, the third and final to be involved in a maritime disaster.

At least *Olympic* had redemption. During the first war, she intentionally rammed into and was responsible for the sinking of a German submarine.

Maybe the White Star Line had hoped to change *Britannic*'s fate, though. I'd read during my years of compulsive research about the sister ships how her name was originally *Gigantic*. But after *Titanic*'s sinking and with passengers suddenly caring much less about size and luxury and more about safety and actually arriving at their destinations alive, her name was changed to *Britannic*.

Little good it did her. Little help it was that she was a hospital ship that should've been left alone. She still went under, and not without her own conspiracy theories. With the improvements made to *Britannic*, it should've taken more than a single mine or torpedo to sink her. But it's said that the ship had portholes left open, ones that should've been tightly closed, that allowed the water to rush into the ship. Some believe there was a second explosion, perhaps involving the highly flammable medical supplies. That led to suggestions of an inside job, someone who wanted to stop the ship from arriving at Mudros, where three thousand sick and wounded were to be rescued, cared for, and if possible, reassigned.

It's not the same, but it's also kind of, sort of similar to how we want to help downed pilots get back into the sky.

I worry our ships will be a target.

I try to shake these thoughts from my overly active brain. While it's not me who is stepping aboard our evacuation ship, I'd die of guilt if I'm the one who arranged for nearly sixty airmen and refugees to board a ship doomed for the bottom of the Atlantic.

"Here we go," Bernez says just as bells begin to chime. It reminds me of Ivana, and how she said that church bells are part of what makes her town in Croatia feel like her home.

Bernez turns the dial on the radio louder. Nine o'clock, the sounds of London's Big Ben tolling the hour. The news broadcast is about to begin and we—Francis, Zacharie, Evan, and I—have all congregated in Bernez's attic to listen to the secret messages that'll follow. Bernez is a fisherman, quite an important fisherman at that, who'll help tactfully lead our evacuees across the mine-ridden beach the night of the escape.

The secret messages come in various forms. An intentionally misquoted poem, dictionary entries, song lyrics, random car parts, and so on.

The result is a bunch of nonsense that means nothing to the Germans but means everything to the various agents scattered around Nazi-occupied Europe who are covertly listening.

Our secret message happens to be a dictionary-esque entry, relating to our network name.

And we hear it.

A heaping of leisure and recreation.

Hands slap the table, run through hair, squeeze a shoulder.

I clasp mine together. "Tonight," I whisper.

Bernez is on his feet. Someone has turned off the radio. "That's that, then," he says and heads for the door. Here, the curfew is nine to five. From the moment he steps out the door, this operation will be a dangerous one. It's why he's the only one going, with exactly fifty-seven pilots and civilians.

Evan and I slip through the shadows back home and onto its peaked roof, our base camp for the evening. From where we sit, I both hope to be able to see nothing but ache to know what is going on. It'll take three hours for Bernez to lead them in the dark, through the wild moors, past a German artillery block-house, down the precarious cliffs, and to the beach.

There, Bernez has identified and discreetly marked seventeen land mines. I can imagine him saying, "Step exactly where I step. Slow now. We'll take it slow."

For those long hours, Evan and I stand watch from afar, my heart in my throat. He wraps an arm around me, his body heat combining with my own, and together we silently urge them on.

Once they're beyond the mines, they'll wait. We wait.

It won't be until after two in the morning that the small row-boats will leave the mother ship discreetly waiting in the bay and cut through the dark waters and toward the shore. We've been told the agents will exchange supplies for our escapees.

I have to think this way, practically, systematically. Other-wise, my imagination will have its way with me.

In the wee hours of the morning, I think I can spot move-ment on the horizon. It could simply be my tired eyes. Beside me, Evan has fallen asleep, his head perched on a knee, the other leg out straight. A strand of his dark hair dangles across his face. Gently I push it aside, feeling an odd sense of ownership over that face.

"Evan," I whisper. When he doesn't stir, I say the most honest thing I've ever said: "I think I may love you."

That's when gunfire erupts, carrying and rising through the cool night. Evan startles. I stiffen, voicing, "Something's gone wrong."

There isn't a full moon for another three nights. It'd be too dangerous to move on such a night. Tonight the moon is waxing, more darkness than light. But in that light I faintly see a shadow move against the black horizon, until it disappears.

"I . . ." Evan pauses, as if he wants to be sure of his words. "I think they made it off."

"You do?"

He nods. *"Beaj vat."*

"What's that mean?"

"Have a nice trip."

Please, I silently plea, massaging one hand into another. Aloud I say, "All the way to Dartmouth."

In the morning, I wake exhausted but satisfied, my limbs tangled with Evan's.

"What will happen between us after this war?" he had asked.

I swallow, bite my lip, then detangle myself, turning my focus back to my mission. We had all decided not to rendezvous with Bernez until the next evening, in case the Germans have a heavier presence in *Breizh* after last night's happenings.

When we eventually meet up, we learn from a very inebriated Bernez that the ship's engines turning on alerted the German patrol boats already in the bay. They opened fire and gave chase, but they were no match for the larger, more powerful steamship.

"Yec'hed mat!" Evan says, raising his own glass.

This phrase is one I've heard before, that I've used before, specifically the night we brought the last pilot into *Breizh* a few days ago. And now those pilots will be safely in England, no doubt eager to once again serve king and country. *"Yec'hed mat!"* I say and clink my glass.

The alcohol burns down my throat and tomorrow I'll have a headache like no other. But this is worth the cheers—multiple of them—and worth the celebration.

Tomorrow we'll begin planning and preparing for our second evacuation. If I have my way, I'll work around the clock and have another batch off in a week's time.

But printing paper, forging those papers, making trips to and from Paris, getting people into *Breizh* all takes time. Then there's the fact the PHYSICIAN network, arguably the largest and most damaging network London has, crumbles. It forces us to take extra precautions and smuggle more men instead of risking the checkpoints.

In July, sixty-two more pilots and citizens make a successful escape with Bernez. That total puts well over a hundred back in England.

We celebrate. We repeat. In August, we hear our secret message again after the nine o'clock news.

"Here we go again," Bernez says, a glint in his eye. I share it.

But things don't go as planned. The Luftwaffe are suddenly everywhere in the sky, seemingly out of nowhere, and the steamship is never able to enter the bay. Thankfully, with the help of a destroyer ship providing anti-aircraft cover, the steamship is able to get away.

My face is in my hands upon receiving the news. "What now?" I ask, not raising my head.

It's just Francis and me at my table.

I jerk up to see him. "Do you think we've been compromised?"

A fear pulses through me. Arrest. Prison. Torture.

Failure to help more evacuees.

He shakes his head. But his words betray his body language. "We have to shift operations as soon as we can. I'm waiting for Zacharie to give me the official word. Then we're out of here and moving . . ." He points toward the window.

"What's that mean?"

"South."

I reposition his arm by forty degrees.

"Like I said, south." His mouth quirks. "Most likely Quiberon Bay."

"Quiberon Bay?" Evan says, entering the room. Never fail, my heart rate picks up whenever he does. Same for when we're alone, exchanging lighthearted stories from our pasts. Same for when we dance around anything more serious, like our future. Francis answers, "It's where we'll likely do our next pickup."

"Oh." It's all Evan says. "Write me?" he says in a casual tone. But nothing about his taut muscles or jawline is easy breezy.

I ask, "You won't be coming with us?"

"Quiberon is hours from here. No friends there," he says.

"No contacts," Francis clarifies.

Evan adds flatly, "Yup. No longer needed."

He's needed by me. But I don't say that. It won't help right now, when I have orders from London to go.

"So, when do you leave?" Evan's question is directed at both of us, but his eyes are only on me.

Francis says, "By the morning we should get word."

That word comes just as Francis said, after a long, silent night with Evan. We've only just arrived at one of the safe houses the next day when Zacharie relays the information. Evan continues not to say a word. Not at the safe house, nor on our walk home for me to pack my things.

But as soon as we enter the shop, he turns to me.

Evan's lips press so firmly against mine I stumble backward. After I regain my footing, I'm the one to push into him, to return his urgency.

I've been waiting *months* for this real kiss. Months.

Now here it is, us finally crossing an unspoken, invisible line.

Breathless, I pull away. "So . . . now what?"

He snorts. "So I want you to come back."

I swallow roughly. "After this trip south? Or after the war?"

"The trip, the war, both."

How can I not smile at that, at the idea that this man wants me?

Evan kisses my smile, a soft growl coming from him. I laugh into our kiss, then I deepen it.

In time, too soon, I say, "Fine, you've convinced me. I'll come back. Happy?"

"No, not yet."

I quirk an eyebrow.

Evan circles behind me. "Months ago you shared part of your-self with me. And I . . . I want to do the same."

A heartbeat later, a necklace dangles in front of my face.

"It was my mother's. It's simple."

"It's beautiful."

"Thank you," he says and fastens the necklace around my neck. I bring a hand to it, pressing it against my skin. "It's a pearl my fa-ther gave to my *maman*. I've never given it to anyone."

I understand what's left unsaid, but I don't understand how this heirloom can be meant for me—and not the woman before me.

Evan's hands fall on my shoulders, him still standing behind me. "I've been saving it. Maybe for my daughter. I don't know." I can hear him scratching the scruff along his jawline. "Claire and I wanted *bugale*. Children. It was maybe the one thing we agreed on. *Breizh* is my home. But Claire never let it become hers. I feel selfish even saying that, considering she left her life behind in Paris and I'll never leave here. But she simply had no interest in learning the language, learning our customs. She once said how she loved me despite all of this."

"Oh, Evan," I say, turning to see his face, his eyes. There's emo-tion there. He smiles faintly.

"Claire was many wonderful things. I loved her immensely. But wanting to be a Breton was simply not one of them." He rubs his forehead, then runs a hand down his face. "But children, a mother, she badly wanted to be that. I tried to give it to her. It wasn't in the cards. That's what people say, right?"

"Right," I say in a small voice.

"One day I guess Claire had enough. Or maybe our love wasn't enough. She left without a word. She took nothing from this life and she disappeared. I tried to find her. I couldn't. It was like Claire Fondeu didn't exist anymore."

I move without thinking, wrapping my arms around him, pulling him into me, hugging him. "That must have been very hard."

It's rhetorical. We both know it. I'm not surprised when he doesn't respond immediately. Eventually he whispers, his face hidden from me, "Just come back."

"I will," I say. "I'll be back as soon as I can."

This, here, with Evan, it's the most honest, heartfelt moment I've had with anyone, as Claire, as Irene, and even as Daphne.

* * *

IN QUIBERON, WE HAVE ONLY THREE MONTHS TO GET OUR operations up and running. We begin by discreetly relocating the eighty-two pilots and civilians to our new location. The quarters are cramped, our number of safe houses cut in half.

I can only trust that the new fishermen we're working with are trustworthy. It's a known fact the Germans offer a sizable reward to anyone who turns in a downed airman.

I can only trust that the people of Quiberon value their freedom the way Evan does. It appears they do. Our November evacuation goes off without a hitch. No air attacks. No gunfire.

Emboldened, we decide to communicate more widely to other networks and through the underground press, and try to get a greater number of pilots and refugees out of France. Gone are the days of striving for a hundred. I want two hundred.

And at the end of December, we put a whopping three hundred on a ship. I could float right off my feet and fly myself anywhere in the world. I know without a doubt that'd be to Evan, a belated Christmas gift.

The thought is comical to me. Terrifying too. It's been four months since I've seen him. No letters, no visits, no nothing. Francis said it'd be too risky to communicate.

What if I return and Evan's interest in me has waned? What's that ridiculous proverb? "Out of sight, out of mind."

Isn't that what Evan did after Claire never came back? Her belongings were screened off in the corner of the room. He never spoke of her. Ronan told me it took months for Evan to smile again.

I'm not Claire, but what if my leaving has gotten tangled up with her leaving in Evan's head? I left so quickly—following orders, of course. But what if Evan thinks it was easy for me to go?

It wasn't.

It was simply necessary.

Was the other Claire's necessary in her eyes?

I want to reassure Evan, right this very second. We've received our next orders, though. March, that's our next pickup date, London pushing us even farther south toward the border of Spain and into the Bay of Biscay.

We begin preparations.

I shouldn't do it. In fact, I don't tell Francis I'm doing it, but I write Evan and tell him my next "fitting" is in Bayonne and I'll be back as soon as I can. I'm not sure when.

Maybe it's all in my head, but soon after, Francis has a suspicious edge to him, and I wonder if he knows what I've done. Or if the stress of the job, of war, or any number of things is getting to him.

Certainly the Germans are making their presence known, both here in Bayonne but also in London.

They've begun bombing there again. We're not even a month into 1944 when the Luftwaffe strikes London at night, then again the next evening. A week later, they're back.

The air strikes continue into February. The last time London was attacked like this was the Blitz, two years prior.

They continue into March.

When will they stop? How much destruction has been done?

Is my father safe? Has our house there been hit? It's said even the prime minister's residence has suffered damage.

One afternoon I'm helping Zacharie code a message when Francis bull-rushes into the safe house, ironically atop a butcher shop.

"There's something I need to tell you both," he starts.

"Sounds serious," Zacharie says, pausing his work. "London get hit again?"

Francis rubs his brow. "Probably. It's not that, though. But it does involve London."

I set down my own pen. "What is it?"

"They're putting an end to our mission. Our next pickup will be our last."

"What?" I exclaim. "But . . ." I look around, as if the hundreds and hundreds of people we've rescued are standing in this very room. "We've been so successful. Why stop now?"

"They claim it's because the nights are shortening. It narrows our window of operation."

"Hogwash," Zacharie grumbles.

Francis sighs. "I think there's something else in play. Some of the other network heads near the coast say they're being asked to lay low."

I scrunch a brow. "Did London tell you that too?"

"No." He clears this throat. "They didn't. But only because there's no need for us to lay low. They're calling us in."

Calling us in? I don't have words. The meaning of what he's actually saying barely registers in my head.

Francis adds, "When the pickup goes down, our orders are to get on the ship too."

My heart sinks, right to my feet, where I feel like it's promptly trampled by the realization that London is telling me to leave, whereas I told Evan I'd be back for him. For us.

CHAPTER 27

Violet

—

HMS *Foxhound*
November 22, 1916

A SMALL ROOM.

Poorly lit.

On a ship.

Despite my head being chiseled in half—or so it feels—I'm able to gather this much.

"Hello?" I croak, unable to turn my head to assess if anyone else is in the room.

The sounds of footsteps are beside me within breaths. "Welcome back. You're on the HMS *Foxhound*. My name's Nurse Jones. How are ya feeling this time?"

The intonation of her voice sounds like she's used that same greeting on me multiple times. "How long?" I ask. There's another question I'm burning to ask, but I'm too afraid.

"Only a day," Nurse Jones says in a soft voice. "Looks like you'll stay with us this time."

"What happened?"

The nurse pokes her tongue into the side of her mouth. "Ya don't remember?"

I'm told *Britannic* sunk in less than an hour. I'm told Captain Bartlett was completely unaware that the lifeboats were lowered without orders and that the ship's propellers were tearing

apart boats and humans alike as he tried to ground his ship. I'm
told I, too, after hitting my head, got swept into the whirl of
the propellers, unbelievably being whipped around the blades
as if I were riding a harmless waterwheel. I'm told I surfaced,
my coat ripped from its back yoke and trailing behind me like a
train and my hair loose and wild, someone calling out, "There's
a woman in the water here!" I'm told a man leapt back in the
waters, swimming with much ferocity to my rescue. I'm told
after the engines were turned off, the remainder of the lifeboats
were safely lowered. I'm told twenty-eight people died in the
first boats that lowered. I'm told 1,100 people survived.

I am one of them. Yet I do not recall any of it.

"Oh, almost forgot. A friend of yours left ya a letter, for when
you're ready." The nurse gestures to a bedside table. I'm slow to
register these new words, still distraught over her last ones. She
goes on, "I'm going to let the doctor know you're finally alert."

I wait for her to leave, then turn my head toward the letter,
cringing at the shooting pain in my temples and neck. The folded
paper is beside Stanley's watch, the cuff links, the bracelet for Eileen, and my mother's figurine. Somehow all my gifts survived the
ordeal.

Somehow I survived.

The question burns in my head: *Did Leo?*

Is he the man who jumped in after me?

I pray the letter is from him. But too many times, those I allow
myself to care for are taken from me.

I'm short of breath by the time I'm half propped against my
pillows. Then I simply hold the paper.

Tanta. I'll never know unless I open it.

Dearest Violet, it begins. But I'm more interested in how it ends.

Yours, Leo

My hands and his letter fall atop my chest. Tears spring to my
eyes. Leo is alive. Leo has written me. And I cannot wait a single
second longer to read his words.

It's happened again, me having to leave while you're sound asleep reenacting a Brothers Grimm fairy tale. Please forgive me for not being with you when you woke. While I tried to delay as long as I could, I'm to be immediately transferred to another hospital ship, those in Mudros still relying on passage to England. Perhaps we've been given a stroke of good fortune, though. My next voyage will be to Malta. I'll write you at your Ealing home as soon as I have word of your brother's recovery.

I hope you'll be fully recovered soon too. I hope you'll allow me to continue to write to you, despite you insisting I don't fit into your life. I know I can be grandiose. I know you stole my heart quickly. But none of it was a farce. And every part of me wants whatever portion of yourself you are able to give me.

Let me write to you, Violet.

Write me back.

Let's find each other again after this war.

So you know where I'll be, I'll return home. For a time, anyway. If I am not there, I'll likely be in Ipswich. Ask for me there. If I'm not at either of those places, my sister will know where to find me. She's lived at the same address for years and she'll never leave it. In fact, start with Alma. I don't want to wait a second longer than necessary to see you again.

Please let me see you again.

I'd ask you to stay off ships, but that suggestion leaves me torn. You are not only Miss Violet but also Miss Unsinkable. Still, I don't know if you should never step foot on a ship again or if you should never fear being on a ship, as you appear invulnerable to maritime disaster. You seem invulnerable to many things life has thrown at you, my darling.

All that matters to me is that you'll give us a chance at a life together.

But I cannot. A chance at a life together . . . the one thing I cannot do. A day, five days. That I'd been able to give. That will have to be enough. I clench at his words. I'll miss Leo. I already feel a void after only a short time together. But I always knew our futures would lead us in different directions. This is merely ripping off the bandage.

"Ah, Miss Jessop, welcome back," a doctor says, walking up at the proper time, pulling me from my thoughts.

Setting aside Leo's letter, I fight for composure. "Violet, please."

He has thick glasses that remind me fondly of Dr. Lowndes. "Well, Miss Violet," he says. "You are truly a marvel. Besides a bump on your head and some gashes on your legs, you're as healthy as a horse."

If that horse had a single lung and a broken heart.

The nurse joins us. "If you're feeling up for it, I can draw you a hot bath. Wash the whole incident off of ya, mind and body."

"That'd be nice," I say.

And it helps, my aching limbs at least. My head still bursts with pain and my heart isn't much better. I'm offered an aspirin, a few times, in fact, but I kindly refuse each time. There are people, nearly thirty of them, who are no longer here to suffer from a splitting headache. So I am more than capable of dealing with the pain for however long it lasts.

After my bath, I ascend to the deck, in need of a lungful of salt air, when I see the sea scout. I do not know his name. I do not know anything about him. But my chest swells. He's made it.

I give him a wave, thinking that'll be the end of it, but upon seeing me, he rushes my way, a steaming mug in his hand.

"Miss Violet," he begins.

I immediately apologize, "I'm sorry, I never got your name."

"Zander." His grin is toothy. "Everyone knows your name. Everyone's talking about you, how you went toe to toe with that propeller and won."

"*Ay, Dios.*"

He chuckles, but softly. The decks are quiet, respectful, even as the crewmen and medics pat each other on the backs and continue to relish in their reunions. Zander clears his throat, then says, "I wanted to thank you, though. You and the officer you were with."

"Leo," I supply.

He nods. "I wish there was a way for me to repay you for giving me a kick in the pants."

"That's not necessary."

He looks down, then shoves his mug at me. "Here. I didn't have any yet. Navy cocoa. If you've never had it, it's something."

I'm not usually on the receiving end, but I can see this means something to Zander. I accept the mug. "Thank you."

He tips his hat to me, then he's off, ideally to get a replacement cup.

The drink looks delicious, so thick that a spoon could stand on its own. I inhale deeply, enjoying the aroma of chocolate mixed with the salt air.

Just then there's a gust of wind, not only giving me more fresh air than I bargained for, but also taking with it the entire contents of my cup.

At a loss for what else to do, I laugh.

* * *

I'M REPATRIATED, SENT BACK TO ENGLAND TO FULLY RECOVER, though not swiftly. I transfer from ship to shore to ship until I'm offloaded at Marseilles. From there, I spend two very long days on an unheated train until I finally reach Le Havre, and then I am sent on to England.

Ealing is familiar, depressingly so. My brothers at war, my sister away at school, Mother by her window.

She doesn't know I was aboard *Britannic* and I intend to keep it that way. Her nurse says she doesn't even know of William's illness. It's for the best.

Days pass, ones where I feel unmoored with idle hands. I'm

under strict orders not to exert myself. That means, according to the *Britannic*'s Dr. Beaumont, no work.

Right away I balked, "But I must," speaking so sharply my head rung. Then I remembered how my position with the VAD had been a volunteer with no salary. It's my brothers who are earning pay and who are currently without tuition bills. But of course, we still have other bills. We have Eileen's schooling, Mother's live-in nurse. Now that I have the opportunity to secure paying work again, I should be pursuing it; not doing so goes against every instinct.

"Heal," Dr. Beaumont had implored of me. "You'll do your family no good as a corpse."

It's as if he knew what would get through to me.

In following doctor's orders, I feel of no more use than a houseplant. I check the post daily for Leo's letter, telling myself it's only an update on my brother that I'm after. I tend to the gashes on my legs. I rest my eyes, preferring dark rooms that don't make my head scream. I spend hours doing nothing more than tapping my foot. I tidy—Mother's nurse, who also acts as a housemaid with Mother a simple charge, consistently insisting I do no such thing. When I can, I read the daily paper, news of *Britannic*'s sinking given only a brief outcry. Soon it's all but forgotten.

There's not a mention in today's paper. I've restlessly folded and unfolded the pages, leaving the small adverts page face up. I'm about to feed it to the fire when my eye catches something that tickles my brain.

The London branch of the Banco Español del Rio de la Plata of Buenos Aires is looking to fill a role.

It's an Argentine bank, one my father took me to once in Buenos Aires. I don't anticipate the emotion that comes over me at the memory. But I'm certainly thankful to have this moment where I remember my father, where I remember another proverb he loved to recite.

"Wherever you go and whatever you do, may the luck of the Irish be there with you."

And right now, seeing this ad feels fortuitous.

Should I ignore it? Dr. Beaumont would say so. He'd likely insist I'm testing fate.

But I'd chuckle in turn and say, "She and I are quite familiar."

So I go down to the bank. Even more fortuitous, I'm given the job in the Information Department, all because I can speak Spanish, all because my father moved us from Dublin to Bahía Blanca on a sheep-farming whim.

Thank you, Father.

And maybe he's pulling strings for us from heaven because I return home to find a post from Leo. I run a finger over my scripted name, knowing Leo wrote it while thinking of me. But I only allow myself to linger in the time we spent together for an instant, too eager to know what he's written: joyous news.

William is well. He's recovered. He's on a troopship bound for Salonika. I wish my brother was here in Ealing with me. I wish he was starting Jessop Brothers with Philip, Patrick, and Jack this very moment instead of them fighting. But for now I'll be satisfied with knowing he's beaten malaria. And finally, after seemingly holding my breath for weeks, I feel as if I can breathe.

In regard to my brother, at least. Leo ends with his hope—there's that word again—that I'll write back and reconsider my decision.

But I have not.

I settle into working at the bank. The work is easy enough. Enough to keep me busy. Enough to help pay the majority of our bills. I'll risk a late payment and the lights going out. Enough to distract me from thoughts of Leo, of my brothers, even of Eileen. She'll be out of school soon, with a future that's positively unknown.

A year passes. A year's worth of letters from Leo I leave unopened. A year's worth of battles: in Arras, Vimy Ridge, Aisne, Messines, Ypres, La Malmaison, Cambrai.

With each one, I scour the newspaper for any inklings about

my brothers. After each one, I'm overcome with relief when we receive no official letter.

That is, until April of 1918.

The tenth of April used to be a happy day. I remember, back when I was a child, that had been the exact date Father decided we'd move from Buenos Aires to the Andes to try to save my life.

How, for me, had the tenth of April meant a new beginning but, for my brother Philip, it'd been his ending?

The only details I'm given are in black and white. Philip was a corporal with the King Edward Light Horse division. He volunteered with four companions to man a machine-gun post that kept a crucial retreat road open for his comrades to use. They kept it open for three days. He didn't survive the fourth. Not Philip, nor his companions.

I don't know how long I hold the letter. I opened it in my bedroom, sitting next to the window. I know Mother sits by another window. But I cannot go to her. I cannot grieve with her.

Mother's nurse said, early on, that if one of my brothers should fall, she thought it'd be too much for my mother to bear.

She was not wrong. Mother is so lost to herself that the rise and fall of her chest and an intermittent blink are her only signs of life.

But I ache to go to her. I ache to be the child who lost her brother, consoled in the arms of her mother. Instead, I dress for work.

At the bank, my main task is to translate letters for Mr. Samson. He's a man who on any other day would bring a smile to my lips from his pleasant disposition. He always has a roll of Pep-O-Mints in his pocket, a joke on the tip of his tongue, his clothes impeccably pressed. A very put-together man.

But on this morning as I enter his office, he looks very much the opposite. His hair is disheveled. His eyes are unfocused. He grasps a letter, though I don't think he sees it. His mind is elsewhere.

"Good morning, Mr. Samson," I say, as is my routine, distracted by my grief. When he doesn't answer, I add, "Is that a letter you'd like me to translate?"

Still nothing from him. I carefully slip the letter from his hands. Taking charge in this way is second nature after so many years assisting women aboard my various ships.

What will never be second nature, no matter how many times I encounter it, is reading about death.

Mr. Samson's youngest son has also been killed, in the same engagement that took my brother from me. The unthinkable coincidence, the sheer unfairness of it, has me wrapping my arms around my superior.

Together, we weep.

Months later, we weep again. In a railroad car outside a French town, the Germans signed an armistice agreement. The war is finally over. Mr. Samson has two sons who survived. I have three brothers. But still, we both mourn our one who will not be coming home, imagining my Philip and his James together in their final moments.

In the end, Mr. Samson doesn't make a fuss when I tell him I received notice from White Star. They're to resume service and they'd like me to return.

Historically, the ocean has allowed me to love and care for my family from afar. In my grief, I need that distance. With one of my brothers no longer on this earth, I also need the possibility of tips. I'm determined that Jack, William, and Patrick will still have Jessop Brothers. I'm more determined than ever.

All Mr. Samson does upon my resignation is unwrap a Pep-O-Mint and offer me both the candy and fatherly advice. "Miss Violet, I still find no coincidence in you seeing my advert. You were without your mother and father. I, without my wife. We survived on account of our shared grief. But if you go back to the sea, promise me you're going for yourself and not because you feel you must."

I wish it were a promise I could make to Mr. Samson, but it is not. I already made another promise long ago that trumps all.

CHAPTER 28

Daphne

CODE NAME CLAIRE
Alias Madame Claire Fondeu

Bayonne, Brittany, France
March 24, 1944

I'M BEING TOLD TO RETURN TO LONDON. NO MATTER HOW many times I repeat it, it still doesn't make sense.

If I'd been called back as Katherine, sure. Absolutely. That would've been fair. I'd been compromised. I'd broken out of prison.

But as Claire?

That doesn't add up for me. I'm doing good work as Claire. We've helped hundreds of people. We've moved to a new location in Bayonne, where the Germans won't be expecting us. Claire has become a part of Brittany.

She's fallen in love with her husband.

I press my fingers into my eyes.

I know it . . . I can feel it in my gut that tonight's radio announcements will include our secret message. A nail in the coffin to end my time here.

I wrote Evan a second time. I had to. It'd be unfair to leave him without a word, the same way the other Claire had done.

But I don't see how my vague explanation that "my family

is asking me to come visit" will be a consolation. I don't know if he'll believe me when I say, "I'll be back as soon as I can."

I've already said this once.

But I meant it then, and I mean it now. I mean it so much. I'll come back for him after this is all over.

London's secret message for us comes during that night's nine o'clock broadcast.

There's a flurry of excitement. The Bernez here is named Goustan. It'll be my first and last time working with him.

Every inch of me feels heavy, my heart feeling it the greatest. There's too much here I don't want to leave. Too much here left undone, unsaid, unfinished.

But I've committed myself to this war and the orders that follow.

At that, I begin to follow Goustan through the night. Hitler's Atlantic Wall stretches all the way to Spain, but his fortifications are the strongest around major ports. Bayonne is not one of them.

We need to take caution nevertheless. There are still machine-gun towers, mines, and barbed wire. There will still be Germans lying in wait in the Bay of Biscay.

But tonight is a new moon. That'll help. Francis, Zacharie, and I, along with forty-two others, skulk through the darkness toward the beach.

I'll miss the salt air. I'll miss the sounds of the port. I'll miss the people of *Breizh*. I thumb my necklace. There's one person I will miss the most.

Goustan must've held up his hand. In front of me, Zacharie stops. I run into his back.

"Ouch," he says in a dramatic whisper.

"That didn't hurt."

He chuckles slightly. It's a tick I've noticed of his. Zacharie laughs when he's nervous. Francis becomes quiet. Evan fidgets, often touching his face.

All thoughts always seem to return to Evan.

We begin moving again. The ground turns to sand. Like a life-or-death game of follow the leader, we painstakingly make our way across the mine-infested beach.

Waves crash.

My pulse thuds.

It's funny how boarding a ship has become secondary to my angst at leaving.

My own tick is a restless brain.

We stop, the waves lapping at our feet. I back up to drier ground and perch on my suitcase. All that's left to do is wait for the rowboats to come for us. I bite my lip, feeling the emotion building in me again. This time I stare into the inky night, my terror at stepping aboard a ship again finally dwarfing my other emotions.

My breath quickens. My skin is clammy.

I hear a whispered, "Claire."

The voice is agonizingly familiar. A cruel trick.

A second voice cuts through the darkness, Francis's. "Evan?"

Evan?

It couldn't be.

I hear my name—my code name, I correct—again and again, his voice still whispered but drawing nearer.

"She's here," Zacharie says.

Then hands frame my face—and Evan is before me, kneeling in the sand.

"You're here," I gasp. "How is that possible?"

"I have my ways."

"You're coming with us?"

Evan smiles and whispers, "Always so many questions."

"I'm serious."

I can't think why else he'd be here, if not to run away with me. Evan lowers his hands from my face to my hands, squeezing them. I wish I could see his expression more clearly. He's here, only inches from me, but I can't read his cheekbones, the lines of his forehead. The cleft in his chin is lost to the night.

"No, I'm not coming. But I couldn't let you leave without say-ing goodbye."

Hearing him say that word is an ambush to my thoughts. But all I can seem to utter is "You're here to say goodbye, that's it?"

"I had to come before you left."

I furrow my brow. "You're here . . . and you're content to only say goodbye?" This whole situation is so unexpected. I'm still playing catch-up. But a question weasels its way in. "Are you fine with me leaving?"

And suddenly it feels like the ground has been ripped out from beneath me. I've fallen for this man, yet he's content for me to leave—now that he's said goodbye? Is that what is happening here? I had every intent to leave tonight, but it was killing me inside. After reading my letter, I imagined Evan as upset as I was. But his voice is sure. Have I been wrong?

It feels too similar. It feels like anytime my father is happy to send me on my way after a brief time with me.

Did Evan actually only want me for the time I'd be in France? Is he just like the other men in my life? Was I only a diversion, like with the married man I'd dated?

I rephrase my question into a statement. "You're fine with me leaving."

"Listen to me. You need to go."

I need to go? But wasn't I already set to go? He didn't need to risk coming here to tell me that. I look away. My voice is barely more than a whisper when I question, "Why are you really here?"

"What?" His brows furrow, then he grips my arms, refocus-ing. "Claire, listen, it won't be safe here soon."

I slowly turn my head from side to side, confused, frustrated. "When has it ever been safe in France, Evan?"

"There's a reason they want their pilots."

"London has always wanted our pilots back."

"Sure, maybe, but I've heard other whispers."

I clench my eyes shut. Why does it feel like he has an answer for everything? And also like this conversation has an expiration that's quickly approaching? "If it's not safe for me, it's not safe for you. You're here." He's still holding my hands. I shake them. I want to shake sense into him. "Get on this ship with me. We'll leave together and come back when it's safe."

"I can't."

"Why the hell not?"

"This is my home, Claire. I'm not leaving it."

That's a punch to the gut. Of course I know it's his home, but after the last year, it feels like mine too. And here Evan is, telling me that I need to go, yet insisting he must stay. And if he's staying, why not ask me to weather this storm with him?

"Ask me to stay, Evan."

"What?"

"Ask me."

"You have orders. You followed them before when you left Plouha."

"Yes, but that was to help more people. This time I'm being pulled out."

"But you'll still go."

"I don't have to," I snap. I blow out a breath, trying to regain composure. My emotions and logic feel as erratic as the waves. What am I doing?

Sabotaging, I know it. But I cannot stop, driven by a lifetime of feeling unwanted. "Ask me, Evan. Ask me to stay and I will."

I can sense the others listening, but I don't care. All that matters is what Evan says next.

"I won't ask you to stay."

I rip my hands from his. Tears build in my eyes. Anger builds too. "Maybe if you asked your wife to stay, she wouldn't have left."

I regret the words immediately.

"I'm sorry."

Evan is still right in front of me, but he might as well be a mile away. His voice comes low. "That's where you're wrong. I did ask her to stay. It did nothing. She left anyway. She never came back. And eventually you'd leave too. You already left for months."

"I had a job to do."

"Exactly. You came here for a reason, and that reason is not me."

"That's not fair."

"I'm not pointing fingers or saying you've done anything wrong. But that's the reality. You came here for a mission. That mission is now over."

What it feels like he's saying is that this—us—we—are now over.

The air suddenly feels colder, the wind whipping at my hair, my damp cheeks. The shadows of the others around me are no longer here.

"Claire," I hear. It's Francis. "The boats . . . the others are already boarding."

I nod. "Perfect timing, it seems."

Evan reaches for my hand. "Claire, after this war—"

"Oh, you'll want me then?"

It's never my terms. It's always theirs.

Both Evan and Francis speak my name at the same time.

"Goodbye, Evan. I'll be sure to *beaj vat*." Then I wade into the water.

★ ★ ★

NO PART OF ME BELIEVES I'LL HAVE A NICE TRIP. IT'S NO secret I've long feared ships and bodies of water.

I don't trust Mother Nature and those rogue waves, icebergs, and deadly storms of hers.

Furthermore, I have too much trust that the Germans who have engineered the mines and torpedoes to sink our ships are overly competent at their jobs. I've read of their successes too many times.

Regretfully, a hand helps me from a ladder to the deck of the *Visenda*.

I'm numb, my emotions mangled. Angry at myself for letting myself fall for another man. Heartbroken that what felt to be forever had only been temporary. Ashamed that I'd said things I didn't mean. Frustrated that I made an utter mess of our final exchange.

I barely remember boarding the lifeboat, being rowed through the dead of night, and being told to climb.

"You're trembling," a sailor says to me now in English. It's the first I've heard the language in over five hundred days, an extremely stark reminder that I am no longer on French soil. "Let me fetch a blanket."

One is wrapped around me.

"Here, come sit down."

I'm guided through the pitch blackness into a chair.

"Better?" I'm asked.

"I will be," I mumble, staring blankly.

I hear his long breath, likely reluctant to leave the unstable woman sitting alone.

I don't know where Francis and Zacharie have gone. I don't care.

The ship's engine roars to life. We begin moving at such a great speed that I bang into the chair's arm, nothing more than a rag doll.

A shot rings out.

The sailors yell to take cover. This yanks me from my somber state. I fall from the seat to my knees, covering my head. The shots keep firing. But it's dark, the middle of the night, and I can't tell where they're coming from, if the bullets are hitting their marks.

As quickly as the gunfire began, it ends.

The sailor's rushed breaths are suddenly beside me. "Are you okay? Have you been hit?"

"No," I say.

"Brilliant," he says, no doubt relieved I'm no worse than I was when he left me. "The warship cleared the way for us. Are you well enough to move inside? It'll be more comfortable. We should arrive in Cork in—"

"Cork?"

"Yes. Our original course was set for Plymouth, but the bombing in England is still ongoing. We've been rerouted to Ireland. We'll ferry you to land, then we'll continue to Newfoundland."

"Canada?"

"We're loaded to the gills with macaroni and kraut, set for a POW camp there. They shouldn't be a bother, though, ma'am. Shall we?"

The sailor helps me to my feet and escorts me to a stateroom. It's small. Two wicker chairs, a sink, a dressing table, and a bed, raised as if another should be underneath.

I thank him before he leaves.

For a moment I simply stand there. Feeling overwhelmed, not knowing where to start in my head. A rock of the ship forces me forward. Instinctively I cover my mouth, knowing seasickness is going to hit me like a ton of bricks. I stagger to the sink, splashing cold water on my face.

The draperies are closed at the bedside porthole. I'm thankful for that. If I pretend, this is any old room—and not a room on a ship that is getting increasingly farther from shore and deeper into the Atlantic.

How long had the sailor said the trip would take? Then I remember, he didn't. I had cut him off. But I suspect a day, give or take a few hours.

I can do this.

If I can sleep, that'll already remove a chunk of my time at sea. And I'm not cutting across all of the Atlantic, like I was meant to do in the past. I'm merely cutting the corner to Cork.

I toddle toward the bed, sliding a hand along the sink until I can transfer to the mattress. I climb—literally climb up and in.

Then I plead for sleep. I'm desperate for sleep. I do not want to remember the stories I've been told about *Titanic* thirty-some years ago. Neither do I want to remember the words exchanged with Evan only hours ago. One sends me into a panic, the other into heartbreak. Then the emotions reverse. Panic over never seeing Evan again. Heartbreak over that night on *Titanic*. I would've said so many things differently to Evan. My life would've gone so differently if not for my *maman* wanting to start again overseas. To think I'd be American. To think I may not have been in Paris when Marie walked in. To think I never would have met Evan.

I plead harder for sleep.

* * *

"KNOCK, KNOCK," I HEAR ON THE OTHER SIDE OF MY STATE-room door. His words come in English instead of French, another dagger to my morale.

I sit up in bed. No need to dress. I never changed last night.

"Come in, Francis," I call in French.

His head pokes through the cracked door first, then his whole body. "How'd you know it's me?"

I frown. It's now I switch to English. "I used to be a secret agent and trained for such things."

He sighs. "I'm not happy about this either. But hey, how about some grub?"

"I'm not hungry."

"Some fresh air, then."

I wonder aloud, "What time is it?"

"Nearly seven."

"In the morning?" No wonder I'm exhausted. What on earth is this man doing up and knocking on my door? I nudge aside the curtain. Daylight. And a nerve-racking, expansive sight of the sea. I swallow. "Yes, some fresh air."

Really, I want to count the *Visenda*'s lifeboats.

"Let me check," I begin in French. I pause, sigh. I continue in English. "I'll meet you on deck."

I take care of my morning necessities, then find Francis with both hands on the railing, gazing yonder. I stop a few paces behind him, thumbing the pearl around my neck, missing Evan, blaming Evan, maybe blaming myself even more. "I'm ready," I say to Francis.

We stroll, with Francis glancing at me every few steps. "Being on the water doesn't seem to suit you."

"Am I that green?"

"At least the trip is short."

"At least there's that," I say, distracted. A row of lifeboats is ahead. As we pass, I count. Fourteen. "Do you know how many people are on board?"

"Oh, I don't know."

Yeah, me neither. I grab the arm of a soldier passing by. "Sir, hello, sorry, hi. Do you know how many are aboard this ship?" I press my lips together. Then add another, "Sorry," because the sailor looks startled at the intensity of my question.

"Um, a crew of one hundred seventy-four, over a thousand detainees, a few hundred to guard them, then our addition last night of—"

"Forty-five."

"Well," he says, "there you have it."

"And the number of lifeboats? Are there enough?"

"With the ninety life rafts, yes."

"Thank you," I say, achieving a minuscule level of calm. It's something.

"Is there anything else I can help you with, ma'am?"

"No. No, that's—"

I'm thrown off my feet. A sound rings out, so consuming my eardrums could burst. My hip screams. My head, I've hit it.

Then I hear nothing. My cheek is against the deck. Feet rush by. I lie there. Stunned. Shocked. Suspended in time.

Francis's face is in front of mine. His mouth moves.

I push onto my elbow, wincing at a pain in my shoulder.

Francis's mouth still moves. There's a trail of blood running down the side of his face.

I touch my own head and wince again. An egg has already formed.

I push against my ears. I shake my head. A mistake. I cringe. I press again on my ears. I still hear nothing.

Then with a *pop* I hear everything. Screams. Fragments of directions being yelled. My name.

"Francis." My voice sounds far away.

He leans closer. "Are you okay?"

I adjust from my elbow to my hand. "I think so. What happened?"

"We hit a mine, I think."

I whip my head toward the lifeboats. My vision is blurred, making the sight I see even more horrifying. "No," I whisper.

"What's wrong?" Francis asks, but then I see awareness bloom on his face. I blink, focusing my eyes. One lifeboat has been damaged in the blast, and also a davit is split in half. Without the crane-like device, the lifeboat it's meant to lower is useless.

That's two lifeboats lost.

"There are other lifeboats," Francis asserts. "Here," he says, standing to his own feet, wobbling a step to the left, then extending me a hand, "let's get you on your feet." I take his hand. "Easy now."

"Easy now," I repeat, my eyes still locked on the lifeboats.

The crew is already preparing to launch them. A crowd is forming.

Someone yells how the engine room is flooding.

I squeeze on either side of my nose, closing my eyes, wishing for the pain in my head to subside.

A distress signal is launched into the sky. Today's sky is beautiful.

On my feet I sway, but I manage a step forward. Lifeboats save lives. I know this. I've experienced this. My father has told me stories of this.

His stories are all I have to rely on. I was too young to remember *Titanic*. Too young to remember somehow leaving my *maman*'s arms and being passed to countless others, until I eventually reached the arms of someone in lifeboat sixteen.

"Afterward," my father had told me when I was old enough, "your *au pair* searched for you on *Carpathia*. Remarkably, she found you and brought you to me in London."

"And my *maman*?"

"She was never found. I don't know what happened to her. I only know she cherished you."

Emotion pricks at my eyes.

A davit is getting the first lifeboat into place, about ready to load people. There's a loud snap, a crunch, then the lifeboat plummets toward the sea. The resulting sound is less splash and more crash.

I run, my footfalls wayward, toward the ship's side. The lifeboat is in pieces. I notice, too, we're closer to the surface. "We're sinking." I press a hand over my heart. "Francis, we're sinking."

He nods, his own fear evident in bulging veins along his temples. "We'll get a lifeboat."

"Yes," I say. "Yes. Just not that one."

"My God, Claire," Francis says, incredulous. "Even now you joke."

But I need to. I think I may need to become a full-blown comedian when another lifeboat is shifted into place and, again, the davit fails.

A second lifeboat meets the water's surface.

There are ten left.

I've taken to clutching Francis's hand without even realizing it. He pulls me forward. A life vest is pushed at each of us as a sailor runs by.

I waste no time putting it on over my coat.

The third lifeboat is lowered. Everyone watching collectively holds their breath. When it doesn't plummet, a sailor calls, "First to load, step forward."

No one moves.

"Claire," Francis prods.

Logically, I know I must get on. But I shake my head.

The boat loads with a few nurses, some sailors, one of which is very young. It's only half full.

The sailor calls out, "No one else for this boat?"

"The next one," I say to Francis. "We'll get that one."

Together we watch as the lifeboat lowers, and lowers, and lowers. The ship lists. The lifeboat bangs against the ship's side. But then it hits the water's surface, just as it should.

The many, many people on deck push forward to the next lifeboat getting moved into place.

There are nine left.

And those rafts. But I am not getting in a life raft in the middle of the Atlantic.

"Come on, Francis," I say, tugging him forward.

"Now she wants on," I hear him say.

"Women first!" is called.

The next boat is filled entirely with nurses and women I hear referred to as Wrens.

Eight left.

"Any other women?" is called.

"Is the ship still moving?" I ask no one in particular. I ask because of *Britannic*, because I've read how boats and people alike were pulled into the propeller. Miraculously, a woman survived the incident. I bet she hasn't gone near water ever since. I wouldn't. I want no part of it even now. "Are we still moving?" I call louder, more frantic.

"No," someone answers. "The turbine is blown. We're going down, you fool."

I ignore the barb.

The sailor calls out, "No more women?"

"Here!" I yell, noticing I am one of the last. They'll have to begin taking men too. "Here!" I shoulder myself to the front, not letting go of Francis's hand. "But with him too." I whip my head around. "Where's Zacharie?"

"I haven't seen him," Francis says into my ear, otherwise I'd never hear him. The volume of the men has increased, everyone now jockeying to get on.

"Get in then, woman!" someone hollers. "We're sinking, for the love of God."

I very well plan to get in.

I eye the sailor manning the lifeboat. "Him too?" I repeat.

"The both of you," the sailor confirms. "Go on, what are you waiting for?"

I step into the boat.

Francis is right behind me.

I wrap my fingers around and under the seat bench. More men are loaded. And more and more. Finally, we begin to lower.

I'm glad I don't remember this from my first sinking. How outlandish to even be able to say *my first sinking* . . .

But here I am again.

The lifeboat tilts left, then right, then left again. We thud onto the water's surface.

"Away!" is yelled by one of the two sailors at the helm of our boat. They begin rowing.

I let out a long-held breath.

We've made it.

As we distance, I keep an eye trained on each lifeboat that goes down thereafter until . . . Zacharie is on the third remaining boat. I recognize many of our forty-three.

It's only then that my grip is loosened, though not entirely, from my seat. Still, there are hundreds on board. The majority are detainees, but I don't wish for anyone to be lost to the sea. Better for them to rot in a cell for what they've done during this war.

The second to last boat lowers, filled to such a degree that it begins to immediately take on water.

We watch in horror as the water level rises and the boat lowers, until the men are within the freezing water and the boat is fully submerged. Then gone. The men splash and flail. Some swim for the nearest lifeboats.

Panic seizes me at our boat being ambushed—and sunk. I'm relieved to feel the motion of our boat moving away, not closer. I'm also relieved it is not me but the oarsmen who have made this decision.

When the final lifeboat hits the water, it's overwhelmed with men. I have to look away as that boat, too, succumbs to the over-abundance of weight, leaving even more splashing within the icy water.

Life rafts begin to be thrown like candy. The men in the water latch on and climb in. They'll be saved. Each of them. Yet another relief.

But still, there are more on board. Prisoners, made clear by their clothing, descend the side ladders like ants, one after another in a line, moving quickly.

The ship groans and lists farther.

She tilts so severely that half the ship is soon fully in the water. Men cling to the ship's side. Men begin sliding off the deck and into the water. I gasp when I see the captain do this very thing. He simply steps off, letting the frigid water have him.

Only a sliver of the ship remains, the last refuge for the remaining men. Italian internees is my best guess. They don't move. They don't enter the water. They remain exactly where they are when suddenly the ship rolls, her bow raises, and then she's gone, taking the men with her.

I stare in disbelief at what has occurred in only a matter of minutes.

Visenda has sunk, and now I am once again stranded at sea.

CHAPTER 29

Violet

—

At sea aboard *Majestic*
October 13, 1925

MANY WOULD'VE CALLED ME A FOOL FOR RETURNING TO SEA after surviving three disasters. But the land doesn't feel any safer. Illness, death, and war can still find me there.

So can Leo, but I couldn't let him find me. I told myself selling our London house and moving us to the country was only for Mother's health. Dr. Cree did insist the fresh air would be good for her. But in reality, I knew it was because I'd been too much a coward to face Leo if he had come looking for me in Ealing after the war. He could've easily learned of my whereabouts aboard a ship, then. My brothers would've gladly given me away, both my location at sea and also my hand in marriage.

No, imposible.

I reasoned: How could I give myself to him when my life was still not my own to give? As such, years have passed and Leo's letters have remained unopened and tucked away in a small shoebox that has journeyed with me through each new voyage.

Though, on these voyages, I am delighted to receive news from my brothers. The twins moved to Australia shortly after the war, with the totality of our meager savings, to begin Jessop Brothers. William chose his own path, marrying a nurse he'd met while serving.

It's just as it should be. *Family first,* I pride myself on . . . I have prided myself on that for the past seven years, culminating to sixty-nine voyages, seventy if I count this current passage, one that is fortunately ripe with gratuities. My brothers send small stipends home, but they have their own debts, their own lives to see to. I wouldn't dare rob them of that.

I focus on the woman in front of me. She's known as Bear Woman. It's no wonder why. Her face is covered in straight black hair. The same hair, only coarser, is present on the rest of her visible skin. Her eyes, nose, and teeth are unusually large. She does, for all intents and purposes, resemble a bear. And it's been quite profitable for her.

"How long was your tour in America, Miss Perez?" I ask her in Spanish as I lead her to a stateroom. Usually she'd be in second-class lodgings, but when I realize we share a language and when I learn a room is vacant in first class, I come here instead. I'll deal with Mr. Hampton's disapproval later.

Her mouth falls open at the opulence of the stateroom.

I smile genuinely.

"Um," Miss Perez begins. Her voice is beautiful, melodic. In her circus act, she sings. It's no wonder. "Nearly a year. I'm eager to return."

"Oh?"

I have a firm rule that prying should be confined to this single word. If they wish to say more, which they generally do, they will.

"A sweetheart's waiting for me," Miss Perez all but gushes.

I fluff a pillow that's gone flat. "How wonderful. Now, should you need anything, there's a bell just there for you."

She thanks me and I'm on my way to another room. Word has it that a Mr. Capone is also on this voyage. Not that I'd be able to pick him out. The ship is not short of bootleggers in dark suits and fedoras, now that America is firmly in Prohibition and a passenger line is a viable option for exportation, as long as customs is dodged.

In general, the vibe of the ship has altered. Gone are the days of mass immigration, and now there are the many who simply wish to visit abroad, inexpensively at that.

I don't mind, as long as they tip well.

Most do, though many of the other stewards insist a longer, multi-destination voyage—a world tour—is ripe with good tippers. I suppose it makes sense, as I'd be with the same passengers for nearly half a year. It'd be rather awkward, for us all, if they were tight with the purse strings. An enticing endeavor.

And I jump at the chance after my voyage ends, deciding on a change of pace, of scenery, of income.

I decide to do my first world tour, then more. And more. The years accumulate. I lose track of how many exactly. I travel to the most fascinating of places: Japan, China, Indonesia, all over Asia.

I decide to do something completely rash. I marry on a lark. Then I divorce even quicker, knowing it'd never last beyond the ship. I wish to say little about him, only that the tendrils of time must've wrapped around me and clouded my judgment.

It was the sombrero, the spurs, the lifestyle of lassoing sheep and spending more time in a saddle than out . . . and he reminded me of my father.

Everyone is entitled to one *loca* decision in their lives. This was mine, a moment of weakness that compelled me to say *sí* when he asked.

But maybe there was more to it. Maybe I ached for a thrill while the world—and even I myself—suffered a depression. Maybe it was because I received news that my baby sister, Eileen, had married. Maybe it was because I was lonely, even while spending twenty-four hours a day, seven days a week surrounded by a sea of people, whom I resolve to keep as nothing more than acquaintances. Maybe it was because much of my life simply repeats itself.

At land.

At sea.

At war.

At land.

At sea.

And now, again, at war.

My ship is once more recommissioned. I am once more out of a job. I'm once again en route to the house I share with my mother, with me somehow recently crossing fifty years of life. Yet it's my younger, wedded sister who greets me as I enter our country home.

"Violet! You're here," Eileen says, pulling me into a hug, the rhinestone bracelet I'd given her years ago cold against my neck.

I startle at her touch, stiffening. How long has it been since I've been hugged? I've embraced Mother in recent years, but I cannot recall when I've been the recipient of such affection. Well, besides my ex-husband, whom I'd rather put out of mind.

I soften into her hug, returning it. My eyes flick toward the window, knowing Mother will be there. There's a man—who I presume to be my sister's husband, Chester—in a chair, reading the newspaper.

He stands, the two of us quickly exchanging a cordial *how do you do.*

My sister and Chester had a small ceremony not long ago, not wanting to make a fuss. Or spend the money. I'd been in Athens.

Eileen hugs me again.

"Congratulations," I say, realizing she likely cannot hear me and that she needs to see my lips. I pull back and repeat myself.

"Thank you, Vi."

And when she touches her stomach, I realize I've congratulated her on the wrong thing. I squeeze her hands, my cheeks pushing out into a grin. "And a baby," I muse.

For a moment I simply stare at my baby sister, no longer little. Gone is the cherublike girl with red curls and forget-me-not blue eyes who ran everywhere she went when we lived at the convent together. Every evening at six o'clock we'd be reunited, her curls bouncing as she hurried toward me with outstretched arms. We called that hour "our very own."

It's been so long since we've spent any significant time together. Somehow Eileen is in her midthirties, specks of gray to her hair, with eyes that have seen her own life's ups and downs.

Married. With a child on the way.

I hold a plethora of emotions, ranging from pride to happiness to jealousy.

"It's so good to see you," I say, cognizant of the speed of my diction, enunciating each word, aspiring not to insult Eileen in the process. "Though it is not quite six o'clock."

It takes her a moment, but I see the recognition spark behind her eyes. "Regardless, I'm happy for our very own time together." Despite Mother sitting wistfully in the room's corner and my sister's husband only a few paces away. "Oh! And I have more news too. I've gotten us clerical jobs. Well, Chester has with a few connections. Nothing fancy. Ill-paid, I'm afraid." She laughs and I match her. "But it's something. And, Vi . . ." Eileen pauses, glancing at her husband. "I'm glad not to be a burden anymore."

"No," I cry out, louder than intended. Chester jars at my volume. Mother even quirks at the noise. "Never," I insist, leaning closer. "Never, ever. I love you, our family. Mother." My voice chokes.

"But you've done so much, given up so much."

I only shake my head. Being there for my family may have begun as a promise to my father, but it's become my existence. Sister and daughter is who I am. I don't begrudge anyone that. We all need to be somebody. "No. Now, tell me more about this job."

★ ★ ★

THE JOB IS AS POOR AS EILEEN DESCRIBED. THOUGH, WHEN the war demands for women to work in factories and I begin there, I can argue that work is far worse.

Both are better than being at the forefront of this second war.

Women much younger than me are now contributing as nurses, as shipbuilders, as ambulance drivers, even as spies. Or so I hear.

It's comforting to think my brothers are too old. Leo is too old.

Leo . . .

Maybe it's the existence of another war. Maybe it's my loneliness. Maybe it's my failed marriage or my baby sister's successful matrimony. It matters little; Leo is consistently in my head. And I wonder what he wrote in his letters to me all those years ago, if he put more of what our future could've looked like on paper. If perhaps it's not too late to indulge in the fantasy of a future together.

For the first time I set the shoebox with his letters on my bed and think I may open it.

Sí, I will.

Heart pounding, breath bated, hands shaking, I flip through the twenty-four letters I received in the two years Leo wrote me between sinking alongside the *Britannic* and the first war's end.

I land on the most recent letter.

I trace a finger over my name. Unable to wait a second more, I rip open the envelope and unfold the pristine paper.

It could be a scene straight from a motion picture. But in this story, the girl does not get the man. No, the man has already gotten the girl—and it is not me.

I've met someone, I read.

There's more to what he's written, a tear landing, expanding, eating up more of his words. But what's the point in continuing? I don't need to read any of the others. None of the other letters matter, when it'll lead to those three words.

Over the years, I had imagined what had become of Leo's life after the war. I assumed he eventually would've married. He'd have children, maybe even grandchildren.

I wanted that for him.

Likewise, it never has been in the cards for me, never more clear than in this moment. Life really is better alone, because pain is inevitable and we might as well minimize it.

I twist my lips and nose, stifling the emotions I unleashed from my very own Pandora's box.

The next day I'm on the bus after a long day at the factory, ignoring the book that's been sitting on my lap, too dark to read. The holidays are approaching. Instantly, I think of Naples. Instantly, I chastise myself.

With a sigh, I gaze out the window as we come to my stop. I ready myself for the short walk down our lane and toward the house.

I'm surprised to find an unknown auto in the dirt drive. I quicken my pace. Inside, Mother's nurse has a hand over her mouth. She's pacing by the entry door.

"What is it?" I ask her, noticing Mother is not in her usual chair. "Where's my mother?"

She stutters out a response. I think I must've heard her incorrectly. But then she repeats, "She's gone."

"Gone? Where could she have gone?"

Mother needs help walking. She needs encouragement to eat. Mother needs prodding and aid to do all aspects of her life.

"No." The nurse shakes her head. "She's gone, Miss Violet. She's passed on."

Passed on.

They are two words I never expected to hear, though I've heard them too many times in my life, though Mother is eighty-two years old. But now she's gone, the most foreign of concepts. "Where is she?" I need to know.

"I helped her to bed early today. She seemed more tired than usual. I called the doctor when . . ." Her eyes tear and a sob spills out.

I touch her arm. "I know, Janice. I know."

Then I go to my mother in her bedroom, fully aware that it'll be one of the very last times I set my eyes on her.

She's still beautiful. Long auburn hair, much like my own in youth, that's gone snow white. It's down instead of coiled into a knot. She looks only to be resting. A strong-willed woman who moved to Argentina instead of losing the man she loved. Not knowing a lick of Spanish. Who scrupulously dressed every afternoon at four o'clock for all the world to see, as if she expected the king of England. It was only ever Father.

That was Mother . . . until Ray, then Denis, Molly, and then, completely shattering her, Father. She still knows nothing of Philip.

Now Mother joins them.

And me . . . I realize with an emotion so strong that I brace myself against her bed . . . I no longer have a promise to uphold to my father. My sister is married. My brothers are grown. Mother's soul is no longer on this earth. I've been living for them for as long as I can remember.

And now, it is only me.

CHAPTER 30

Daphne

CODE NAME CLAIRE
Alias Madame Claire Fondeu

Atlantic Ocean
March 25, 1944

IT'S CRAZY HOW QUICKLY THE TIDES CAN TURN. ONE MOMENT *Visenda* was there, the next she was gone, leaving only churning, bubbling water. And now the water is settled, calm, the sea an accomplice to what's happened only an hour ago.

A plane's engine is heard above our lifeboats. I react so quickly, everyone reacts so quickly, upturning our heads, that our tiny boat rocks.

I clench the bench seat, fighting through waves of nausea, as I watch as bags are dropped, containing first aid kits, food, cigarettes, and a message that help is coming.

There's nothing on the horizon.

The plane circles, the engines roaring in my head, a dull, seemingly endless throbbing pain.

Four long hours pass, my emotions feeling frayed, hanging on by a thread.

But then . . . a vessel on the horizon. I could cry, despite my reluctance to get on another ship. Anything to get out of this tiny lifeboat.

Within hours, I'm stepping onto Irish soil. I'd be fine never to leave again, never to board another boat. In fact, I now live in Ireland. I'll promptly learn Gaelic.

As it turns out, in theory I'd have ample time to learn the language. Francis, Zacharie, and I are brought north to the base of the British Expeditionary Force, a branch of the British Army meant to help protect Ireland's valuable ports and coastlines.

There, we're told to do nothing but recuperate, while the pilots we freed from France are flown back to London. I'm left with little to do but twiddle my thumbs, replay my final conversation with Evan, and apparently recover from a concussion. I'm told that's my priority.

But recovery is not my personal preference. I'd rather torture myself—about a multitude of things. Evan, yes. But also how I felt relief as our lifeboat distanced from *Visenda*. So many drowned, while I survived. For the next month I'm reminded of that each time I hear of how another body washes ashore. Most cannot be identified.

I ask for work to occupy my mind. There are alleged intelligence-gathering trips happening here to glean information on the rail system south of the border. However, I'm placated.

"Hang tight," I'm told.

Hang tight? When have I ever hung tight?

My whole life I've been chasing the next challenge, the next opportunity to prove myself.

When what's being called "the baby Blitz" ends in London in May, I expect we'll be sent back to London. But, no. We're kept in Ireland.

By this time I truly have learned a smattering of Gaelic.

One afternoon I'm half-heartedly paging through a book when Francis and Zacharie rush into the common room. They jostle to be the one to dial on the radio.

I set aside my book.

Francis answers my unasked question. "General de Gaulle is doing a broadcast."

Zacharie shushes him.

"The Supreme Battle is underway," General de Gaulle is saying. "Of course, this is the Battle of France and the Battle for France. For the sons of France, wherever they are, and whoever they are, the simple and sacred duty is to fight the enemy by all the means at their disposal."

Sons of France. Evan immediately comes to mind, along with that pang in my stomach that happens whenever I think of him. I focus on the broadcast, more information slowly trickling in. Our invasion of France is underway. Quite successfully, at that. On five beaches along a fifty-mile stretch in northern France, Hitler's Atlantic Wall has been breached.

Francis speculates this is why we were forced to leave the coast, even with Brittany farther beneath the attack.

I'd be naive to think what happens next will be easy. It's not. The reports we receive paint a picture of fighting gone rampant. Cities are gutted and burned to the ground. Many perish. But by the end of August, all of northern France has been liberated.

Bayeux. Cherbourg. Caen. Saint-Lô. Finally, Paris.

"Is it over, then?" I ask, my excitement getting the better of me.

Francis is quiet. I know this tell of his. "What is it?" I demand. "Tell me." I feel like I'm on an island on this island, only ever on the receiving end of news.

He sighs. "With the north under control, I suspect the fighting will move south. Specifically, southwest."

"You mean . . . to Brittany."

He nods. "We'll need to take back the ports there too."

"We should go," I spit out. "We can help."

"Claire," Francis says, "we're not trained for battle."

"Neither is he."

We both know who I am talking of. Francis doesn't say a

word. Nor do we receive sufficient updates on what is happening in *Breizh* with the Americans leading the charge. All I know for certain is when the Battle for Brittany is finally over. It took three long months.

Three long months when a multitude of dangers could have befallen Evan. Bombings, ground fighting, pillaging. Evan would have sooner died . . . He would've done whatever necessary to help the Americans remove the Germans from his home.

I contact London, asking them about his welfare. They think me a foolish woman. There are over twenty thousand men and women of the Resistance based in Brittany and I want an update on a specific one?

Yes.

They tell me to be patient. They'll bring us back to London soon.

That doesn't happen for another seven months, after the Battle of the Bulge, which puts the Germans officially on the retreat, and not until after the very last bomb falls on Britain.

A plane is sent for us in May, ironically the very day Germany surrenders. There are even rumors that Hitler has taken his own life. A coward's way out—and a way out I refused even before I entered the war, leaving that L-pill on the colonel's desk.

When we arrive in London, the city is in a state of celebration. To think I had a hand in this, doing my small part with our acts of sabotage and rescue missions.

What a feeling.

What a smile Young Allan Jeayes gives me when I approach the SOE headquarters on Baker Street.

"Mr. Dewitt, Mr. Edwards, Miss Chaundanson, welcome home."

"Oh, I'm Daphne again?"

He laughs. "If you wish."

"Daphne," Francis says. "How odd for you to not be Claire."

"And for you to be Mr. Dewitt."

It truly is odd and simultaneously poignant to hear my real last name, to say my real first name. Part of me had become Claire. Evan's Claire. But that's no more. I've no reason to ever be Claire again. I'll likely never see Evan again. And there's that familiar pit in my stomach, wondering if he came out of the battle unscathed. Now that my actions are my own to do with as I will, I vow to find out. Young Allan Jeayes—looking a little less *young* and more *middle-aged*—won't know Evan's fate. But maybe he'll know about the others I've grown to care for during this war.

Before our small group heads inside, I stop him. "Do you have news of Gabriel? Has he returned too?"

"Mr. Harrington has been in Portsmouth for quite some time now."

"Portsmouth. How grand." I recall him saying his Evelyn was doing secret stuff there. "And Louis?"

"Back with his daughter."

I warm even more. "Well, what about the rest? Adele, Suzanne, Denise, Marie?"

"We were able to evacuate Adele only recently. And even more recently, she reunited with her husband—"

"That's a relief," I cut in. I recall how Adele was adamant she only joined up for him and how she'd do anything to ensure his survival.

"Almost a tragedy, though. Her husband was imprisoned, but he was also able to escape."

"You're telling me I'm not the only escapee? Here I was, hoping to be the sole owner of that title."

Middle-Aged Allan Jeayes laughs.

"And Suzanne?"

His laughter fades. "Yvonne Rudellat was her real name. Sadly, she didn't make it. Miss Rudellat and her partner were stopped at a roadblock. Things escalated and they tried to break through the barricade. Unfortunately, Miss Rudellat was shot and hospitalized. We had plans to rescue her, but she was moved to a prison before we could. This is where our path goes a bit cold, but we believe she was taken to Ravensbrück, then to Bergen-Belsen, where she succumbed to an illness. We believe she's in a mass grave there."

"No," I utter.

How horrible. How frightening too. My own imprisonment could have ended so differently.

He removes his spectacles, wiping away a smudge with his sleeve, then returns the glasses to his face, a solemn expression there. "I wish I could say things fared better for Miss Borrel, whom you knew as Denise. She, too, was captured."

All I can do is shake my head, consumed by myriad emotions: shock, remorse, sadness for a woman with such strong convictions.

"We know more of her fate," he goes on, "as she was taken to a men's camp. The presence of a woman there—women, actually, as she was with three of our other female agents—wasn't a close-kept secret." He swallows hard. "All of them were executed. Witnesses, however, said Miss Borrel put up quite a fight."

I say in a small voice, "That sounds like her."

"It does, doesn't it." He clears his throat. "I can fortunately end with good news. We called Marie of Lyon back, as you may know."

"Did she return to France? She wanted to."

He snorts. "She wanted to very much. We refused, so Miss Hall weaseled her way back to France through the American Office of Strategic Services. She had a hand in Normandy, I surmise. Last I heard, she's in Paris, quite alive and well."

"Well, that's a relief. I must say, I don't envy all you know."

He shakes his head again. "Neither do I. But enough catching up. You have a life to return to, yeah? Back to being Miss Chaundanson, one of the lucky ones."

I smile, because that's what he wants from me in this moment. And I do feel lucky. I survived.

He extends his hand to me, and our time together ends the same way it began.

* * *

AS I APPROACH THE LONDON TOWN HOUSE, I KNOW THE woman I am now is different from the woman who left three years ago. There's something powerful in knowing that.

There's also something sad. I left not realizing how badly I craved a feeling of home. And now, more than ever, I feel displaced.

It didn't help that on the way here, my stomach turned at seeing great portions of London destroyed. Many buildings are lined with scaffolding, with renovation already underway. Some buildings are gone completely, reduced to rubble. Others have obvious water and fire damage.

It dawns on me I would've been told if my house no longer stood, a reassuring thought. In fact, I was given a key to the townhome before leaving the London headquarters. Of course they'd have a key.

The lamps are on when I step inside. I scrunch my brows and pause. My first instinct is to run. But no, I'm being silly. There are no Germans here. I'm not to be arrested or imprisoned. No one is hunting me anymore.

"Hello?" I call out.

I'm met with silence. I notice how the dust coverings have been removed from the furniture and a newspaper sits unfolded. Perhaps my father had been here, forgetting to close down the house before he dashed off to his next project. It's the most logical explanation.

I've nothing to unpack. All my belongings were lost in Lyon, then lost again at sea. It seems all that remains from my time in France is Evan's necklace.

I thumb the pearl, thinking of him. It's been just over a year since our ending on the beach, and while I'd only just vowed to learn of his fate, part of me wonders if I'm setting myself up for another dose of heartbreak. He very likely has put me out of his head. I saw him do exactly that with his first Claire. What's more, I've spent my whole life being rebuffed by men, mostly my father, but still, on that beach, I all but begged Evan to leave with me before changing my tactics and begging him to ask me to stay. I just wanted him to want me. He said no to both.

I'm too drained to further dissect the ins and outs of those rejections. I slump down on a sofa, my breath puffing out of me.

It's then that a man walks into the room.

He's absentmindedly flipping through a bound set of papers.

"Father?" I ask, launching to my feet.

He startles and the stack of papers lands on the ground with a *thunk*. "K-Katherine?"

My father is usually very put together. Lush, dark hair coiffed perfectly so. To my great astonishment, he looks a mess, his face unshaven and his hair standing on end.

"Oh, Katherine," he laments, rushing to me. My father has never rushed to me. He's never held me so tightly before either. "Finally, finally, you're home."

I dislodge myself from his embrace. I'm still so shocked to see him. Strange, as this is also one of his homes and there's the half-read newspaper . . . but he's rarely here. All I can think to say again is "Father?"

"Sit, sit," he says. "Are you well? You look well."

Along with being put together, his diction is usually composed. This man is foreign to me.

I sit. "What's wrong?"

"I've been so worried."

"About what?" The war is over.

"About you. How can you even ask that? About you, Katherine. I've been trying to find you for the past year."

It's as if I've stepped into an alternate universe. "I didn't know. I've only just been allowed to return."

"Where have you been?" He runs a hand through his hair, mussing it further. "It seemed strange when I hadn't heard from you. Usually you have something or other to share with me. With all the bombings, I became worried. I asked Higgins to check on you, but he said you weren't here. I feared you never left Paris. But no, he said there were signs that you'd been here. I contacted Josette."

"You remember Josette?"

"Well, Higgins recalled her name," he says, averting his eyes. "But Josette hadn't heard from you either. At that point, I figured you'd joined up in some way. I assumed something with languages or decoding here in London. You certainly have the mind for it. But you never came home. No one would tell me anything. All the volunteer groups swore they didn't have a Daphne Chaundanson signed up with them."

"I'm surprised you didn't ask for Katherine."

"Truly, you think I don't know your given name?" He pins me with a disappointed look, still standing. I wish he'd sit. Or better yet, leave. He will anyway. But then he continues, "I wagered you were part of some clandestine organization. I used every contact I had. I knocked on every door made available to me. Eventually some bigwig in the army put me on house arrest."

"No," I say, astonished. And because all of this is so out of character for my father, I break out into laughter.

"Katherine," my father admonishes me, his forehead overly creased. "This is serious. I have been a nervous wreck."

My laughter fades. "You have been, haven't you?"

"Yes. Why does that come at such a surprise?"

I rub my lips together. My father has always been honest with me, to a fault at times. But I realize now it's been my own mistake that I haven't always been honest with him about how I feel. I'd been too afraid to push him any further away. "I didn't think you'd notice my absence."

His shoulders stiffen, but I see his composure fall back into place before he says, "Well, I did."

Finally he sits, but far enough away that there's a gulf left between us.

"Father, I was gone for three years. You noticed after two." I can tell he's about to protest and I hold up my hand. "But I don't blame you. Well, that's a lie. I do, but only partially. I've never held you accountable as a father. I'd do something remarkable to impress you, you'd be momentarily dazzled, then the shine dulled and you discarded me. I was your daughter only when convenient for you."

"I discarded you?"

"Yes, our time together always had an expiration. Two, three days maybe."

"That can't be true—"

"And it was never just the two of us. There were always hordes of people and fans around. No one knows you *have* a daughter. Besides Higgins. But he doesn't count." I roll my eyes at my tangent and refocus. My heart is pounding with every honest word I get off my chest, and I need to keep going, to say it all. "You told me not to tell anyone that I'm your daughter. What makes me the angriest, though, is that I'm the one who let this all happen, again and again. You're the reason I can speak six languages."

Actually, I can now add Croatian, Breton, and Gaelic. But those additions have nothing to do with my father and every-thing to do with me. Funny thing is, I have no desire to change my total to nine. I have no desire to tell my father about *any* of my contributions in helping to end the war. Nor will I tell him about my imprisonment, sinking, or all the other incredibly dangerous situations I've faced, merely to have him momentarily fawn over me with concern.

"Oh, Katherine."

"It's Daphne," I correct. "My name is Daphne."

His head dips. "It is, I'm sorry. You may be the first person who's spoken to me like this. Well, besides your mother." His lips quirk into a small smile. "I see so much of her in you."

"I wouldn't know."

"Another of my mistakes, I'm afraid." He clears his throat and rubs beneath his nose. "If it weren't for me, your mother would likely still be here."

I scrunch my brows, not understanding. "What does that mean?"

He clears his throat again and he repositions on the sofa, inching closer to me. "I've told you a lot about that night, about *Titanic*, but not everything." My father looks pained, literally pained, as he says, "If it weren't for me, your mother wouldn't have been on that ship. I told you how your mother wanted to start a new life."

"Yes, you didn't want me."

He closes his eyes. "That's not the full truth."

I narrow my eyes.

He rubs beneath his nose again, a tell of his. He's choosing his next words carefully. "Have you ever wondered why there's no account of you on *Titanic*? I know you've done your research over the years."

I nod slowly. In the past, I reasoned away my absence from the passenger list. Many bodies were never accounted for, but even their names were on the manifest. Yet I've never been able to find mine. I say, "I assumed *Maman* used a different name for me, with her wanting to start fresh."

But even as I say it, I know it's not true. I've debunked that theory myself. I've found *Maman*'s name, so why would only mine have been altered?

"She did want to start a new life. That portion is heartbreakingly accurate. And I've told you how your mother wanted no part of mine. But there's more to it. She wanted *you* to have no involvement in my life either. I fought her on it. I wanted you from the first moment I laid eyes on you." His gaze drops to the cleft in my chin, the attribute we both share. "I fought your mother very hard about it, in fact. But your mother was insistent she didn't want you to be the daughter of Charles Labine. I didn't know her scheme. No, not scheme. That sounds too callous, and your mother was anything but cruel. I'll say I didn't know her plan until afterward. When your *au pair* brought you to me. She said a ticket was never purchased for you."

"No ticket? But why?"

"Your mother didn't want a record of you existing before America, so she snuck you on board."

"What? Why?"

"She wanted to quickly marry in New York, and have that man adopt you as his own. Your mother desperately didn't want there to be an account of you until you were living a new life, no connection to a life with me. Instead, a real family, a real father." He swallows roughly. "I'm sorry I've failed at that, at being a real father. I failed terribly, I see now. I thought I was fulfilling your mother's wishes by keeping you out of my world."

"So you never hid me because you weren't proud of me?"

"My God, no, Daphne. It was never that. I gave you your mother's family name and the name she chose for you. But I selfishly called you Katherine. I've made so many mistakes. If I had just let you go from the beginning, your mother never would have gotten on that ship. It haunts me."

My mind is still processing. My father had always wanted me? He feels responsible for my *maman*'s death? I lay a hand over his. "*Maman* dying on that ship wasn't your fault."

"She wanted to put an ocean between us."

"But it was her choice. You didn't ask her to go."

"It almost cost your life. I *never* would have forgiven myself for that. What's worse, I don't think I ever would have known." He sniffs. "But somehow, someone kept you safe that night. Then I continued to make sure there was always a safe place for you to live, to learn."

"But not with you."

"No. In part because of needing to keep you out of my world. But I see now I easily justified it because you've always been so intelligent. You thrived wherever you were. I didn't think you needed me to be more than I was."

"I did."

"I see that now. I regret that now. If I'd been a present part of your life, you would have told me when you returned to England. You would have told me you signed up for the war. Because those are things an involved father would know."

I nod. It's true. I would have written him those letters.

My father's eyes are wet with emotion. This may be the longest conversation we've ever had. It's easily the most important. Which, naturally, is why I cannot help a small quip. "It appears being on house arrest has done you a world of good."

He reaches over the gulf between us and squeezes my hand. "Can I make it up to you? Anything."

"I don't need anything from you. I never did. I mean, I won't say no to macarons, but . . ."

He laughs.

"But no," I finish. "I've only ever wanted you to want to be my father."

"You have me," he says. "I want that. I have an idea. Why don't we take a trip, just the two of us?"

"A trip?"

"Yes, I'll admit it's a bit of a selfish ask. If I don't get out of this house soon, I may lose my mind."

It's my turn to laugh. I'd rather get to know my father in a more normal environment—like this house that maybe could be a home—but I can see he's trying.

"What do you say, Daphne? Someplace neither of us has been. And not just for two or three days. We'll make an event of it."

"Okay," I say. "A trip sounds nice. Your choice. But before we go, I need to do something."

"Go on, you've piqued my interest. Anything I can help with?"

"Actually," I say, thinking. "Maybe you can. I met someone during the war and—"

"Like a man?"

I shake my head. "You certainly are taking this 'being a father' thing to heart."

He smiles. "I take it you lost touch with this man."

I wring my hands together. "You could say that. He could be where I left him. But there's a chance, with all the fighting in that part of France at the end of the war, that his home was destroyed or he's living somewhere else or he's in hospital or . . ." I let that train of thought die and instead say, "You mentioned all those contacts of yours that you used when you tried to find me . . ."

"Of course, of course. I'd be happy to help."

"Thank you. I just need to make sure he's okay. That'll be enough."

The way my father watches me, I think we both know that's not true. But it's time for me to be Daphne Chaundanson—and not stuck in the past as Claire Fondeu.

CHAPTER 31

Violet

—

Southampton Port aboard *Andes*
January 7, 1946

WE ALL NEED TO BE SOMEBODY. IT'S A THOUGHT I'VE HAD before. I'm a sister. I've been a daughter. I've been a breadwinner, a provider, a protector.

But now I can be something all my own. I can do and be whatever I decide. On the heel of my mother's death, it's a bittersweet realization.

All those years ago on *Titanic*, I had ruminated on what Madeleine Astor would be like. I applauded her for turning a blind eye and ear to all the naysayers about an eighteen-year-old marrying a forty-seven-year-old man.

I like a woman who goes after what she wants.

That's the thought I had back then.

Yet I hadn't done that myself.

That needed to change.

The problem was, for the life of me, I hadn't a clue what I wished for that to be. Nor did I know where there'd be a place for me. All of Europe is still dusting itself off after the war.

England is rebuilding.

Germany is dividing.

The sea, though . . . the sea still remains as it was, wide and expansive.

But is the sea for me? It almost sunk me three times. I left it because of illness. I left it because of war. I returned out of necessity. I returned because I still needed it. Did I need it even now?

One evening I was paging through Mother's prayer book. I'd found it with her possessions. And in the margins, my father's chicken-scratch had written, "Every eye forms its own fancy."

Then, not a day later, I was walking about town, and right there on a job board was a posting about the RMS *Andes* taking to the seas.

The Andes.

I couldn't believe it. I stopped right there, a woman running into me, and slapped a hand on my thigh in disbelief. The Andes was the very place that had breathed life into me as a child. In my memories I've gone back to our dinner table there many times. The Andes was the last place that ever felt like home.

And now there was the ship of the very same name.

Increíble. Fortuita. Too much of a coincidence to ignore.

In fact, I decided right then and there that if I applied and got the position, it'd be my last ship to work. My farewell voyage, on my own terms, sailing because I wanted to, not because anyone needed me to.

The Andes had been a beginning, and it would be my ending too.

I got the job.

And here I am, the ship preparing to leave within the hour. Actually, any minute now, I realize. Sailing day is always the most chaotic of days. There's luggage being delivered, vases to be found, questions to be answered, errands to be run, tea to be fetched, clothing and possessions to be put away.

But I don't mind; an old broom knows the dirty corners best. I put on a megawatt smile, pausing long enough to wind my watch from Stanley.

Another moment is forthcoming, I tell myself, then I offer a welcome to everyone I pass. I'll relish these encounters because they'll be my last of a very long career at sea, one I wasn't certain would ever come to an end.

I think of the bright-eyed young woman who once tacked a photograph of Mary Pickford on *Titanic*'s walls. I huff a chuckle at how starry-eyed I'd been. I had one of Charles Labine, too, vowing I'd one day have him sign it if he ever sailed during one of my voyages.

Shame he never did. That would've been something. He directed many a wartime film to boost morale. Seeing him now would be just as dazzling as it would've been in my twenties.

My brows furrow. Two passengers approach. And I must be caught up in my daydreams, because the man, even wearing sunglasses and a fedora that covers his trademark hair, could be a dead ringer for Charles Labine, though a bit longer in the tooth, as many of us are now. On his arm is a younger woman. However, she doesn't cling to him like the women I've seen in the magazines do.

I eye him—them—as they approach. My heartbeat quickens. It *is* him. The woman is young enough to be his daughter, lighter brown hair to his darker features. Tall, both of them. His head falls back in a laugh and the woman watches him admiringly.

Do I have the nerve to stop them?

"I'm sorry to intrude," I could say, "but could I trouble you for an autograph?"

But what would I have him sign? I pat my apron. Stanley's watch clatters—and now I know I must work up the courage, even if it is just to say hello and not let the next moment pass me by.

They're only feet away.

"Excuse me," I say. "I am a huge fan of your work, Mr. Labine, and I only wish to tell you so."

"Ah, it appears the incognito has failed."

But then he winks and the woman lets out a deep-sounding laugh. "Foiled, Papa." The woman turns to me. "We're on holiday."

"A birthday cruise," Mr. Labine says. "My daughter's birthday is in two days."

"A brilliant way to celebrate," I acknowledge. "Have you ever been to South America?"

"No," the woman says warmly. "Neither of us have. The real question is whether my father can handle three straight months with me."

The last question is directed toward him. She's being playful. Funny, I didn't know he had a daughter.

He smiles. "I most certainly can. It's not as if I'll jump overboard."

I laugh, his attention drawing back to me. His daughter's, too, her saying, rather, her offering, "How about an autograph?"

I pat my apron again. "Just a hello is enough, thank you. And should you need any—"

"No," the woman says, "that won't do. We have photographs in our rooms. Why don't I fetch one for you?"

I shake my head. "That's very kind of you, but—"

"Nonsense." The woman raises her chin. "I'll be right back."

"No," Mr. Labine says hastily. "You stay here in the fresh air, Daphne. I'll go."

"Oh, so now your paternal instincts kick in?" Again there's a playfulness in her voice.

He rolls his eyes, the most peculiar of responses for a man his age, and off he goes.

The woman turns to me. "I've already been struck with some motion sickness. A unique ability, as we haven't even left port yet."

I step closer. "Is there anything I can get you? Is it Miss Labine?"

"Chaundanson," she corrects, not unkindly. "But no, I'll be right as rain. The fresh air is already doing wonders. And it'll pass. It's happened to me every time I'm aboard a ship. That I can remember, that is. I was still in swaddles the first time I sailed,

I'm told. That ship sank." She punctuates the statement with a disbelieving shake of her head. "But I've already counted the lifeboats and we've more than enough."

"How scary," I remark. "I'm afraid I've been in your position." I hesitate, but then I add, "On more than one occasion."

"How peculiar," Miss Chaundanson says. "I've sunk twice myself. We both must be mad to be aboard yet another ship."

I let out a huff. "A young man once told me that he'd ask me to stay off ships, but it appears I'm invulnerable to maritime disasters. He called me Miss Unsinkable."

Miss Chaundanson guffaws. "The best yet the worst of nicknames. This trip was my father's very enthusiastic doing, and I didn't have the heart to tell him I was scared to my core. So here I am, facing my fears."

"Quite admirable. You, too, seem invulnerable to what life throws at you. I feel it's only fair to extend the notion of being unsinkable to you as well."

"I'm uncertain if I should thank you," Miss Chaundanson says with a smile. "Can I be forward and ask you something personal?"

I cock my head. I've been asked a number of intimate things throughout the years. My shoe size. My heritage. My hand in marriage.

"Go on," I say, wholeheartedly enjoying my conversation with this woman. A kinship, perhaps.

"When you mentioned that young man a moment ago, your eyes all but sparkled. Are you still in touch?"

I purse my lips, caught between emotions.

Miss Chaundanson grabs my hands. "Oh, I'm sorry, I never should've asked."

"It's okay. No, we are not. But I think of him often. A missed opportunity, you could say."

Miss Chaundanson's face changes, losing some of its animation. "And do you regret it?"

"*Regret* may not be the correct word. I'd make the same choice again. I suppose I only wish I could've traveled two paths, been two separate people, lived two lives."

"And you know nothing of him now?"

"That young man is no longer young. Nor am I."

"Age is nothing. Do you know my father and I only formed a relationship in recent months? If that old dog can learn new tricks . . ."

She smiles, and I laugh. Miss Chaundanson grows more serious. "What if you tried to find him? Gave that other path a try? How unbelievably romantic would that be if he's been waiting for you too?"

"That I know to be impossible. Leo wrote me years ago, speaking of having met someone."

"The young man has a name," Miss Chaundanson says with a wink that's so much like her father's, apparently ignoring the second half of my statement.

"He does," I say, prepared to make my exit.

"But I wonder," she says, a tap to her lip with her finger, "if this Leo of yours also wished he could've lived two lives. You said years ago. Much could've changed since then."

And now she's gotten in my head. Or maybe being aboard *Andes*, with all her serendipity, has relit a fire within me. Ever the pragmatic, I've always put one foot in front of the other, carrying on. But what if I choose more for myself? What if I choose running blindly, with abandon, toward my own possible happiness? And what if that happiness could be Leo? *One day . . . someday . . .* could be now.

I could go in search of him, even if only to say a friendly hello, to apologize for pushing him away, to tell him that my life is my own to do with as I want now.

And that I never stopped wanting him.

After all these years, he's still the something I want that could be all my own.

How vulnerable a thing to want. How presumptuous. I tell

myself again: *Leo is likely married to that someone from long ago.* He may not even be living in England anymore.

But I choose to hope. How Leo of me.

I'll return home, he had said in his letter. If he's not there, he'll likely be in Ipswich. Ask for him there. If he's not at either of those places, his sister would know where to find him. She's lived in the same address for years. She'd never leave it. In fact, he told me to start with Alma. He said he didn't want to wait a second longer than necessary to see me again.

And I don't want to wait a second longer than necessary to see him again either, no matter what happens once I find him. The horn of the ship blows, a final warning before the ship's departure.

CHAPTER 32

Daphne

Southampton Port aboard *Andes*
January 7, 1946

THE STEWARDESS—I RUDELY FAILED TO ASK HER NAME, though her nickname of Miss Unsinkable is truly one for the books—jerks her head toward the sound of the ship's horn.

Her hand goes to her chest.

I touch her arm. "Are you all right?"

But she doesn't answer. She mutters, *"Perdón,"* then turns. Her pace quickens. Tiny, quick footsteps. If I didn't know any better, her destination is the gangway to leave the ship.

But then I hear "Violet!" called—and she stops. Her back is to the voice, who I see now is a man.

It couldn't be. My hand flies to my mouth. This is something straight out of one of my father's films. The man's eyes are locked on her, on Violet.

She turns. "Leo?" she says, clearly astonished at his presence. *"Increíble."*

I look back and forth between the two of them.

"Violet." He jogs the remaining distance to her, hesitating only a moment before taking her hands in his. She stares at their hands, a perplexed expression on her face.

"I don't understand. I was just going to . . ." She points in the direction of the gangway. "But you're here. How . . . I can't believe you are here. How are you?"

"I'm well. I'm nervous. But yes, I'm here, Violet." He takes a step closer. "I've found you. I'm so glad I never asked you to stay off ships. Do you realize there are various lines?"

She chuckles, then nods.

"Well, I did not. For the record, I now know there are four."

"How many did you try?"

"Lucky number three."

She laughs, a sound I can see bolsters her Leo. He pulls her a step closer. "I've missed that laugh. Violet, this is going to sound forward, but I don't want to live without that laugh any longer. I'm an old man now. Maybe a foolish old man."

"You aren't the only one who has aged."

He chuckles. "I know you have responsibilities. Maybe that hasn't changed. Maybe this timing won't be any better. But leaving you after *Britannic* was one of the hardest things I ever had to do," Leo goes on, oblivious to me and the others who have stopped to—inappropriately, perhaps—witness their reunion. "But I meant what I said in my first letter. I would've been happy with whatever sliver of yourself you were able to give me. I wrote you. I wrote you for two years until—"

"You met someone. It's the only letter I could bear reading. Actually, just that single line."

"None of the others?"

She shakes her head, her response a whisper. "I couldn't, not back then."

Leo's jaw is tight. At first blush, it looks like anger. But no, I see it is composure he's fighting for. He eventually swallows, then hesitantly touches his forehead to hers. "Timing. Life is all about timing, isn't it? I married. I loved Maribelle deeply, but she passed away seven years ago. Then the war broke out. So many emotions were stirred up inside me. Missing Maribelle. Remembering you from the time we spent together in a different war. I remembered so much of us. I couldn't shake the wondering, those nettlesome what-ifs. My children—I have three of them—they encouraged me to try to find you. I knew Ealing was a long shot, but I looked there first. The only other place I knew to look was a passenger ship. So as soon as the war ended and these cruises began running again . . . well, here I am."

"After three ships. *Ay, Dios*, Leo. Your timing . . . truly. Divine intervention, perhaps. I only just had a conversation that made me realize I couldn't go another minute without searching for you. I was about to run off this ship."

He huffs out a breath. "You were not."

Violet's cheeks push out in a smile, her nod full of conviction. "But you caught me just in time. I thought I was about to send myself on a wild goose chase. And also be out of a job." She touches his cheek, her head tilting as she stares into his green eyes. "That's something that would've once been detrimental to me. So many of my decisions made were because of my family. So much of my fear was entangled in losing them, losing those I cared for. I kept an ocean between them and me to protect myself. That fear is part of the reason I pushed you away."

"But not anymore?"

She steps closer. "Not a chance."

A considerable crowd has grown. One man begins goading that he should kiss her. Soon it's a chant. I can't help but join in. "Kiss her, kiss her," I rally.

Leo's cheeks redden, making this man even more adorable.

"May I?" I think he asks her, his voice lost to the noise.

Violet nods.

And he does.

I clap. It feels like all of the ship is clapping. But in addition to my enthusiasm for these two long-lost loves, something is stirring inside me. My own second chance with Evan. I begin to backpedal, bumping into a woman behind me, blindly apologizing.

I told myself I was merely content to know if Evan was okay after the war. But that's a lie. I now know he's uninjured, though the butcher shop didn't fare as well. But he'd rebuild.

This is the information my father had told me, after he'd found him. But inserting myself back into his life would only cause us both pain. Or that's what I've been telling myself these past few months. But really what was keeping me away from him was my own fear. I was afraid he'd say no to me again.

I didn't think my heart could take it, not after I allowed myself to love him. Not after knowing what it felt like to be loved back.

But now I need to know if I can have that feeling again, if we can build a home together, even if it means an encore of heartbreak.

I realize the ship's moving. On our way to Buenos Aires. Apparently *my* timing is not as serendipitous as Violet and Leo's. But Violet is right. I am unsinkable. The minute we dock, I'll board yet another boat to get to France. The things we do for love.

Glancing once more at Violet and Leo, I crack a smile. They give me hope.

I look up to see my father down the deck. The crowd has thinned some, the show now over.

My father mouths, "I love you," and then he steps to the side, revealing a man behind him.

It couldn't be. I'm tempted to search for movie cameras because I'm now convinced there's little chance this is not one of my father's films.

"Evan?"

I'm truly agog.

He steps toward me, leaning on a cane.

I run to him, stopping short of barreling him over. I hesitate, then wrap my arms around his neck. "How . . . I can't believe you are here."

"This is a good surprise, then?" he says into my ear in French.

I pull back and look beyond him to where my father is seemingly mighty proud with himself.

"Were you two in cahoots?" I ask in French.

Evan waggles a brow.

As I'd done to him—poorly—when we'd first met. And now here we are again. "But I'm confused."

Evan explains, "Your father found me, apparently. But I didn't know he did. I was out of town for building supplies. Ever since our last conversation, though"—he blows out a breath—"it's been weighing on me. I would've said so many things differently. But I was scared."

"Me too," I admit.

"You'd already left for months, and I'd barely survived that. I was petrified that I was just a distraction for you."

"You weren't."

"Or that I wasn't anything meaningful to you."

"You were."

"But still I had to risk going to the beach that night to see you. I had to say goodbye—and apparently do a terrible job of expressing myself."

"You close down," I say, not judgmentally, and he gets that because he replies, "And you don't know your worth."

"We're both something," I whisper, realizing we now have our own audience, my father included. I'm not sure how many can understand our French. I glance at Violet, who is exchanging her own whispers with Leo, his arms around her. Her head turns toward me and she smiles.

"But," I go on, feeling emboldened by her love story, "we have another chance to get this right."

Evan rubs a hand up and down my arm. "I wasn't fair to you. I wouldn't leave, but I wouldn't let you stay. I made it about me and what I needed. But I meant what I started to say about us being together after the war. You know your father tracked me down, but I'd been looking for you too. I tried again and again to contact him with no luck."

My father's head pokes in. "In my defense, there are lots of overzealous fans out there and Higgins is ruthless."

"Papa," I chastise.

He holds up both palms and takes two exaggerated steps backward.

Evan trails his hand down my arm until he reaches my hand. "I remembered what you said, though, about how your father calls you Kitty, and I used that golden nugget to convince Higgins, who speaks horrible French, I should add, to finally let me talk to your father. He wasn't sure if you wanted to see me."

I sigh. "He couldn't have just asked me? She," I say, nodding to Violet, "gets a grand gesture and I get a setup? The two of you thought an ambush on a three-month trip confined to a ship was the best solution?"

He smiles. "Come on, this is grand, no? I was going for the biggest way I could think to tell you and show you that *me az kar*, Daphne."

Not Claire, but Daphne. And with the way he's looking at me, there's no need for the translation from Breton.

"I love you too," I say, a chuckle chasing my words. I'll eat my words. This is pretty damn grand. I've never felt more loved—by both men in my life. I can sense the crowd growing impatient, even without knowing what we've been saying. I'm not going to bother waiting for the chanting to begin. I lean in and kiss Evan, not a second more to be wasted. I'm home.

A NOTE FROM THE AUTHOR

THIS NOVEL IS A WORK OF FICTION, INSPIRED BY ACTUAL events and people whenever possible.

Violet Jessop, a real-life figure, truly survived three maritime disasters aboard the *Olympic*, *Titanic*, and *Britannic*. When I originally came across Violet's story, the first question that came to mind was: *Why?*

Why on earth did she keep getting back on ships?

That story, that motivation, that purpose is what I sought out to tell, which strangely isn't fully explored in Violet's memoir. Violet did, however, talk a great deal about her family, saying how she possessed a "secret hope of helping the family" and how there were moments she wished for that would have to wait "until a day, in fact, when rent and coalman's bills and little pairs of boots did not loom so startlingly on the horizon."

Much of the novel's representation of Violet—her role within her family, her childhood illnesses, the deaths of her family members, her mother's health, her sister's hearing difficulties, her upbringing in South America, the anecdotes of her childhood, the list can go on and on—have all been pulled from the pages of Violet's memoir. If you'd like to learn more about her, it's an excellent place to start. I will note, however, that in some instances, Violet's accounts do not align with historians or other first-person anecdotes. In most cases, I remained true to Violet's experiences as depicted in her memoir.

I find Violet's career at sea astounding. She began working as a stewardess in 1908 and completed her final voyage aboard the *Andes* in 1950, working ashore various times on account of VAD training, repatriation, the Depression, World War II, and various layoffs. She worked more than two hundred voyages.

At the age of sixty-three, Violet retired to Maythorn, her cottage near Suffolk's Great Ashfield. Years after her retirement, Violet received a telephone call from a woman who asked if Violet had saved a baby the night of *Titanic's* sinking. Violet answered that she had. The caller then identified herself as that child before hanging up. The thing is, Violet had never told that story to anyone. And records indicate that the only baby on Violet's boat—lifeboat sixteen—was a boy named Assad Thomas.

There is no account of the child who was handed to Violet before being lowered on a lifeboat and who was taken from Violet's arms once aboard *Carpathia*.

Yet this happened.

The first thing I thought upon learning this was:

What a great opportunity to create a character from this undocumented, secret child.

And thus, Daphne's character was born.

Though my Daphne is fictional, because, again, no one knows who this baby was, she became a composite of the experiences, backgrounds, and accomplishments of the thirty-nine women of the Special Operations Executive, French Section (SOE F).

Specifically:

Daphne's arrest, interrogation, and experiences in prison, including her escape by befriending one of the cleaners, were inspired by Blanche Charlet.

The raid of the depot was inspired by the experiences of Elizabeth Reynolds and of Muriel Byck.

Daphne earned a diploma in Arabic from the University of Cairo like the real-life Mary Herbert.

The friendship with a local bus driver, who saved a seat and warned of the Germans inspecting papers, was based on the experiences of Anne-Marie Walters.

Traveling over the demarcation line in a coal bunker was based on an anecdote from Yvonne Rudellat.

The escape line Daphne helped establish was inspired by

Blanche Charlet and based on the Oaktree Line and the Shelburne Escape Line.

Her sinking was based on the sinking of the SS *Arandora Star.*

The three women Daphne trained with—though I'll note that women didn't begin training with the male agents until 1943, whereas I have them doing so in 1942—were based on Marie-Thérèse Le Chêne, Andrée Borrel, and Yvonne Rudellat.

The Limping Lady, aka Marie of Lyon—and various other monikers—is based on Virginia Hall. She fled France in November 1942 to avoid capture by the Germans. I kept her in France a few months longer to align with my storyline.

The roundup at the Federation of Jewish Societies of France was inspired by the rue Sainte-Catherine Roundup that took place on February 9, 1943. I depict a mother and daughter. This horrific moment was based on the experiences of fourteen-year-old Malvine Lanzet and her mother, Anna Lanzet. As part of the eighty-six rounded up, they were taken to Drancy internment camp. Malvine was released and taken to an orphanage in Paris where she was cared for by the Union. Sadly, her mother was eventually taken to Auschwitz, where she was murdered.

Out of the eighty-six, eighty-three were ultimately deported to the killing camps of Sobibor and Auschwitz.

Malvine eventually was a witness at the trial of Klaus Barbie, who was sentenced to life in prison without parole for crimes against humanity.

I've long wanted to set a book, even partially, aboard *Titanic.* While there are many accounts of the *Titanic's* sinking, the sinking depicted within my book aligns with Violet's portrayal within her memoir. For example, the last song to be played aboard the ship has been long debated. Some accounts claim the waltz "Songe d'Automne," not "Nearer My God to Thee," was the final song.

Accounts of *Britannic's* sinking also come from disparate sources, and sometimes are accompanied by conspiracy theories. Newspaper accounts were often vague and interviews were scarce. It's said this is likely due to wartime censorship and security.

One piece of information I found quite interesting involves Violet's miraculous survival after hitting her head against the ship's hull and being pulled into the ship's propeller. Yes, this happened! But it wasn't until years later that a doctor discovered Violet had fractured her skull in that incident. Not surprising, yet it is surprising that the head injury wasn't discovered straightaway. Violet also claimed she only survived the incident because of her thick auburn hair.

Another shocking moment in Violet's life is that she did indeed marry, as I depict her doing, but within her memoir, she did not tell us his name. This man's presence was such a blip that I gave him equal billing in my story.

But in my telling, I didn't want to leave Violet without love or something all her own. I've written other novels where my characters don't always have a romantic happily ever after and I was determined in *Unsinkable* to give Violet—and also Daphne—a HEA.

Enter Leo and Evan. Both are purely fictional, but I do not love them any less than if they were real. I'll confess to tying up the ending very neatly with a bow. It's what my own heart wanted. Still, I took great care in ensuring the dual reconciliations were completely realistic and unique to the two storylines. Evan's presence on the *Andes* was a wholly orchestrated grand gesture, whereas Leo blindly followed his heart, trying various ships at the first opportunity after the war's end. For Leo and Violet it was always about timing. Finally, he found Violet on the *Andes*, allowing for the second chance they'd both long wanted.

I should also note: because Violet did not have her romantic happily ever after in real life (that she told us, anyway), I wanted to be careful in how I portrayed that scene and it is why I decided to show Violet's reunion with Leo through the eyes of Daphne, instead of through Violet's first-person account.

An early reader mentioned how she smiled the entire time during the novel's end, and I hope you did too.

It was my complete pleasure to tell Violet's story and to create Daphne's character from the incredible women of the SOE.

There are so many I want to thank for going on this journey with me. From my publishing family (Kimberly, Amanda, Kerri, Margaret, Taylor, Caitlin, Savannah, Julie) to my agent, Shannon, to my author friends (Lindsay, Carolyn, Victoria, Lee, J'Nell, Rachel, Joy, Kim, Suzanne, Helen, and aah, so many others I blabbed on and on to about this book), to my IRL friends (you know who you are!), to the uber talented Tall Poppy Writers, to the amazing book community of bloggers and reviewers, and finally, to my incredible husband and kids. I am so unbelievably grateful for the support and excitement for this book. It takes a village, and I have a wonderful one. Readers, I hope you enjoyed reading. Thank you for picking this baby up.

DISCUSSION QUESTIONS

1. The moniker of "Miss Unsinkable" originated from the real-life Violet Jessop. In what ways does it also apply to Daphne's character?

2. What additional parallels can be drawn between Violet and Daphne?

3. Were you familiar with the thirty-nine women of the Special Operations Executive French Section (SOE F)? Did you read more about any of the women mentioned in the author's note?

4. Violet states, " . . . not having to worry about finances would allow for the exploration of what happiness looks like." Paint a picture of what you think this could've been for Violet.

5. Violet suffers from survivor's guilt, relating to both ship disasters and her childhood. How do you think this shaped her sense of duty?

6. Likewise, how do you think Daphne's childhood and relationship with her father played into the novel's theme of duty?

7. Do you agree with Violet's decision to only open Leo's final letter?

8. What, if anything, would motivate you to board a ship after multiple maritime disasters?

9. Daphne's character was born from a mysterious situation. Were you surprised when Daphne's and Violet's connection was revealed?

10. Did you find the Easter Egg from *The Call of the Wrens*?

Written by Marisa Gothie and Nicholle Thery-Williams from the *Bookends and Friends* book club

From the Publisher

GREAT BOOKS

ARE EVEN BETTER WHEN THEY'RE SHARED!

Help other readers find this one:

- Post a review at your favorite online bookseller

- Post a picture on a social media account and share why you enjoyed it

- Send a note to a friend who would also love it—or better yet, give them a copy

Thanks for reading!

ABOUT THE AUTHOR

JENNI L. WALSH WORKED FOR A DECADE ENTICING readers as an award-winning advertising copywriter before becoming an author. Her passion lies in transporting readers to another world, be it in historical or contemporary settings. She is a proud graduate of Villanova University and lives in the Philadelphia suburbs with her husband, daughter, son, and various pets.

Jenni is the author of the historical novels *Becoming Bonnie, Side by Side, A Betting Woman*, and *The Call of the Wrens*. She also writes books for children, including the nonfiction She Dared series and historical novels *Hettie and the London Blitz, I Am Defiance, By the Light of Fireflies*, and *Over and Out*. To learn more about Jenni and her books, please visit jennilwalsh.com or @jennilwalsh on social media.